A PARANORMAL LANDS NOVEL BOOK ONE

LIGHTNING
AND
CURSES

C.C. SOLOMON

CatDog Publications

COPYRIGHT © 2021 BY C.C. SOLOMON

ISBN: 978-1-7361329-7-5

Created with Vellum

ACKNOWLEDGMENTS

Thank you to all my friends and family who supported my dreams. Thank you to my editors at Real Indie Author, you push me to be a better writer. Thank you to my proofreader, for your great eye and my formatters at Yours Truly Book Services for your awesome services at every level. Your quick work and professionalism have consistently come through. And thanks to my readers for keeping me going. Your enthusiasm and feedback has made a huge difference.

A NOTE FROM C.C.

To find information on prior books by C.C. Solomon go to
www.ccsolomon.com

CHAPTER 1

They were biting me. Everywhere. Holding me down so I couldn't move. Vampires. Ghouls. Weres. Even other Fae wanted a part of me. I was nothing more than a source of food to them.

I screamed in agony as teeth tore at my flesh. They weren't gentle. Even the vampires and fae, who only wanted blood gnawed at me. I tried to use my magic, but it ignored me. My mind began to get fuzzy. I wasn't sure if it was due to the pain or the blood loss. It wasn't my concern. I had to get out of there. I didn't even know how I ended up there. Had I been knocked out, drugged?

Now wasn't the time to figure that out. The more important focus was how I could escape.

I looked around the room as the pain grew. Darkness engulfed the large bed. Heavy curtains hid the floor-to-ceiling windows. From the corner of my eye, I noticed movement above the feast that was me. I turned my head, gritting my teeth as fangs dragged down the skin of my neck.

Benjamin Wu, a former boyfriend, my first love, stood there. His hazel eyes were wide and fearful. He twisted, but only his upper body moved, his legs seemingly glued to the ground. He opened his mouth, but I could hear no words, at least not over the chewing noises.

Nausea fought its way up in me, and I dry heaved.

Finally, I heard Benjamin call for me, and then his voice turned into a cough. Repetitive and then thick until I saw him vomit up blood. The liquid poured from his eyes and nose. His eyes yellowed, skin sweaty and hollowed.

It was all happening too fast. It wasn't supposed to move this quickly. I screamed for him, but of course, that did no good.

Benjamin fell to his knees, staring at me now with clouded translucent eyes.

My heart broke. I would lose him again, and there would be nothing I could do. Just like the last time. Except I was even more helpless now. I tried to wiggle against the monsters to seek a way to escape, but I was too weak. I couldn't win, and tears flooded my eyes as I watched Benjamin fall face-first onto the carpeted floor.

He went still.

I shut my eyes, sobbing. Heart-broken, body in mind-numbing pain.

"Lisa?" I heard a familiar male voice call from my left.

Charles Langston raced towards me. His movement too fast for me to track. He pushed the creatures away from me, but they outnumbered him, attacking him in a united front, freeing me. I rolled to my side, my bones feeling too heavy to move. I wanted to try to teleport, but I couldn't—wouldn't leave him.

I rolled to the ground, wincing as my body hit the floor from the bed. All my injuries flared. However, I pushed through the pain and crawled towards him. I had no idea what I would do in this condition, and I was moving at a snail's pace. I couldn't imagine I'd be much help, but I wouldn't give up.

Charles' body stopped fighting against them, and he looked over at me with pain-filled eyes, his arm reaching out in a desperate attempt to touch me.

I had to grab it, had to teleport us away. I couldn't lose him too. It was too much – too much loss.

A ghoul, one I knew too well, turned from the crowded attack and hissed at me. He had jet black hair and coal black eyes that covered up any whiteness. The lower half of his mouth was a horrific mask of razor-sharp teeth. He could tear off an arm with very few bites, but he preferred to carve his food. "Now, where are you going? We don't waste food here," Lorenzo, the ghoul said, in a low, deep voice.

I tried to crawl backwards, but I was still moving too slow.

He raced towards me and was on me in no time. I cursed my weakened state. I hated this helplessness. This heartbreak. I was food. I was nothing.

Lorenzo opened his mouth impossibly wide, rearing his head back before he moved swiftly to rip out my neck.

∼

I woke up in a sweat, my loose hairs from my high bun sticking to the back of my neck. I sat up and rubbed my face, annoyed at how gross I felt. I looked at the bedside table and saw that it was only four a.m. I cursed and swung my legs to the side. I couldn't go back to sleep this sweaty. I needed a shower. I could glamour myself. I was a faerie after all, but I felt a shower would also rinse the ick away from my dream.

Another nightmare. I didn't have them *every* night but anytime was enough. And they were always too vivid, leaving me crying out and sweaty.

A sudden howl ripping through the night shook me. I

should be used to the noises of the night. It had been over ten years since the world had changed to something supernatural, but I hadn't. They might always scare me. Growls, roars, howls, flapping of wings, shaking of the ground from gigantic footsteps. It made me miss the random hoots of an owl or cricket chirps from my youth. Those things still existed, but you couldn't hear them anymore. Nothing was the same anymore.

I let out a breath and walked to my bathroom in my one-bedroom apartment. I took a quick shower, and my nerves settled. Sleep came slightly easier after that. No more nightmares.

When I awoke again, still shaken from my dream, I got dressed, had breakfast and headed to the hospital. I tried to visit as often as I could, though they were becoming less and less, I wasn't giving up hope. I just hated not having a way to fix things every time I visited her.

I walked into the hospital room where my friend, Amina Langston, had been sleeping for almost a year. Her private room was still filled with so many fresh flowers, it looked and smelled like a botanical garden. It was as if her room had become a shrine, which I knew was just the opposite of what she would have wanted. However, it helped us cope with her absence from us.

I placed my purse down on the bedside table and looked at her peaceful face. If I didn't look at the tubes connecting to her, she looked almost like sleeping beauty. Her face was so peaceful, and her curly dark brown hair framed her face. I'd glamoured her into a long white gown that made her look like a sleeping bride. Perhaps it was extra, but she was my friend, and I wanted her to be beautiful even in her magic coma.

Not long ago, we'd won the battle against the original, evil soulmates who, of course, wanted to rule the world and enslave mankind. However, that win came at more cost than I could have imagined. One of those costs was that the new generation soulmates, Amina and Phillip, had to put themselves in a coma to avoid becoming evil themselves. I thought it was too soon to make such a rash decision without us finding help, but they were already becoming overpowered.

I lifted Amina's hand and began to paint her nails a warm peach. "This is a new color I put together at the store. I'm telling you, it looks good on any skin tone. The store's really doing well. I know you would love it." I paused painting her nails and looked to the windows of her room. Talking to her hurt. She couldn't talk back no matter how much I wanted it to happen.

My chest tightened, and I blew out a heavy breath. She was asleep. She was only asleep. I had to keep remembering that.

However, as more time passed, the harder it got for me to keep my hope. Coming to visit her a couple times a month felt like torture, but it was also a way for me to connect and remind me that she wasn't gone. She was still here in this world. A world that had done well at taking so many people from me.

I cleared my throat and got back to painting her nails. "So anyway, I never thought I'd be a business owner. For a girl who didn't go to college, I guess I'm doing okay. Of course, it only took a magical apocalypse for it to happen, but who cares, right?"

Footsteps approach the door, and Erik Bennet entered the room. He looked tired, as always, hazel eyes set in serious mode and hands stuffed in his dark gray jeans. He walked with his shoulders back, as was common with alphas, confident in their being. He tilted his head towards the bed. "I see you changed her look again," he observed with his deep New Zealand accent as he walked further into the room.

I nodded, assessing him. He was like a brother to me and typically looked out for my well-being. Lately, I'd been keeping an eye on him. Ever since Amina had gone into her coma, Erik, her boyfriend, had become something of a robot. He worked, running our town's military police and the pack, took care of his adopted son, Brandon, and looked for ways to safely wake Amina back up. She had been his heart, and everyone in town knew it. Even having Phillip as her fated mate had not changed their love. It was inspiring.

So, despite his extremely attractive looks, not one woman had tried to come on to him. People were indebted to Amina, and she'd garnered the respect of the town due to her sacrifice.

Not that any self-respecting woman would pounce on a man in Erik's situation.

He was in mourning. His hazel eyes were a bit dark, and shadows hung below, letting me know he hadn't been sleeping well. However, he didn't look like he was losing weight anymore, which meant he had to be eating. His usual tanned skin was a little pale, which I assumed meant he hadn't enjoyed the warm weather of the past week. Before we knew it, we'd be back in our new six-month winters. I wanted to suggest he go for a mini-vacation in one of the few resort areas in the world. Those and cruises were safest when it came to travel nowadays. However, I knew that would be fruitless. He would have moved into the hospital to live with Amina if he could.

"Do you like her dress?" I asked, gently blowing on her nails.

He sat down at the foot of the bed on the opposite side of me. "You always make her look good. Not that it's hard to do. Even with her asleep." He began to rub her legs over the comforter.

He believed she could feel we were there through touch.

That wasn't a reach, seeing as we were part of the Special Six. See, when the world had changed, it had brought with it supernatural creatures and a sickness that had wiped out half the world's population. Out of the survivors, the majority had been magically changed into supernatural creatures like myself. Now, we lived in a world with normal humans, fae, vampires, weres, witches, angels, demons and more. I was becoming used to it, and society was rebuilding well.

However, just as I was getting the swing of things, over two years ago, I'd learned I was a member of some super-hero team brought together to protect the world against evil.

Erik began to rub up and down her arms, his eyes softening. "I didn't think I'd be apart from her ever again. Today is her birthday. Did you know?"

I lowered her hand to the bed, feeling like the worst friend in the world. I had forgotten. Truth be told, we'd all met under such extreme circumstances, we barely got to just be normal around each other. I'd met both Erik and Amina because they'd saved my life on two separate occasions. From there, we were always dealing with some lurking danger due to the original soulmates who kept trying to kill us. "No," I said in a barely audible voice.

Erik dug into his pocket and pulled out a small black box.

I gasped. Was he going to propose to her now? She was asleep. "Is that what I think it is?"

"I was going to give her this before..." He hung his head and nodded as he trailed off. He looked so vulnerable. It was not a look I was used to seeing on Erik, who was sporting a full beard now to match his longer black hair that he had combed back. "It's probably not good to give her this on her birthday even if she was awake. It should be a separate day, right?"

I shrugged, hardly the person to give advice on love. My relationships never lasted. Still, I knew how Amina felt about him. "I think she'd be happy regardless of the day. Except probably do this when she's awake."

He nodded again and stuffed the box back in his pocket. "That was the plan. But I always want to have it on me just in case I come one day and find her awake. I miss her, Lisa," he said in a low cracked voice.

It broke my heart. They hadn't known each other super long, and yet their hearts were inseparable. The way he loved her, the way they loved each other, were just goals for me. To have a man care for me like he did was something I couldn't imagine. "I miss her too." I looked down at her nails. "Well, I guess I gave her a birthday manicure."

Erik snorted. "They look nice."

I dabbed at my green eyes, my favorite feature. I'd always thought they were unusual, but when The Event—as most people called the first day of the paranormal apocalypse—occurred, my eyes became an even more vivid green. I chalked it up to the fact that I had become a faerie on that day in my old beauty salon back in New Jersey.

Erik cleared his throat, stroking Amina's hair softly. "Any luck on breaking the spell?"

I already knew what he was asking about, and my stomach twisted in knots. Just the thought of the impending deadline gave me anxiety. I shook my head, wordless, as I watched his judgement-filled eyes. Erik had never approved, and I didn't blame him, but I also didn't think there was a better option. I owed a favor to an elven king to break his curse before the end of the year. One way to break said curse was to let him eat one of my organs.

Erik rolled his eyes. "I can't believe you made that idiotic deal with him."

I cringed. I honestly didn't think it was a bad deal for what we'd gotten from the elf and his people. Not to mention, I wasn't fond of the idea of letting him remain cursed if I could do anything. "You don't have to call it idiotic."

He stopped stroking Amina's hair and glared at me.

Sure, it sounded a little generous, but Joo-won, the aforementioned elven king, had helped us out quite a bit without getting anything in return. It only seemed fair. "Okay, in the non-magic hospitals, people donate organs all the time. That's all this is. I can give him a kidney."

Erik threw his head back and stared up at the ceiling in exasperation. "Lisa, I've told you time and time again, there is power in our blood and our body. You let an elf with questionable morals have *any* part of you, and you don't know what effect that can have."

Logically it made sense, and I struggled with the same thought. However, Joo-won had only shown me kindness, and I had a challenging time ignoring it. He'd never hurt me. He'd saved me. He'd even confessed to loving me. I believed him. I felt his truth even if I wasn't ready to accept it or even process it. It didn't feel like he was lying or using me, but I had to consider that this could be a scheme to steal my power as a faerie and member of The Six. " I hear you, but it's not fair to let him just die or get controlled by the evil witch who cursed him."

Erik shrugged. "Why not?"

I gave him a disapproving frown. I knew Erik wasn't heartless. He was a protector by nature. However, Joo-won had almost killed him a while back so some grudges were a little hard to let go. "Joo-won did fight on our side and save my life more than once. And you don't even have the scar he gave you anymore. He helped us in our time of need. Maybe it's time to let it go."

"That's all well and good, but that doesn't mean you have to sacrifice yourself. Maybe he deserved the curse. He probably stole something from the witch, and that was her payback."

I bared my teeth and turned away. Erik didn't need to know that that was exactly what had happened. Joo-won and his people had a penchant for stealing, and they'd finally messed with the wrong person, a powerful witch.

"Seems like karma to me."

I sighed. "People can change, Erik. What about Phillip?"

Erik grimaced. "I'm still on the fence about him."

I dropped my jaw in shook. "The man is in a coma to protect us."

Erik waved a dismissive hand at me. "Yeah, yeah. Hey, how much time do you have before you 'donate' your kidney to him?" I didn't like how he added quotation marks when he said the word donate.

My stomach knotted in nerves, and I gave it a little rub. Thinking about how little time I had left to fix Joo-won gave me anxiety that I tried my best to push through. "I think a little under a month, maybe a little less."

He muttered a curse. "You're going to end up giving him an organ, aren't you? Can't he just buy one from someone desperate?"

I began to put the nail kit away in my purse. "It can't be sold. It has to be freely and honestly offered. And it can't be another elf, so none of his people can do it."

"If he does something foul because of this, I'll kill him," he growled.

I stood up. I knew he was telling the truth. Erik had a penchant for violence instead of conversation, and he was low on trust these days. Well, most days. Ok, all the time. He hadn't even trusted Amina right after she saved my life the first time we met. "Let's not start any new wars, please."

"You really think you can give him an organ out of the goodness of your heart? Because if you're doing it because you owe him, that wouldn't count either, right?"

I paused, gnawing on my lip. Oh, crap, I hadn't thought about that. Money, favors. It was all an exchange. I wondered if Joo-won had thought about that. I owed him for coming to rescue me when the evil faerie queen, Misandre, had her right-hand ghoul, Lorenzo, kidnapped and tried to eat me alive. I was still livid about that one. Having one's skin sliced and eaten in front of you is not a pleasant experience. I wasn't a killer, but I was glad I'd finally gotten rid of Misandre in the soulmate wars. Now I just had to find Lorenzo, who somehow escaped during our big battle. He'd killed friends of mine and the leader of Hagerstown, a place that had welcomed me. We couldn't let him get away with his murders.

I also owed Joo-won for fighting on our side. He'd gained nothing from joining the fight, especially after he'd removed himself from being an ally. Still, he'd come to my rescue even then. Offering an organ now would clearly be considered a favor. Would the witch be able to sense that? Was she monitoring Joo-won? Did her curse just know that kind of thing? Ten years since The Event, and I still wasn't sure how every type of magic worked. The magic books only now were coming out. All the groups had different rules, and some were more masterful at their magic than others.

Erik smirked. "Didn't think about that, did you?"

I twisted my lips. I loved Erik dearly, but he often liked to believe he was the smartest person in the room. And okay, sometimes he was, but I didn't need him to know that any more than he already did. "Maybe."

Erik lifted his chin, giving me a knowing look. "Uh-huh. You'll tell me before you do something stupid, right?"

He said it more like a demand than a question.

I gave him a curt nod. "Yes, Dad."

"Don't 'yes, Dad' me. You're part of The Six. People have their eyes on us now. People who might try to take advantage of our kindness."

I humphed in annoyance. I really wanted to find the person who decided I needed to be a superhero. That was so not in my life goals. "I'm not naïve."

"No, but you do have feelings for that elf. And I don't think he's above taking advantage of that."

I opened my mouth to protest, but Erik lifted a brow and gave me a look that clearly said he wouldn't believe anything that came out of my mouth.

I humphed again and looked over to Amina. "Happy Birthday," I whispered before leaving the room.

~

"*D*id you try turning your computer off first?" Charles rolled his chocolate brown eyes at me as he listened to the person on his cell phone. He moved his hand in a circular motion as if to hurry the caller up.

I stifled a grin and twirled a black silken lock of my hair over a finger as I stared down at the menu. We were meeting for lunch at our town's Japanese restaurant. It was actually one of the first places we'd visited when the six of us first came to the Silver Spring community in search of a place to belong and get help rescuing other paranormals locked up in a prison run by non-powered humans who used their blood for a power serum.

After the world changed, there was a growing division

between paranormal humans and regular humans, and with the country basically falling apart due to the massive deaths, small towns and communities started to function more as tribes. All this time later, a government federation, made up of government run towns, was reemerging, but there were still many places like this one that did not fall under the government.

At one point, the community was for paranormals only, but in recent months it had expanded to allow humans. This brought forth a whole new list of needs. One being the growing need for magic to help run technology and electricity. When the world changed, technology of any sort disappeared, so the only way to get it back was through magic. Charles, as a tech mage, was always in high demand.

"Ok, ma'am. I'll come over between the hours of 10 and 12 tomorrow morning. That work? Great." He said before swiping his cellphone off and stuffing it in his pocket. He gave me a lopsided grin, and I was reminded yet again how much he looked like his sister, except he was taller. He used to be more lanky, but since becoming an undead vampire, he had filled out a bit more. He also had a bit of a goatee he was growing, and his curly black hair was set in twist that reached his brows, but his hair was still shaved on the sides and the back. I couldn't say I hated this look on him. He'd come a way since I first met the slightly awkward sweetheart. Of course, that was all before he died and rose again as a vampire.

"Sooo, how is she?" he asked, looking down at his menu.

I glanced up at him. "Amina? Beautiful as always. Erik came by. Said it was her birthday today."

Charles gave an indifferent nod. If one didn't know him, one might think he seemed uncaring about his sister being in a magical coma. However, I knew better. He loved his older sister dearly. He was not adjusting well to her absence.

The pair had come a long way together. It wasn't usual for close family members to survive together in this world. I knew he felt a little lost without her now.

"Are you ever going to visit? I'm sure she'd like it."

He glanced up at me from the menu, and his normally expressive eyes were now unreadable. It unsettled me because this was not my Charles. "I can't see her."

I knew he couldn't. He hadn't visited her since that day we'd done the spell she gave us to put her to sleep. None of us wanted to do it, but we also understood why it had to be done. It didn't mean it was easy for us.

He began to scratch at the table with his index finger, looking away from me again. "The longer she's asleep, the more I want to just wake her up. We can find another way to mute their powers so they don't go all psycho. You can't trust me to visit her."

I reached across the table and wrapped a hand over his. His pained expression messed with my heart. I wanted to make it better, but I had no clue how. I just hoped my touch, as a Six, gave him some sort of calm. "I know you wouldn't try to wake her up. We made the deal, and it's what she wants."

He gave me a skeptical look. "You put too much faith in me, Lisa. I'm not that good a man."

I snorted. Charles had his ups and downs since becoming a vampire, but he was still a good man. It was his kindness that made me want to date him. He'd been an excellent boyfriend. I missed those days. The days before he became a vampire and before I'd banished his sister away. We were friends. It was an awkward road to get here, and some days, I did wonder if it was the right decision, but I also knew having him in my life was invaluable to me. Even as a platonic friend. "Well, that's bull. You're textbook good. You're selfless."

The waitress appeared with our drinks and took our orders. Charles took a long gulp of his drink, something dark and alcohol looking, before responding. Charles sat back, reading my eyes. Heck, maybe he was reading my mind. We had a connection that allowed us to communicate telepathically, but we'd agreed not to mind read. Too invasive. "I love our platonic friend dates, but let's get to the real business. Did you find a cure for him yet?"

Ok, maybe he hadn't been reading my mind. Whew. I knew he was talking about Joo-won, and I shook my head. "I'm actually going to go check in on him this evening."

Charles tilted his head and squinted his eyes in a suspicious glare. "You can't just call him?"

I puffed out a breath in annoyance but not at Charles. Charles asked a perfectly reasonable question and yet dealing with Joo-won was anything but. "That jerk won't answer my calls or my emails. He will only respond to me face-to-face."

"Of course. Anything to spend time with you. He's a manipulative one. You know, I'm also looking for a way to break his curse."

I raised my brows in surprise. This was news. What would make Charles care? Then again, I was on the line to lose an organ, and as a friend, I could see him being invested in helping me out of that. "Really? Why haven't you said anything?"

Charles rested his chin on his palm, balanced by his elbow on the table. "There wasn't any point until I found anything."

While it was nice of him to involve himself, it wasn't his obligation. "Why are you doing this?"

"Because you're part of The Six, and we can't have you at the mercy of a cannibal elf. We're family

I lifted a shoulder, cringing at his word choice. "He's not really a cannibal."

"What do you call someone who eats their own kind? He's a subset of the fae. You're a faerie. He needs to eat your organ to beat the curse." He sat back, crossing his arms. "Cannibal."

Ugh, he really did do well at making negative points. And yet still, I couldn't take my mind off that cannibal elven king.

CHAPTER 2

*T*eleporting to Baltimore, where Joo-won and company set up shop, was the easy part. In particular, they'd taken over what was once the luxury district, formerly called Harbor East. It was a collection of expensive high rises, fine dining and shops. When the world had gone to hell, the once growing part of the city fell to chaos and destruction, as did most major cities. In fact, the city of Baltimore was pretty much a nomand's land until recent years. Now there were pockets of tiny communities rebuilding the area.

I stood at the center of the Harbor East area, beside a boarded-up, decrepit building wrapped in graffiti and wiggly, man-eating plant life. A green vine shot out from the building towards me, but I didn't move as it passed through my chest, but I felt nothing. It was like a hologram. Just trickery. I was so used to it now when I visited that I no longer flinched. This was all part of Joo-won's plan to make the town look undesirable so no one would bother them. I thought it was a bit excessive now since the town was no secret, at least locally, that they were there.

A crumbled newspaper flew at my face, and I batted it

away. This time my hand did connect with something solid. It wasn't just an image. This was really too much. There was trash all over the ground, beat-up cars, a large water fountain with a tumbled rusty statute over it and more buildings that looked hazardous. It was the afternoon, but there was no one outside. This wasn't abnormal. It was just part of the glamour.

I wiped a bead of sweat off my forehead. These extended summers could get rough, but I'd take them over the supernatural winters any day. Still, I had second thoughts about that when a whiff of heated stench came my way. These dramatics had to end. "Hey, I'm here. Everyone knows you're here, so the whole theatrics...it's stupid."

My response was met with silence. Every time. Every damn time I came here I had to go through this whole routine. I was certain Joo-won or one of his high-ranking people did this on purpose to get a laugh.

I grumbled and walked over to what appeared to be a deteriorated ice cream parlor and picked up a chair turned sideways on the ground in front of the building. I sat down and crossed my legs, tapping my fingers on my knee in annoyance.

Soon the world changed around me as broken windows became shiny and new. Plant-life receded from the buildings, and graffiti disappeared. The toppled statue over the water fountain rose up to the center, and crystal-clear water began to pour from it. The cars on the street moved to the sides, neatly parallel parked and clean. Trash on the street vanished before my eyes, and even the air smelled fresh and crisp. Soon, people around me began to appear, walking in and out of stores or dining al fresco in front of the restaurants. The knocked-over table in front of me righted itself, and another chair moved up right on the opposite side. I could hear faint pop music playing from the ice cream parlor and saw an older elf waving at me behind the counter.

I gave him a quick wave back before turning to the street. A beautiful woman with long dark brown hair and neon green eyes sat across from me with a smile on her full red lips. She wore a peach A-line dress that complemented her mahogany coloring. The hem hit her knees, showing off her long muscular legs.

"Senna," I replied. The elf and I were developing a slow friendship, so I wasn't unhappy to see her. "So glad to see you pop up out of nowhere. Why do you all put me through this every time?"

Her smile widened. I had rarely ever seen her smile, but for this, she was all grins? "It's fun, isn't it?"

"For who?" I looked around at the busy street. "Do you do this to everyone who visits?"

"Of course not. We have special orders only to do that when you come."

I knew it. I pressed my lips together and raised my brows, hoping she would take my lack of response as the annoyance I felt.

The smell of popcorn from the next-door movie theater filled my nostrils. Seriously, they even had a working theater? The elves really were getting pedestrian.

Senna stood up and offered me her hand. "Shall we take you to who you really came for?"

I really didn't mind her. She was stylish and a warrior. It was impressive. I gave a pretend pout. "Aww, and I always have so much fun talking to you."

She shook her head in disbelief. "Liar."

I stood up and grabbed her hand to teleport us to Joowon's place. "No seriously, the more I get to know you, the more I like you. I thought you hated me at first."

She winked. "I did."

I dropped my shoulders. Well, damn, that hurt. I thought we were friends now. But I guess I wasn't surprised. I had strolled in and distracted her king.

She bumped her hip into mine. "That was then. Now you're ok."

I suppose I'd be fine with an ok. It was better than being hated because I actually did like Senna. She was super confident, smart and stylish.

The scenery around us blurred, and we were transported inside a luxury hotel overlooking the water. The inside was all dark wood, dim lighting and marble floors. If this were the Pre-World, what we called the time before the magic had returned to the world, I wouldn't have been able to afford a posh place like this. Now the elves were just taking up residence here for free. Then again, it had been their magic that had brought the area back from disarray, so I supposed it was only fair.

"He's in his room," Senna said before taking off with a wave of her hand.

I got on the nearest elevator and rode it up to the top of the hotel where his penthouse suite resided. Stepping off, I was met with several guards who then fell back against the wall upon seeing me. I walked down the hall to my right and opened the door, not bothering to knock. He knew I was there.

A statuesque woman dressed head to toe in black walked my way. She had a short, black pixie cut and black painted lips which she used to give me a thin-lipped smile before walking past me. It wasn't a warm greeting, more like something she felt obligated to do so she wouldn't look like a jerk. I decided to give her a wide grin in response to show her I was above her petty acknowledgement. I really shouldn't care about such things, but a jealous note kicked up in me.

Joo-won had every right to date who he wanted, but it didn't mean it didn't sting. I was still struggling with not wanting to get too close to him while he was cursed and wanting to fall into his arms every time I saw him. I was a confused woman.

"New girlfriend?" I asked to the room, still not seeing Joo-won.

I moved to the living area which held a couch, coffee table, large TV to the right and a dining set and kitchenette to the left. Floor to ceiling windows took up a wall across from the entrance, and a cracked door beside the mounted TV held Joo-won's bedroom.

I flopped down on the beige couch, suddenly feeling stupid for coming there. I should have insisted we have a phone conversation so I wouldn't have to barge into him doing whatever he was doing with other women.

The bedroom door opened wide and Joo-won appeared looking as hot as ever. Seriously, I had known this man a year, and he never ever looked bad. Never a bad hair day or a breakout. Never baggy sweat pants or scuffed shoes. Yes, I knew he had his elven magic, however, it would have been nice to see his perfect image scratched up a bit. Without such, I found it hard to think of him as even close to human. He became this intimidating being, kind of like a celebrity. But even celebrities pretended to be just like the rest of us common folk from time to time.

Today he had the audacity to come out of his room with wet hair, a big, fluffy white towel over his bare shoulders, a pair of loose black pajama pants and bare feet. I mean, I assume they were PJs. I was too caught up in staring at his defined chest, six-pack and muscled arms accented by droplets of sweat or water.

I placed my hand under my chin to make sure my mouth wasn't hanging open. However, I wasn't going to be swayed by him. Well, not today, at least. During most of my visits, I successfully kept him at an arms-length to focus on me.

But it was so hard. I gave an exaggerated roll of my eyes to show how unbothered I was. I was the queen of lies. "I could have waited for you to put a shirt on."

Joo-won's full lips went into a smirk as he walked towards me. "I didn't want to keep my butterfly waiting," he said in that deep voice of his that did something to my lady parts.

Seriously, I really hated him. "Oh please," I stated as he sat down next to me. Damn, he even smelled good – like a mixture of licorice and spices. I wanted to put my nose in the crook of his neck and sniff him for as long as I could.

And now I sounded like a creeper. I moved away from him until my hip hit the couch arm.

Joo-won's mouth parted slightly, and he rubbed his bottom lip with his thumb, appearing to enjoy that he was getting to me. "And to answer your earlier question, I do not have a new girlfriend. I'm waiting for a certain someone to come to her senses about who she rightfully belongs to— I mean, with." He gave a slight upturn of his lips that had the unfortunate effect of sending a tingle to my core. It really didn't take much from him, and he knew it.

Did I mention he was crazy arrogant? He'd gotten by in his many supernatural years on his wealth and looks and didn't know what the word no was all about.

I flipped my hair over my shoulders to continue my pretense of being unaffected by his glistening bare chest. "Well then, I guess having female visitors and being half-naked is your thing."

He scooted closer to me until we were only a couple of inches apart. Stupid tingles again. I scooted away from him.

The mix of blues and greens that I always found

mesmerizing in his alien eyes dimmed a bit. He pushed his wet, black hair back from his forehead. "Actually, that woman was a witch all the way from Germany. We were hoping she could get rid of my curse. She has a good reputation for breaking curses."

It was still good to know he was finding a way to break his curse. He wasn't just resting on eating my organ. It seemed he really did want to find another way, and that made me like him more. "I'm guessing by your face, it didn't work."

He tilted his head back on the couch, propping a foot up on his coffee table. This was the most relaxed I'd ever seen him. It made him seem almost human, and I liked it. "No. And she doused me in the blood of some animal, hence the need for a shower."

I scrunched my face in disapproval. I was so not about harming animals. Unless it was food. For the first time, I noticed his left forearm was bandaged in a wrap. I was really focused on the wrong thing. "Was that part of breaking the curse?"

He looked down at his arm, his upper lip turned up in disgust. "No. It's part of the curse. I've been having growing effects as my timeline draws to a close. I awoke to a nice scar this morning. It's really a marking etched into my skin."

I frowned. I had no clue he was already suffering effects. I could only begin to guess what surprises this witch was putting him under to remind him of his remaining time until he would be her slave. Why had he kept his suffering secret from me? He was so stubborn, especially when it came to getting my help. No matter how conflicted I felt about him, I didn't like seeing him suffer. "I can heal it."

"Thank you, but it won't work. It's resistant. As are most of the effects."

I touched his arm, feeling a rush of sympathy and help-lessness. "Are you in pain?"

He looked over to me, giving a slight flash of teeth, his confident mask returning.

That disappointed me. It was the vulnerable side of him that I liked and saw too little of; then again, it also added to my confusion about how I felt about him. If he remained the mysterious, arrogant jerk, I could keep myself protected. Better to keep my heart my own.

He let out a breath. "I can handle it. But it looks like I'm going to have to eat you after all. Your organ, not anything else. Unless you ask me to."

I made a gagging noise and waved my hands in front of me. He really was insufferable. "You are so inappropriate. But seriously, there was something I wanted to call to your attention. It's why I came here. So, like, a person can't sell their organ to you. It has to be of their own altruistic giving. And, I actually owe you a couple of favors. If I'm giving an organ to you, it's kind of like payment for those favors. Maybe it won't count then."

He looked away from me to the ceiling, contemplating. "Yes, I've come to realize that. But we can get around it. Pay me back in another way, and then we'd be even when you give me an organ."

I puffed out a breath, trying to think of what I could offer that would make his fighting on our side to defeat the big soulmate evil and saving my life settled. "Hmm, you could jump in front of an angry troll, and I can save your life." Trolls were typically giants. Like some were as tall as a house, so this was nothing light weight. Of course, if I failed, he'd be squashed.

He chuckled. Guess that was no good. I kind of knew that before suggesting it, but it was nice I could get a laugh out of him. Actually, it just made him sexier, and I didn't need that.

"Or, you could drink a poison, and I can find the elixir to bring you to health."

He glared at me before looking away. Yeah, ok, I knew that wasn't a good one. Who wanted that kind of risk, but I was running out of ideas. This wasn't my expertise, and time hadn't helped me at all. "Well, do you have a better idea? I'm not sleeping with you as payment, if that's what you're thinking."

Joo-won stood up, raising his arms over his head in a stretch. More of his stomach became exposed, and I could see the V of his pelvis peaking through.

I quickly looked away so he wouldn't notice me ogling him.

"Silly butterfly, I flirt but there is a limit. You're far too precious to me than to use sex as a bartering tool. I want your heart, but I want it willingly."

Ok, maybe he wasn't a total jerk. And there went my heart, skipping a beat under the intensity of his gaze. I swallowed, trying to catch my breath. I couldn't have that. The idea of getting attached to him when he could possibly disappear to serve a witch or toss me to the side after he ate my kidney didn't sit right with me. I was not ready for that emotional risk. I never had the best track record when it came to falling for guys. The men that stole my heart didn't stick around. They tended to die.

I was beginning to feel like a black widow. It wasn't because I didn't trust in Joo-won; he'd proven through his actions time and time again that he was here for me. No, what I didn't trust was love. I didn't trust that I could truly make an elven king happy, and I didn't trust that love would remain in this horrible world. I hadn't seen anything last. Someone always died or disappeared.

Even though Charles had come back from death, I couldn't forget the pain of watching him die. I couldn't forget the pain I'd seen in other couples I knew when a partner left or died. I thought of Erik and how melancholy he had become with Amina in her sleep. It was scary. Love was scary. It was risky. To love a man like Joo-won, one so desired by such powerful beings like Misandre and the original soulmates, was even more terrifying. I wanted him, but I couldn't let myself chance the pain that would surely come.

I honestly believed that the best thing for Joo-won was for us to stay at a flirty superficial level. Lisa's heart was closed for business. Even when I was staying with him to get him to our side in the soulmate war, I'd maintained my decorum. He walked to his kitchenette and pulled out two glasses from a cabinet above the counter. "Drink?"

I got up and walked towards him, confused. "Sure. How are we even?"

He poured what looked like a cloudy pink liquid into the glasses from a dark, nameless bottle sitting on the counter with several other liquors serving as a makeshift bar. "You saved me when we fought Lorenzo at Misandre's castle."

I knew that well, but I was about to get eaten alive by Lorenzo when Joo-won showed up. "You only got hurt because you were rescuing me."

He offered the glass to me, face unreadable. "You killed Misandre, and she was a pain in my ass. So, we are even. In fact, it might be that I owed you and paid it off when I aided you in battle. Us saving each other in the fight doesn't count. It's part of battle."

I narrowed my eyes before taking the glass. I sniffed it and raised my brows. It smelled like nothing. I took a small sip. It was like a sweeter version of tequila. This is the kind of drink that would sneak up on you and have you on your butt before you knew what happened. I'd have to drink slowly. "I think you're reaching. Do you want to risk your life on that hope?"

He tilted his head, his eyes now thoughtful as he considered my words.

Man, even thoughtful-eyed Joo-won was gorgeous. I imagined he was looking at me and thinking of all the ways we could do things that did not involve talking. Things on the bed, floor, shower, table. Him surrounding me with his muscular arms. My legs wrapped around his waist.

Ok, Lisa, get it all the way together. My heart kept fluttering around him. I rubbed my chest as if stamping out impending heartburn. Could he, like, fart or something so I could get out of his trance. This is why I liked to keep my visits short with him. Here he was talking about serious things, and I couldn't even remain focused. My brain was becoming a jumbling pile of naughty thoughts of him and the matter at hand.

"What choice do I really have?"

What was he talking about? Oh, right, the curse and eating organs. I took another sip of my drink to refocus. This was probably not the right thing to do. I needed to stay sober around him. "We still have time."

Joo-won reached over and traced a finger up my arm.

A shocking tingle went through my body. Did he just use magic or was I just in lust? It was probably both.

"Why do I feel like you're backing out of your promise?"

I moved slightly away from him. Joo-won had always been good to me. Even when I did things that should have pissed him off, like stopping his fight with Erik in the past. However, I didn't want to test him much more. He was powerful, even with the curse on him. While I was no weakling, I'd much rather have an ally Joo-won than an enemy Joo-won. "I'm not. It's no big deal giving you an organ. I'm just a little nervous about..." I trailed off. Did he know that he could have some type of power over me by having my organ in him? Would he try to control or use me? I hoped he wasn't the type, but I couldn't be a fool.

He leaned in towards me, searching my eyes. Once again ignoring my personal space.

I wished I hated it, but my racing heart said otherwise. I kind of wanted to lick the water droplets from his neck. Seriously, was I in heat?

"Nervous about what? Do you think we'll have a connection if I have a part of you in me?" The warmth of his breath skipped across my skin, and my body throbbed with a desire I so didn't need right now. "That might be nice."

No. Nope, it would not be nice. I moved away from him and fought to get some air in my lungs. Now I was beginning to wonder if he was really making his best effort to get out of this curse. I needed to take the lead and put in a greater effort now. Maybe I should have one of my salespeople run the shop while I hit the road looking for a cure.

Joo-won cleared his throat, grabbing my attention. "By the way, I need you to accompany me to a gathering."

I lifted an eyebrow in suspicion. "You really aren't focused. You don't have time for parties."

He gave me a cocky wink. "There's always time for a party, and I can multitask. So, you'll come, yes?"

While I loved a good party and any chance to dress up, I no longer had the down to party attitude. Well mostly. "If I don't come, will you bug me about it?"

He cocked a brow and leaned back as if he were insulted by my question. "Do I seem like the type to be a nuisance?"

My mind went back to the time we first met, and he afterward proceeded to fill the house I was staying at with every manner of gift he thought I would like to get me to fall for him. He wasn't exactly a nuisance, but he was persistent.

28

Still, I couldn't believe he was inviting me because he had to have some arm candy for this event. He didn't seem like the type to need such a thing. "What's the catch?"

He tossed a hand to the side. "I have no ulterior motives. I just like seeing you dressed up." His marble-colored eyes glowed with mischief. "It excites me. Also, this can be the favor you owe me."

Kind of seemed like I was getting let off the hook here. This couldn't possibly rise to the same level as what he'd done for me. He must have really wanted me to come. The pit of my stomach tightened. The man was a flirt, and it really didn't take much. Those eyes did most of the work for him. Then there was his smile, his lean, muscular build and even his pointed ears were a turn on. Maybe I was a little excited myself. And because I seemed to relish in bad decisions, I decided to say yes.

I gave him a curt nod. I was going to an elven affair. This would be fun.

CHAPTER 3

*E*lves didn't live in different realms like the fae, so I had no real idea of where this party would be. Honestly, I didn't know much about it. Now, because I already agreed, Joo-won was back to being his secretive self and wouldn't tell me anything more. Like, why the elves were partying. How big was this event? Was it the V.I.P. elves? Was it regional? Was it a birthday party? An award's ceremony? How did elves party? I knew elves liked their liquor, but I didn't know if they were as notorious as some of the faerie parties, which involved hedonism. However, I couldn't assume they just walked around with glasses of alcohol and small plates listening to a DJ or live band.

Of course, that then lead to more pressure of how I should look. Joo-won wanted arm candy. That was an outdated kind of request, but I had to admit, I didn't mind it. I liked looking cute, and it would be a great way to advertise a gown I designed. Anyway, I decided to pull out all the stops. If I was going to look good, I wanted to turn some heads while doing it, and I prided myself on being able to make others glamourous. I'd do no less for myself.

When Joo-won came to take me to the undisclosed location, I was dressed in an off-the-shoulder, floor-length electric blue gown. The back was all lace, including the train that swept behind it, and the front held a thigh-high split. I paired the dress with thin-strapped skin-toned sandals and magically added some extra inches to my hair, sweeping it all to the side, down to just below my chest. I added a bold red lip as the final touch. Ok, and a little faerie sparkle to my skin. I really wanted some iridescent wings to finish off my look, but this fairy had no wings. I still held out hope that it would come one day. I was still a young faerie, and as my power grew, I figured they would appear. I was getting stronger every week as I continued my strength training in my free time.

When Joo-won showed up at my apartment door, he raised a brow, and a slow smile lifted the corners of his lips as he gazed at every inch of me.

A normal girl would have been uncomfortable under his stare, but I was way too confident for that. This is the reaction that I wanted. Faerie glamour did a lot for a gal, and I was making the most of it. This was how I made my living, after all.

He reached out a hand. "Thank you for agreeing to come with me. You take my breath away, butterfly. I almost don't want to show you to anyone else. I'm not in the mood to fight off others tonight."

I snorted and took his hand. A warmth of pleasure raced through me, forcing a wide grin on my face. "I didn't look this good just for you. I like to be seen."

He leaned forward and kissed my hand, eyes still on me. "Oh, you will be."

I tried to keep up the air of confidence I had so carefully curated, but I had to admit, Joo-won wasn't looking too shabby himself. He wore a wine-colored suit that was tailored to the gods with a crisp white shirt and iridescent tie and pocket square. His hair was parted and combed back, showcasing his beautiful bone structure. A hint of black liner rimmed his eyes, and his lips seemed more red than normal. The whole look made my stomach clench. Seriously, why did this man have to look so beautiful?

As if he seemed to know what I was thinking, he had the audacity to smirk before gripping my hand more securely. "We will have to go through a portal to get there. My people are already at the event, so we'll make a nice, slightly late entrance."

He snapped his fingers, and a floor-to-ceiling circle grew before my eyes, leading to a cloudy, baby blue environment. I could see nothing else beyond the mist.

Using a portal to arrive made me wonder if we were going to another realm, although this was the way elves teleported. This was really going to be a surprise.

When we stepped through, the setting quickly transformed, giving way to a navy blue evening sky full of shockingly bright stars. However, that wasn't the amazing part. We were now standing at the entrance of a glass mansion that seemed to sit on top of a large body of water. It didn't sway like it should have. It was not a boat. It sat as solid on the water as if it were ground, but I could see low waves lap against the pristine glass.

Inside there were many areas that seemed to be covered in clouds or a translucent film. I assumed those were bedrooms and bathrooms. The foyer around us was grand. People passed by us to go towards the back of the mansion, which opened to a massive living and dining area. I could already see a large gathering of people mixing and mingling through the glass walls.

I leaned towards Joo-won. "Where are we?"

He glanced down at me without moving his head. He brushed the back of my hand gently with his own, and my mind momentarily grew to distraction at the zing of electricity from the small contact. "It's a secret."

I walked ahead of him, slightly frustrated. It was no surprise he wouldn't tell me. He liked the power he held over me when he knew things I didn't. "You're annoying." I really wanted to hate him for it, but it was like my body refused to care about what my brain said. His very height alone; he was least a foot taller than my 5'1 frame, made me want to climb him like a tree and ride him like a horse. *Lisa, what has gotten into you? You aren't even drunk.* He had to be using magic. That was the only explanation of why even after all these months, my mind refused to get out of the gutter around him. But would he really do that? He said he wanted me willingly. Was I really this horny?

He easily caught up to me with his long legs and took my hand in his. "Don't go leaving me, butterfly."

His hand was warm and soft, and instantly, my body buzzed to attention, stomach clenching in desire. I snatched my hand back. "I am available."

He laced his fingers between mine, making it harder for me to pull away.

He stopped walking, causing me to stop moving as well, and I looked up at him with questioning eyes. He leaned towards me, and my breath caught.

Was he going to kiss me? In front of all these people?

His face betrayed no emotion, so I really had no idea what he meant to do. However, instead of putting his lips to mine, he moved his face beside mine and whispered. "We both know that's not true. I've declared my intentions for you. I know you like me, too. I'm a patient man, but don't fool yourself into thinking that you are anyone's but mine."

I cursed my body for tingling at his egotistical and possessive words. I was not a thing that belonged to anyone, and he needed to know that. He was always so damn cocky

33

and self-assured. I'd never seen him off his game, even when he almost died fighting Lorenzo. He made even death seem like it was on his terms. And now he had the audacity to think that he ran everything, including my heart.

Before I could open my mouth to tell him just what I thought of his cocky attitude, I heard someone call his name behind us. We both turned to see Senna and Yuri, Joo-won's other trusted high-ranking member, walk towards us.

Senna looked stunning, as usual, in an orange halter gown and had a slit so high, I thought we might see her goodies. Her almost waist-length deep brown locks were piled high in a bun on top of her head except for a couple locks that framed her face.

Yuri stood in stark contrast to her. He matched her height in her heels and was lean and muscular with skin devoid of melanin with equally white hair that laid in long loose curls around his face. He was strangely handsome with a strong jaw, large, almond-shaped eyes and full lips. Against the paleness of his skin were electric blue eyes that always seemed to look right through you, as if you didn't exist. His face was a constant mask of boredom and irritation. Tonight, he also wore a well-tailored burnt orange three-piece suit with a multicolored tie and pocket square. He looked pretty darn dapper even with the multiple piercings in his pointed ears and the septum piercing in his nose.

The pair actually seemed like a couple going to the high school prom with their matching colors. To annoy Senna, I thought it was best to say something about my observation. "Did you both coordinate what you were going to wear like a gorgeous couple?" I gave them a toothy smile.

Senna glared at me.

Yuri, whose face was usually even more devoid of emotion than Joo-won's, actually lit up. His eyes widened, and I saw just the slightest turn up of his lips. "This was purely a coincidence," he replied in his thick Russian accent. "However, great minds must think alike." He looked over to Senna as he spoke, and there was a wistfulness in his eyes as he gazed at her. I found him absolutely adorable when he looked at her like that. His coldness was just an inch less frigid. He looked like a puppy dog that just wanted to be petted by her.

Senna, however, refused to meet his eyes, her scowl still in place. Either she was really clueless about Yuri's crush on her, or she was purposefully ignoring it. I was betting on the latter. "We clearly spend too much time together. Now we look like backup dancers for the King."

Joo-won chuckled. "That seems appropriate. You both really do look quite stunning. How lucky am I to be surrounded by not only highly capable and superior fighters but also such beautiful ones."

Oh, he knew how to lay on the charm.

"What have we missed?" he asked them as the four of us began to walk towards the gala space.

We passed several elves mingling about the building. Everyone seemed like giants to me. As most elves were near six feet and up, I was glad I decided to wear my highest heels tonight, even if my feet would kill me later. I was still a little person compared to them, but at least I didn't have to strain my neck looking up as high as I would have in flats. The Pre-World had gotten elves all wrong. They were not little people who made yummy chocolate cookies or toys for Santa's sleigh. The only thing we'd gotten right was the pointy ears and the partying.

Senna nodded in response to his question. "You should know that Martin is here. I'm surprised he's here. I didn't think this would be his type of event."

Joo-won's fingers tightened around mine.

I winched slightly.

He quickly relaxed his hold, lifting the back of my hand to his lips with an apologetic kiss. "It isn't. He's only here for one reason."

I looked into his eyes, but he gave nothing away, ever the cool one.

Yuri shook his head. "He is a scoundrel. He means no good."

Joo-won rolled his shoulders back, seemingly unbothered. "Let's go."

We began to walk again towards the festivities. So, he wasn't going to tell me anything about this Martin guy, huh? I would have to press a little later. Clearly, this guy was not a friend based on their reactions.

When we arrived at the grand area, my mouth dropped open in awe at the space. While I'd seen from the front of the mansion that it was an open design for the dining room and living area, the glass walls facing the back were actually all floor to ceiling doors that swung open to what appeared to be more seating, an infinity pool and a rose garden. Vines of roses and greenery hung from the ceiling and wrapped around the edges of the room. I looked up at the tall ceilings and noticed that the space was lit only by floating orbs of various sizes that gave off a warm glow. It was like we were in a dazzling greenhouse.

The globes continued to the outside, where several guests also resided. On a glass platform over the pool, also stable, was a DJ and several elves danced around her on the glass platform, not afraid of it breaking under their weight.

This felt like a fairy tale, and I was the princess. Now to hope there was no evil stepmother out to kill me.

An elf walked over to us, balancing two large trays of food and drink in the air above their open palms. We each took a flute of what appeared to be a bubbly red liquid. I also grabbed a tiny plate filled with three mysterious bites of something I hoped was tasty. I'd failed to eat before I came here assuming it would be a sit-down affair.

I took a sip of the drink and was pleased to find it crisp and slightly sweet. "So, what is this whole thing for anyway?"

Senna gave a nod to the waiter elf that we were done partaking, and he walked away. "This is just a reminder that we are all family. We only get together like this every decade."

"So, it's like a high school reunion? You look to see who got fat, who got married, who's doing well?"

"Interesting reference but not wrong. It's a power play as well. Elves stick to their own territories, which can be hard since we had to be mobile. Some tribes had subgroups, but there was one king. There were many mergers and marriages for power. Sometimes we use these events to broker deals and arrangements. See who we can combine with."

"Are you looking to expand?" I looked up at Joo-won for an answer to that question, but he wasn't paying attention.

Instead, he was starring across the room with an intense look, but I couldn't figure out who he was gazing at. He suddenly glanced down at me. "Excuse me for one moment. I have to speak to an old friend. Stay here."

Senna took a step towards him. "Are you sure that's wise?"

He flashed her a brief look of annoyance. "Are you questioning my decision?"

She looked undeterred by his mood. I had to give it to her, Senna never appeared fearful. She was loyal to Joo-won without question, but she didn't cater to him. "Not at all, my King. I simply want to ensure your safety."

Joo-won's face relaxed back to its neutral setting. "Come with me then." He looked over to Yuri. "Stay with our butterfly." He then gave me a wink before turning and leaving.

Yuri stood rigid. "I will guard her with my life." He looked as if he was just told to bodyguard the president.

I patted him on the shoulder. "Calm down, I'm not that important."

He gave me wide eyes as if I'd said the most idiotic thing in the world. "You are most precious to our King."

I had to admit, that gave me a pop of delight in my stomach. A girl could be confused about her feelings for an elf, but she sure did enjoy the attention he gave. I was so vain. I took a nibble of one of the pastries on my plate and was delighted to find it tasted like a mini chicken pot pie. As I chewed, I looked to Joo-won and Senna as they approached a small group.

In the center stood a man with a clean-shaven tanned face, thick, dark brows above large lavender eyes that appeared strangely haunted and captivating. I could barely tear my eyes from them to assess the rest of him. He had long chocolate brown hair that grazed his broad shoulders. He was also handsome. Actually, like Joo-won, that description wasn't really fitting. He was beautiful. Like, maybe I was a little jealous of his flawless skin and those amazing eyes. Even his hair seemed to shine. Granted, magic was a thing now, so we could all be beautiful people, but he had something I wasn't sure even glamour could provide. And did I mention his lips? They were actually rosy and naturally upturned in the slightest pout. I wanted to be inappropriate and touch them. He was dressed simply in black slacks and a silky white tunic. Around his neck was a colorful, long beaded necklace. He was just one shade removed from looking like a 70's hippie, like in the old movies.

Joo-won reached out to offer his hand to him, and the man took it, but instead of shaking it, he pulled Joo-won to him and wrapped his other hand around Joo-won's back in a tight embrace. I wished I could have seen Joo-won's face to see how he reacted to that. Something told me he wasn't expecting that kind of greeting. Joo-won wasn't really a toucher beyond me. At least not in my presence.

"Who's the hot guy Joo-won is talking to?" I asked before stuffing another pastry in my mouth. This one was sweet, like a cinnamon bun. I needed to find more of these things. Three weren't going to cut it.

Yuri narrowed his eyes at the man. "Danger."

Well, that explained nothing at all. "Ok, but does danger have a name?"

"Martin Dupont."

I tapped my chin, trying to place the last name. "French?"

Yuri nodded.

"Does he have an accent?"

"Yes."

"That's hot."

Yuri cut his eyes at me. "Accents are hot?"

I scrunched my face. Some accents were hot. I wasn't a huge fan of Yuri's accent, but there was no need to hurt his feelings and qualify my response.

So Joo-won had a friend, of sorts, who was almost as handsome as he was but more dangerous. I was very curious. Not for any dating purposes. My feelings for Joo-won were already complex enough, I certainly didn't need another mysterious, bad boy elf to drive me to distraction. However, I was extremely nosey. "So, what makes Martian so dangerous?"

"He is a dark elf." He took a sip of his drink and continued to glare.

"That's it? That's all I get?"

"He is also master of bugs and rodents."

I bared my teeth in disgust. "By master, do you mean he can control them?"

Yuri furrowed his brows. "Yes. It is disgusting. I never liked the infestations he would cause. They were effective but nauseating."

Interesting how such a beautiful man could have such gross power. In my mind, a guy who could control roaches and rats should be slimy looking with yellow teeth. But there had to be more to him than being a dark elf and a bug master. "Anything more?"

He turned slightly and gave me an apologetic frown. "Apologies, Lisa, but I am not one to gossip. It is best you learn about such things directly from the King."

I pouted. He was loyal. I shouldn't have been surprised. "You're no fun."

"Fun is not my specialty." He looked almost solemn when he said it, and his face relaxed.

Well, if I wasn't going to get the goods on Joo-won's past acquaintances, I might as well get in the business of his wingman to keep me occupied. And I knew just where to start. "So, you have a thing for Senna?"

At my question, Yuri nearly spit out his drink, instead of going for a cough. "I know not what you are meaning."

I gave him a playful roll of my eyes. He looked hard on the outside, but he was a big softie when it came to Senna. I would get the truth out of him. "English may not be your first language, but you command it pretty well. You know what I mean. The way you look at her, it's totally obvious."

He looked almost appalled when he stared down at me. "Tell me you lie."

I shook my head with a smug smile. "Sorry, dude, you look totally love struck."

He dropped his shoulders like a sad child. "She is the moon to my stars."

I sighed. Aww, the poetry of it all. "That was beautiful."

"Sadly, as just a small star of many, she will never notice me. I am simply a friend to her. A brother of arms."

"Have you tried telling her how you feel?"

He shook his head quickly. "I could never take such a risk. She is a serious woman. She would see our joining as unprofessional."

Now that I believed. It didn't initially dawn on me that Joo-won, Senna and Yuri were really like a working team with Joo-won as the boss. My group of Six all mixed it up, but I guess it ran its risk of going to disaster if there were any lover's quarrels. Well, it actually had almost gone that route. Amina and Erik had their spats, but it never threatened to break us apart. I had my situation with Charles, and that made things awkward, but we were able to work together for the greater good. I couldn't imagine what would happen if we all just couldn't get along to provide aid when needed. Did Senna really think that a romance could prevent her from doing her job? Or maybe she just wasn't into him.

"I know we live long lives, but tomorrow is never guaranteed. You should let her know how you feel one day soon. You never know what could happen. She seems like the type that likes for the man to make the first move."

Yuri gave me a wary look as if he seriously doubted the accuracy of my words. He would be right in his suspicion as I had no idea what I was talking about. Almost a year after meeting her and I had no clue about who Senna really was. Not that I'd ever bothered to find out.

Another waiter passed by, and I grabbed another plate of food, starting to get a little restless. Trying to get Yuri a love life was not the best use of my time. With Joo-won being gone for so long, I was beginning to believe that eye candy was not really what I was here for. I knew it was too good to be true. My presence here was more than cutie in a dress.

"Am I really here just as eye candy?"

Yuri studied a pastry, sniffing it before deciding it was okay to eat, and popped it in his mouth. He chewed slowly, as if deciding on whether he liked the food. I wanted to wring him by the neck and get him to hurry with a response. "Do not tell the king this," he finally stated. "But I suspect he brought you here to let others know he has friends in places that are high. You are part of Six."

I snorted. I got it now. It made the most sense, and it was a bit of a let-down. He was using me. "Oh, so he was trying to show off."

Yuri nodded his head swiftly. "Yes, this is right. Other's will believe he is quite formidable if you are here. They may want to align with him. The bigger our tribe, the safer we are."

"I get it, but I think he should be focusing on other things like his survival. None of this will matter if he's not around to rule it." Not to mention that there could be people here that could help Amina.

Yuri's eyes darkened, and his mouth thinned into a tight line. "I fear that he is doing this for that very reason. If he does not survive, he wants his people to be safe. We are strong now, but perhaps he believes that if we are larger, we would be even more protected."

I looked back in Joo-won's direction. The longer I'd come to know the elven king, the more I learned that he cared about his people and did what he thought was best to protect. Even if sometimes that was misguided, like siding with evil ancient beings because he thought they were stronger than my friends and me. He, at the last minute, figured out he was wrong on that one. So at least he was able to course correct. It kind of made me like him more.

Joo-won and Senna returned to us, this time with Martin and a couple others. Joo-won removed my now empty plate from my hand, giving it to Yuri, and grabbed my hand.

I raised my brows in surprise. Yes, Joo-won was more touchy-feely with me, but this felt almost like a necessity. What was that all about? I'd have to find out later.

Martin looked to me, a spark in his eyes. "There is a room on the second floor where we can talk more freely without the loud music."

The way he was just looking at me as he spoke was disconcerting, sending an icy chill through me that was a mix of pain and pleasure. Confusing. Was he talking to me? We hadn't even met yet. I was getting weird vibes. Still, I was more than curious about this mystery man. Maybe this little private talk would open up some mysteries about Joo-won's past.

CHAPTER 4

*H*ave you ever climbed glass steps in a glass mansion before? I am not a fan. The staircase had the audacity to be wide and winding. It was very grand, and if I was a performer on stage, it would make for a very impressive look. However, with each step, I thought I would drop through the building. And yes, I know it was all psychological, but it still didn't stop my stomach from clenching. Maybe I was a tad afraid of heights. I did want my faerie wings but maybe flying wasn't all it was cracked up to be. Though the wings would make an awesome accessory.

Once we made it up the staircase, we made a left down the hall past rooms filled with white clouds, or something very similar to it, that preserved privacy. At the end of the hall, we faced a door, and Yuri opened it to let us into what appeared to be a small library filled with books and comfortable seating and tables that were not made of glass but rather leather and dark wood. We gathered ourselves near a window that faced the pool. I sat flanked by Joo-won to my right and Senna to my left. Yuri sat on the edge of the arm of the couch near Senna. Martin and his two people, two men dressed in a similar fashion to him, sat on the opposite couch.

Martin turned his attention back to me, his eyes smiling and crinkling at the corner as he grinned. He was assessing me.

I was used to that type of look. What I couldn't tell was what he was thinking. Did he like what he saw?

Joo-won moved my hand to his thigh and placed his hand on top of mine, probably knowing I would have moved it away. I wasn't super comfortable with public displays of affection.

Martin suddenly broke the growing silence in the room. "Before we talk about anything else, I want to formally meet this beautiful woman sitting in front of me," he stated with a melodic French accent. Actually, I could have heard him read an instruction manual and drifted off to a peaceful sleep. His voice was just that soothing and, ok, a little damn sexy.

I put my drink down on the coffee table and gave him a quick wave, unsure if touching was okay. In most cases, elves were particular about that. In the past, a handshake was not an issue. In this new world, magic had the potential to be exchanged just by touch, and I wasn't sure how I felt about this guy. He was a dark elf, after all. In the world of the fae, being dark, and I wasn't talking skin complexion, meant that you were evil. I really hated calling negative things dark, but not everyone knew the significance of unseelie, which was more appropriate to what this Martin guy fell into. It really meant that he had some evil tendencies at the most or at the least, just wasn't a fan of the human world. I wasn't sure which he fell into. Joo-won was not seelie himself and fell right in the middle. He didn't harm humans, but he didn't help them either.

I kept waiving like a buffoon. "I'm Lisa. Small business

owner, faerie, and member of The Six, as I'm sure you know."

Martin's grin widened, and he gave me a head nod. "I'm Martin, an elven leader from France. I see you've been captured by our friend Joo-won. He has a way of stealing hearts, like so many other things, does he not?"

While one of Joo-won's more negative qualities was that his tribe was known for pilfering things, I wasn't totally sure I got what he was saying in this context. What exactly did he know about Joo-won? I'd heard he was a ladies' man, so maybe that was it. He certainly wasn't shy with his flirtation game.

When I didn't respond, Martin leaned forward, still with the pleasantries. "Did you know much about our friend here before recent years? I knew him before he was a proper king. We shared many good times together." He glanced over at Joo-won, and there was something in his eyes that made me still.

Desire.

I tilted my head to the side but kept quiet. Now this was a new development. Did this guy have a thing for Joo-won? No, wait. Did they have a thing for each other? Was Martin actually an ex-lover?

I turned my head to Joo-won, whose eyes betrayed no information. I would really hate to play poker with him.

Joo-won crossed one leg over the over, leaning back in his seat. "I agreed to speak to you because you said you were able to help me break this curse."

Ah, so that's what this was about.

Martin leaned back, looking back at me once more before addressing Joo-won's statement. "Yes, I can access some magic that could possibly break that curse."

Senna shifted in her seat beside me. "I'm assuming it

would be evil magic. Something that would no doubt require killing or summoning something demonic?"

Martin kept his eyes on Joo-won. "As much as that disgusts you, Senna, dark magic is the strongest magic there is. I don't think anything else will be good enough to break his curse. Or would you rather your leader die so you can maintain a moral high ground?" He finally looked to Senna, and his eyes were anything but friendly now. There was clearly no love lost between those two.

"That's a stupid question. It's about more than morals. Evil magic always comes with a price. The more potent it is, the heavier the price. We would never go into any kind of deal like that without knowing the full consequences."

Martin snorted. "Joo-won, since when did you let your underlings speak on your behalf?"

Joo-won tilted his head back slightly, looking mildly bothered as his eyes iced over in a cold glare. "They don't. However, Senna is no underling, she is my advisor, and I don't take her words lightly."

"But you are in a desperate situation."

"I am never desperate."

Yikes, I could feel Joo-won's anger radiating next to me. Seemed Martin knew exactly how to push his buttons. I really wanted to know more about their past.

Martin raised his hands in surrender. "Very well, but what are your options, mon ami? My heart would break if such a dear friend were to leave this world so young."

Joo-won was hundreds of years old, in theory, he had already worn out his welcome. Not that I was anxious to lose him either.

Joo-won looked down to his glass of alcohol and appeared to study it before speaking. "What would this magic consist of? What would be the price, and why do you want to help me?"

Martin smiled again, encouraged by Joo-won's curiosity. "It is a potion. The price is something we cannot control. And because I am your friend who cares about your well-being."

"Why would I take a potion with an unknown price? I could very well end up in the same predicament. Death or life-long servitude to someone else."

"It is a fair concern. This potion doesn't always have a price. You have a good chance at having no negative outcome at all."

I'd want to know percentages. What was the likelihood that he'd be cured with no consequences? This seemed like a risky deal and from an alleged friend. By Joo-won's behavior, I couldn't really tell if he actually liked Martin. He certainly didn't seem pleased to see him. At the mere mention of his name, he'd put my hand in a vice grip.

Joo-won put on a gentle smile and brushed the side of my hand with his thumb.

I think he did it more to settle his mood than as an affection towards me.

"I'll keep in mind your offer after I explore other options."

Martin looked down at our interlocked hands, and there was a flash of disapproval or maybe jealousy there. "Well, you know how to contact me should you change your mind."

Yuri stood up with a grunt like an old man. He meant to get noticed, and it worked because we all looked at him. "Well, now that that is over. You can leave."

Martin chuckled, leaning back to show he had no intentions of leaving. "I've only just gotten here. Not happy to see me?"

"Never. I am never happy to see you. That was a silly question."

"I know you, and we have had our differences, but I'm not a bad guy."

Yuri scoffed and crossed his arms. "You are the very definition of a bad guy. Why are you here?"

Yeah, this is what I wanted to know as well. Very little was coincidence in this world.

Martin crossed his legs and looked around the room, very unbothered by Yuri's cold demeanor. "I like a grand affair like any other. And I was hoping to see my dear friend. I know I usually don't go to such things, but I thought it time for a nice change of pace. I am not the elf I once was."

Yuri snorted again and looked to Joo-won for our next moves.

Joo-won let go of my hand and rose, and I decided that was my cue, along with Senna, to rise as well. He looked down to Martin with his normal cold eyes. "Be well," he said simply and began to walk away.

I wasn't a nosey person. Ok, who was I kidding? I was a very nosey person. There was a lot happening here that I wanted confirmation about. I knew Joo-won had a past. He was hundreds of years old, and he'd been married before. Had kids and everything. I also knew he was a neutral fae. That didn't mean he was always good. In fact, many unseelie fae who gave up their unseelie side just became neutrals. When you looked at it that way and threw in Joo-won's tribe being known as thieves and siding with ancient evils, him being a former bad boy wasn't out of the realm of possibility.

I looked back at Martin, who gave me a wink. "I'll be seeing you again, my friend. And hopefully, your lovely woman too."

Joo-won paused, his body going rigid for a moment. This guy was really getting to him, and it made me all the more curious about who Joo-won really was.

*J*oo-won was a man who liked to have everything in order. Every hair was in place, everything in his territory was immaculate, and he never seemed out of sorts. He maintained the upper hand with me because he didn't share information, and he knew I wanted to know things about him.

So how could I find out about him without making it seem like I wanted to know? Senna and Yuri would only say so much. I could really put in the work when it came to me minding the business of others. It was like my non-lucrative side hustle. I decided that the best way to get what I wanted was to not say anything at all. He was used to me blabbing away all the time. I think he found it amusing. However, if I gave him the silent treatment, I stood a good chance of breaking him just a tiny bit, and that would allow me to go in for the kill. Of course, me being silent for any long period of time would be a feat in itself. I really was dying to know more about the elven world.

Unfortunately, one hour later into the party and Joo-won seemed truly unbothered by my silence. He really did treat me like a little kid and he, the wiser adult. And in some ways, it was true since he was old enough to be my great great great on and on grandfather. However, I was no kid. It was time to level up.

Before Joo-won could start yet another conversation with yet another tall, pointy-eared elf, I tapped him on the shoulder. He looked down at me, mouth slightly parted in the barest of a grin like he already knew what I was about to say. He probably thought I was going to ask him some questions about Martin and the elves. However, I was going to give him just the opposite. "I've been here for over two hours. I'm going home now."

He didn't seem fazed at all. Instead, he gave me a tsk-tsk. "You can't leave now."

I gave a short chuckle. "Sure, I can. Did you forget that I can teleport? I don't need your portal."

He lowered his brows, lips turned down at the corners in disappointment. "Why leave, butterfly? Have I angered you?"

Ok, he was playing innocent. Well, I wasn't going to fall for it. "I suddenly realized that although I've known you for nearly a year now, you keep very important things about yourself hidden from me. I never know what's going in that head of yours. I had no idea that you were going to change your mind and help us fight the soulmates. You like being all mysterious, and I don't care for any of it."

He didn't look like he was buying what I was selling. "Honestly?"

I jutted my chin out, puffing out a deep breath. I was starting to get annoyed. Against my better judgement, I was falling for a man who I couldn't allow myself to fully trust. I had no idea if giving him my organ would unleash another villain into the world. And yet, my heart refused to listen to my brain. I really liked him, and I hated that I couldn't trust him. It drove me insane, actually gave me sleepless nights. I couldn't defend him to my friends. I couldn't even think of giving him my heart, let alone any other organ, if I didn't really know him. And all he wanted to do was to play the mysterious flirt. It was unhelpful. "Yes. Honestly. I have better things to do than chase after you all the time. I have a friend lying in a magic-induced coma, and I have no way of figuring out how to fix it so she won't go all evil. She's saved my life, cleaned up my mistakes, and forgiven me for betraying her. I've been a shit friend, and all the while, I'm running after you just to amuse you. It's getting old. You are getting old."

I was actually shaking now. This had gone in a direction I hadn't anticipated ,but it was my truth, and I needed to be real if I was going to make any impact on this frigid elf. And, the truth was, if he still didn't care, then this still would be worth it. It would mean that there would never be anything between us because I couldn't be with a man who was so cocky and stubborn that he couldn't give an inch. That would actually make my attraction to him easier to ignore.

When I didn't see a change in his face, I turned away and clapped my hands. A swirl of what looked like colorful glitter, but was actually faerie dust, surrounded me and prepared to send me home when I felt a hand on my forearm. I looked down at the large hand and then looked up at Joo-won, but his face was masterfully unreadable, as usual. "Don't go."

I wasn't sure if this was a command or him being vulnerable. Curiosity got the better of me. "Why?"

He squinted his eyes at me, wrinkling his nose in the process. It was playful but not in an arrogant or cocky manner. He was being cute, and the look might be effective on me, as were most of his looks. "I wanted you to stay the night."

Of course, it would be about fulfilling his needs. I shook my head swiftly. "I'm not staying overnight with you anymore. You think you're eventually going to wear me down, but you won't."

He lost the playful glint in his eyes, and I saw a very brief flash of hurt beneath them. "Can you not see yourself in love with me?"

"Not if you can't ever be vulnerable with me."

He let go of my arm, giving a short, dry chuckle. "If I tell you something you want to know, will you stay with me this weekend? I just...like to be near you. Does that bother you? I like your presence."

52

He ran a hand through his hair before looking away from me, his shoulders dropped. Maybe it was an act, but he would have no reason to put on a show. Joo-won had always been transparent with his feelings. And he was respectful. Most of the time we were together, it was very PG-13. He accepted my limits without pushing them or trying to convince me differently. He always seemed to just want me around. Damn it. It was moments like this that made me like him. "Fine, but it doesn't mean sex will be involved."

He lifted a brow, in shock or offense. I couldn't tell. "Is it ever? And yet, I still want you by me. More than you know." He shook his head, pressing his lips together as if to stop himself from admitting more.

Now that sounded like a sweet thing to say. The last time Joo-won had confessed any sort of feelings for me was when I saved him from dying when we battled Lorenzo. I'd played it off then as him still being in a haze of recovery.

I snapped my fingers, and the fae dust disappeared, giving me a better vision of the beautiful man in front of me.

"What would you like to know first?" he asked, opening his arms.

"I want to know about you and Martin. Everything. The whole back story." I needed to know why he almost cracked my fingers with just the mention of this elf's name.

A flash of dismay crossed Joo-won's eyes, but he didn't argue. "Fine, when we get back to my place, I will tell you all."

And so, we stayed at the party a couple more hours before returning to his place. Before leaving the event, I learned that elves knew how to throw a party. They got drunk, they danced, some wound up in the ocean partying like this was some magical MTV spring break special from way back in the day. Even Senna and Yuri let loose. A drunk Yuri talked way too much about nothing you wanted to know about, and a drunk Senna was a big flirt, though not with Yuri, much to his dismay.

Joo-won, however, seemed to still be totally in control. It was crazy annoying. When we got back to his hotel, we entered his suite, and I collapsed on the couch, ready for his truth-telling.

CHAPTER 5

*J*oo-won loosened his tie and ran a hand through his hair, tousling it before sitting beside me. "Are you hungry?" he asked, stretching his long legs in front of him and laying his head on the back of the couch. He seemed very tired, either physically or from our conversation. I couldn't tell, but I wouldn't be surprised if it was both.

I squinted my eyes and took another look at him. Hmm, maybe he wasn't as sober as I thought. There was a little more relaxation in him that I'd never seen from the poised elf. He seemed totally at ease. I felt suddenly happy that I'd monitored my own drinking. Now was the perfect time to get the goods on who Joo-won really was.

I shook my head. "Nope, I'm full." I'd eaten an unknown number of pastries despite my form-fitting gown. If Joo-won really did like me, he was going to like my food belly as well. "So, Martin…"

Joo-won lifted his head and rubbed his jaw, eyes still closed. "You are relentless."

I wordlessly folded my arms, not letting his exhaustion

dissuade me. He was going to tell me what I wanted to know. We'd made a deal.

He opened his eyes, leaning forward with his forearms on his thighs. He stared at the floor, preventing me from seeing his eyes, which I believed was purposeful. Showing one's eyes made them vulnerable, and he was about to do just that. "I met him years after my marriage to my now deceased wife, In Ha. At the time, I was no one's king. I had not even met Senna yet, and Yuri was fairly new to my life. Elves run in tribes, but when we don't, we search for our kind, as we don't do well alone."

"I would have thought Senna was with you first." She was his second or at least a trusted advisor. Was Yuri really above her?

"No, I've known Yuri longer. Met him in Russia in the late 1600s. Moscow."

"How old were you then?"

He sat up, and I caught a wistful smile on his face as he remembered his past days. "Almost 150 years old. Then I met Senna in the 1780s in Jamaica, almost a hundred years later. She's a powerful elf. Very wise. Her magic is strong, but her mind is what makes her shine. She was barely 18 when she asked to join us, and I couldn't turn her away. Yuri is stronger. but he isn't as smart. However, his heart and loyalty are second to none. He is my brother."

I adjusted in my seat, facing him. Giddiness spread through me. He was being so open. I'd never even heard him talk much of his people. Most of our chats were random tales of his past but without too many identifiers and he never talked of feelings except for In Ha. "So where does Martin come in?"

Joo-won took his tie off and threw it on his lap as if it were a snake trying to strangle him.

I wasn't sure if he actually hated the tie or hated this conversation.

"I met him a couple decades later after Yuri in the south of France. At the time, the three of us took a liking to each other and became The Three Musketeers, of sorts."

"And what did the three of you do?" I had a feeling they weren't out fighting injustice.

He grimaced. "Things I no longer do."

Ugh, he was going to make this like pulling teeth. I wound my hands in front of me, one over the other to calm my growing frustration. *Patience, Lisa.* I was going to get him to talk if it was the last thing I did tonight. "Uh, care to elaborate?"

He side-eyed me. "Not really."

I know he hated to talk about his past, but I needed him to move this along despite his clear displeasure at it. At the very least, I could be happy he was even agreeing to speak at all. Of course, him being so vulnerable also upped my confusion factor. I was struggling between wanting to shake him so he could hurry his story along and at the same time jump on his lap and kiss him all over.

He slouched down on the sofa. "You won't let this rest, will you?"

"No, sir."

He crossed his arms and widened his legs, getting more comfortable as he stared out of the window. " We were criminals of sorts. We stole, we threatened, we hurt people. Martin found our jobs, I planned them out, Yuri was our muscle, in case we ran into trouble. He was also our conscious that we mostly didn't listen to. He had more of a moral code than we did."

"And what does that mean?"

He threw a forearm over his eyes as if to block out the light from the living area. He really was letting himself get unraveled with this discussion. I kind of liked it. It was the most human I'd ever seen him.

"I am not a good man, butterfly. I have much to atone for."

"Did you kill someone?" He had tried to kill Amina, Blake and Erik at one point, so it wasn't a wild guess. If he had killed an innocent person, I didn't think I would be able to look past it. I really hoped he answered no. A yes would be easier but, I didn't think I really wanted easy.

"I have not killed an innocent but events I caused did result in the death of innocents. I started to lose a taste for crimes that caused harm to those who did not deserve it. Yuri was always a proponent of being more selective and going after evil-doers. I eventually came to his side, much to Martin's displeasure. Yuri and he always had such tension. Martin assumed it was jealousy, but I knew different."

I raised a hand to pause him, moving closer until my knee was touching his thigh. He pushed closer to me, but I didn't let the contact distract me. Ok, it did distract me a little. Even through his pants, I could feel how warm he was. He was his own little mini furnace that I wanted to snuggle up against. But now we were getting to the good part, and I wasn't going to let him skim over it. I'd seen the way Martin looked at him. "What's the real deal with you and Martin? You were more than just cohorts in crime. I saw the way he looked at you back at the party."

He uncovered his face and looked down at me with lowered lids. "We were...close. He fell in love with me. I cared for him deeply, but I didn't love him. I couldn't love anyone like I loved In Ha. At least not then."

He looked down at his hands like a sad child, mouth in a tight frown. Did he think I'd look at him differently because of his past relationships? I'd like to think of myself as pretty open-minded. Plus, Martin was hot. Who could blame him?

"When I was seventeen, I made out with Candace, she was the head cheerleader. She had a total crush on me, and she was crazy cute. I was experimenting then and figuring out who I was. She was an amazing kisser but then I somehow made out with her boyfriend, Tom. I think they wanted to have an open relationship. We were doing the absolute most in twelfth grade. Anyway, things just got messy from there, and I broke it off. Didn't even last a month. I don't judge."

Joo-won gave me a bored look.

That was not the reaction I was expecting. There I was, trying to connect, and he looked very unmoved. Perhaps he didn't need my understanding. Elves weren't human.

"Did you tell me that story for a reason?"

I thought we were getting closer, but there he went, back to being his arrogant self. He didn't need me to approve of his relationship choices, but I just wanted to bond. Now I was feeling awkward and a tad silly. Time to turn this ship around. "I was trying to let you know that I was cool with whatever relationship you had with Martin because you were looking like a sad puppy, and I thought maybe you were feeling a little weird about telling me."

He tilted his head and gave me a lopsided grin. "I don't feel weird, as you say, about discussing my past relationship with Martin. I do not feel ashamed. The rules of man didn't apply to us. We love who we want. Always have. And butterfly, I never expected you to judge me. I hold you in too high a regard. Although your story was cute. Polyamorous relationships aren't for everyone, especially at such a young age."

I crossed my arms and twisted my lips. Way to make me feel like an amateur. "We didn't even do anything. All the drama without the fun except for some low-key make-out sessions. So, what was with the sad face then?"

"Memories."

Now that made sense. I wondered if he still had a thing for Martin. Had seeing him stirred up old emotions? "How many years were you together?"

"One hundred."

Well, damn. He said it like it wasn't that long. My mind was having a hard time trying to process living that long, let alone being in a relationship for that many years. I was still getting used to the idea of us paranormals living longer lives than regular humans. I was 31, but I hadn't aged since The Event. That part, I was quite pleased with. I was getting the wisdom without the wrinkles. But Joo-won was always an elf. Magic had never been removed or muted from him like it was us humans turned paranormal. And because his magic had never been touched, he was immortal. Part of me was peeved that whoever had ended magic all those years ago had deprived me of immortality. However, their cause, eradicating supernatural evil, was good, so I couldn't say much. Plus, I could still possibly live for hundreds of years. It was still too early in this new world to exactly tell beyond what psychics foresaw.

I shook my head and focused back on the conversation while I still had him. He'd been with Martin longer than my inseparable grandparents had been together, and they'd only been together 66 years. What kind of relationship could Martin and Joo-won have had? And how could Joo-won never have fallen in love with him in all that time? Was he even able to really love then? Was In Ha it for him? If that was the truth, then what were all the sweet words he was saying to me? Perhaps I was right to keep him at a distance.

I wanted to ask him so much more about their relationship, but I also didn't want to know. My stomach churned and not in a nervous way. I was uneasy. Crap. I was jealous. My stupid body cared nothing about what my head wanted.

Joo-won studied me as I rubbed my stomach. "Everything okay?"

I nodded, straightening up. Time to focus on the non-specifics of the relationship for now. "So, Senna knew him from before as well?"

"Things changed when she joined. The group expanded. She thought I was a leader and meant for more than just traveling the world and causing mayhem."

I still couldn't reconcile a rogue Joo-won out there like some globetrotting criminal. He seemed too sophisticated now. I wondered if that was Senna's doing. "I'm assuming Martin didn't want that. Guessing Martin didn't like sharing you."

He glanced over at me and opened his hand, palm up. I gave him a quizzical look. "Give me your hand. I want to feel you."

Something about the way he said that tightened my core, and my queasiness vanished. So simple, and yet it implied so much more. He wanted to touch me. He wanted to be with me. I hated that I got any happiness out of that.

I gave him my hand, and he quickly kissed it before lowering our joined hands on the couch space between us. "He did not like it at all. He was jealous of Senna. I'm pretty sure he would have killed her if he didn't think it would hurt me and Yuri. She never argued with him. Always poised. Yuri fell in love with her from the start. He acted like her bodyguard anytime Martin or really any of the males in our group came too close."

"Yuri's loved her for that long? I can't even fathom that."

Joo-won's lips turned slightly up, and he squeezed my hand. "We live long, but time goes so fast for us. It seems but a blink of the eye. Yuri has loved her non-stop, but he has had other relationships, as did she. But their bond is solid. Maybe she does not care for him in the romantic way, but she cares for him as if he were her mate." He gave a shrug. "Maybe that's what keeps giving him hope. Anyway, whenever anyone confronted her, he argued on her behalf, and while he did that, she went ahead and implemented her plan."

I held in a yawn. I was getting tired, but I didn't know when I'd have another opportunity to get this much intel from Joo-won again, so I pushed through. "And her plan was to make you a king?"

He nodded. "Now you will ask why she fought so hard to make someone else a leader. No one is that selfless."

"Exactly."

"She is an adviser. Not a leader. But she needed someone who would listen to her while also being an effective leader. I didn't fault her for her ambitions. Senna and Yuri have made me better. In a way, so has Martin."

Like I already knew, Senna was a smart woman, and Yuri was really a good guy. Now this Martin, I still needed to understand.

He looked reflective again, and I felt a tiny stab; okay, a large poking shank of jealousy. If he cared for him so much, what had Martin done to make him walk away? I moved even closer, and he smiled, moving my legs over his muscular thighs, and I could feel my body already relaxing. He began to take off my shoes. He was going to get me comfortable, but it would not distract me. "So, what was the last straw with you and Martin?"

Joo-won gave me a sly smile as she slowly rubbed my legs. Just the touch of his warm hands loosened the nerves in my body. "Wouldn't you much rather be doing something else?"

"I thought I said I wasn't having sex with you?"

He looked down and ran his hand up my leg and over my knee, pausing at the top of my thigh just as my body clenched at his touch. He seemed to know his effect on me because he was already grinning. "There are many other things we can do. As you know."

He must really hate this conversation, and also, there was the drunk part. I kind of didn't want him to stop moving his hand, but the sober part of me knew that this might be my only shot in a long while to get him to talk. "What did Martin do?"

Joo-won rolled his eyes but kept his hands on my thighs. "My butterfly has lost her fun. You would like to hear a tragedy instead? Very well. We wanted riches. Martin wanted chaos. He knew no end to his desire for it. He grew up very poor. His life was one of hardship. He came from a smaller and weaker tribe, and many of his loved ones were killed by larger, stronger tribes. He ended up being enslaved to a larger tribe, and no one in the hierarchy cared to rescue his people. Elves have a basic power system. There is a hierarchy, and tribes like his were at the bottom. I came from a high-ranking tribe, so I can't say I understood all the struggles that he endured. But I could empathize. It's why I typically don't interact within the structure. And why I had no problem stealing from higher-ranking elves to get my riches at one time. We don't treat our lower ranks very well."

I laid my head on the back of the couch as I listened to him talk. Thankful that he was sharing so much. It felt good to see him this open, and I was learning so much. "What group does? We should protect the weaker, but instead, we take advantage of them. I'm going to assume the party tonight was only for the powerful ranks?"

Joo-won nodded, thrumming his fingers on my thigh, and each beat of his fingers tingled my core. Damn, it didn't take much tonight. Or ever with him. "That would be an accurate guess. I'm honestly surprised Martin didn't cause a commotion tonight. That would have been his style in the face of the elites."

"Maybe he's changed. Like you did?"

"Perhaps, but then I'd want to know why. He's not that simple. And his hatred of hierarchies and power structures ran deeper than mine. I eventually went right. I worked within the system by gathering weaker tribes and making them part of my own, as equals. Martin wanted more than that."

It seemed to me that Joo-won had been more noble than I had given him credit for. It made me like him more. However, I could only imagine what Martin could have wanted for his own revenge. I'd want to destroy things too if my family was killed off. I was enslaved, and no one helped me. I'd want to burn down the system and make everyone uncomfortable.

Joo-won continued. "We had formed a large tribe, we were gaining wealth that allowed us to live comfortably and independently of the humans, but it wasn't enough for him. We weren't enough for him. He brought forth a plan to steal from a very high-ranking family. One that was a blend of human royalty and elven. It was a large mission and too risky. We'd never done a crime that high up. It would have upset not only the elven power structure but also human politics. Possibly exposed us or caused turmoil within their lands through suspicion of each other. And it would involve attacking their palace with many innocents beyond the soldiers and guards. I didn't approve it. But he gathered several of my people and went anyway."

So, Martin had betrayed him and then had the audacity to talk to him like they were still besties. And just as importantly, Joo-won was fine indulging him. Why? Were there still feelings there? I had to know more. "How did he think just a few elves could take on a whole palace?"

"Magic. He made a deal with some powerful witches and a few others for help. He had more alliances than I knew about. I never knew about his side deals for certain, but Yuri had shared rumors of such, but we could never verify."

So, Martin was determined and sneaky. That reminded me of Phillip. You didn't want a person like that going against you. Too dangerous. I suddenly began to feel even more uncomfortable with Martin's sudden reappearance in Joo-won's life. "Did they storm the castle?"

Joo-won closed his eyes, body tensing. He was either reliving the memory or trying his best to think of something else. "Yes. And killed everyone, including the defenseless. He destroyed a dynasty in one night, taking everything of value. What he did started a war between the humans and made the elven tribes fight not only each other, out of suspicion on who murdered that family, but also a battle with the humans. We exposed ourselves out of rage."

I shook my head slowly, horrified. I tentatively reached out to touch his arm. His shoulders relaxed, and I was pleased that my touch seemed to settle him. "I thought magic was gone or at least diluted in those days. How were they that strong?"

"Magic was never fully gone, especially in other realms that had portals to the human world. As long as the other realms like the fae, the heavens and the underworld existed, then power could always be tapped from there."

"So, what did you do when you found out what he did?"

"I imprisoned him and killed many of his allies. It took decades to do so, but I couldn't let it go. I do have a bit of a conscience."

I already knew that. Joo-won had always come through on the side of right when push came to shove. "Why didn't you kill him too?"

He ran a hand over his face, exhaustion growing in from

our late night. I should have let him sleep, but I knew if we stopped now, I'd never get the full story.

"I cared about him. It was a weak point for me. Instead, I had his powers removed. Much like mine will be if I do not find a cure."

"Then how is he free now? Does he have his powers back?"

"It seems I did not kill all of his allies. After over 100 years confined, he escaped."

A hundred years in lock up. I could not even fathom. I had no idea how Joo-won treated his prisoners. There was no bad area of his town that I could see. Then again, he might have treated Martin slightly better. Maybe he'd been under house arrest and not, instead, in a small concrete cell. On one hand, I found myself sympathizing with Martin's need to bring destruction to the elite. However, on the other hand, I could not support his violent ways. Not everyone deserved pain, and Martin didn't seem to understand that.

I studied Joo-won's sleepy-eyed face, determined to read his mind and failing. "You still care about him?"

"Do you still care about Charles?"

I bared my teeth at him. He really loved getting a rise out of me. "This conversation is about you and your evil ex, who we can't trust."

Joo-won began to stroke my thigh, and my body melted. He really knew when to distract me.

"He wants to save my life."

"At a price. What if he tries to draw you back into doing evil again? You are starting to turn over a new leaf. You've made good decisions that your tribe has prospered from. You aren't a thug anymore. You think he's just doing this out of the goodness of his heart? He'll want something from you. You broke up with him, killed his allies and imprisoned him for a century. You don't just let bygones be bygones after that. You can't tell me he doesn't want payback. And if he doesn't, you elves are officially weird to me."

He stood up and offered me a hand, unbothered by my comment. I was a lot dismayed that he was no longer stroking me. His hands were impossibly relaxing and seductive at the same time. I wanted the heat of him back.

"I know he doesn't want me dead. He may want to torture me and lock me up for a hundred years, but death is not his desire."

I took his hand and stood up. I was thoroughly confused. Elves definitely thought in different ways because I could not understand his confidence in Martin's motives. "Why do you trust him so much?"

He gave a slight smile and traced my cheek with the back of a finger. "You wouldn't understand."

I leaned into his touch in spite of myself. My body couldn't help wanting his touch, and I wasn't putting up much of a fight against it. "Maybe, but promise me you'll give this more time before you accept his offer. Something doesn't feel right, and you're smarter than this."

Before I could say another word, he pulled me into him and pressed his lips against mine. They were warm and tasted slightly sweet from all the liquor he'd been drinking. He playfully licked my top lip before deepening his kiss until his tongue delved inside my mouth, twirling and sending a warm flush through me. He was trying to distract me. I knew it.

I was not going to let him fully distract me. Something burned in me to keep him away from whatever Martin planned to do. I needed Joo-won to be good. "Are you going to listen to me and stay away from Martin?"

Without warning, he picked me up and walked us to the counter in his kitchenette. "You are so small; it hurts my back to lean over to kiss you. This is better." He then tilted my head sideways and sprinkled kisses over my neck.

Desire sizzled through me with each touch of his lips. I couldn't have this. If we did anymore, it would be over, and I wouldn't be able to let him go. "I'm not having sex with you," I said through panting breaths.

"So you've said," he replied, a hand slowly moving up my thigh.

My legs spread farther apart at his touch, and he pressed closer to me until my breasts were smashed against his solid chest.

Crap, his body was a heated solid mass, and I wanted him on me. Covering me. I moved my head back, quick breaths releasing from me as I struggled to regain control. This was not what needed to happen right now. Yet my fingers still found themselves laced in his silky black hair, refusing to let go. "Let me continue to work on getting you a cure or letting you eat my kidney or something."

He pulled away from my collarbone and quickly ran his tongue over my lips, and just like that, my body was a ball of fiery heat. "Eating your kidney. This is not sexy. You are ruining the mood." He moved his hands higher up my thighs, closer to my center, before dipping his tongue to my cleavage.

I let out a moan of anticipation as he closed in on my erogenous zones. Without thinking, I moved my hand from his shoulder and began to trace the outside of his ear, lingering slowly over the pointy tip. "And you are avoiding the topic."

I heard Joo-won groan into my chest, not answering my question. The vibration from his mouth only turned me on more.

Elven ears were very sensitive to the touch. Seeing Joo-won come a bit undone was kind of exciting. I pulled his head up towards me and flicked the tip of his ear with my tongue. "What do you say?"

His eyes fluttered, and he pressed himself closer to my apex. I could feel he was very much alive now. "I say keep doing what you're doing," he whispered in response, his hands surrounding my back in a desperate grasp.

I pulled away slightly, removing my mouth from his ear, but he held on tight to me. "And I will keep exploring alternatives, but if nothing else works, I will not go with his option."

He didn't sound very convincing to me, but I would make him keep his promise one way or another.

CHAPTER 6

*J*awoke the next morning to darkness. I knew it was morning because I peeked at the clock, and it said 10:35am, but Joo-won had his black-out curtains closed, and I could barely see a thing. It really was warm and cozy in his room. His bed, a California king bed, always put me immediately to sleep, and my body was devoid of any aches when I woke up. It was no wonder I always woke up late morning at his place.

Currently, his arm was wrapped around my midsection, my back pressed against his chest. And I was clothed, thank you, in a large shirt of his. Really, I was impressed by my own strength at resisting Joo-won.

I rolled towards the edge of the bed.

He pulled me back to him.

"You can't keep me here."

His baritone chuckle pierced through the darkness. The sound slid down my spine like silk, and I instantly started to relax again. This man was sexiness incarnate. Maybe it wasn't impossible to believe that Martin would give up any vendetta he had against him to keep Joo-won alive. Not that I would actually let my guard down around the French elf.

"I would never trap a butterfly." He snapped his fingers, and the curtains opened, revealing the bright, sunny day.

I squinted my eyes and turned to look at his beautiful face. His hair was tousled to perfection, and he didn't have any morning crud in the corners of his eyes. His breath never even smelled bad in the morning. Did he get up and wash when I was asleep?

He was only wearing silk pajamas, leaving his chest exposed. His ab definition was drool-worthy, and with the smooth, hairless skin, it was almost lickable. I shut my eyes tightly and looked away before temptation won.

I heard him move slightly on the bed. "Will you not even stay the weekend?"

"I can't lounge around. I have a store to run and cures to find for you and Amina." I sat up and moved to the edge of the bed, swinging my legs over the side.

He slid up behind me.

"No, no, no. Don't try to prolong this with another make-out session."

"While your willpower is impressive, that is not what I plan to do." He then picked up my hand, turned it over and kissed the inside of my wrist. "Ok, you can go now."

I squeezed my legs together in response. I turned slightly to him, startled that he was so close I could brush my lips against his. "Why did you do that?" "I marked you." He gave a slight shrug and laid back down on the bed, resting a muscled arm behind his head.

I closed my eyes in disbelief. I could not be hearing right. I wasn't going to get enraged because there was no way he would do such a thing for real. "Come again?"

"You need protecting."

It was my turn to chuckle now. "Clearly, you are joking. I need no protection. I am a member of The Six, thank you very much. Plus, you gave me the emerald necklace to contact you, so if I were to find myself needing help, I could reach you that way."

"You rarely wear it and I know you won't use it."

This was true. I really didn't want to be dependent on him or anyone, really. "And what the hell was the kiss about?"

"I need to know when you are in danger. It will let me know. " He nodded towards my hand. "Touch your wrist where I kissed you."

I touched my wrist, and a pinkish-red imprint of his lips appeared like a tattoo. I gritted my teeth, and fury swept through me. "Get this off of me."

"Sorry, butterfly. Once it's done, it's done."

I glared at him, almost paralyzed with anger. Why did he insist on making me feel like I was his property? "You didn't even ask me."

With an unapologetic face, he brushed a strand of hair from my face, and I slapped it away.

"I knew you would say no."

"Why do you think I'm suddenly in danger?"

"Until I talk to Martin again, he might not care for our... relationship. I thought it best to add extra protection. I know you are capable, but I do worry."

I was almost buying it. I knew he really did care about me, but his methods were not okay, and he had to know that. I snarled and shoved him in the ribcage. He really thought I was an idiot. I knew he could be a jerk, but this was ridiculous. "This is bullshit. You could have told me to wear the necklace if you were really concerned about Martin. You're using him as an excuse." I lifted my hand in the air to stop him from talking. "I know I might seem like I was born yesterday, but I wasn't. You marked me. This is a kiss tattoo. I've read about them. It isn't just to alert you if I'm in danger. This is to ward off anyone else from trying to get with me. It's laced in magic, and any paranormal will sense it. Why did you do this?"

Joo-won gave me a slight smirk. "You're mine, butterfly. You can go back to your Charles, but he will know now that you are no longer his."

Charles? Was he still jealous of our friendship? This asshole. I jumped up and grabbed my dress and heels. "I'm no one's anything. I'm my own woman. You aren't the Joo-won that I know. I don't know why you're acting like this now."

He closed his eyes, smiling wider. "You know that I am not a good man. You shouldn't be surprised."

But I was surprised. Curses made people darker versions of themselves. And with Joo-won's curse nearing its climax, things would only get worse for him. I had to find him a cure soon. If he kept this up, I might kill him before the curse took effect.

~

*A*fter getting back to my apartment and showering up, I went to my store. I really felt like an absentee boss. My store was still new, and I was relying heavily on my two employees to keep it going when I was out. I should have waited until things settled down to start a business, but I needed to make money, and things just never seemed to quiet in my life.

When I arrived at my store, called Revamp, it was empty except for one of my employees, Peter. This was unsurprising since it was almost twelve in the afternoon. Soon we'd be getting people in who wanted a variety of things. Specialty-made garments, hairstyles, makeup looks. We offered it all, and it didn't take long. Just a consultation and some damn good magic. I was pretty proud of myself.

"Afternoon, sunshine," Peter said with a wave as he folded up a small pile of clothes at the counter.

I paused, surprised to find him there. "I thought Tasha would be opening up today."

He shook his head, continuing to fold. "Just because I'm a vampire doesn't mean I can't do daytime. I'm a living vampire, remember?"

I should have remembered, but my mind wasn't focused like it should be. Living vampires didn't go up in flames under the sun, although they couldn't be outside for long either, and they could still eat and procreate. It's the vampires that were killed while human or something else, that were more limited.

I really felt like a bad boss for not tracking my employee's schedules. I only had two of them. Peter and a witch named Tasha.

I sighed and threw my purse behind the counter. "Sorry, Pete, my mind isn't focused today."

"Still worried about Amina? Or maybe your lover?"

I gagged. Not because of Amina but because of the last part. "He is not my lover."

Peter stopped folding and gave me a look of disbelief. "You rushed off to be his arm candy yesterday, and he's always showing up here."

I looked down at my wrist. The tattoo was invisible, thankfully, but I still knew it was there. I couldn't feel it but just knowing made my wrist itch. I scratched at it and grumbled curses under my breath. Who could I get to take this thing off of me?

Peter leaned towards me with squinted eyes. "Everything not going well with prince charming?"

I snorted. "He's no prince."

"Yes, yes, he's a king."

"Not a good one."

He crossed his arms. "Ah, so you did have a fight."

I shoved my wrist in his face, and Peter reared back with furrowed brows. "Your hand smells like nutmeg. Why do you smell like an old lady?"

I sniffed my wrist, and it indeed smelled like spices. I smelled my other wrist, it was my normal flowery scent. I would kill him. No, I would strike him with lightning and then kill him.

"Joo-won marked me with an invisible tattoo."

Peter's eyes widened, and his mouth dropped open. He grabbed my wrists, and his jaw dropped even more. "He claimed you? I didn't know things were that serious. "

I grumbled. "Things are not that serious. He did this without my approval. And I don't want anyone to know, so keep it quiet."

Peter scrunched his face up. "Well, then you probably shouldn't have told me. You really are distracted."

I closed my eyes and slapped my forehead. I forgot Peter was the town gossip. I really was off my game. I'd have to get in front of this before he made it into something more. By this evening, the town would think I was now a married elven queen.

"Look, this is only a temporary situation because he thought I needed to be safe from his enemies." In a way, that was true.

Peter gave me doubtful eyes. "That fine specimen of a paranormal man wants more than just to protect you."

I rolled my eyes and stepped away from the counter to begin my normal look around *Revamp*. My place was bright and classy with white walls, marbled floors, glass chandeliers and splashes of pastel artwork and furniture. It was very much like my own home space and was the dream store/salon I'd always wanted.

Peter made a tsk-tsk noise. "You didn't ask me, but I

think you're afraid to get hurt. You're intimidated by Joo-won. I get it. Who wants to risk a broken heart? We have enough pressures in our world. However, I think if you give in, you might like it. I mean, the sex would probably be very stress-relieving."

I rubbed the bridge of my nose. I really didn't want to talk about my crazy love life right now. "Do you want to work in fashion or be a psychiatrist?"

Peter glanced over at me with a raised brow. "Was that a veiled threat to fire me if I keep talking?"

"I'm sorry. I didn't mean to make it veiled."

Peter raised his hands in surrender. "Sorry. I just like to call things like I see them."

"Thanks for the advice."

He smirked at me. "Can I get a raise for my advice?"

I chuckled. "No, but you can get not fired."

"Figures. By the way, ask Tasha if she can get that claiming off of you or knows a witch who can. That's pretty messed up that Joo-won would do that without your approval. Wonder what that's about?"

Oh, now he wanted to be sympathetic. Joo-won was cursed, at least that was what I hoped was wrong with him. Maybe claiming a woman was who he really was? He was a thief, after all. He liked to take without permission. Eww, that made him such an asshole. I had to get that curse off of him and find out if this was really his way of doing things. It would make my complex feelings on not getting into another serious relationship with him a lot easier.

I continued to pace my store, turning away from Peter. "I have no idea what got into him," I said in an innocent voice. There was no way I was telling that gossip that Joo-won was cursed. I was already mad at myself for talking to him about Joo-won marking me.

The next few hours remained uneventful until I got a surprise guest around 6 p.m.

Charles strolled into the store, which was now fairly busy. He was wearing his usual sunglasses, and I had no idea why he was out so early.

I rang the last customer in line and raised a brow as he leaned against the counter. "Why are you out so early?"

He looked up at me from the top of his sunglasses. "Word on the street is that you're marrying the elf?"

I looked over to Peter, who quickly spun around and ran up to assist a customer. "How?" I yelled. He must have run his mouth during his lunch break.

Charles leaned on the counter, eyes narrowed in suspicion. "So, it's not true?"

"No, it's not true. Don't believe everything you hear on the street."

"That's where you're wrong. I saw it on The Page."

"The Page? Really?" I shouted, loud enough so Peter would hear.

The Page was the equivalent of our own little social media. Like a smaller, local version of Facebook. Now I knew how word traveled so fast. Peter just had to use his phone. It was time to go back to landlines.

A customer came to the register, and Charles moved out of the way, waiting patiently as I rang up her purchase.

He moved back in front of me when I was done. "Well, I'm glad to hear that. I won't lecture you on him. You'll do what you want." He held up a hand before I could respond, not liking his tone. "And I'm not here because of that. Feel like taking a visit to New York?"

The last time I'd been in New York, we'd been in hiding from the original soulmates. "What's there?"

"The vampire, Niles. I've been reaching out to him for

help, and maybe he can provide some assistance for our elf problem."

I scratched my head, not making the connection. Niles had a powerful base, but we'd already reached out to them. "How?"

"I was going to talk to him about what they've found when I get there. Really, I just want to get out of town for a bit and see something different."

Now, this was news. If they'd made progress in helping Amina, I was all game to hear about it. However, this could have been a phone call. I eyed him suspiciously. Why was he so dead set on leaving right now? He'd been adamant about not going anywhere unless it was to get a cure for Amina. Niles and his people were welcome to visit us anytime, so Charles didn't have to go there. He couldn't possibly care that much about Joo-won. Or really at all about him. Further, as popular as Niles was, I couldn't believe that he would have more resources than our town. It would be nice if Charles finally took a break, but because I was nosey, I wanted to know what changed his mind.

I reached across the counter and placed a hand over his. He flinched slightly but kept his hand in place. It was cold, as was common of undead vampires. I knew he was self-conscious about it, but I wanted him to know I didn't mind, and I really didn't. "Charles, what's this really about?"

He tilted his head back down but avoided my eyes. "It's exactly as I said."

I squeezed his hand, and he looked down at it with saddened eyes. "Be honest with me, Charles. After all we've been through, we can at least do that much."

"These past eleven months, I've tried everything, contacted everyone, put requests out on the internet. No one knows how to help her. I feel like a waste just sitting here and not accomplishing anything. I know finding cures isn't my specialty. And I know others are out there roaming the world to find help, but I hate feeling useless. She's my sister. Maybe a change of scenery will do me good. I don't know if visiting Niles would get answers any more than just communicating with him from a distance, but–"

"It's better than sitting around waiting for answers to come to you. I can understand that." And maybe going to Niles might turn up something unexpected. He had people who helped us before. I gave Charles a wide smile. "Let's go on a trip. Just the two of us."

I'd never traveled with just Charles before. This was going to be interesting.

CHAPTER 7

ile's town was in a section of Manhattan, New York. Actually, his community was a collection of many communities in New York that were not part of the federation and worked as allies with each other. Since the big fight with the originals, they'd begun to advertise their area and bring more life back to a city that had been decimated after The event. Although the federation had taken over most of New York City, getting there was not the same as in the Pre-world since most of the bridges and tunnels were now destroyed, although repairs were being done on some.

Like most cities, New York was a victim of a large amount of supernatural destruction. Cities were prime locations for monster infestations because of the amount of people there. It was also a super spreader location for sicknesses like the ones that took out most ungifted humans and the paranormal sickness threatening paranormals now.

In fact, the suburbs had become the most desirable locals. The countryside had its risk of more rural-based creatures like giants, wild were packs and more aggressive man-eating plant life, some that actually moved and chased you.

The last time we visited, Niles had us meet in an abandoned, run-down part of town that was formally one of the artsy parts of town. When we arrived this time, I was shocked to see that it looked like its former glory with tall shiny buildings, fancy brownstones, storefronts and restaurants.

"Looks like they expanded," I observed, turning around in a circle.

However, it wasn't just that the area looked like its old Pre-World days. There were people. Not nearly as many as there used to be, but still, one could say the area was bustling with activity. It was a Saturday evening, and I could see restaurants busy with patrons and shops open for business. A bit of nostalgia from the old days panged in my chest. A lot had changed in just a year.

Charles pointed to a pizza place across from us and began to walk. "Pizza!"

"You aren't focused. We are supposed to meet Niles here."

"I can meet him with a NY slice in my hand. You think it's going to taste like the old days?"

I huffed and followed him, rolling my small suitcase behind me. I may or may not have overpacked, but we weren't sure how long we were going to be there, and Niles was a former celebrity. "Does anything taste like the old days?" I paused suddenly, narrowing my eyes at him. "Are you still taking those drugs to eat? I thought you were doing them in moderation? You just took some when we went to dinner the other day."

As an undead vampire, he shouldn't have been able to retain food.

Charles paid for two giant slices of pepperoni pizza.

I crossed my arms and glared at him as he walked over with the pizza on two paper plates. He handed one to me, and I accepted. It actually smelled heavenly.

"I'm on a new one that lasts five days. I got it from the apothecary back home. I can only take it once a month without getting sick. Don't worry, I'm not up to anything bad."

His explanation sounded plausible. However, I also knew that since becoming a vampire, he'd gone a little rouge and into a depression, doing harmful drugs and using his vampire glamour to hypnotize people into letting them drink their blood. It was for this reason that Amina had bespelled him. Against his wishes, she had placed a spell over him to make him accepting of his new status as an undead vampire. It was that act that was the catalyst for her asking to be put to sleep. She thought it was a slippery slope to becoming evil and controlling people like the original soulmates.

However, I didn't blame her for worrying. I'd been concerned about Charles for a while, especially after he bit me without my consent some time ago. Yet, since Amina's sleep, he'd been on the up and up as far as I could see. Then again, he didn't ask to remove her spell either, so that could have played a role. It was funny, Joo-won had a curse that would make him the dark souled guy he used to be, and Charles had a spell that made him the old lovable guy he used to be. Magic was a hell of a thing.

My attention was moved back to the present when I heard Charles make an inappropriate moan, closing his eyes as he chomped into the pizza. "We've gotta take some pizza back home before we leave."

Was it that good? I gave him a look of doubt before I bit into my slice as well. And...he wasn't lying. The grease to bread to cheese ratio was perfection. "Maybe we should just live he–"

My words were cut off by loud screams coming from two blocks up. A crowd of people running our way with looks of terror a moment later. Charles and I moved to the side of the street, back towards the pizza shop. What was going on?

It didn't take long for my question to be answered. Behind the crowd of people were at least fifty rats. And I'm not talking about cat-sized rats that were not unknown to haunt cities. No, these rats were as big as wolves. Actually, they weren't exactly like were-rats. There was something off about them. They were dark brown in color, but their coating wasn't like that of rats. It was something different. Hard and plated, like an armadillo. How?

Charles swore, then took a few more bites from his pizza.

I looked at him with astonishment as I put my pizza on a nearby table and pushed my suitcase in the corner. "How can you continue to eat with an attack out there? We have to help those people."

I looked back out of the store and saw the giant rat-things pouncing on people, scratching and biting. Were-rats didn't necessarily have a taste for people, although they would eat them if starving. They would also attack if they felt trapped. However, that couldn't be the situation now. They were in a busy city around tons of restaurants and shops. They could get food easily. And they were out in the open, so they weren't trapped. Were they all loupe, having lost their minds? Or maybe all sick from the paranormal sickness? That would be odd. How could a whole were pack get sick or go loupe?

A smaller group I could understand, but were-rats usually had the largest numbers in their packs. It was too many for them to all go bad at once. Then again, if that wasn't the issue, what was going on?

I turned my attention back to the inside of the shop. Charles had placed his bookbag on top of my suitcase, but he was still eating. "Don't look at me Lisa, I'm eating my pizza." He looked over to the man behind the counter, who stood paralyzed with fear at the scene outside. Something crashed against the window, and I looked to see a giant rat slide to the ground. Luckily the glass was not shattered, unsurprising as people were fortifying their buildings against paranormal attacks nowadays.

"Can you put her pizza in a to-go box?" Charles asked, pointing to my slice.

The man looked at him like he'd lost his mind.

I wondered the same. I walked over to our bags and did a glamour spell to make them invisible as Charles gave the man my slice and the rest of his for boxing.

"Alright, let's go fight some rats," he grumbled. "I hope we don't catch anything from them."

Oh, right. The worst thing about were-rats, besides the obvious of being a rodent thing and traveling in mass numbers, was that they also carried disease. They didn't usually spread it haphazardly, but it was one of their lycanthrope gifts. Usually, it was something plaguy and very unpleasant that could kill a normal human and many paranormals if left untreated.

"Well, you are already dead, so you can't catch a disease, and I'm a faerie, so I can use magic to heal."

Charles walked to my side and surveyed the attack. "Are they wearing armor? I've never seen skin like that on rats before, and what steroids are they taking? These dudes are huge!"

I tried to curb my annoyance that he was only just now noticing how different they were.

"What if it's the paranormal sickness? We aren't immune to that, and so far, the only people who can heal that are sleeping. We gotta be careful, Lisa."

It was true that reports were saying were-rats were super-spreaders of the different supernatural sicknesses that affected humans and paranormals. I had no doubt that all those people currently being attacked would get infected as well, and there was no cure, just tests. We had to stop this now. Of course, I had no plan on how, other than just using my powers to kill them as they came. That was better than nothing for now. I immediately turned to my left and sent a wave of lightning from my hands to a giant rat about to pounce on a teenage boy running in my direction. The creature shook, smoke rising from it before dropping to the ground.

Charles gave a curt nod as if hearing what I was thinking. He shrugged his light jacket off, and I saw for the first time that he was wearing shoulder and waist holsters for the various guns he was sporting. "I was hoping I wouldn't need to use these, but you never know." It had become his habit some time ago to always stay strapped. He was a weapons mage, after all, and part of his power came from his ability to create and utilize weapons to the best of his ability. He could shoot and never miss. We would definitely need him today.

He pulled out a handgun from his waist holster, and I raised a brow in doubt. "Is that enough?"

He grinned. "Oh, this is just the appetizer. Let's take out as many as we can until they retreat. There are a lot of people fighting out there, so we aren't alone. Maybe if we find the leader and kill him, that will cut this short. Look for the scariest one." He looked like he was about to have some fun.

I followed him, less enthused. They all looked scary to

me, and I really hated fighting. How anyone thought I'd be a good member of The Six was still curious to me. I'd just done my nails, and I was very much not feeling this.

The area smelled putrid, like garbage that had been sitting under the sun too long. Was this from the were-rats? They didn't normally carry an odor. Between the smell and the platted skin, I was beginning to think we were dealing with something different.

I gagged but tried to be professional and push through. Charles shot a rat in the stomach that was in a mid-air leap over an elderly man. He barely looked at his aim before turning and hitting another target with ease. I watched as the first hit rat dropped to the ground but pushed forward as if unbothered by the bullet, but I knew what was coming. A second later, the rat's stomach burst open, releasing the contents of his bowels mixed with blood and gore. It splattered over the old man, who stumbled to the ground in horror.

Charles' magical exploding bullets. They did the job, but it wasn't clean. It was impressive, but not to toot my own horn, I wasn't any slouch either.

Several were-rats surrounded a terrified looking family to my left. The father shot at the beast with a handgun, but they were regular bullets, and they weren't slowing the weres down through their armor. If he wanted impact, he'd need silver bullets or exploding bullets like Charles usually used, and those were hard to come by. Not to mention, I wasn't sure if they could piece through this new skin these creatures had.

The mother swung an axe at one of the beasts, and the two children, no more than fourteen years old for the boy and maybe twelve years old for the girl, also stabbed at the creatures with daggers. They must have been human, but I wasn't surprised they were all armed. In this world, no one went around defenseless. Not man, woman or child. We used to try to keep guns away from children in the Pre-World, now we were handing weapons to them as soon as they could walk.

It still didn't mean I was going to turn my back on the family. They tried to attack between the plates and the exposed underbelly, but the rat creatures weren't making it easy. I could take those super rodents out a lot faster than this family could. I clapped my hands together, and a burst of lightning erupted from the sky. Thick white-yellow strips shot down and electrified all the rats surrounding the family, frying them in one go.

My body buzzed with the electricity, and I felt nausea grow in the pit of my stomach. I didn't like killing of any kind, and I didn't take lightly that I had just taken the lives of several paranormals in one go, but I knew it had to be done. It just would take a toll on my body to do this much damage and killing in one go, which I was hoping to avoid.

Something large and hard, like a car, pushed into me and sent me flying down the street. I landed on my arm, feeling the break in the bone. Sizzling pain raced up to my shoulder, and I fought a round of dizziness. It could have been worse. I could have hit my head. I didn't need to be passed out right now. I struggled to my feet just in time to see what I assumed was the offending rat creature gallop towards me. I pushed my good arm out to send it flying back with my magic wind. It slid on the ground but quickly recovered before hawking what looked like a large yellow phlegm the size of a basketball at me.

I teleported down the street in horror as the disgusting glob landed on the ground. What in all of the world? Hot steam rose from the mass of grossness, and a nauseating fume hit my nose. I wanted to vomit. What was it? I didn't want to know. I shot my hand out again and electrocuted the creature. It shook several times before dropping to its side, dead.

Another creature shot towards me and stumbled to the side as a man in a police uniform shot at it with a semi-automatic. The rat spit at him, and this time, the man didn't get away fast enough. The gross phlegm landed on his forearm. The man yelled as the liquid expanded and wrapped around his arm, going up his shoulder.

I looked back to the rat who was opening its giant maw, preparing to bite the poor man's head off. Oh, hell no. I lifted it high in the air before pushing it down again with a full-force wind. When it dropped, it was nothing but a splattered mess. I then ran over to the man, who was still screaming and struggling to remove the phlegm that was apparently consuming his body. It stuck to his free hand like a fly trap, melting his skin.

I poured healing fae magic into him, and the glop began to retreat, falling off of him. However, what was left under the disgusting mess was ripped clothing and burned skin. Some skin burned so bad I could see bone. His whole right arm, shoulder and part of his chest were seriously injured, and his left hand was no better.

Another man ran over to him and began to push his own healing magic over the injuries to aid the process, but the injuries were too serious for this to be a quick healing.

Charles ran over to me. "Seriously, why do rats have to travel so deep? How many are there? I kill one, and two more pop up, and they are taking up a lot of my bullets trying to pierce that armor. Plus, they spit some kind of toxin."

I knew all too well about the toxic phlegm. "I'm healing someone now," I replied through gritted teeth. I looked around us again, and he was right, there were still so many. The townspeople were fighting back the best they could, but several were, rightly so, running inside buildings to safety. The few who couldn't get inside fast enough were holding their own. They weren't all humans. Several weres, witches, vampires and orcs pushed back against our attackers. All this killing, and I couldn't make sense of it. Maybe we could get rid of them, but I certainly didn't want a town full of large dead rats for a clean-up either. Especially when we didn't know why they were attacking. We needed another tactic.

"Charles, can you give that man some vampire blood to help his healing. I need to stop these guys with something bigger."

He nodded and ran over to the man as I pushed up my hands and conjured a tornado-like wind above me. I pushed it down, and my magic-made tornado swooped up the were-rats in a zig-zag pattern, carefully leaving out everyone else. Minutes later, there was a large tornado of were-rats spinning in the air above us like Dorthy in Kansas.

Charles sucked his teeth. "That's going to be some messy shit if they all fall to the ground," he muttered before digging into his pocket with a free hand.

I kept my hands, my broken arm already healing but still very painful with the movement, focused on the tornado. I hadn't thought out what exactly I'd do with them once rounded up. Find a large enclosure to trap them in, perhaps?

Charles pulled out three flat disks the size of cookies. He reared his hand back behind his head as if he were about to pitch a baseball and threw the disk towards the rat tornado. The disks separated and surrounded the rats, equal distance from each other. Seconds later, I saw a translucent blue wall surround the tornado on all sides as well as above and below.

What was that? I gave Charles a raised brow with a questioning look.

He returned my look with a self-appreciating grin. "Containment field. One of my latest inventions. My little disks up there act like a ward. Nothing can get out, including a flying were-rat."

I patted him on the shoulder. That was kind of awesome. "Teamwork makes the dream work. So I'm assuming no leader?"

He shrugged, brows furrowed in an agitated frown. "None that I could find. Maybe the asshole just let his pack go without him. But if we keep them contained in a mass like this, it'll thin out the herd, and the rest will retreat since they will be outnumbered."

Before I could ask just how long I had to keep my tornado going, I felt the ground shake. I stumbled slightly but maintained control of my magic.

"The calvary has finally arrived," Charles stated, looking behind me.

I turned and saw a small crowd of paranormals of all kinds racing our way. However, it wasn't the crowd that shook the ground. It was the great beast leading the way. It was shaped like a brachiosaurus. Only I don't think it was a herbivore. It was over 30 feet tall, except it was a splotchy purple and had long, scaled black wings and a horn on top of its head. The first time seeing the creature was pretty scary. I never stopped being terrified of large creatures. However, since I now knew Barney was friendly, I was only slightly less nervous. I still didn't like it.

Sitting on the dinosaur was the man we had come to see. Former pop star, Niles Davis. He looked every bit the rock star he once was. His blond hair was longer now, reaching his ears but still, white highlighted. His eyes were the color of rubies beneath long, thick lashes, and his skin was pale and shimmering. What appeared to be a fine glitter or mica covered every inch of him. He wore black leather pants and a barely buttoned purple shirt to match his pet beast, I guessed.

Niles jumped down to the street, barely affected by the distance. He was a vampire, after all. His people were dispatched all around to help the injured. He looked up at my tornado, scratching his chin with a hand covered in rings. "What am I looking at?"

"A temporary fix until you and Puff the Magic Dragon over there came," Charles answered.

Niles smiled, a flash of fang showing. "Sorry for our delay, friend. We got here as fast as we could but seems you two are quite efficient. These bastard wererats have been giving this town the blues for a while now."

As much as I wanted to know more, like why they were large, armored and spitting toxic phlegm, I really needed a decision to be made because maintaining a swirling mass of were-rats in the sky was no easy feat, and I was losing energy. "Where should I put them?"

Niles clapped his hands once and then turned to me. "Sorry, hon. I was so impressed by what you did here. Lower it down slowly. I'll have one of my witches wrap them in a transport ward and send them to our prison. It'll hold them." He raised a hand above his head. "Fiona!"

Barely a second later, a petite woman with waist-length strawberry blond hair and a face full of freckles appeared. "Yes."

"Please transport our friends to the prison."

I lowered the mass. There were at least 20-30 of them. I guessed it was a proper prison then and not some makeshift one like I was used to seeing. Once Fiona had wrapped her magic around the disk-reinforced tornado, I let go of my magic. I sighed as the growing tension on my shoulders relaxed, and feeling returned to my broken arm, which had been numb from the pain.

Niles walked towards us, his beast remaining in place. The creature looked very disturbed by the weres as it flapped its wings and snorted out puffs of smoke. "I can't think you both enough for helping. Here I thought we were going to help you."

I flexed my tight fingers. Magic really did do some wear and tear on the body, especially strong magic. "It's what we do. But any idea why a pack of rats attacked? Do you have some kind of fight with them?"

Niles shook his head. "Not one that would warrant a random attack on this scale. Sure, we've been having disagreements but to attack innocent people is just...tacky."

Charles snorted. "That's one way of putting it. What would be their gain from fighting here? Why not fight closer to your part of town?"

"Because it's not just me they hate but the other leaders in our alliance as well. This, I guess, is a good middle ground. Still, an attack was unexpected. I didn't think it would come to this."

I was sort of relieved that this attack had nothing to do with me. I really hated the idea of us bringing yet another attack to Niles and his people like we did when we first came to New York. It didn't improve the situation, but it lessened my guilt. A small part of me had wondered if maybe a certain chaotic elf had tried to dispose of me while I was far away from Joo-won. Good to know that wasn't the case. "Why are you fighting with them?"

He let out a breath and turned around in a slow circle as he looked at all of the surrounding destruction. Beyond people being harmed, there was also heavy property and ground damage. Nothing that couldn't be easily fixed with magic.

"The main thing that many of us argue about nowadays. Resources."

"Why do they look like that?"

"That relates to the resources. They like to eat people, paranormal and not. That we can't ignore."

"That's not normal."

Niles frowned, looking on as recovery kept in motion. "No, it is not. In the beginning, it was just that they didn't like to play by the rules. Which is unfortunate because they are our largest were population. Since they didn't abide, we asked them to leave our community. We've been trying to reason with them and at least coincide peacefully. We even had a meeting set up with their leadership. It seemed like things could resolve. And then, two weeks ago, we discovered they were attacking people and eating them. They weren't starving, so it made no sense."

I scrunched my face. What would make a pack of weres change their diets like that? For the most part, weres did not eat humans. At least not sane ones. "Are we ruling out that they just didn't all go loupe or get infected?"

"No, it's possible. But it doesn't make it any easier for us. They started off looking like regular were-rats, and the main thing they wanted was land and normal food. Then recently, they started to change. Got a little bigger every time we saw them. Then there was the plated skin. The toxin is new. They must have made a deal with someone with a modification power to make them stronger and harder to take down. That is not good for us."

Great, just what this hellish world needed, new ways for the already scary guys to get scarier. Who the hell was out there selling modifications? I shouldn't have been surprised. People would find all sorts of ways to make money even if they were harmful. They did it before magic, so why stop now?

Charles let out a low curse. "Just what we need, paranormals getting more paranormal. I heard about things like that. There's a growing underground business for enhancements. It's strong magic, and it's not cheap."

Niles shook his head. "They got money from somewhere."

"Are there more of them?"

"Yes. I am not sure how long we can hold them off. We might have to get the federation to step in, and I won't want that. They'll want us to join."

He was right. The federation's number one goal was to grow. They made few alliances, and a prime area in New York City was not something they'd let sit uncontrolled by them. Niles would have to work this on his own or seek further help. Our town, perhaps. "You have to destroy the nest then. I can talk to our council and get them to help."

Niles flashed a smile that seemed out of place. "Yes, we have some leads on their location. Don't worry, we aren't going to let them get another jump on us."

He was so confident. I was sure it was an act. He was an entertainer, after all. However, that confidence made people at ease and want him as a leader. He was a smart guy, and I knew he hated asking for assistance, but we owed his people. "We can also find who made them so strong. Maybe it's a drug, and it's not permanent. Taking out their source of strength could be a big help. It's got to be a witch, mage or demon."

Niles gave a light pat on my shoulder. "We're working on that as well but the more help, the better. Now, this is not why you all came here. This should be a relaxing break for you, and it's been far from it. What can we do to make up for it."

Before I could say anything, Charles spoke up. "I'm going to need more pizza."

CHAPTER 8

A moment later, Charles walked up beside me, holding what appeared to be the rest of his jumbo slice.

I looked at him with astonishment. When had he raced back in and gotten food? Why was that important for him to do now? We were trying to handle a mutant wererat situation. "Seriously?"

He shrugged. "I'm not wasting the medicine."

It was at that moment that I was certain that so-called medicine was also killing some brain cells of his.

Niles stuffed his hands into the pockets of his tight pants. "I can give you a bunch to take home for free for your help here." He glanced over to me. "Many of my undead citizens take the medicinal powder to eat as well. It's become very popular. And lucrative. We sell it. Different strengths have more long-lasting effects. Ours last up to10 days per dosage with only a weeks rest between."

Charles' jaw dropped open. "What? I'm on it."

I side-eyed him and gave a twist of my lips. He didn't need to take anything else.

Niles gave him a wink before turning back to his giant

beast, who had just taken a thunderous sit down, resulting in a slight tremor. "Come, let's go to town and catch up. Do you need a ride?"

I pointed to the beast. "Not on that thing."

Niles chuckled. "Aww, she's harmless. But no, I was going to offer that one of my people take you." He waved a man over and asked him to give us a ride into town.

The last time we visited New York, there was much secrecy. This time, everything was open and seemingly accessible. Well, I did feel the full-body tingle of a ward when we got closer to Niles' section of the city. I was guessing that all the communes were warded, and only certain areas, like the area we were just in, was unwarded.

Inside the town, our escort showed us to our hotel, the same one as last time – a luxury high rise in the busiest section of town. The concierge let us know that Niles would catch up with us for dinner at seven p.m. in an Italian restaurant at the end of the block.

That was a few hours away, so in the meantime, we got settled in and then met up with a witch named Fiona and other magic users for the assistance we came to get.

She met us at the receptionist desk an hour after we arrived dressed in a colorful maxi dress, combat boots with waist-length honey blond curls and large smile. Most people in town seemed optimistic. This was a far cry from the busy New Yorker that didn't acknowledge another person on the street back in the Pre-World. However, for all intents and purposes, Manhattan had become a small city.

She extended her hand in a greeting. "It's nice to see you both again."

I shook her hand and kept my face neutral. I didn't recall meeting her last time. However, that didn't mean I hadn't. We were in a challenging space at the time, so it was possible I forgot many faces around me.

I guess my face wasn't neutral enough because she waved a hand in front of her face. "Oh, it's okay if you don't remember me. The Six are somewhat celebrities. In fact, Erik and Phillip were named in the top 50 Sexiest Men Alive in the New People magazine."

Charles grumbled behind me. "That's some bullshit."

Again, his priorities were really suspect.

Fiona crinkled her eyes at him. "You're actually my favorite. Your mage abilities are amazing. I've never seen anything like it. Tech mages are one thing. They're not as common but still prevalent. However, a tech mage *and* a weapons mage? That's unheard of. You really are special. And those ward disks are damn solid. Mind if we keep them? We used them with our warded cells."

Charles cleared his throat and puffed out his chest. "Thank you for your appreciation. And yes, you can keep those. There are more back home. I was thinking of selling them."

"You should." She lifted her shoulders. "Now, I hope Niles told you that we are making some headway in finding help for Amina and Phillip's side effects." She escorted us to a collection of big soft chairs off to the corner of the lobby. We sat down as she continued recounting her progress. "We've been working on how to lessen the negative side effects of the soulmate power. We're doing a lot of work with loupes and those affected by the paranormal sickness. The common thread is that their powers have turned dark. We hope that's a good angle to work with."

"Sounds smart."

"We aren't as far in that as we hoped, but we continue to push forward."

Charles leaned forward, a serious look darkening his eyes. "I thank you for all the effort you're putting in. I really appreciate it. If I had any say, I would have never agreed to using the sleeping spell on her. But she was terrified of what she would become. I didn't blame her. Those original soulmates were messed up. I just wish she'd let us try to find a cure while she was still awake."

I rubbed his back, sympathizing with his feelings. I think we all felt the same way, but Amina was stubborn. Then there was Phillip, whose good nature came and went at the drop of a hat. It was plausible he would have easily dragged her down into insane, power-tripping psychopaths. She was smart to be cautious. It just sucked.

But something Fiona said did pique my interest. Perhaps baby steps could lead to bigger discoveries. "Do you think any of the research and testing you've been working on would work on a curse that might be making someone go dark?"

Charles turned fully to me with raised brows. "The Keebler going evil?"

I rolled my eyes. "I feel like calling him that might be racist or something."

Charles tilted his head. "Fair point."

"Anyway, the curse he's under does aim him towards negativity. And in the end, he becomes a slave to a witch."

"It doesn't seem like an angry slave is ideal."

I agreed. It made no sense, but until I met this witch, I wouldn't understand the full truth. "Maybe it's a side effect of her curse?" I shrugged. "Seems like everything comes with a catch nowadays."

Fiona tapped her nose in thought. "I'd have to meet him to get a better idea of the curse, but they are tricky things. Spells are straightforward. Still challenging to break, don't get me wrong. However, curses are deceptive. It's like they have booby traps set in them. You think you broke the curse that makes you a frog, and you're now human again. Except you age 50 years and die the next day."

I touched my collar bone in shock. That was terrifying. "Well, I don't want that. Could that really happen?"

Fiona gave a solemn nod. "That was a real example."

Charles muttered something unintelligible under his breath. I was guessing it was rude. "So let me get this straight. We could break this curse of his, and he's free, but a side effect could be death. Or maybe he becomes a dog."

"Well, yes. Or there could be no side effects. You never know. I haven't been able to find the booby trap in a curse. I haven't come across anyone in person or in my online groups who have either. It's kind of like picking the prize behind a closed door. You might get a new car or just a life-time supply of lima bean soup."

"Have you had lima bean soup with turkey or bacon, though?" He rubbed his stomach. "I'm just saying. That's good eating."

I cut my eyes at him. Clearly, he was in jokes mode. "Not the point, greedy. If we break this curse, we could be making things worse for him."

Fiona gave a sympathetic sigh. "It's possible." She narrowed her eyes at me and leaned forward, peering at my wrist. "A claiming." She gave a large grin and pointed a finger at Charles. "Did you do that?"

Oh crap. It was invisible. How did she know? I didn't think she was interested in me.

Charles furrowed his brows, glancing over at my wrist. "No." He crossed his arms and sat back, an amused look in his eyes. "Santa's little helper do that to you? You did tell him we're just friends, right?"

I rolled my eyes, face flushed with embarrassment. I really didn't want to talk about this with him or Fiona, for that matter. However, I knew he'd never let it go. "I don't know what to think, Charles. I get torn between hoping he really is the good guy he presents himself to be and then wondering if doing things like marking me is who he really is." After all, he used to be a criminal and involved himself with someone who killed people.

"That's some barbaric shit."

"Yes, yes, I know that. Hence, why I'm talking to Fiona about it." I waved a hand towards the witch as if he needed reminding that she was there.

Fiona gave me a sympathetic smile. "Is he cute?"

I smooshed my cheeks together, so very uncomfortable. "Not the point."

She gave me expectant eyes, head tilted.

Charles waved a hand in front of his face as if he was hot. "Oh, he's so cute," he said in a fake teenage girl accent.

Fiona giggled, slapping Charles lightly on the knee in the way we women do when we are trying to be flirty. I wouldn't be surprised if she had a real crush on Charles. "Well, Lisa, have you thought about just visiting the witch and asking her to lift the curse? You never know, maybe she could change her mind. Offer her something in exchange."

That was a great idea and one I'd thought of. Unfortunately, her whereabouts were unknown.

"Or we could just kill her," Charles added.

We both glared at him.

Charles widened his eyes giving us his best impression of an innocent man. "I'm not suggesting you do that. I'm just saying that works, too. But I'm banking your elf guy would have done that by now if he thought he could."

"Who's the witch?" Fiona asked, taking out her phone. I was guessing she planned to look her up. I knew there were many witches who advertised their services or were part of databases online, but I doubt this woman would be on any list.

As for the witch's name, I couldn't fully recall it. "Her name is Mercedes Mann? No, that doesn't sound right.

Mercedes Mona. Mercedes Benz. Nope, that's definitely not right." My mind went blank. What was her last name again? Crap, I was apparently horrible at remembering faces and names.

Fiona paused, looking down at her phone. "Mercedes Mana?"

I snapped my fingers in recognition. "Yes, that's it. You've heard of her?"

Fiona nodded her head vigorously. "Yes. Now that woman there is not to be messed with. She's super powerful. Heck, I think her last name actually means supernatural power in Hawaiian or something. She was practicing witchcraft before The Event, and now she's even stronger with magic's full return. Your guy must have really done something wrong to piss her off. I don't hear much about her cursing people. She's not a dark witch."

I took a tiny bit of relief that at least she wasn't an evil witch. That means she had morals and possibly could be reasoned with. "Yeah well, he stole from her."

Fiona let out a low whistle. "Must have stolen something important for her to curse him with enslavement. Guessing whatever he stole, he wasn't able to give it back?"

"Oh no, that's the funny part. She was able to retrieve it."

"Wait, so she has it back, and she *still* kept the curse on him? What'd he take?"

I shrugged, not understanding the significance either. "Some powerful pendant. She had a tracking spell on it, so that's how she was able to find him and get it back."

Fiona scrunched her face up in confusion. "And she still put that heavy a curse on him? That doesn't sound right. Now, I don't know Mercedes personally. I've communicated with her online for guidance on spells and such, but each time, she was very pleasant to talk to. She doesn't have a bad reputation. In fact, people seem to fiercely respect her. No one messes with her though, because she's wicked strong. I've heard of some folks testing her and it not ending well for them. We'd be stupid to not fear her on some level."

"Like the elf," Charles cracked to which Fiona tilted her head to him in agreement.

I rolled my eyes but nodded along. He wasn't wrong. Joo-won had gotten in over his head on that one. Incidentally, it had gotten him to go good. "So, I'm guessing this pendant was super important, and just the act of taking it was bad enough to warrant enslavement."

Charles blew out a razzberry and slouched in his seat, looking bored. "Maybe he didn't apologize. Maybe that's all she needs."

I gave him a squinty-eyed stare. He enjoyed testing my patience. "Are you being serious?"

"It's not out of the realm of possibility. I'm just saying, don't rule it out."

"I just can't think of anything I would have that would make me want to curse someone to a lifetime of servitude after I got it back."

Fiona hummed and tapped her nose again, which I was beginning to believe was her thinking gesture. "Maybe he broke the pendant somehow, and it no longer works right. Maybe it had sentimental value. Who knows? I would just ask her."

Could it really be that simple? Joo-won had to have tried it, but maybe all that was needed was a different voice. One that wasn't involved in stealing from her. One that was obviously on the side of good. "Should I just call her or email her? The elf doesn't have her contact information anymore, and she moved, but maybe you could give it to me?"

Fiona lifted her lip in the corner and tilted her head from side to side, obviously not liking my idea. "For this, you need to see her face to face, and I'm not talking over the internet. She's old school, and I think you going to see her will go a long way. I know she lives in Hawaii now, not sure where, but I can reach out to her and get her locale. Well, I can try. I'm not sure how receptive she'll be to a visit, but maybe she can be enticed if it's from a member of The Six."

She stood up, and we did the same. "I have to get back to checking in on those were-rats, but I'll also see if there is anything I have that can help with his curse, but I wouldn't hold your breath on that."

Well, crap, there went my hopes.

"If it's from Mercedes, then I know my magic doesn't match up. I'd like to think that I have a healthy sense of my limits. If I don't get Mercedes information before you leave, I'll email it to you. It might take a while to convince her."

"We have less than a month left until the curse kicks in, but we appreciate anything you can do," I replied. "Sorry we waited so late to get to you about this.

Fiona nodded. "Yes, reaching out earlier would have been helpful, not just to me but maybe for convincing Mercedes. I'm not sure how open she'd be now that almost a year has passed but never say never." She gave a slight wave before turning and leaving.

I dropped my shoulders, feeling exhausted from just the half-day. "Maybe we should go home. I don't know if there is anything more we can get here."

Charles threw his head back in frustration. "Oh, come on, Lisa. We are here for a little break. Also, we're supposed to meet Niles for dinner. Don't give up hope on helping Joo-won or Amina. His time isn't out yet. Don't give up the fight. Now let's enjoy New York and pretend it's like the good old times."

I let him push me to the exit so we could explore. "Maybe a little retail therapy would cheer me up. And I might find some good things for my shop."

He cursed. "That's not what I meant, though. Damn it."

⁓

When we entered the restaurant that evening, it was not what I expected. I thought we'd go into some dimly lit space with piano bar music and quiet conversation. There was someone at the piano, but it wasn't who I expected. Niles sat behind the keys wearing something as flashy as usual. His sparkly skin was especially glittery that evening. Vampires didn't naturally have sparkly skin, however, Niles had gotten glitter magically added to his body to appease his fans, who were also lovers of certain vampire books from the Pre-World.

He was currently singing a piano version of one of his hit songs from his boy band days, and the entire restaurant was joining him in one giant sing-a-long. I wondered when we first met him how a pop star had become a town leader. He had the charisma for sure but he was also a smart guy. He surrounded himself with competent people, and he was a good fighter. People could easily take him for granted, but they'd learn the hard way. He also had a town full of citizens who loved him to almost a cult-like degree.

He got up from the piano for his next song, one from his solo days, and music played from the restaurant speakers as he walked around the room greeting the patrons who swooned or swayed at his touch.

Charles leaned towards me. "What the hell did we walk into? Is he putting on a concert?"

I shook my head slowly, not sure myself. Our hostess came to our side and escorted us to a table off to the side, near the window. It was actually a nice location.

Niles continued making his way through the room, at times putting his equally glittery microphone up to people so they could sing. I was not surprised that everyone knew the words perfectly.

"I hope he doesn't walk over here signing," Charles muttered, looking at his menu. "I don't know these songs."

"I do," I smiled as I continued to look at Niles work the crowd.

Charles looked at me with disappointment before glancing back down at his menu.

"I will not be shamed. Niles' music got me through some tough days in high school. Oh, who are you to judge me? You like anime."

Charles slapped his menu down. "Anime is an art form that is for all ages. The beauty of the artistry, the plotlines, the character development, the passion from the voice actors– and I do subbed, not dubbed– the action. It's all just...chef's kiss." He brought his fingers to his lips and made a kissing noise.

I gave him an open-mouthed stare. "Nerd."

He winked at me. "You like this nerd."

Of course, I liked him, he'd always have a place in my heart. And he still had a way of lightening a mood. Just hanging out with him being silly made me feel better. Like maybe things weren't too bad or hopeless.

His eyes widened, and he tilted his head up, staring behind me. "Oh shit, he's floating."

I turned in my seat to find Niles floating above our heads as he belted out an impressive high note. From somewhere, a wind blew, tossing his ankle-length jacket back and blowing his hair. Ok, this was a bit much, and the crowd was eating it up as they oohed and clapped.

When he was done, he floated down to the ground and gave his mic to a waiter before heading our way. Naturally, all eyes in the room turned to us as he greeted us and took a seat.

He tossed his hands out to the side. "So, what did you think?" he asked with a wide grin.

I channeled my inner sixteen-year-old and touched my chest, eyes wide. "That was freaking amazing. Like, you transported me back to my high school days for a moment."

Charles snorted. "Even when he was floating?"

Niles nodded. "Thank you, darling. No, I know it seems a bit much, but my band and I did a show back in the day where we swung from wires and glided through the air above the audience. It was amazing. Now I can do it with my vampire powers."

Charles gave a chuckle. "Maybe you should get the band back together and do a reunion tour, flying and all."

Niles' smile dropped, and he looked down at the table. "Sadly, none of them survived. Two succumbed to the different supernatural illnesses, one went loupe and another was killed by a demon."

I shook my head. I'd heard as much. I cut my eyes at Charles, who frowned with bared teeth. I guess I shouldn't be surprised he didn't know, but still, it was not a good look.

"Sorry, man. I didn't know."

Niles straightened up in his seat and raised his hand for the waiter's attention. "It's all good, friend. These times have brought loss to us all." The waiter arrived, and Niles put in an order for a bottle of wine for the table as well as an array of other dishes for us to eat. "No need looking at the menu. I know what's good here. I've ordered us a mix of a ton of stuff. You'll love it."

Charles snapped his menu closed, looking impressed. "I'm about to get drunk on food today!" he sang, wiggling in his seat.

Niles laughed and sat back in his seat, resting an elbow on the back of his chair. He looked so comfortable. I wondered if he ever got stressed. "So, we have much to catch up on. Fiona mentioned that you have an elf friend who is cursed, and she's working to help you."

I scooted closer to the table. "Yes, and thanks for letting your people help us."

Niles waved a hand. "Anything for a friend. Hey, I heard the elves had some big shindig on the water in some floating glass mansion. We have an elf tribe out in Brooklyn that we work well with. Did you get to go?"

I gave a slight smile, remembering the glamorous evening and the steamy time after. I cleared my throat before I spoke, feeling my body already buzzing from the memory. "Yes, it was beautiful."

"I'll bet. You know, I admire the elves. They have no divisions. Dark elves, neutral elves, light elves, they still can come together and party, man. That's the dream. The rest of us can't get over our differences to even be in the same room."

I thought of Martin. I wasn't so sure that the elves coming together was such a good thing. Especially if they were going to stir up old emotions and be a bad influence on each other. Something in my face must have given away my thoughts because Niles was studying me.

"You don't agree?" His brows raised, and he gave me an amused grin.

Damn, now I had to say something, and I hated feeling like a gossip. I mean, I will absolutely gossip, I just hated feeling like one. Plus, I didn't know how fast word got around in mixed communities. I didn't want to say I didn't like Martin, and then he find out and come for me.

"Oh, uhm. It's just that my friend, Joo-won, has some interesting associates."

Our waiter came back and poured our wine. We sat silently until he left. Niles then turned his attention back to me. "By associates do you mean Martin?" he said before taking a sip from his glass.

I had already taken a swig of my wine and nearly spit it out when he mentioned his name. How the hell did he know? "You know Martin?"

"Eh, I know about him. I'm not keeping tabs on you. As I said, we get along well with the Brooklyn elven tribe. I was told you were there with Joo-won and that Martin met with you. It was only of note because Martin has a certain...reputation." He briefly lifted his upper lip in a soundless snarl before regaining his composure. Guess Martin had another enemy to add to the list.

Charles scrunched his face and put his glass down. I already knew he wanted to drink something else. He was never a wine guy. However, he was polite and didn't complain. "What's the deal with him?"

"He's basically a gangster. And the worse kind. He and his thugs do immoral businesses, kill, pillage. I've heard rumors of darker things as well. I'd suggest staying clear of him. If he's sniffing around, I can't imagine it's to do any good."

I couldn't say I was surprised, and it made me all the more concerned for Joo-won if he took him up on his offer. "Did you have any personal dealings with him?" I needed Joo-won to understand that this guy wasn't just a problem from his past but was still a criminal to stay clear of. Perhaps if I had a recent example, he'd think twice.

Niles nodded. "About a month ago, he attacked some of our people while they were reentering town from a trade. The ones who survive think they might have been followed from New Jersey, where they'd gone to trade. They took everything and killed any who tried to fight back."

Right, so clearly Martin had not turned over a new leaf, and if he knew of Niles and his people, maybe it wasn't so far-fetched to believe he had a connection to the were-rats. "Oh, my God."

"Yeah. One of the only two survivors remembers him saying, 'I like what you have. See you soon.' I think the only reason those two were left alive was to carry that message back. He wanted us to know he's coming for us again. Coming for our town."

"Do you think he has that many people to fight you? I mean, it's not just this community, you are part of a collective."

Charles laid an arm on the table. "And then you have your allies like our town. He has to know this town fought against the originals. If you didn't let us fall, we aren't going to let you fall."

Niles gave him an appreciative nod. "Thanks, man. And I honestly don't know how many people he has. He outnumbered the group he attacked. He could be using this time to collect more allies for a battle." He glanced over to me. "Stay away from Martin. For your own good. Think about the timing. Of everything. I don't believe in coincidences."

Neither did I. Not anymore.

CHAPTER 9

*A*fter dinner, Niles invited us back to his place, where he was hosting what he described as a small gathering of friends. For a leader whose people were recently attacked, he seemed very chill. I guessed this was just another way he kept the masses calm because even in the mix, he was still very alert. There was no being distracted or too relaxed with him.

When we arrived to his luxury penthouse apartment, there were already several people there, listening to music, drinking, exchanging blood openly.

Niles placed a hand on my shoulder. "You're safe here. Everything is consensual. Tonight, we relax. Tomorrow and the day after that, I get back to continuing the work of our defenses."

I nodded absentmindedly, still looking around his immaculate apartment. It wasn't opulent. In fact, it was modern minimal. The exact opposite of his rock-glam. It made me wonder if this was the real him and the outward Niles was really a fake. We knew he got the glitter skin for show, why not everything else?

A woman came up to him and whispered something in

his ear. By his reaction, I was banking it was not work-related. He waved his hand around. "Enjoy yourself. Have a look around. Mi casa es su casa and all that." He then turned and walked away, an arm wrapped around the waist of the woman.

As soon as he left, a man and a woman came over to us. They were young and eager-looking. She was wearing a sparkly, off-the-shoulder mini dress with a swirling rainbow pattern.

I raised my brows in approval. I remembered designing that dress a couple of months ago. "That dress is gorg on you."

The woman's eyes widened. "I love your online boutique." She waved a hand downwards. "I got this dress from there."

I beamed. I really was almost famous. Someone who I didn't know, in a place I didn't live, was wearing my design and knew me on sight."

The man extended a hand. "You're Charles and Lisa, aren't you? We're big fans."

I looked him over. He wasn't wearing anything of mine. How did he know me? I shook his hand. "You're fans of ours? Why?"

"You're The Six. You're like superheroes."

Oh yeah, the super group thing. I did have that going on, didn't I? I'd still rather be known for my clothes.

The man cleared his throat, and she looked up at him. He tilted his head towards Charles, and she nodded. "So, we were wondering if you were...thirsty."

Charles formed an O with his mouth. "Uh, I could always go for a drink."

It was clear to both of us that she wasn't talking about a cocktail. He turned to me, and I tried my best to not have a judgmental face. He had a right to drink blood. He was a vampire after all. But I didn't want to see it. I was freaked out enough being surrounded by people getting bit on the neck, arms, wrists. I guess I had a bit of PTSD from the many times I'd been bitten by various creatures. My first one was a vampire years ago.

"You know what? Maybe later," Charles replied.

I placed a hand on his back. "No, Charles, if people are offering, you should take it."

The woman clasped her hands together. "Yes. We've both been told our blood is really good. I'm a blood mage, and he's a wereswan."

Blood mage? That was new. "What kind of power does a blood mage have?"

"I can manipulate blood, including my own. Make a weapon out of it, take it away, give it."

"That dope," Charles replied, a fist over his mouth.

I could tell he wanted to sample her power. But he wasn't going to do it in front of me. I suppose if I were a vampire, tasting the blood of a blood mage would be pretty darn tempting.

"I'm going to go on a self-guided tour of the apartment. See how the other half lives."

I thought I had with my visits to Joo-won, but I was nosey. Mostly, I wanted to give Charles an opening to do his vampire thing without being self-conscious about it.

I didn't wait around for his response and turned to walk away.

Since the living area and his wrap-around balcony were full of people, I decided to go down the hall and check out his rooms. Just as his front rooms, the other rooms were also minimalist. He had a workout room, an owner's suite with floor-to-ceiling windows, a guest room and an office.

I looked out of his bedroom window at the lights from the bustling city below. I wondered how Niles afforded all of this. The same way leaders in other communities did, I supposed. They exported and traded. If they weren't part of the federation, they secured the resources, materials and magic to be self-sustaining. With the amount of people living back in the cities, they had to be doing fine. No wonder the federation wanted to reclaim this territory.

The government was the majority of this country and a good portion of New York outside of the city. They weren't the bad guys, but if they came for Silver Spring or even Joo-won's territory, I wasn't sure what we would do. It wasn't a fight I was interested in taking on. After I helped Joo-won and Amina, I was going to focus my energy totally on getting back to the Lisa I used to be before this world changed. I didn't want to stay in Silver Spring, and with New York returning to its former glory, this is where I wanted to be.

"Hey, I need to talk to you about something," came a voice behind me.

I jumped and spun around. I dropped my shoulders and cursed as Charles stood at the entrance of the bedroom.

He walked further in and flopped down on the bed.

"How was the...drink?"

He side-eyed me with a skeptical look. "You really want to know?"

"I asked."

"It was delicious. She should bottle it."

I squinted my eyes, spotting something on his chin. Blood. I tightened my lips, fighting against the disgust I was feeling. "You have a little something on your chin."

Charles wiped at his face. "Oh, thanks." He licked his fingers and then stopped midway. He gave me an embarrassed laugh. "Sorry about that. I wasn't thinking."

I waved my hands in front of me. "No, no. it's fine."

Charles looked down at his lap. "It's not, I know. You look like you want to hurl."

Crap, I really didn't want him to know. I walked over to the bed and sat down next to him. "I'm sorry. I just have to work through some trauma."

"I get it. It's kind of related to what I wanted to talk to you about. I'm beginning to be fine with being what I am. Yeah, I loved being human. Just a mage. But being a vampire is better than the alternative, which was me staying dead. It was great seeing loved ones. Not so great getting a vision of us getting annihilated by the originals. Glad that vision never happened."

I was ecstatic that he was coming back to himself again. I'd missed the old Charles.

He twisted so that he was facing me. "We've had a while now to sort out our feelings for one another. You don't have to feel weird around me talking about the elf. You could have told me about the claiming thing. It's okay if you guys are together."

I opened my mouth to say something. I had no idea what. I couldn't ever imagine talking about my complicated feelings for Joo-won with Charles. I wasn't sure I was that progressive.

He shook his head. "It's true. You can help him from afar, but you visit him, you hang out with him. You really care about the guy. It's not like it was with Blake and me. We were both just filling a void. You know she's dating Jerry."

Blake was the head vampire of Silver Spring, and he'd become a sort of friends-with-benefits with her when he thought I'd betrayed him by running off to the fae realm and then coming back only to banish Amina. "Wait, Blake's with Jerry, the orc?"

Charles nodded. "Yeah, you know he hates to be called that. He doesn't look like an orc unless he transforms, but he finds it really offensive for some reason. Then again, if I got called 'the black guy' all the time, I'd be pissed."

"Good for her. But Charles, you're reading too much into things."

"Nah, I'm not. Whatever we had, we don't have it anymore. It's no one's fault. Things happen. I'll survive just being your friend. As long as I have you in my life, then I'm good. But if you found someone you really care about, you shouldn't keep wasting time by fighting it. Our lives aren't guaranteed."

I felt a flood of relief. I wouldn't lose him as my friend if things ever changed between Joo-won and me, and that mattered more to me than anything. I rested my head on his shoulder. Charles was a good man. Whoever ended up with him would be a lucky gal. "Did I ever tell you I'm glad you're in my life?"

He tapped his cheek against the top of my head. "Not nearly enough. And hey, just because you have a new guy, don't act like you don't know us anymore. Life is changing for you. Now that we have this new normal, you're going to move to New York and get back to being this internet celeb, making all the people shiny and new. I'll maybe move to a government town, if it all doesn't become government, and maybe start my own gaming company. Who knows? This is all after we wake up Amina and Phillip."

I frowned. This was new. But why was I surprised? The world was becoming more mobile again. Why did I think we were relegated to staying in just one place? Why did I think Charles would never grow? "Would you leave Amina in Silver Spring? She's part of the council, I don't think she'd leave. Even if it got swallowed by the federation, you know they'd make her and Erik some sort of officials. I don't know about Phillip."

Charles rubbed my arm slowly, a comfort I didn't know I needed. "Yeah, I suspect she'd stay. I really don't know, Lisa. I'm just talking. I need to find my way. Everyone's finding their path, I have to find mine too," he said the last part with a tightness in his voice.

I nodded. Not sure what more to say and afraid I would cry if I did say anything. The thought of The Six going our separate ways was kind of scary to me.

"And for the record, I still think Joo-won is trash, but you have to find that out on your own. Just don't let him drag you down. You're a member of The Six. You have an image to upload. It's part of your brand or some shit."

I snorted. "He could be like Phillip was when he was bespelled. Let's give him the benefit of the doubt. But I'll be careful."

I looked down at my wrist where the invisible kiss tattoo was stamped. I was really hoping this was all because of the curse and Joo-won was as good a man as Charles. I needed to find that witch.

CHAPTER 10

*T*he rest of the weekend was actually fun. No attacks and just the rest and relaxation I needed. Niles even let us use the luxury spa in the hotel free of charge. Charles and I were making profits in our respective jobs, but nothing felt sweeter than free.

So, when I arrived home, I was thoroughly able to focus on my job and finding a cure for Joo-won for the week. However, time was running out, and my refreshed week didn't bring me any new leads, nor had Fiona been able to get the witch's new contact information, but I would not give up. And the week was on my side, because until Friday, everything was normal. Then I got a surprise visitor at my store just as I was closing up for the night.

I didn't notice the sound of the car door opening behind me, at first, because my store was on a busy shopping and dining district, so there was plenty of life going on that evening. Usually, I kept the store open a little later on weekend nights because people tended to shop later, especially after a few drinks at dinner.

My block consisted mostly of shops, so it was a bit darker now but still packed with cars parallel parked on either side from people going to the nearby bars and restaurants. When I turned, Senna stood there, crossed arms and leaning against a regular red sedan, looking very pedestrian. She was, however, still fashionable in a white jumpsuit. She looked almost human since her long locks were covering her ears, and her eyes were covered in sunglasses like she was some celebrity.

"Hi?" I said more as a question than a greeting.

"Busy?" she asked, looking up and down the street.

"I know it's lame for a Friday night, but I was going to go home and just rest for the night. But I can recommend you some great spots if you're looking for a turn up."

She pushed away from her car. "We need to talk about Joo-won."

I closed my eyes. What could I say to her about him? I had nothing good to report. Time was ticking away to help him, and I was failing. I was already thinking about life with one kidney. "I don't really have anything to tell ya. Sorry. By the way, do you know what he did to me?"

Senna took off her sunglasses and narrowed her eyes with suspicion. "No, tell me."

I shoved my right wrist at her. "Can you see this?"

She inspected my arm and then sighed. "He marked you. Are you serious?"

I balled my hands into fists, getting angry all over again. "Am I serious? No, is *he* serious?"

"Yeah, that's what I meant. This is crazy. I've never seen him mark anyone before. He's had other women–"

I lifted an index finger in the air. "He hasn't had me." I was not about to be lumped in with his groupies.

She paused and looked at me with amazed eyes, which was unnerving given how astonishingly inhuman they were. "Are you serious?"

"Are you going to keep saying that?"

She shook her head and placed a hand on her collar-bone, seeming thoroughly perplexed. "Apologies, but this is most unlike him. Never has he marked anyone he was seeing, and never would he see someone he was romantically interested in and not sleep with them for this long. I can't imagine he's actually been celibate this long."

"Well, he wanted to, but I said no."

"He would have tried to seduce you."

I lifted a shoulder. I was no first-timer to admirers. I didn't bend at the knees just because a guy winked at me or bought me jewelry. "He tried. I mean, we did some *things,* but we don't get to the end game."

She studied me for a moment, speechless. Then she relaxed her face. "Impressive. Now I understand why he's so taken with you. You are a challenge. You are making him strong in ways he hasn't ever had to be. Will-power is a great power."

A waved a hand in front of my face, still stuck on her earlier words and slightly offended. "Wait, you didn't understand what he saw in me before?"

She cocked a brow and tightened her lips. "Sorry, not sorry. I'm slow to trust."

I could understand that. I wasn't really upset. Ok, yes, I was, but I would have to get over it now. Time had passed, and Senna was now well aware of the fabulousness that was me. "Back to me being marked like some animal in the wilderness. If this isn't like him, then why did he do this to me?"

"This goes to why I wanted to speak with you, but I'd rather not stand in the streets and talk about such delicate things."

"No one in this town cares about Joo-won."

She shifted in her stance and kicked out a heeled foot, flexing. "I realize that."

I smirked. "You just want to go sit down because your feet hurt?"

She threw her hands out in exasperation. "Yes."

"Who told you to wear six-inch heels?"

She placed her hands on her hips and eyed me up and down as if I insulted her. "And ruin this outfit with...flats?" she said the word flats as if it were a curse. "You are the fashion person, you should know that."

She had a fair point. Her outfit was fire, and flats would have dragged them down. I never understood why she was always dressed up like we weren't living in apocalyptic times, but since we'd become more used to things, even I dressed up normally now, so I guess I couldn't fault her for that. And the fact that she came out looking this good meant only one thing: she wanted to be seen.

"Fine, there's a fancy rooftop bar about two blocks from here. We can teleport there, but I've got to change. You aren't going to have me looking like your wicked step-sister." I closed my eyes and clapped my hands, feeling the wind of my fae magic incircle me. I opened my eyes again and soon went from jeans, an off-the-shoulder blouse and ballet flats to a red off-the-shoulder romper with black open-toed sandals.

Senna appeared impressed and gave me a thumbs up. "Now, can we teleport there?"

I grabbed her hand. "Absolutely."

Our town had only two rooftop bars, which was pretty good seeing how small we were, and I think that's all that there were prior to the world going all supernatural. This bar was a relic to the old days of the 1920s and even had a speakeasy in the basement. There was a dress code, and the owner didn't care if it alienated our citizens and lessened business.

Actually, there were a few people who came from other

towns to visit our growing nightlife, and we'd gone from being exclusively an invitation-only town for just paranormals to being more open for those seeking refuge, even if they were only human. That new rule came about after Amina and Phillip went to sleep. It was something Amina had pushed for but didn't get a lot of traffic on. Then after the battle, I guess the council felt a little guilty and changed things up.

Because we prided ourselves on our paranormal identity, our nightlife was like no other. Everything had a magic-based vibe to it. Even though this rooftop was old school, it still had magic. There was a mage who could bring art to life. There was also a medium who worked in a separate room, and apparently, he was exceptional. I'd never gone. Both my parents didn't make it, killed in a supernatural earthquake. My siblings, I'd never found. My best guess was that they didn't make it through either. I'd found extended family, but to this day, they had received no word from my brother and sister. I was too scared to confirm it by talking to any psychics. Some part of me chose to believe that they were living and couldn't reach me. Maybe they even lost their memories, like Felix had. I didn't want to know if I was wrong by trying to communicate with the dead.

Fingers snapped in front of my face, and I focused back on Senna. We sat at a table under a moving Monet artwork. "Where is your mind?" she asked before taking a sip of her cocktail.

I rolled my shoulders back. "Sorry. Hey, can you take this marking off of me?"

She placed her drink down. "No. Even if I could, I wouldn't go against my King and do such a thing. But I will try to reason with him."

I dropped my shoulders in disappointment. "So, what did you want to talk about?"

121

"Martin." "He visited you?"

She scowled. "Not only did he visit our town, but he took Joo-won away from us. This was two days ago. They were supposedly going out for drinks. However, that is not what happened."

I eyed her waiting for more, but she didn't continue. "Well, what happened?"

"I don't know, but Joo-won came back to the hotel with his clothes a mess and bloody. He wouldn't say what happened, but it couldn't have been anything good. Then Yuri came across a news report that several homes in an all gargoyle community not far from us, Charles Village, was attacked and robbed the same night Martin and Joo-won were out."

Yikes, I didn't want my mind to go there, but I couldn't help but wonder if the elves were behind that attack after speaking to Niles. "Why do you tie them to that? It could be a coincidence."

Senna leaned into the table. "The report said that it was done by masked elves and large never before seen creatures."

We'd just been attacked by modified wererats in New York, and Martin had attacked Niles' people as well. Now we were hearing about odd creatures and elves again. No, this couldn't be a coincidence.

Senna looked at my face and nodded. "You think it's them too, huh?"

I told her about the attack in New York and Nile's robbery. I looked down at my drink. The ice was beginning to melt, but I couldn't bring myself to take another sip. I was starting to feel sick. I couldn't let this curse make Joo-won do something he couldn't come back from. As much as I wanted to deny how I felt, I really liked Joo-won. As questionable as he could sometimes be, it would hurt if he turned out to be the baddie that Erik and Charles thought. "Maybe Joo-won was high and asleep in the car or something when Martin and his thugs attacked. Or he was a part of it, and it's the curse."

Senna looked up at the animated artwork, her face saddened, a far cry from her usual cold features. "Everything has a side effect. He'll be rotten by the time the witch comes for him."

"Why would she want that of him?"

"Who can say? Maybe it'll make her feel less guilty for turning him into a slave if he actually is evil. Lisa, if he does something that he can't repair, we will lose him completely. Our people will never follow him. We aren't saints, but we do have a code of ethics. He'll taint us, and we won't remain neutral. We will lose some of the alliances we've built, like the one with your town."

I rubbed my temples. I could absolutely not deal with this. "We need to find this witch and get her to change her mind. I've put out some feelers that I hope come to something."

Senna glanced back down at me. "Do you honestly think she would change her mind? Without a cost?"

"I'm sure there will be, but we will figure it out. We can't just let Joo-won go out like this."

"He's tried convincing her before."

"Why wouldn't she budge?"

"Maybe she did, but he wouldn't give her what she wanted. He never said. Joo-won likes his secrets."

No surprise there. "So, what do you think *I* can do?"

Senna raised a brow, giving me a knowing look. "It's clear Joo-won is in love with you. If you stay around him, that might keep Martin away. You can't stop the curse from making him go dark, but maybe you can at least prevent him from acting on those impulses."

I waved my tatted wrist at her to show her that I had no power over making Joo-won do the right thing. He never asked for my opinion on anything. I couldn't stop him from doing bad.

She rolled her eyes. "Well, at least preventing him from doing something really bad. Something he can't take back."

I choked back a laugh. "I've seen this movie before. Only the righteous woman can keep a man struggling with inner demons from going bad. That was Amina and Phillip's story, and I bought into it."

Senna pressed her lips together and raised a brow. She didn't say the thing that I'd just thought about. She was annoying that way. Like a teacher that wanted me to say the answer instead of telling it.

I grumbled. "Yes, it worked for them, but that doesn't mean it will work in this case. I have sacrificed my freedom, in a sense, to appeasing Joo-won before. To prevent him from killing Amina and Erik, I stayed with him. I do want to get rid of that curse, because I consider him a friend when he's not tracking me for migration purposes. But I can't give up my life. I have a store to run. I need to pay bills. I wish they'd left bills in the Pre-World, but apparently, they are necessary, or so they say."

Senna threw out her hands to the side, a look of frustration on her face. "Then what shall we do? He won't listen to me or Yuri. He adores you and will listen. You stopped him from fighting with the originals. You have power over him. Believe it or not."

When she said it like that, it did sound good. But that power came at a cost. I didn't want to have to be glued to him for me to wield my charms. I still felt bad for my role in making Amina do the same for Phillip. A woman's goal in life was not to help a man live his best life. Sure, she could help out but not at the expense of her freedom. I wanted to end that narrative.

A cold air brushed my arm, and I rubbed it absentmindedly. I soon found out where it came from.

"My two favorite women out without me even knowing. Now how did this happen?" Joo-won stated, suddenly appearing in front of our table.

Martin by his side. He looked between the two of us with an amused grin. There was nothing funny or happy right now, so I assumed it was a mask. Scary.

Right now wouldn't be the best time to faint, but they scared me so bad that I almost did. Had they heard us? This would not be good. I looked over to Senna, whose face expertly betrayed nothing.

She gave him a slight smile. "Hello, your majesty. I'm sorry we didn't invite you. I simply wanted some girl talk with Lisa. All this time and she and I never had any one-on-one time. She might one day be queen, and I wanted to know her better."

"Yeah, girl's night out," I said, raising my hands towards the roof awkwardly.

Joo-won furrowed his brows, either confused from my actions or not buying it. "Girl's night out," he said slowly, as if trying to comprehend it.

Martin snickered, leaning toward Joo-won. "It's when females dress up, drink cosmos and talk about men."

He'd been watching way too many TV shows. Although, he was frustratingly on point right now. Joo-won nodded in understanding.

"How'd you know we were here?" Senna asked.

His popping up wasn't random. He never came to this town unless he was looking for me. It was the stupid tattoo.

Joo-won me with a sly grin. I wanted to punch him.

Senna put a hand on the table, and I looked down at it in

an effort to refocus my attention because I was still reeling. "Were you looking for Lisa, your majesty?"

He kept his eyes on me as he responded. "You are very formal tonight, Senna. Why is that?" He finally looked to the other elf.

Senna didn't give away any emotion. "Because we are in public." She didn't miss a beat.

He patted her arm. "Relax. It's Friday night. I did come to find Lisa. I heard you had a weekend away with your ex. I got a little jealous and decided to spend some time with you."

He was full of crap. He was keeping tabs on me, and I didn't like it. "Oh, please. I heard you were partying it up with your ex as well. Who cares?"

I glared at Martin, whose eyes were only for Joo-won up until that moment, and they were not innocent eyes. There was a heat behind them that was quite inappropriate for public display. I had no clue what this man was up to, but I knew one thing for sure; he was very much still in love with Joo-won. Even with their falling out, it had not dimmed his desire.

As if noticing my own eyes on his, he glanced over to me and winked. "I told him you might be upset. I did want to spend time with you, but it seems our Joo-won wanted to keep you all to himself." Martin leaned forward and reached a hand out towards me. I got a whiff of his scent, an oak and cinnamon mix that wasn't unpleasant.

I sat rigid, unsure of what he was about to do. He gently touched my cheek with his index finger, his skin feeling light as a feather and smooth. I fought the desire to tremble.

"Eyelash." He showed me my lash on his finger. "Aren't you supposed to make a wish and blow?"

He moved his hand towards me, and I looked down at his finger. I glanced up at Joo-won, who was giving us cool

126

eyes, except I noticed his hands were in white-knuckled fists. It seemed he was breaking his mask and he didn't really like this exchange. Interesting. I looked back to Martin, who gave me a gentle smile. He really was quite charming. But then most sociopaths were, weren't they? I wouldn't be swayed. I closed my eyes and made my wish that we would find all the cures we needed, and blew.

"I hope your wish comes true."

I stared up at him, and it appeared like he genuinely meant it.

Senna stood up. "I'm going to get another cocktail. Need anything?"

Joo-won shook his drink at her and took her seat. I had a feeling she wouldn't be back soon.

She cleared her throat and eyed Martin, who bobbed his head to the music, ignoring her look. She walked over to him and hip bumped him, to which he chuckled. "Ah, yes, it seems I'm being summoned by your beautiful right hand. I'll leave you two love birds alone." He looked to me and gave a head nod. "I hope in the future we can spend some time together. I am not who I once was. I am hoping I can show you that." He then turned and walked away with Senna.

Joo-won, whose eyes had never left me, leaned towards me from across the circular table. "I don't know why you think I don't care. I thought we had something."

I took a sip of my cocktail and then placed it down on the table before I read him for filth. It didn't matter how I was starting to feel about him, I had to let him know that he couldn't do whatever he wanted when it came to me. I was not a possession. Not his or anyone's. "Let me make this perfectly clear because I think there has been some misunderstanding here. I am not yours. I am my own woman. We might have had an inkling of something, but since you decided to tag me like I'm some whale in the ocean, you can forget that."

He tilted his head, a slight smile still present. His cockiness made me want to punch him. Just like the first time we met. It annoyed me then, but as I got to know him, I'd come to realize he wasn't such a pompous jerk. He had a moral code and a heart. Therefore, claiming me against my will didn't fit with his style. I had to remind myself that it was just the curse. Even Senna seemed to believe he was acting differently. But it was so hard to do when he was looking at me like I was some small-minded idiot.

"Are you listening to anything I'm saying?" I spat.

He traced the back of a finger along my arm, sending chills through me, but I refused to move away and let him know how much he was getting to me with such a small touch. "Of course. You're mad."

He didn't seem bothered that I was mad at all. "Are you even remorseful for what you did?"

"I think if I said yes, you would still be upset."

He was maddening. Why did I have to fall for someone so cocky? I had to remember that maybe this was all the curse. Perhaps, like some fairytale, once it was broken, he'd be my own knight in shining armor. I felt ridiculous thinking it. Life wasn't that easy, and he enjoyed toying with me way too much for my comfort. I needed to back away and keep my head on straight.

I got up for my escape, but he grabbed my wrist. The contact over his mark sent a shiver through my body and not an uncomfortable one either. What the hell? He rubbed his thumb over my wrist, back and forth slowly. It sent tingles to my nether regions, and I could have exploded right then in front of everyone.

I shook free of his grasp and took in a deep breath to calm myself.

He gave me curious eyes. "Everything okay?"

I rubbed my wrist on the side of my hip as if that would erase the lingering feeling. "You know damn well it is not. What the hell just happened?"

He took a sip of his drink. It was dark in color, and something sweet no doubt, as most elves preferred. I watched as he gulped it down, his Adam's apple on his smooth long neck moving, and even that transfixed me. He removed the short glass from his mouth and ran his long, pink tongue over those full lips of his in a slow movement, capturing the residual liquid from his drink. The theatrics of it all served their purpose because I actually sucked in a breath, imagining that tongue on me and in various places. I hated him. Not really.

His eyes sparkled when he glanced up at me again. Oh, he knew what he was doing, and he knew how it affected me. "One of the other benefits of a marking. When I touch it, you...feel things. Pleasant things. You are a faerie. You can mark me as well. I'd like it." He bit his lower lip.

I hated that his movements made my stomach clench. "Pass. Get this marking off of me!"

He put down his drink. "We continuously go back and forth with each other. Why the limbo? We both like each other. We have chemistry. Stop running from me." He reached out for me again.

I stepped back. I couldn't let him touch me again. He confused me too much. I wanted to jump on him in private, and feel every part of him. I also wanted to slap some good back into him. The need to have Joo-won be the good man that I dreamed him to be was almost overpowering. I had to get him cured and see if he was who I hoped he was. "Let me stop you right now, ok? Whatever we have? I'm not going to explore any of it while you are still cursed because this version of you is not so likable anymore. And I don't want to hate you. So, I'm going to fix you, and then we'll see if there really is anything between us."

I turned and walked away, feeling a mix of emotions. I should have just gone home. What did Senna expect me to do for Joo-won while he was in this state? He was hundreds of years old. Surely, he could maintain some type of control. If they had to knock him over the head and tie him up until we found a way to break the curse, then we should try that.

A buzzing from my purse tore me away from my angry thoughts. I dug through my bag and pulled out my cell-phone. A text message from Fiona. She'd gotten Mercedes' address, and we were to go see her tomorrow. Wow, not a lot of time, but I wouldn't waste this opportunity.

I swung past the bar where Senna appeared on the verge of a coma while listening to a man trying to impress her with his big talk.

I shook my phone at her. "I got Mercedes' address, and we have to go tomorrow. I'll text you the details. Let's go save your guy."

CHAPTER 11

*T*urns out Mercedes wasn't in Hawaii. She was on vacation in New Orleans for some kind of magic conference. We didn't know exactly where we would meet her once in town, but Fiona assured us that she would be able to get in touch with us at some point that day, and from there, we wouldn't have much of a window to get to her, and teleporting would not be an option. Most of Louisiana, including New Orleans, was part of the federation, and you couldn't just teleport inside, and even while there, teleportation was prohibited. More and more places were banning teleportation unless it was for longer travel because of breaking and entering and privacy issues.

In any event, so that we didn't miss her call – I had no real idea how she would get in touch with us- we arrived super early to also account for the time zone difference. Senna thought bringing Yuri was a good idea to avoid any possible traps. I talked Charles into also joining so that we could have another member of The Six present since that's what Fiona promised her. I'd have asked for someone else, but Erik wasn't leaving town while Amina was asleep, and Felix and Faith were on some mission with the angels or something. With the four of us, we would be prepared to take on whatever this witch threw at us. All I knew about her was that she was super powerful, and I didn't like walking into things totally unprepared without support.

We got through the usual rigamarole of entering a government town by having ourselves tested for magical disease before entering. Normally we'd have to get a sponsor and get stripped of our powers for 24 hours if we didn't have proof of being from another government town. However, Charles and I were considered honorary citizens under the federation because of our relationship with the Hagerstown government town back home. Senna and Yuri refused to go powerless, but we got around that by getting temporarily magically bound to them to prevent them from causing trouble. If they did, we would all get jailed.

After we were allowed to enter, the four of us sat inside a local coffee shop way too early in the morning. Charles had his sunglasses on and head tilted back, I was sure he was asleep. Senna sat alert, reading a book. Yuri busied himself with some sort of activity on his laptop.

I looked at the time. I was bored. It was after nine in the morning local time, and we'd already been in the shop over an hour. I huffed and picked a corner off my beignet to nibble on. I could no longer worry my brain about my last encounter with Joo-won or the fact that although I wanted to be repulsed by his ways, I was still stupidly turned on by him. I wanted to slap myself, and if I did so now, they would think I was crazy. Maybe I really was.

"What is the problem?" Yuri asked, eyes still on his laptop. What could he possibly be working on? What did it take to help run a mini kingdom, and why was Senna not working then?

Damn, this elf was more observant than I gave him credit for. "I mean, how long are we going to wait for

Mercedes to respond to us? What if we are here all day? They're going to kick us out of this shop."

"We've only been here thirty minutes. Read a book like Senna or sleep like Charles."

I leaned into the square table. "What are you doing?"

He looked up, blue eyes their usual coldness. "Work."

I gave him a tight smile. "Thanks for explaining."

He looked back at his laptop. "You are quite welcome."

I huffed again. "You're mean."

He frowned. That actually seemed to bother him. I was kind of joking, but he appeared to not get it.

"I have done nothing wrong. I have answered your question. You are a troublemaker."

Senna lowered her book to her lap, a patient smile on her face. "The princess needs to be entertained, can't you see?"

Why did that feel like a dig at me? *Because it probably was, Lisa.*

Senna's response seemed to only further trouble Yuri, whose eyebrows knitted together in a deeper look of displeasure. "She is an adult. She can entertain herself. Go shopping. That is your thing, yes?"

While shopping was one of my many passions, when he said it like that, I kind of sounded like a frivolous teenager. "I do not shop. I curate items for my store and gather inspiration for my creations and brand."

Yuri tilted his head. "You do this by shopping, no?"

Senna chuckled and then slowly closed Yuri's laptop. "You work too hard. It is a Saturday. Take a moment. Our future queen wants something to do. Go shopping with her."

Yuri and I both called out in disagreement at the same time, but Senna raised a hand to silence us. "You need to bond."

I cut my eyes at her. "We are already bonded through magic."

"You know that's not what I meant, now go."

Shopping seemed like a frivolous thing to be doing now. We were on a mission to save an elf and maybe Amina if this witch was that powerful. I needed to stay focused. I gestured to my pastry. "What about my beignet? I haven't finished eating it. Also, what if Mercedes shows up here like we asked her to, and I'm not here? "

Senna lifted her book back up. "Take your food with you, and we will contact you if Mercedes shows. Bye."

We stared at her for a beat. "I won't repeat myself."

We both got up grumbling. Why was I afraid of her? I was a super powerful faerie. I took a large bite of my beignet and left the rest there. I wasn't one to walk and eat, but I did bring my coffee.

Yuri and I left my shop and walked a short while in awkward silence. After a while, he pointed across from me to a store. "There is a shop there. It is open."

I looked, then scrunched my face. "It's a tourist souvenir shop."

He lowered his hand and looked away. "You cannot curate your brand in there?"

Something told me that was more a smart-ass comment than a genuine question. Why did it feel like Yuri didn't like me? I thought we had bonded at the elf party. "Did I do something wrong?"

He paused and looked down at me. "No."

He didn't say anything more. This guy really wasn't a talker. I had to pull words from him to make this less awkward.

Yuri cleared his throat. "Nice weather, isn't it?"

While the weather was pretty darn perfect for being on the cusp of our long winter, we weren't about to have a lame weather conversation, and I didn't think he had more to say about getting a cure of any sort. "We can do better than that. Joo-won told me that you didn't get along with Martin? You were all cohorts back in the day."

His shoulders rose, clearly agitated by the mention of Martin's name. "Yes."

It was like pulling teeth, I tell you. "Well, since you've known him for so long, have you noticed him behaving differently lately?"

He gave a quick twitch of his lips. I was hitting a nerve. "Yes."

I would jump on him. I would jump on him and maul him like a bear. "Care to elaborate?" You turd.

Yuri gave a long-suffering sigh with stern eyes fixed on me. "He is not the Joo-won that I know right now. But...he is not an impossible Joo-won either."

I kept my mouth closed as I tried to patiently wait for him to continue. He was a whole foot taller than me, but I could float off the ground and make up the height difference so my hands could easily wrap around his throat.

Yuri turned from me and pointed again. "Store."

I followed his hand and was happy to see a cute boutique. I grunted to save face but still walked in that direction.

To my surprise, Yuri continued to speak as we walked, seemingly more relaxed than before. "Joo-won had a questionable moral code a long time ago. Did you know that he was originally a light elf? There are really only two kinds of elves: light and dark. He became neutral because of his past crimes. If he kept going down that path, he would be a dark elf like Martin."

He held the door to the shop open for me, and I walked in, eyes immediately growing as I looked at all of the stylish clothes and knick-knacks. "So, you were his Jimminy Cricket?"

"What? I do not shapeshift."

"He's from a fairy tale. Pinocchio?"

Yuri gave me a blank stare and then walked over to a frilly pastel pink dress. "What about this?"

In spite of my frustration with him, I chuckled. He was an odd elf, but there was something endearing about him. And, as I looked at the dress, it actually was cute. "Hold on to that. Doesn't matter what size." I could magic it up so it would fit whoever bought it.

Yuri looked up from his phone. "I understand now. I was his conscious, and I tried to be his guide."

Had he just looked up Jimminy Cricket and Pinocchio? "Ok, yeah."

He put his phone in his pocket. "Now he has no guide because he is cursed. The cricket that is me can no longer be heard." He actually sounded really sad when he said that. It kind of made me sad too. "If we cannot save him, he will not live. Our King must not be a slave."

I put down the necklace I was holding and poked Yuri in the chest. There were options. Even if we ran out of time, we could still work on ways to get Joo-won out of servitude and return his powers. I hadn't come all this way and spent all this time to just give up on him. I wasn't ready. "We aren't offing him. No matter what."

"He won't give us a choice."

"Then we tie him up." I stomped away to continue my shopping, an unsettled feeling growing in my stomach. If we couldn't get Mercedes to change her mind, I was really running out of options. Sure, Joo-won was a pain in my butt right now but the thought of him dying actually scared me. It made me want to ensure he was monitored at all times.

Once we got back, we'd have to do just that if things didn't go our way here.

A beautiful indigo blouse appeared in front of me.

Yuri gave me neutral eyes as he held the blouse up for me to inspect. "You think I want my friend to die? He is our leader, but he is my brother first. You know him better now, but not like I do. I've seen him in good times and bad. He is not the perfect man he presents himself to be. He has hurt, and he has been hurt. He is loyal and giving. Sometimes too giving. He loves freely but is guarded at the same time. When he shows his heart, it is a controlled process. I only say this to you because I know he cherishes you the most. We must not fail."

My heart tightened at his determination. His hope somehow made me a little less worried. Ok, Yuri was deep and observant. I'd definitely have to pick his brain more. I took the blouse. Crap, he had a good sense of style. "I'll continue to do everything I can to protect him," I replied. And I meant it.

When we returned to the coffee shop two hours later, Charles was awake and chatting it up with Senna. It appeared they were having their own little bonding session.

"No word from Mercedes?" I asked, setting my bags down. The only reason I was carrying anything was because Yuri also had an armful and not just things for me, mind you. The shopping actually did the job of calming me a little, and it made me like Yuri. He wasn't the uptight meanie like I always thought. And I suspected Senna wanted us to bond all along.

Senna shook her head and got up. "I can't stay here all day. Let's book a room for now, and you can drop those bags. Maybe we should stay the night. My treat."

Charles stood up and stretched as well. "I like having rich friends."

So, did I.

We found a hotel near Bourbon St and secured two rooms. Senna and I shared a room, and Yuri and Charles got the other. I sat on my bed, looking through my purchases. "Well, since we're still waiting, we should go sightseeing and grab some food."

Senna looked at herself in the mirror near the bathroom. "Might as well. So how did things go with you and Yuri?"

"He's actually a cool guy. Great sense of style. Tell me again, why you don't like him?"

Senna turned slightly to me, a look of confusion on her face. "Of course, I like Yuri. He is my best friend, if such things exist between elves. I'm just not in love with him. I can't control that."

Just like I wasn't able to control not falling for Joo-won. We had a similar issue in a way. "No, I guess you can't."

"I would assume the same goes for you and Charles."

I paused, looking through my items. Well, that's not what I thought she would bring up. I knew they were looking a little too cozy in the café. "Why do you ask?"

She turned back to the mirror, applying a lipstick I had not seen her remove from her purse. "He seems like a fun guy. And he's cute."

"Yes and yes. But we just didn't work out."

"Mind if I make a play?"

My heart froze. I wasn't surprised, and it wasn't that I didn't want Charles to move on. It just felt weird if Senna was the one he moved on with. Then again, Senna and I were not best friends, and I had no claim on her loyalty. By the time she'd come around to even liking me, Charles was already hanging around. If he liked her, who was I to stand in the way? Plus, we both had moved on and what we had was brief. If the two of them could develop something long-lasting and strong, I was all for it. Charles deserved it, and from what I knew of Senna, she did too. I waved a hand at her. "Have at it. Just don't be so obvious about it in front of Yuri. He's going to be so heartbroken."

Senna lowered her head, but I saw her face scrunch at my words. "I've already broken his heart. I wish he'd let me go. I hate hurting him."

I gave her a sympathetic frown. "Yep, magic doesn't stop love from being complicated." I knew that first hand.

CHAPTER 12

We'd explored the city, ate way too much food and still no word from Mercedes. I was beginning to think we'd been played. I went to bed angry and feeling darn near hopeless at helping Joo-won.

Hours later, my eyes opened to the darkness of the hotel room. I looked at the digital clock near me, and it read 3:01 a.m.

Someone was humming. It sounded like a woman, and I didn't think it was Senna by the tone of the voice.

I followed the location of the sound and soon could make out the shape of a figure sitting at the table next to my bed.

The lights turned on.

Senna jumped up from the corner of my eye. "Mercedes."

The woman slouched in the chair looked very relaxed. She was not what I expected. She was maybe in her early fifties with tanned skin, long, wavy black hair and hazel eyes. Mercedes stretched her long legs in front of her and let out a yawn. "Sorry about the lateness, dolls. This is the witching hour though, so it's quite poetic."

Senna sat on my bed beside me. "Were you out dancing the night away?"

Mercedes gave her a wink. She was dressed in black leather pants and a billowy white blouse. She certainly looked like she'd been hitting the streets. "Naturally."

She seemed kinder towards Senna than I expected. For someone who had cursed her leader, I'd have thought Mercedes wouldn't want anything to do with the elf.

"Well, we wanted to thank you for agreeing to meet with us. We know you have every right to ignore us and continue with what you have planned."

Mercedes lifted a shoulder and looked over to me. "I'm here to meet The Six." She sat up and reached across to grab my hand. She then closed her eyes and made a little humming noise.

I sat motionless, not sure how to respond.

When she opened her eyes again, she patted my hand and let it go. "You have amazing energy. You're lucky I can't siphon it because that would be tempting. I wanted to see if you were indeed magically bonded. You are. Whoever was able to bond six strangers together like they did had some magical range. I wish I could." She then made a show of looking around. "Where's the other? I was told there would be two members here?"

I gave a quick nod then closed my eyes – time to use our mental telepathy that The Six shared.

Charles, are you up? I called in my mind.

Yes, I'm up, watching TV and listening to Yuri snore like a bear. He needed his own room.

Come to our room. Mercedes is here.

On it.

I opened my eyes and smiled. "Charles is on the way."

Mercedes settled into her seat again, looking pleased.

She was comfortable, but I was excited. I twisted my

fingers together, nervous. I had so many things I wanted to talk to her about. I could hardly organize my thoughts. "While we wait, I wanted to talk about Joo-won."

She lost her smile. "Ack, can't it wait? I really don't understand why you aligned yourself with that cocky bastard anyway."

I opened my mouth to reply.

She cut me off. "I didn't want to meet you to discuss that elf." She tilted her head towards Senna. "The only reason I don't mind her being here is because she's reasonable. That and the pale one."

Senna grimaced. "You mean Yuri?"

As if on cue, we heard a knock at the door.

I snapped my fingers, and it opened, letting Charles and Yuri in.

Charles was wide awake and alert, but Yuri looked like he'd literally gotten out of bed, his hair was tousled and his eyes were hardly open.

Mercedes clapped her hands. "Wonderful." She extended her hand, and Charles swiftly approached her for the greeting. "I'm so sorry about your sister. It was quite noble what she and Phillip did. I'm not sure I could have done the same thing. Magic is a tricky beast. Nothing comes without a cost. The trick to saving her is to find how much of the price you can reduce and still have her maintain most of what she is."

That sounded more complicated than she was making it.

Charles seemed to ponder that, lowering his eyes and searching the floor. "There's always been a negative cost associated with magic."

She lightly tapped his cheek with her palm. "There's a science to this magic, as silly as it sounds. Actually, I wanted to meet you both because I have something to say. It was quite fortuitous that Fiona reached out to me. The Six have more to do."

I dropped my shoulders. That was the last thing I wanted to hear. The words exhausted me already. "Don't tell me that."

She shrugged. "I know, I know, but you couldn't possibly think you'd be a one and done."

"Actually, yeah, I did. That was a pretty big one, so I did think I was done."

She snorted and dug in her pocket, producing what looked like a cigarette. She waved her hand over the end of it, lighting it quickly. "I'm sure someone told you about the purpose of The Six. You save the world against evil. Those original soulmates aren't the only evil in the world. The worlds a fucked-up place now. Well, it was a fucked-up place before too." She then brought the cigarette to her lips.

Charles lifted his chin and sniffed the air. "Is that marijuana?"

Mercedes winked again. "A magically laced version of it. Wanna hit?"

Charles walked closer and took the drug from her to inhale. "Hells yeah."

No, really, she was definitely not what I expected. I'd thought I'd be meeting some old crone who looked like she lived in the middle of a forest and ate children. What I got was a hip auntie type. I raised my hand. "Sorry, moving past the thought that I'm not sure how much world-saving we can do with Amina sleep, and I really wanted to retire from the whole superhero game, but can we finally talk about why we're here?"

Charles returned the weed to Mercedes, who then offered it to me.

I quickly shook my head. Drinking was my only vice.

"Ah, Lisa no fun?"

Lisa no fun? Lisa was up in the middle of the night with a room full of people. Lisa was barely coherent. "Yeah, I'm the party pooper in the group and not the elf to my left giving off so much chilly air I could catch a cold."

Yuri, who up until that moment had been leaning against the dresser with his regular scowl, straightened up and pointed at himself. "I assume you are talking about me?"

"Give that man a prize." I rolled my eyes and looked back to Mercedes. "Can we discuss what we came here for now?"

Mercedes took another hit of her joint before speaking. "I see you want me to lose my buzz. Let me save you some time. I will not change my mind about cursing that elven king."

I scooted to the end of the bed. "But might it be too harsh for the crime? I mean, you got your pendant back."

Mercedes lowered her lids. "I've had this discussion with those two before." She pointed to Yuri and Senna. "When someone commits a crime, they have to do the time. If they break in a person's house and steal their jewelry, they go to jail for a period of time." Mercedes passed her joint back to Charles, who gladly accepted it.

He was no help.

Charles took a hit before speaking. "Ok, I see your logic. So, are you saying Joo-won would only have to be powerless and serve you for a limited time? Like a few months or something?"

Mercedes gave a bored sigh. "No. A lifetime. His evil ways are over."

I shook my head. This was really crazy. The punishment wasn't fitting the crime. We were missing something that she wasn't telling us. "He's not evil, Mercedes." Well, that's what I was banking on. "What really happened that day? I know the pendant was very special but did him taking it really warrant a lifetime of servitude? I need to understand. Joo-won's a...friend, and he's done good. I think he's worth saving."

Mercedes retrieved the weed from Charles and then put it out on the window ledger before inserting the remainder of it back in her pocket. "It wasn't that he took the pendant. It was that he touched it. Held on to it. If anyone else had touched that pendant, I would have cursed them too."

"Why was the act of touching it so bad?"

"Because that is how the pendant becomes powerful. Joo-won is tainted. One touch of that item and it turns you into the worst kind of creature. An ugly, evil menace that causes nothing but death and destruction. My curse on him was an attempt to prevent that. The window to stop his downfall was short. I did what needed to be done."

Yuri shifted in his stance. "Why would you make something so horrific in the first place?"

Mercedes sneered at him in disdain. "I would not. It is a demonic object. Whatever hell-spawn created it was using it to drain the holder of their energy while turning that person into a creature that would follow them and cause mayhem on their behalf. That demon is no longer, but the object still holds power. I was calling myself keeping it safe from the clutches of anyone who would use it to harm others since the object cannot be destroyed. Only a very select few can touch it without being harmed – the deceased demon and super powerful witches. Even I dared not touch it with my bare hands. Once you turn evil, there isn't a cure. When I found it missing, I knew I had to find it, or all hell could break loose. There's enough evil in the world without an object roaming out there turning more people bad."

Now that she explained it, things made sense. She really wasn't an evil old hag. Joo-won was infected, for lack of a better word, and she'd found a way of getting around having to kill him. She was basically going to force him under her power so she could keep him in line. In a way, she had spared him because she could have killed him. I felt some relief with that. Perhaps things weren't so dire. "Is there a way to stop him from becoming a creature?"

"Thus far, I can't find a complete cure. The only thing that I've seen work is overlapping him with another controlling magic."

Senna crossed her legs, looking way too poised and perfect for this time of night. "The pendant controls those who touch it, so you cursed him to trump the pendant's control."

Mercedes nodded, leaning back in her chair. "I'd think my control would be better than his fate. He's lucky if you ask me. I caught him early. The change is not immediate. I have actually helped him because at least my curse gave him time before it takes hold. Time he wouldn't have had otherwise."

"I understand completely what you have told us. Why didn't you say this before now?"

Mercedes raised her brows and lifted her chin in a show of haughtiness. "Because I was pissed at you all for breaking into my house in the first place."

I couldn't say I blamed her. Here she had someone steal from her, then she had to search for it. and I was sure Joo-won didn't easily give it back. She most likely went through a lot to get that pendant back. And then, to top it off, she didn't try to kill Joo-won, she instead thought to save his life. I had no idea what being a powerless servant would be like for him, but it had to be better than turning into a horrible creature. Still, one thing did confuse me.

"Why tell them there was a way to break the curse if it was done to save him?"

"Honey, because I don't care about him being a servant to me. I don't have a need for some pretty boy running behind me all day, getting in my way. The person who gives him an organ can control him. Since they have to do it for no payment or obligation, my hope was that it would mean his master would not be an asshole. Even if they knew that offering an organ would get them control of Joo-won, it wouldn't work because that would mean it wasn't altruistic. It has to be a caring soul."

Whoa, this was news. So, I really could save him with an organ. I wouldn't control him. He could be himself again. It sucked that there was no other option, but I suppose it was time to accept that this was the only way. I squished my cheeks together, feeling even more exhausted.

Mercedes tapped her fingers on the arm of her chair, eyes squinted as she looked at me. "Would you be willing to give him one of your organs?"

"Yes, but I thought the person had to give up their organ with no favor or price. I owe him for saving my life."

She tilted her head from side to side. "There are loopholes, but he didn't need to know all of that. Plus, you are a member of The Six, so you can do certain things others can't. It's in the handbook."

I widened my eyes. "There's a handbook."

She chuckled, waving her hand at me. "No, just messing with you. Seriously, The Six, through their bonds, have more abilities together than individually. I'm not sure if that is the case now with Amina asleep, but in theory, that's the way it works."

Charles nodded, crossing his arms. "Yeah, we were told that before."

I cut in, feeling somewhat renewed. "So, I can give Joo-won my organ, and he'll be free of the pendant curse and your curse?"

Senna narrowed her eyes in displeasure. "But then she would control our King."

Mercedes yawned. "Better her than a stranger."

"He would never go for being controlled."

If anyone could do it, why not have Senna or Yuri give an organ. Surely that would be better than me. "What about another elf giving an organ?"

Mercedes inspected her nails. "They aren't as special as The Six. They don't get through the loopholes." She looked up and winked at me. "You're the best deal in town."

I looked around the room, and the elves didn't look like they fell on a good deal. Now that we all knew what the cure entailed, giving up an organ probably seemed a lot less ideal than before. I'd have to get them to realize that they had nothing to worry about. Controlling people wasn't my style. "I would never try to control Joo-won. But I am a firm believer of people doing what they want." I looked to the elves in the room so that they would see the seriousness on my face and understand that I was being sincere. "You can lock me up if I do otherwise. You could also put a spell on me to prevent me from controlling him."

Mercedes tilted her head back but said nothing.

What did that mean? Was I assuming too much? Would a binding spell even work on me with something like this?

She slapped her thighs and stood up. "Well, children, my turn up has reached its limits, and I must get my beauty rest."

I jumped up, suddenly remembering something. I lifted my right wrist in the air. "Can you tell me how to remove a mark?"

She gave me a wiry smile. "Laser surgery, honey."

She really was full of jokes.

"I kid. Must be the joint. Anywho, if you are talking

about being claimed, you can kill the person who claimed you."

Well, that wouldn't work.

"Why type of marking is it?"

I showed her my wrist.

She grabbed it, inspecting my arm. "An invisible symbol. Those are removable. Much easier to end the bond than, say a were or vampire bond. Was it our handsome King that did this to you?"

I hesitated, not wanting to shine a bad light on Joo-won in front of her.

Mercedes glanced up at me. "I'll take that as a yes." She let go of my hand. "Keep it. It will probably help ensure you can break the curse because of your bond."

I frowned. "I thought you said being a part of The Six was enough?"

"Eh, having extra can't hurt. Use all of this to your advantage." She tapped my nose with her index finger.

What did that mean? Were we not equals now? Was there something more she wasn't telling us? I wondered if Senna and Yuri weren't here, if she would be more open. I kicked myself internally for bringing them. I thought they could offer perspective to her that I couldn't, but really, I didn't need them. I rarely took the lead on things, but it seemed others didn't have more answers than I did.

Senna stood up, hands on her hips but eyes looking very tired. Even elves needed their res. "How will we know it works?"

Mercedes clapped her hands and began to fade before our eyes. "Well, when the curse is set to take full effect, it would teleport him directly to me. If that doesn't happen, then it worked," she replied before disappearing before our eyes.

CHAPTER 13

*O*nce we teleported back to Silver Spring, we used the elven portal to go to Baltimore. I could have teleported us there as well, but that would have taken more energy. Teleporting was a major convenience, but it didn't come without weakening my magic for a time. Portals took a bit more time to create, but we weren't on a time crunch right then, although I was looking forward to breaking Joo-won's curse. I was not looking forward to how he would react to me having power over him. Would he not take the cure? If he did, would he behave differently around me? Maybe not even want to be around me? I wouldn't blame him. Distance would probably bring him comfort from worrying about being controlled.

Senna and Yuri came with me to my apartment so I could drop off my purchases from the prior day. I dropped my bags off in my bedroom, really wanting to take a shower but also wanting to get this over with. When I returned, I found the two inspecting my space like nosey parents.

Senna replaced the lid to a scented candle after sniffing it and put it back down on my coffee table. "I'm assuming no one has thought about how we will present this to Joo-won."

Yuri continued to flip through my design pad. "I'd assume we tell the truth, no?"

I snatched my pad back from him. It felt kind of like he was reading my diary. I didn't want to share it right now, and since I didn't get many visitors, I didn't think about hiding it. "Joo-won has an ego as large as this planet. If he thought I'd have any power over him, he would say no. But right now, we have almost zero time left, and other than Martin's mysterious offer, we don't have any other options."

Senna made a grumbling noise. "For all we know, Martin's offer would be the same. I can't possibly imagine Joo-won being controlled by him."

Yuri folded his arms and barred his teeth. "I would sooner kill Martin than have him hold power over our King."

Senna nodded. "So, we all agree that Lisa is the best option. And since that is the case, we might want to be selective about what we share with Joo-won."

"We would lie?" Yuri looked at us with wide, concerned eyes. For a being that was hundreds of years old, he still possessed an innocence about him that was quite endearing.

I placed my design pad back down on the coffee table. "We wouldn't lie, we'd just omit the whole truth. For his own good. Honestly, he'll never know. I'm never going to exert any power over him. But who wants the hassle of trying to convince Joo-won of this? I know I don't."

Senna placed a hand on her chest. "I know I don't either."

We looked to Yuri.

The elf looked down at the rug, scrunching his face. "He will kill us if he finds out."

I raised a brow. "Then don't ever tell him. So, is that a yes?"

Yuri dropped his shoulders and kept his head down. "What choice do we have? He's never going to take the cure if he knows that he could be controlled. And we can't lose him."

I shook my head. "No, we can't. And we're pretty much out of time to do any convincing with him. So, where should I go to take out my kidney?"

Yuri grimaced, and Senna raised a brow. Oh, they thought that was a gross question? Well, they weren't the ones about to lose an organ. I rubbed my hands over my face and shook. I really wasn't looking forward to this.

Senna walked over to me and placed a comforting arm over my shoulders. "You're scared. I didn't think you would be, but I suppose this wouldn't be pleasant for you. We'll have a witch or a fae remove it magically. They'll put you to sleep and heal you up. You won't feel a thing."

I nodded, barely hearing her words. I was nervous about the surgery, magical or not, but I was also worried about the after-effects. Had Mercedes told us everything? Would another surprise pop up that I wasn't prepared for? Mercedes was so cryptic about it all. Would Joo-won just eat my kidney, and things would go back to normal? Would he disappear once he got what he needed?

Senna leaned in towards me. "Thank you for this. It's going to work out."

I gave her a weak smile. It had to work out. We had no other choice.

∼

*W*hen we returned to Joo-won's place, he was in the bathroom. Yuri and Senna excused themselves and left me alone with him to do what needed to be done.

"You can come in," Joo-won called.

"No, thank you," I replied back, taking a seat in the living area.

"I'm dressed."

"I don't believe you."

"I've never lied to you."

This was true. I sighed and walked to the cracked bathroom door. I placed a hand on the knob but didn't push it. "If you are clothed, what are you doing in there? Are you on the toilet?"

I heard him make a noise of irritation. "No, Lisa. I am simply relaxing."

Clothed but relaxing in the bathroom? I opened, more intrigued than anything. The bathroom was large with the toilet behind another closed door and a separate shower from the bath. When I stepped onto the white tiled floor, I had no idea what to expect. Seeing Joo-won fully dressed except for his socks and shoes and sitting in the large jacuzzi tub filled with just water was not on the list of things I'd thought I'd see.

And it was hot. Ugh, even doing something as odd as this made him look appealing. His wet clothes clung to every part of him, his thin, white shirt practically looking like paint on his skin as his tone abs and chest showed clearly through the fabric. His head leaned against the gray wall tile, and his wet jet-black hair hung near his closed eyes. His black trouser-covered legs were spread wide, one hanging off the side of the tub. He certainly didn't look evil right now. Maybe it hadn't crept in yet. Maybe it would happen at the final moment of the year. Or maybe Mercedes was just wrong. Although, I doubted the latter. Right now, all he looked was sexy.

I crossed my arms. "What am I looking at?"

A smile covered his lips. "Me in a tub."

153

"Fully dressed."

"Yes, that is true."

Although I wasn't inviting him to strip, it was still an odd sight. "Why?"

"I needed to be in the water right now. I was naked, but you arrived, so now I'm not."

By the way he said it, I just assumed he used magic to clothe himself quickly. It didn't explain why he didn't just get out of the tub. "Well, that was thoughtful, but why do you need to be in the water?"

He opened his eyes, and I was once again ensnared by their beauty. It was like staring into the ocean. "Because my body is hot."

I snorted, looking away from him. The man sure had a lot of confidence.

"Not in the way you are thinking, butterfly. I am saying I am physically hot. I felt like my body was on fire. It's been happening more and more lately due to the curse. I expect I might one day erupt in flames if I don't get to the witch by the end of this month. It's one of many ailments I've recently dealt with."

I knew he had ailments from the curse, but he did a great job at keeping me in the dark when he was suffering. How many other issues had popped up for him? "What else?"

He lowered slightly in the water. "I also get chills that cannot be ended by any amount of heat. Constricting of the heart and an unsightly rash on my back."

I lowered my shoulders and walked over to the tub, sitting down on the ledge. He looked so peaceful in the water now, his eyes closed again. I brushed my fingers over one of his hands, resting on the ledge. I felt sorry for him. Sure, I was pissed about him marking me, but his pain affected me. Hurt me.

He turned his hand so that he was now gripping my fingers. "Do you feel sorry for me, butterfly?" he asked in a barely audible voice that stirred my insides.

"Maybe."

He quickly reached up, pulling me on top of him in the water.

I screamed in surprise, shoving at him. "You jerk."

He pulled me to his chest and chuckled in my ear. "I'm sorry, I couldn't help it. I wanted you near me."

I smacked his chest, although it was not nearly as hard as I could have hit him. Maybe, I didn't mind being wet in the water with him. "There were other ways."

His cool lips made a trail on my cheek. "But this is the most fun."

I adjusted so that I now straddled him in the cold water. I should have been freezing, but his body was, as he said, hot. It was like being close to a stove. Not enough that it burned me to touch him, but I was sure prolonged contact would get very uncomfortable. There was no way he was comfortable now.

I knew something that could aid in cooling him down. I lowered my head and closed my eyes, bringing forth my magic over the elements, and soon felt bits of coldness touch my skin.

"Snow?" Joo-won asked.

I opened my eyes and saw now that the room was filled with a light flurry that I had conjured with my seasonal fae magic. "Is it helping?"

He looked up at the ceiling, grinning in a sort of child-like wonderment that I had never seen before. I really enjoyed when he let his guard down. "Yes. Thank you, butterfly. I suppose you aren't still mad at me then?" He ran his hands lazily up and down my back.

I relaxed in his arms in spite of my anger at him. "Yes, I am. And you are going to remove this stupid tattoo."

"I'd rather not." He lifted my hand and kissed my wrist where the invisible tattoo lay.

A shiver went through my body, clenching my core.

"The way you react to me..." Joo-won didn't finish his sentence. Instead, he gave me a wicked grin, biting down on his lower lip.

My cheeks heated as I focused in on those pillowy lips. I wanted to taste them. He was driving me to distraction. I had to remain focused. "You should stop being an ass because I can cure your curse."

His smile faltered, and his eyes enlarged. "Go on?"

I wiggled in my position to get as comfortable as I could while sitting in cold water over his lap.

"If you keep moving like that, you might feel more than you anticipated."

Too late. I could feel him between my legs, and his body was very much responsive to mine. More distraction. I cleared my throat. "Don't ask me any more questions, but I know for a fact the curse will be broken if you eat me. Wait, that sounded very inappropriate."

He cocked a brow. "How can you expect me not to ask questions?"

I jutted out my chin. "Very easily."

He placed a hot hand on my arm and began to rub. "You are a last resort. I don't want to take anything from you."

I rolled my eyes. Not this again. He loved reminding me of me owing him an organ, yet when it was time to seriously talk about it, he fell back. "Are you kidding me? We are running low on time, and I am giving you a cure."

He lifted his upper lip slightly in a snarl. He really didn't like this idea. "I refuse."

I splashed him with water, annoyed. "Well, it's too late." I then clapped my hands, and a large glass full of a thick pink liquid hovered in the air in front of him. "This is my kidney smoothie. I tried to make it sweet so it wouldn't be gross, but I'm not sure it worked. I didn't taste it because I'm not a cannibal. It still smells vomitous, though."

Joo-won looked at the concoction with curious eyes, but there was something else there. Sadness? This was really upsetting to him? My heart fluttered at the thought. "You amaze me, butterfly. Why would you do this for me?"

I looked away from those beautiful eyes and shrugged. I was feeling flushed and not just from the heat he was radiating. "Maybe I don't want you to die. Maybe I want you around longer so I can kick your ass properly for this tattoo."

He wiggled his brows. "I wouldn't mind a good spank on the ass."

I tossed my head back. He really was incorrigible. "Clearly, I said kick your ass, not spank your ass. Are you going to drink it or not? I can't put it back together and insert it back in. I went through surgery and everything. They put me to sleep. I woke up in a bed with an IV, which I really think was for show because I was able to leave the hospital the same day, but that's not the point. I had magical surgery to save you, so please don't let my kidney go to waste." I chuckled to myself. "There's a sentence you don't hear every da–"

I didn't finish my sentence because soon his lips were on mine, his hand on my cheek and the other hand on my lower back, moving me closer to him. His lips were soft and full, and I gave in to the urge to flick my tongue over his top lip, which only encouraged him to suck on my lower lip. His tongue pressed into my mouth, dancing across my own. He tasted like wine, and I let myself float into him because it felt too damn good not to.

The air left my lungs, making my mind all mushy. I had to get him to drink and focus on kissing later. I pulled away slowly. Very reluctantly. "I can only hold this glass up with my magic for so long. Can you please hurry up and drink this stuff before it falls? Then you will have to lick it up from the floor, glass and all, because I am not giving up another organ."

Joo-won released me and let out an exasperated breath. "You do know how to kill a mood."

I batted my lashes with a tight smile, feeling worried. I really needed him to drink this potion. "I do so try."

Displaying what I could only deem his athletic prowl, Joo-won wrapped his hands around me again and stood up in the tub in one smooth go.

I yelped and wrapped my legs around his waist, but he seemed totally in control. It was impressive.

He moved us out of the jacuzzi and stood on the floor. He then gave me an amused grin. "Shall you stay wrapped around me? I suppose I don't mind, but I was hoping to drink this in private, so you wouldn't see any unpleasantries."

Such as him gagging on my kidney? Yeah, I'd take a pass on that even though I think I liked being wrapped around him. Not that he needed to know that.

I quickly left the bathroom and did a clap of magic to dry my clothes. I flopped down on the couch, crossing my legs as I waited for Joo-won to reappear. A few minutes in and I felt a tingling wave pass through my body like a buzz of energy. My nostrils filled with a familiar scent, his scent. I then felt the taste of him on my tongue. It was as if he was surrounding me, only I could not see him. What the?

Shortly after, the elven king reappeared, his clothes now dry.

I narrowed my eyes, catching what looked like a dollop of pink goo on his chin. I pointed in a circle at him. "You don't feel that?"

He tilted his head. "Feel what?"

"A piece of my kidney juice is on your chin."

He wiped the goo off his chin with a finger and then put it in his mouth, eyeing me with an unbothered look that also somehow managed to look sexy. How?

He grinned at me. "If you would be so kind as to not refer to it as kidney juice again, that would be wonderful."

I lifted a shoulder. Toying with him was actually fun. I liked messing with his perfectly curated façade. "Feel any different?"

He sat down beside me and tapped his chest slowly before responding. "It feels like a vise gripe has been released from my heart."

My fingers ached to touch him, but I remained composed. I wished I'd gotten more details from Mercedes about what the breaking of the curse would entail. "Well, that's good, right?"

"How'd you know it would work?"

I didn't see the point in lying to him. At least not about that. "I asked the witch who cursed you."

He side-eyed me. "And you trusted her?"

I nodded. "You know, you really should apologize to her."

He made a pfft noise and looked away.

"She isn't a bad person, and you were in the wrong. It might be good for you to fix your aura. Without there being anything in it for you."

"I don't see the need for that."

I rolled my eyes, uncrossing my legs. Why did he have to make himself likable one minute and then a jerk another? There was a good guy somewhere in him, and maybe I wanted him to be good to justify my attraction to him. I tried all this time to keep things between us casual and PG-13ish, but the more time I spent with him, the harder it was.

I lifted my wrist to his face. "Then take this tattoo off of me."

He smirked and stretched. "No, I don't think so."

This son of- "Are you kidding me? After what I just did?"

"You didn't make it conditional. Plus, it's just another form of protection."

"How? You marked me."

"It keeps us connected."

I growled. It did a hell of a lot more than that. "It keeps other guys away from me."

He shrugged. "Win-win."

I balled my fist in anger. He really wanted to make me regret my decision today. "For you, maybe. We are not a couple."

"Now that I don't have the stress of the curse over me, we should be."

"You aren't a nice man."

"Never said that I was."

Rage burned my insides, and I took in a deep breath. I was not a violent woman, but I wanted to jump up and kick him in the chin. I hated that I had any type of feelings for him. Why was he being such a jerk? "Do you really want to control me?"

He snarled, upset by my words. "I would never."

Oh, he could take offense to that but not to marking me like some animal in the wild. He had to be smarter than this. Surely, he was playing me. "You do realize that marking me as yours against my will is a form of control. I'm more than a pretty face. I do have a brain."

Joo-won scooted closer to me, and I leaned back, lips tight. I would not kiss him again. He could forget it. "I know you are intelligent. It's why I like you. Look, butterfly, I like you. And I know you like me. So why are you fighting this? I know you aren't enticed by material things, but I can't help but want to at least protect you. Especially after what you've just done for me."

I wasn't buying his gentle words. "Then give me what I want. It doesn't matter to me what kind of chemistry we have. I don't like jerks who think they know what's good for me."

He looked down at my hand, but I caught a look of sadness cloud his eyes before he did. Was he really that bothered? "Why won't you listen to me when I say it's to protect you?"

I crossed my arms and closed my eyes, reaching my limit with his games and doubts of my abilities. "You think Martin would hurt me? He's been kind so far. You think it's an act?"

"I think I would not put much past him. While he hasn't suggested anything harmful, I need this safeguard for my own peace of mind. If you really don't want it, then I suggest you leave this region and never contact me again. For your own safety."

I looked out of the window. Now he was pushing me away. I couldn't keep up. "There is no way I'm leaving. I have a business, friends."

He tossed his hands out to the side as if resigned. "Then I cannot remove it. I am sorry."

Sorry my butt. I could make him. I had control now that he'd broken the curse by eating my kidney. At least that's what Mercedes had said. I promised I wouldn't use that magic, but perhaps this one time, I could make the exception. As much as I thought I cared for Joo-won, I could not have him claim me. Not now, perhaps not ever. I wasn't ready to fall into him. It was too scary. Even more so now that he was cured. I had to move at my own pace and protect my heart. "Remove the tattoo now."

Joo-won furrowed his brows together in a frown. He lifted his hand up slowly, but his face showed a tight strain. He looked at his hand in surprise, as if he disagreed with what his body was doing. His arm hovered in the air, and he looked over to me with darkened eyes. "Butterfly...what have you done?"

The way he asked the question held more than just curiosity. A panic overtook me, and I instantly began to regret my actions. Perhaps I should have shown more patience and pursued the removal another way. There was a careful stillness in his voice that felt very uneasy. As if he would pounce at any moment and I would not be prepared, even if I knew that was his intention. I couldn't recall ever being afraid of Joo-won, but something in the way he looked at me now gave me goosebumps. I didn't think he would hurt me, but I wasn't sure of his limits. Perhaps, control was one of them, ironically.

"Nothing," I replied in a singsong tone. It wasn't that I thought he would believe me, but maybe playing cute would make it go over better? Doubtful.

His arm, still outstretched, began to shake against my order. He really was strong, but was he strong enough to defeat Mercedes' spell? "The witch didn't lift her curse, did she?"

I stood up, intending to leave. If I pushed this, he would know I had power over him, and I wasn't sure I was ready to let him know. I honestly didn't want to control him, and I'd

162

just done the thing I promised I wouldn't do. I could have kicked myself, but I was just so mad at his stubbornness.

I'd give him a little time to get his shit together, but not much. And when he found out what breaking the curse had cost him, I might lose him. As conflicted as I was about him, I knew I did not want him out of my life.

CHAPTER 14

*R*unning away, well teleporting away, from Joo-won was the coward's way out, but I knew I couldn't lie to him if I kept looking at him.

A week later, my guilt or something worse had gotten the best of me. Leaving the town hospital, I looked down at the potion the mage doctor had prescribed for me. For the past week and a half, I'd been suffering from stomach cramps off and on, and it wasn't that time of the month, and I knew I was recovered from the kidney surgery. Just because we were paranormal didn't make us invincible, especially when there were tons of supernatural illnesses out there to hurt us.

The doctor didn't seem to believe it was anything serious because after some quick tests, they couldn't see anything concerning. She thought it was just stress. That made me feel only slightly better. Weird pains coming out of nowhere were still disturbing. After all, I'd been through in the past year, or even the past ten years, I never got stress pains. I decided that my guilt over what I'd done to Joo-won was stabbing me from the inside.

I was a horrible person for breaking my word, and now I

was being punished for it. I thought maybe my request didn't count but control was control. He didn't want to remove the tattoo, and I tried to force him. Granted, he was super strong, and controlling him wasn't as easy as I thought, but if I'd pushed further, I knew I could get him to do what I wanted. However, my conscience got the better of me, and here I was, still punished, even though I didn't get the tattoo removed. Joo-won had to have known I was exerting power over him. I ruined everything because I couldn't stand to be claimed. Rightfully so, but still, it was supposed to be a secret.

Now, I had been dodging his attempts to contact me. I was crashing at Faith's place and even got it warded so he couldn't come in. What was I running for? There was no way I could dodge this man forever. I would have to fess up to what the cure was really about. I really could not keep a plan together. Senna and Yuri were going to be so pissed at me. Maybe they'd understand? Who wanted to be claimed? Joo-won and I weren't even dating yet. At this rate, we probably never would.

Another stabbing cramp hit me in my side. I wanted to down the potion right there, but the doctor said I had to take it with food, so I went to the nearest fast-food shop and grabbed an order of fries. I suppose a salad would have sufficed, but that was no fun.

With my food and medicine, I sat at a small table and chomped away at a few fries before opening the vial and drinking down the potion. Instantly the cramping went away. Here's to hoping it didn't come back.

I felt a sudden presence over me and looked up.

A man I had never seen before stood in front of me with a nervous smile. He wiped at his sweaty forehead. It was not hot inside, but the guy was practically dripping.

"Can I help you?"

"Sorry, Lisa, right? I just wanted to tell you that I think you're amazing. All that you've done and all."

Oh, he was a fan. It felt weird that people thought of us as celebrities. It was good for business, but sometimes it was a little uncomfortable. I was cool with being known for my creations but not for fighting. I didn't feel like any type of superhero.

I gave the guy a slight smile. "Thanks. Did you want an autograph?"

He scratched his head, hair thin and oily. "Well, that would be nice, but I wanted to ask if maybe you would be open to joining me for coffee sometime. You're really hot." He gave a flash of fang, and his eyes went straight to my cleavage peeking out of my V neck T-shirt.

Ugh, pervert. I grabbed my bag of fries and stood up. "No, thanks," I muttered, turning away.

He grabbed my wrist in a painful hold. "You think you're too good for me?" He spat.

Like, literally, spittle was flying out of his mouth, and I leaned back to avoid getting hit.

There was a wild look to his eyes, and the pupils dilated. Was he on drugs? There was that new street drug still going around that I'd heard was the catalyst for the paranormal sickness.

I shook my arm. "No, now get off me."

He licked his lips, and his eyes bled red. Not good. Red eyes on a vampire meant they were about to feed.

Whoa, this went serious way too quickly. Crap, there was no cure for the illness, and if he somehow caught it, that put everyone in here in jeopardy who hadn't been healed by or placed under Phillip and Amina's magic. Seeing as the pair had only gotten the mass healing ability after the original soulmates died, and then they went into their magical slumber the same day, I didn't think a lot of people were in the clear.

From my peripheral vision, I saw the patrons in the restaurant move about, call for him to let me go and whisper that he must be one of the sick. I didn't expect anyone to move closer, it would risk their health. Plus, I didn't need a knight in shining armor. I was my own savior.

I pushed out my hand and sent the man sliding back on the floor. He hissed and charged at me. "You stuck up bitch!"

I shot out bolts of lightning with my magic, which shook his body as he slowed his run to a walk. He pushed slowly, as if trudging through mud. The infected were always stronger in their attack moments. They didn't usually attack during the day. The height of their violence symptom seemed to mostly come at night, but it was evening, and the sun was setting early now that we were hitting the supernatural winter.

I wrapped the lightning I conjured around the man like rope, binding his arms, hands, legs and ankles. He tumbled to the floor of the restaurant as he bucked and wiggled against my magical binds. His red eyes glared at me, mouth now dripping with rabid foam. He had fully gone blood lust, his incisors longer than before, reaching his chin, nails like black talons. He was horrifying as he screeched nonsensically at me. At this point, he had devolved to almost an animal right before my eyes.

A wind blew my hair but I didn't turn, keeping my attention on the man. Then suddenly Joo-won appeared at my side. I wasn't surprised since he could feel when I was in danger due to the tattoo. Except he wasn't alone.

Martin flanked my other side.

Fuck.

Martin gave a tsk-tsk. "I thought this place was safe."

It was, but we couldn't prevent the paranormal illness

from getting out there. Not that I needed to give an explanation to him.

Joo-won leaned forward, inspecting the creature on the ground. "I don't know how long those bindings will hold, butterfly."

Martin walked closer to the creature. "A plus for creativity, though."

Agitation grew in me. I didn't like Martin being so close to the guy and not because I was worried about Martin's safety. "Keep away from him. We need to sedate him and take him to an isolation facility."

Martin, looking very unconcerned, turned slightly to me. "You keep the sick alive? But there's no cure, and it's my understanding that anyone who can reduce the symptoms is no more."

The man was defenseless now, and he couldn't help if his mind was broken because of being ill. I'd gotten the situation under control. "We can easily put him to sleep until we get a cure."

"Seems like a waste of resources."

"Well, it's no concern of yours. The police will be here soon."

Joo-won lifted my hand gently.

I winced in pain.

"Did he do this?"

I glanced down and only now noticed the fresh bruising on my wrist. It was much better than a bite, which is what I was used to. "It's nothing."

He narrowed his eyes in anger and touched it again

I yelped from the sharp pain.

"Lisa, this is broken. Do you not feel it?"

Well, I was feeling it now. Perhaps the adrenaline from the attack had kept the obvious pain at bay. Now it was full-on. Still, I needed to ensure the vampire was contained long enough for the police to arrive.

Joo-won swiped his arm over my wrist, and an instant healing warmth spread over it. But the warmth was interrupted by what felt like a slight plucking in the back of my head. My bindings!

"Whoa!" Martin took a step back towards us and clapped his hands.

I looked up to see the man now on his feet, my magical bindings hanging off him. Damn it, he was even stronger than I thought. I needed the police to get here faster.

I pushed out my magic, and the man slammed against the wall. I had hoped the force would knock him out, but he was darn near indestructible. This was not uncommon for those sick with the paranormal illness or on the street drug, which was why most encounters with them ended in death.

The man regained his footing and raced towards the nearest patron, a teenage boy too busy filming the vampire on his camera phone to realize his life was in danger.

The boy dropped the phone and hopped back towards a table and chairs. He was too far from the door to make it. I couldn't tell what he was, but if he had teleportation magic or speed, I was sure he would have used it by now. I teleported to the boy and stood in front of him before the vampire could slice him up.

The vampire swiped at us, but before I could make another move, Martin grabbed the creature by the back of the neck in what looked like a vice grip because the vampire was squirming. Martin looked past me and wiggled his fingers at the boy. "Run along now, child."

The boy bent forward to grab his phone.

"Leave it," Martin spat. "Before I let him go."

The boy straightened up and ran out of the restaurant,

and I noticed what looked like slits around his neck. Gills. Perhaps he was a were amphibian of some sort.

The vampire twisted out of Martin's hold and tried to get away.

Joo-won was suddenly in front of him, his glowing blue sword unsheathed. He pressed the tip of the blade into the chest of the vampire but not deep.

The vampire winced and paused, looking between the two elves with red confused eyes. Martin pinned his arms back so far, I thought they would break off. Elven strength was stronger than I could have imagined, but I didn't want this going deadly.

"I can handle it from here, guys," I said, stepping forward.

Martin pouted. "Aw, no need. Let us do a good deed for the day. Take a rest."

Like hell, I would. He needed to be contained, not killed, if we could help it. Especially, because the vampire hadn't killed anyone yet. The color of red began to spread through the center of the vampire's white T-shirt. I raised my hands to subdue him more tightly this time when Joo-won pressed his sword deeper into the chest of the vampire. "Let me help you put him down with a little more force," he stated in a calm voice.

I had no idea what that meant, but I didn't want him touching the guy. Joo-won didn't capture people, he conquered them, and the blaze in his eyes let me know he had no intention of just subduing him. "Wait!" I shouted, raising my arm out in front of me.

But it was too late. Joo-won paused but didn't look at me. I sighed. He'd listened to me, and I didn't even have to use my control over him. He really wasn't a bad guy after all.

Martin punched his fist through the back of the

vampire. His hand appeared through the vampire's chest, holding his heart. "Still salvageable."

I screamed in shock, joining the exclamations of surprise and fear from the crowd around us and soon the sirens of our police force.

"Why?" I screamed. "I said wait!"

What the hell did he mean by salvageable? What was he going to do with the heart? I leaned on a chair near me, feeling queasy. This didn't have to happen like that. We couldn't go around killing everyone who got sick unless it was the last resort. That vampire hadn't hurt anyone yet. I knew Martin was despicable, but I hated the fact that I thought he was ever charming. "You shouldn't have done that."

Joo-won looked over to me with a slight pity in his eyes, his mouth in a wrinkled frown. I wasn't expecting that reaction from him. He actually seemed sad, although I wasn't sure if it was for the vampire or me. "There's no helping the sick, Lisa."

Martin kept the heart as he withdrew his hand from the chest of the vampire, who then fell forward dead. Why was he keeping the heart? "Should we have waited until he killed someone? This was preventative measures." He looked behind me at what I assumed were the police. "We've done your job today, my friends. No need to thank us."

Joo-won's sword disappeared from his hand, and he made a circular motion with his fist, a portal appearing. Martin walked through, still with that damn heart. Joo-won, seemingly unperturbed by his friend's new parting gift, tilted his head, staring at me. "Come."

I scrunched my face in annoyance. Did he think I was some kind of flunky he could order around? "No," I huffed, straightening up.

A tingling warmth spread in my nether regions. My eyes widened, and I backed away as my body buzzed with the private sensation. This was his doing.

Joo-won lifted a brow with a thin smile on his lips, looking too amused. I hated that his cockiness was still so sexy to me. And I hated that he had that kind of power over me just because of this damn tattoo.

I felt a presence at my side and looked up. Erik. He surveyed the scene with darkened eyes. "What the hell happened here?"

I looked back to Joo-won, who still remained beside his portal. "I need to talk to the police. I'll talk with you at your place after I'm done,"

The elf only smirked before walking through his portal. "Don't be long."

He said it in such a confident way, and it was irritatingly hot. I opened my mouth to respond, but the portal snapped shut. Of course, he would get the last word.

"Do I need to have his access to town revoked?" Erik asked, moving me to the side as officers and the clean-up crew walked towards the deceased body.

I shook my head slowly, not totally sure the answer was no. "They killed a vampire who I believe was either high on that violent drug or who had the illness. I think we have to do mandatory testing more often."

Erik sighed. "I would agree. Was death the only option?"

I paused before stating no. The vampire was clearly out of control, and in the past, there was zero-tolerance if the infected had killed someone. I wanted to condemn Martin and Joo-won's actions, but I wasn't sure I had enough support to feel that way. By the look of the other patrons relief, I'd be on my own in thinking the elves weren't help-ful. "If I had been better at restraining him, then maybe not."

He patted my shoulder. "It's not your fault. There has been an uptick in cases recently, even with the tests and Amina and Phillip curing all those people. We're going to have to close our doors soon and shut down traveling."

I groaned, turning away from the gruesome scene. I didn't want to be heartless but being stuck in our small town when I had a business to run that depended, in part, on outside sales wasn't something I needed right now. That and our finding a cure for Amina couldn't be done just by sitting at home. "For how long?"

Erik ran a hand through his hair, shaking his head. "No idea. But I just wanted to give you a heads up. I gotta go." He began to walk but stopped suddenly. "Hey, be careful of Joo-won. Charles mentioned you have the power to control him now. That's a powerful person to control.

There are people who might want to manipulate that or do you harm. Don't make yourself a target. We have enough problems."

He was right on that point. Playing with Joo-won was a dangerous game.

~

When I arrived at Joo-won's hotel, I was dismayed to see Martin still around. Sans heart. I could only assume he put it away for safekeeping. I wanted to ask about that, but that would probably open up a can of worms that I didn't want to deal with. More than likely, he was going to sell it. There were witches who could use a vampire heart to make a powerful, dark potion.

They were both sitting on the couch watching the large TV – some basketball game. It was odd to see ancient elves doing something so pedestrian. I walked in front of the TV, hands on my hips. "Why were you in my town today?"

Martin put his drink down on the coffee table. "You're welcome for saving you."

I scrunched my face. The nerve of him. I had the situation under control before they made everything messy. "You didn't save me." I glanced over to Joo-won. "Does he need to be here? I thought you wanted to talk to me."

Joo-won crossed his legs and balanced his drink on his knee. "Is there anything private we needed to discuss?"

Yeah, my feelings about him. My frustration that he was hanging around his upsettingly hot yet psycho murdering ex-lover.

Martin widened his large lavender eyes in mock innocence. "Are you going to talk about me? Are you mad about what I did? I thought I was doing the right thing. There was no cure for that vampire."

I rubbed my forehead. It wasn't his to decide how to handle the situation. That was up to Erik and leadership. "Why were you even there, Joo-won? Because of the tattoo?"

Joo-won lifted a shoulder. "I came because you were in trouble."

How did he know I was getting attacked? He'd given me an emerald necklace that I could use to immediately reach him when I needed to, but I hadn't put it on today. It clashed with my orange mini dress. I pointed to my wrist. "Because of the tattoo? I thought I had to touch it?"

His face remained neutral. "No. The tattoo is mostly a ward against those who may try to claim you. It would have prevented that vampire from biting you as well. However, the tattoo is not as good as a full claiming where we would be able to connect on every level. It is a pale substitute."

Martin swung his glass in front of his face. There was something cold in his eyes that made me more than uncomfortable. He didn't like that I was claimed. Perhaps he was even jealous. "Would you like him to properly claim you?"

I didn't even know what an elven or fae claiming consisted of, but I definitely didn't want one now, and I was sure as hell not going to talk to Martin about it. I was sure he'd sooner punch my heart out as well than have me any closer to Joo-won.

But if it wasn't the tattoo that alerted him, then what was it? Oh, crap. The kidney connection. Mercedes left that bit out.

Joo-won rested the back of his head on the couch and looked up at the ceiling. "Tell me, butterfly, did the witch tell you of any...side effects to the cure?"

Oh crap, oh crap. He knew. I knew it! No more running now. Time to face the music. No, I had to play it cool and not give my hand away. I scratched the back of my neck and looked at the carpeted floor. "Not that I recall. Why?"

"Might it be that the power of her curse simply transferred from her to you?"

I dropped my hands and bit my lip, thinking of my next move. Maybe now was the time to tell the truth. Where was he going with this question? Did he already suspect? I would just make things worse if I lied. I could always calm his fears that I wouldn't control him. Well, not any more than I already tried to do. I'd have to figure out another way to get him to remove the tattoo. Maybe guilt. I came from a long line of guilt-making experts through my mom.

Martin chuckled. For the first time, I noticed what looked like a colorful ring, the size of my thumb, on his middle finger. It shimmered in multi-colors in the light. It was kind of beautiful, in a gaudy way, except it, crap, it moved across his fingers. A bug. No, no no. "Look at her, my friend, she is practically trembling. Don't bother lying. We will know. The truth will set you free, as they say, no?"

I groaned inwardly, eyes still on the large bug that now

crawled up his arm and perched at his shoulder. If that thing hoped or flew, I was going to pass out.

I tore my eyes from the giant creature and looked to Joo-won, who gave me expectant eyes. Since I was already exposed, it was time to give in. "Yes, I have control over you. But you don't have to worry. I'm not going to use it. Anymore. Better me than the witch or someone else."

Joo-won 's eyes blazed with suppressed anger. He uncrossed his legs and placed his drink down on the table. "I will not be controlled."

I rolled my eyes. Did he hear anything I said? "I said I wouldn't."

He stood up. Why was he standing? What was he about to do? "Ah, but you did. When you tried to get me to remove the tattoo. Only you stopped. Why?"

I stood my ground, although every muscle in me wanted to back away. "Because it's wrong."

He approached me like a stalking cat, and the nerves in my body blared to attention. I didn't believe he would hurt me, but I did believe he wouldn't understand, and by his reaction now, I was right.

He gazed at me fully, as if assessing me, before taking my chin in his hand and lifting it slightly. He then moved towards me slowly, seemingly to kiss me. But instead of meeting my lips, he kissed me on the cheek and then moved to my ear. "You kept the truth from me, butterfly. You have broken my heart."

I felt a crack in my heart. Anger, I expected. I prepared for that. But this I wasn't ready for. Nor was I ready for the crushing weight I felt from hurting him. It was for his own good, but I didn't think he'd understand. "I was trying to protect you. I wanted you healed, and you're so stubborn."

He slowly leaned back from me, a deceiving smile on his lips, eyes still darkened. "Ah, yes, but you still didn't tell me even after I drank the potion. Was it because you wanted to have an edge over me? A little payback for the tattoo?"

My jaw dropped in shock. He really thought me more cunning than I actually was. It both hurt and pissed me off. "No. I just didn't want to upset you. I care about you."

He sighed, the smile still on his face, but his eyes seemed to soften, and for a moment, I thought he might forgive me. "I care about you too, butterfly. But I don't think I can trust you. And clearly, you don't trust me. I don't think you ever have. So where does that leave us?"

I was still numb. Was this it? Were things over between us? I'd just gotten him free of his curse. I was now ready to really face my feelings about him and whether it was all worth the risk of loving someone again, and he just pushed me to the side without so much as a private discussion. My eyes burned with hurt and fury, tears threatening to force their way down my face. Martin gave a smug smile and waved. "Goodbye, little butterfly. Flutter away now."

The mysterious bug on his arm sprouted wings and zoomed towards me. I let out a terrified scream and teleported away.

I had not thought I was in a battle for Joo-won's heart, but all this time, I had been, and I had lost.

It hurt as much as I feared it would.

CHAPTER 15

I let out an exhale and put on a wide grin for a customer as I rang up her purchase. It had been busy recently, which I only saw as part of the improvement of our economy. Between my sales and going to other towns to peddle my goods at pop-up shops and markets as well as my online store, I was keeping plenty busy.

Busy was a good thing. It kept my mind off of Joo-won, who I had not seen in over two weeks. I was moving robotically now, trying not to let my mind focus too much on him. When it did, I just hurt. Bedtime was the worst. That was when I found out that even with all my loss in the past, I still had more room to cry. I hoped there would be some relief with finally having a decision made about Joo-won, but I was wrong. Instead, I had fear and sadness. Fear that he was still angry at me and sadness that he now hated me. Perhaps hate was a strong word. He had yet to remove the tattoo, but I was beginning to wonder if that was because he wanted to mentally torture me with it. It was certainly a man repellant. Meanwhile, he was free to roam around and date and bed whoever. That part pissed me off the most. I wanted to try again to request him to remove it, but I thought more time apart would be better before I tried. Perhaps once he saw that I really wasn't going to control him, he'd relax.

The familiar chime of yet another customer entering the store recaptured my attention, and I looked over to the entrance to see Senna stroll in. "Oh, shit."

She gave me a squinty-eyed smile. "And hello to you, too."

"I'm sorry. I didn't mean for you to hear that. I'm just assuming your visit isn't to buy clothes and accessories."

A dull cramp hit my stomach, and I rubbed at it. Whatever the witch at the hospital gave me for these cramps, it wasn't working. God, I hoped it wasn't something serious.

Senna picked up a beaded choker and admired it. "Oh, this is cute. I'll take it." She walked over to the counter and placed the choker on my counter. "It's a bit pricey, but I can afford it."

I grabbed it and began to ring it up. "Yeah, remind me what you do for a living again?"

"I help run one of our tribe's very lucrative businesses. In particular, I run a high-end auction house. I also get paid as his right hand in running the town."

I nodded. She told me this before, but I always forgot. I just knew it was something very white-collar, and if she was making tons of profit from something that wasn't about our basic needs, then I knew the world was getting on track.

I gave her her purchase wrapped up in a cute tiny reusable bag. Most communities nowadays sold nothing that wasn't made to be reusable or recycled. Who knew it would take an apocalypse to get us on the right track about the environment? "Thanks for shopping with us. Now why are you really here?"

She lifted a shoulder and gave a hollow giggle. "You are so funny, Lisa."

I gave her deadpan eyes, not buying her act. She was

acting very far from herself. "Yeah, I'm a barrel of laughs. You didn't come here to go shopping."

She waved a hand over her body. She was dressed fashionably in a fitted, peach pantsuit and shiny black heel. "Well, clearly I love fashion so– Oh, okay, I did not come here to shop."

I put my hands on my cheeks. "I am shocked," I replied in a robotic tone.

She placed her hands on her hips, but just then, a customer walked up behind her. I shooed her to the side and rang up the next purchase. When the customer left, Senna leaned against the counter. "It's really nice that you're busy. That's so wonderful."

I twisted my lips. Why was she drawing this out? It must be really bad. "Cut the crap."

She let out a breath. "I hate to bother you about Joo-won. You don't owe him anything anymore, and he told us to leave you alone. He seemed pissed we went to see Mercedes, even though it seemed to heal him. Did you tell him about the whole control thing?"

I so didn't want to talk about this. My heart panged at just the mention of Joo-won's name. Heck, I felt a cloud of gloom weight on me just seeing Senna's face. "A little."

Senna turned her head and side-eyed me with a questioning glance. "What does that mean?"

I recapped how I tried to get him to remove the tattoo.

She rubbed her forehead. "He read us for filth, as you say, for keeping things secret. I think Yuri cried. A tear dropped from his eye, anyway. He's barely speaking to us."

A stupid little twinge hit my heart. Did he hate me? That didn't sit right with me. I'd rather me be angry with him than the other way around. "So, what made you disobey his order to keep away from me?"

"He's not the same. I thought it was because of the curse,

but if you cured him, then he should be better. He's been making business deals with unsavory characters. And Martin is still lurking around."

I ran a hand through my hair, suddenly feeling exhausted from the emotional weight I kept dodging. "Maybe this is who he really is, and you just don't want to face it."

Senna grimaced. "He was better before the curse."

"He stole from someone. Be honest with yourself."

"I am. We were going in the right direction. Slowly, yes, but still, we were moving right. I thought he would change his ways after breaking our truce with Misandre, but that's not the case. He might need a little nudge." She gave me an expectant look.

Was she implying what I think she was implying? After my last meeting with him, there was no way I was stepping in. I was fragile enough as it was. I couldn't take looking at those beautiful eyes of his looking at me in disappointment. I'd barely recovered from that. I shook my head quickly. "No, nope, no way, not going to happen. He is all your problem."

"Please rethink that." She swung the small shopping bag in the air. "After I patronized your store?"

"I can refund you."

"I think he might get persuaded to combine our kingdom with Martins. While growing in size is always good, it won't be if our town becomes full of degenerates and criminals. We've worked hard to become a respectable tribe. Plus, the bugs and rodents."

We both shivered at the same time. I was reminded of Martin's pet bug monster the last time I saw Joo-won. It still made me shake all over. I was just thankful Martin hadn't brought any along when he helped take down the infected vampire. That would not have been good for the restaurant.

Another pinching in my stomach, and I massaged at it. I needed to find another doctor.

Senna zoned in on my stomach. "What's wrong?"

"Nothing, just some recurring cramping."

She sucked her teeth and shook her head. "It's worse than I thought."

I narrowed my eyes at her. What did she mean by that? Did she know what was going on with me? "What's worse than you thought? Did you do this to me?"

She waved a dismissive hand. "Of course not. Mercedes said this would happen. Whenever Joo-won does something evil-like, you'd feel it."

I looked up at the ceiling. When had Mercedes said that? Granted, I wasn't fully awake when she came by, so it was probable that I would have missed something. Also, I was never good at paying attention to people for long. School was torture for me. "So, are you telling me I've been suffering with these stomach pains all this time because that jerk can't stay away from being bad?"

Senna gave a sympathetic pout. "That would seem to be it. You should go tell him that he is causing you pain."

I didn't know anymore. After that threat, I couldn't assume I was in Joo-won's good graces anymore. "What if he doesn't care? If I try anything with him, he'll kill me. He said so himself."

Another customer walked up, looking at us with wide eyes.

I took the items from her to ring up. "I'm just helping her rehearse some lines from an upcoming play she's in. Believable, right?"

The customer gave me doubtful eyes as she glanced over at Senna, who had moved to the side.

Senna waited until the customer left before responding.

"The man is in love with you. I can't see how that's possible. It was just an empty threat."

"I'm not interested in betting my life to take that chance."

"So, you want to deal with stomach pain for the rest of your days? If he does something really bad, it could put you down. You'd feel like you had appendicitis."

I jutted my chin out. "Ha, I got you there. I had my appendix taken out some years ago."

Senna closed her eyes and shook her head. "It wouldn't actually be appendicitis. The point is, you would feel really bad. Suffering indefinitely."

"How do you know that? Did Mercedes mention it, and I forgot that too?"

"No. It can happen with connection magic. I had an elven friend who was the consort of an unscrupulous vampire. She talked about it all the time. Finally, he was murdered." She gave a wave of a hand like she'd said they just got a divorce. "Luckily, she survived the breaking of the bond. Didn't it happen with your soulmates?"

I squinted my eyes in thought. I couldn't recall Amina ever feeling pain from Phillip's bad deeds, although they could psychically hurt each other.

Maybe it was time to see the elven king again and get him to calm down. There had to be some kind of compromise. And I had to admit, I wanted to see him again, even if he did hate me.

❧

*W*hen I arrived to Joo-won's that evening, the hotel was lit up with festive lights and music. I looked around the lobby at the colorful floating lights and numerous guests standing about noshing on finger foods and drinks.

I buzzed with a bit of excitement, always loving a good party. "What's all this?" I asked Senna.

She nodded. "Ah, right. Open house night. It's leadership's way of connecting with the people. Makes Joo-won more accessible even though he barely shows his face at these things."

I spotted Yuri through the crowd, and he walked over to us, holding two drinks in his hand. He smiled and gave us each one. "Lisa, it's good seeing you again. It's been too long."

I accepted the drink. "It's been less than a month."

"A month is too long." He looked around the room with large eyes before leaning forward. "When you aren't around, our leader surrounds himself with unsavory characters doing not so pleasant things."

"Like?"

"He's planning a takeover of another elven kingdom but not a friendly one."

Now that was new. Joo-won never seemed the type to overtake a community. He'd grown his tribe through the freedom and choice of his citizens. I took a sip of my drink as liquid courage for my confrontation. The concurring thing was new, and I didn't like it.

Yuri nodded as if hearing my thoughts. "We also were trying to strengthen diplomatic ties and trade with Hagerstown. That would have been big because they are Federation. However, our talks fell through due to his unnecessary stubbornness and some rumors about his association with Martin."

"I'm not into politics, but he's not thinking straight and–" I cried out, doubling over in pain and spilling my drink. Yuri caught my glass before it fell and Senna steadied me. My stomach felt like someone was stabbing it over and over again.

"Cramps?" Senna asked, rubbing my back.

I nodded, dropping low into a squat. Senna lowered down with me.

"It's him," Yuri said with darkened eyes.

This pain was worse than usual. Why hadn't Joo-won come to see what was wrong with me if we were so connected? "Shouldn't he know if I'm in trouble?"

Senna shrugged. "I'm guessing not when it's pain he caused."

A cool breeze brushed my hair, and I knew it was him. Senna rose and moved to the side, and soon, I felt strong arms lift me up. Joo-won looked down at me with concerned eyes, brows furrowed together. The lobby went quiet except for the music. He paid them no mind as he carried me out of the room to his suite. I closed my eyes, clenching my teeth from the pain that I was hoping would soon go away.

When we finally got to his room, he gently laid me down on his bed before sitting beside me. "What hurts?"

"Stomach."

He rested his hand on my abdomen. I knew I was in a lot of pain because I would have sucked in my stomach, but I couldn't even bother now. Moments later, the pain subsided, and I opened my eyes. Joo-won leaned forward and lightly kissed my shirt-covered stomach. "How did I cause this?"

Did he really not know? How could he be so gentle in one light and threaten to kill me in another? I never could reconcile that, and I didn't want to have to. "I could never figure you out. I wanted you to be a good person."

He straightened up. "Sorry to disappoint you."

"Yuri and Senna think so much of you. Why did you change? I gave you my organ because I couldn't imagine that you would go wrong like this. I would have thought twice if I had known better." I sat up and noticed for the first time that there was a splash of blood on his neck. "What have you been up to?"

Joo-won tilted his head, looking away from me so I couldn't try to figure out what he was thinking. "Nothing of your concern."

Bull crap. "Except whatever you were doing nearly caused me to pass out."

He stood up. "I'm simply engaging in negotiations at the moment. Stay here and rest."

Yeah, right. He was little more than a gangster at this point. He was probably beating up some poor soul until they agreed to his demands. I'd had enough. "Rest while you go back and do what you were doing? And hurt me again?"

"I'm done with that part."

I swung my feet to the side of the bed. "Yeah, for today, maybe. Whatever you are doing, stop it."

He gave me a chiding look. "Butterfly, you won't tell me what to do."

I paused. Something about the way he phrased that didn't sit right with me. "What do you mean, I won't?" Of course, I knew. He'd made it very clear the last time we spoke. I just wanted him to say it again because this time, I wasn't going to cower. If I was going to be in pain, then I might as well face his threats anyway.

He tilted forward and brushed a lock of hair from my face. He then kissed my forehead before straightening up and turning. He thought this was a game. I was done with him taking me for granted. Here I was, not using the power I got to prevent him from doing the very thing Mercedes wanted to stop him from doing.

Well, it was now or never. "Stop!" I commanded, lifting a

hand towards him. I wasn't sure if the hand was needed, but I was all about the dramatics.

Joo-won stopped in his tracks. He turned to look at me, his face visibly strained.

"Stop with those alleged negotiations you're in. What you are doing is evil."

His eyes blazed with anger, and for a minute, panic gripped me because I didn't know what he was thinking. "You have no idea what I am doing," he said through gritted teeth.

I knew enough from the fact that I almost passed out in pain. "Explain it to me."

He stood glaring at me for a moment before finally speaking. "We have a problematic town nearby that has encroached on some of our lands. Their leader was not very agreeable. So, we are going to absorb them."

Absorb. I knew what that meant, and it didn't sound like a fitting response. "So, you got a couple of trespassers, and you decide the fix is to take over the whole community."

The fire in his eyes died, and he gave me lifeless eyes. He was becoming unreadable again, and that was a dangerous thing. "Let it be a lesson to others."

I was sure he wasn't telling me the whole truth. If he was just getting deserved revenge, then I wouldn't have doubled over in pain. The truth was that there were probably some rogue people from this town, and he was punishing them all because of it. Was this really who he was? "Lesson's over. You are to let whoever you are torturing free or at least put the appropriate offenders in lockup until they serve their sentence. And stop letting Martin advise you on these things. Because I know he's behind this. You weren't this guy before."

He gave me a closed-mouth grin, and suddenly, my core awakened. My thighs tensed, and I grabbed the bedsheets with white knuckles. My body hummed with desire, and I threw my head back against my will. He was turning me on with this stupid tattoo, and I was putty in his hands. My legs spread, and I cursed myself as I felt a dampness flood my lower half.

"Are you alright, butterfly?" Joo-won asked in a playful tone, eyes sparkling.

He knew good and well I was not okay. "Stop what you're doing."

He lifted a brow. "What am I doing?"

I screamed in frustration, and to my horror, it turned into a moan. I felt warmth on my cheeks from embarrassment. "You know what you are doing to me. Stop it now," I said through clenched teeth.

He gazed at me with lowered lids, appearing to really enjoy the show. My nipples pressed against my blouse, bordering on a painful pleasure. Yup, I would ruin him. Why the hell hadn't my power over him stopped this? Did his claiming nullify my hold when it came to our bond?

My body was now a mass of nerves, and I would explode at any moment. I could barely think. What was I doing? Ah, yes, trying to stop him from doing evil. And he was getting me back by attempting to give me an orgasm. While in theory, that wasn't such a bad punishment, this was hardly a friendly situation, and I did not agree to him pleasing me.

He sat beside me, and his hand trailed up my arm farthest from him, my hands still clutching the sheets. "Let's call a truce."

I shook my head and pulled away from him. Somehow, I managed to get to my feet, although my legs felt like jelly. I needed to be home and alone. Away from him. "I'm not giving in."

I began to teleport away, but Joo-won grabbed my hand

and teleported along with me. When we reappeared in my apartment, I shook him loose. "Leave!"

He ignored me and went to sit on the couch, gazing at me with those unreadable eyes. I was far from in control right now, and I leaned against a dining room chair, crossing my legs. This was humiliating.

I heard Joo-won give a light snort. "Just give in."

Give in? I'd had enough of this. Two could play this game. I glared over at him, wanting to smack the cockiness off his face. "Unbutton your pants and touch yourself." I gave him a sinister grin.

The smile disappeared from his face as his right hand jerked up and went to the top of his pants. He barred his teeth against the action. "Stop this."

"You first."

Seconds later, just as he began to unbutton his pants, the tingling in my core subsided. I let out a breath of relief and mild disappointment. Hey, the feeling was quite pleasurable, it was just the circumstances. If things were better between us, I wouldn't have minded at all. I let go of my control of him, and he buttoned his pants, glaring at me the whole time.

I sat down in my chair, feeling more than frustrated. Why did it have to be this way? I had saved him. "I thought... I thought you cared about me."

His face relaxed, and he reached out for me with a raised hand. "Come, please."

I shook my head and stayed where I was.

He dropped his hand and got up, walking over to me. I tensed, wanting to keep my distance from him, as if that would really matter. He crouched in front of me. "Do you hate me now?"

I scrunched my face in frustration. Why would he ask me that? Is that what he wanted? I suppose it would be better for him if I wasn't around to foil his plans, and he was doing a grand job of making that happen. "Do you want me to hate you?"

"I think it would be good if you did."

I let out a short breath, the emotional pain from the last two weeks sharpening in my heart. He was pushing me away on purpose. To protect me? I had to understand. "I don't get you. I thought you wanted us to be together."

He tapped my knee with an index finger in a slow rhythmic pace before he answered. It was a move that wasn't normal for him. Was he nervous or worried? About what? "We need to sever our link. Did you know that with your control, my powers are weaker?"

Ah, that's what this was about. I couldn't recall Mercedes mentioning that transferring the curse to me would make him weaker, but I hadn't recalled the whole stomach pain thing either, so my attention was as problematic as the teachers in school used to say. Still, I just thought that since she no longer had the curse over him, then him getting weaker wouldn't continue. I certainly didn't want that for him. "I honestly don't recall her telling me that. I would have given you a heads up."

He studied me, still tapping his finger. "Would you have? Perhaps you thought keeping it a secret would be better so that I would accept your cure. You were maybe afraid I wouldn't find another solution before my time ran out? Or were afraid another option wouldn't be as agreeable to you?"

I poked my lips out in confusion. I really wasn't that devious or calculating. Okay, I had been sort of devious, indirectly, when I sent Amina and Phillip to Ireland to bond. Still, after that betrayal, I didn't plan on repeating such a mistake. It had technically cost me my relationship with Charles, and things had never been the same. Perhaps our breakup would have happened down the line anyway, but I would never know. "While your suspicion of me is fair, I wouldn't do that. I can't imagine Senna or Yuri would let me keep that white lie."

As soon as I said it, I wished I hadn't. They had most certainly kept secret that I could control Joo-won.

Sensing where my mind was going, Joo-won gave a tiny smile. "I took the deal before conferring with them, so no need to fear my wrath upon them. However, they didn't know about my weakening power." He sighed, stopping his tapping. "No matter, I believe you. However, the fact still remains that I cannot be weakened."

What could I do about it? As far as I knew, this was it. Fear stabbed me in the stomach. Was he going to try to kill me to get free? Was that why he was being an ass? So, we'd hate each other and make it easier for his attack. I jumped up and backed away from him. "My death won't help you. The curse will just revert back to Mercedes, and she'd be pissed you killed me. No telling what she'd make you do."

He slowly rose, lids lowered. "How horrible do you think I am?"

"I don't know anymore."

He ran a hand through his hair and looked away, another move that was unlike him. Seriously, what was going on with him? "I need you to hate me."

If he kept up this behavior, it would happen sooner than he thought. What was going on? "What are you keeping from me?"

"I can't protect you like I need to, butterfly."

What the hell was he talking about? What or who did I need protection from? Outside of Lorenzo, all my enemies were dead, and I could better handle him on my own now. At least, I thought. "Why do I need protection?"

He looked around the room as if seeing it for the first

time. "He was greedy, this was always true but not for power. For riches. Anything else never interested him. Seems his mind had changed since being locked up all those years. I underestimated him. I should have known when he showed up at the ball."

I shook my head. "Wait, are you talking about Martin? I thought you two were ok now."

He looked at me, eyes steely. "I am appeasing him until I can gain the upper hand."

A heaviness lifted from, and I straightened up, feeling a wave of relief. He didn't hate me. He was protecting me. Not that I needed it, but the fact that he cared enough to try meant so much to me. It also worried me that he was putting himself through this. Being around Martin was too much of a risk. "Are you saying he's stronger?"

He nodded. "Unfortunately, I am."

I massaged my head with both hands as my mind processed what he was telling me. Suddenly his behavior made more sense. He was afraid for me because of Martin. He was being a dick so that I would stay clear, thus making Martin happy. Although he hadn't shown it, Martin was threatened by me.

Joo-won lowered his head, looking resigned to his fate. "Tattooing you was a mistake in the darker hours of my curse. In fact, it might be that very action that caused you to be in greater harm. Martin was already jealous of you when you escorted me to the ball. My claim on you only made him that much angrier. I'd never done such a thing with anyone else. His interest peaked more when he found out you were part of The Six."

"So, this is all about me?"

He placed his hands on my arms. The look in his eyes was one full of worry, and it scared me. "You are a part of it. I know now that things have been placed in motion by him that were beyond my thought. He's grown smarter. It was he who indirectly put into my head the jewel to steal from the witch. He had to have known what would happen. And he's up to something far more sinister than I know. He is rapidly growing power over other elven and fae communities."

My eyes widened in realization. "He was the threat discussed at the ball? The one who is absorbing the power of other elves? How?"

He dropped his hands to his sides. "I suspect. And I can't figure that part out, but I need to. I can't underestimate him any further. Or put you in danger. Until I understand him and how he's gotten this strength, I cannot allow you to be at risk."

Fear mixed with relief swelled in me. Relief that Joo-won really wasn't the asshole I thought he was and fear because he seemed actually scared of Martin. The original soul-mates did bring him concern. It was why he sided with them, to protect his people. However, he never appeared concerned. But the man I was looking at now actually looked troubled. Was Martin stronger than the original soulmates? I couldn't believe that. "Why are you more worried now than about the original soulmates?"

He raised a hand and placed it on my cheek, his eyes softer now. Just that small shift in him slightly settled me. It was crazy how much I'd come to enjoy his comforting ways. It made sense why the pain he caused me hurt even more. "Isn't it obvious, my butterfly? I'm worried because of you. It's because I love you, and I can't have anything happen to you. Let me protect you the best way I can now."

Love. He'd used that word sparingly with me. Several months ago was the first time he had professed to love me, but he was heavily drugged at the time so he could heal after fighting Misandre's pet ghoul, Lorenzo. He had claimed at the time it wasn't because of the drugs, and since that time, he'd uttered those words again. Each time, I found it hard to accept. He was no longer the elf only trying to seduce me, yet there was something that prevented me from fully accepting him as more than a casual distraction. I was scared. Scared to face all that he offered me and scared to lose what he gave, like I had with others before.

I grabbed his hand on my cheek. I needed to change the mood. I needed to make him understand that I wasn't fragile and that the woman he thought he loved wasn't the woman he should bend for. "Or maybe you let me help you. I know I seem all delicate, but I'd think by now that I've proven I'm not. And I certainly don't want to live my life navigating out of fear of what other people might do." I would ignore the irony of how I had no problem letting fear dictate my love life. That was different. And don't ask. It just was. "I won't be stupid, but I can't be scared. You have resources, Joo-won. Allies. I can even talk to Queen Arwa. You still have that alliance. We'll find a way to boost your strength. Maybe we can even make it so Martin doesn't want to bother with you anymore. Part your hair down the middle and slick it down, wear suspenders and a bow tie."

He threw his head back with a laugh before quickly leaning forward and kissing me deeply on the lips. And just like that, my legs turned to jello again. To my dismay, he pulled away all too quickly. "I'm sorry. For everything. I keep needing reminders that you are different. It's why I love you. Will you forgive me?"

He loved me, and I felt it to be true, but it scared me deeply to admit the same. He was so complicated, and the ups and downs we had were too risky. I sighed and looked down at my wrist where the invisible tattoo lay. I wanted to forgive him now that I understood it all. And since he'd apologized, there was no need to hang on to the anger. Still, something nagged at me. I wouldn't have felt pain if this was all an act. "If you weren't really doing evil, why did I still hurt?"

"I never said I hadn't. I had to maintain the act to be believable to Martin. To make him think that my behavior would not appeal to you."

"So, I can assume Senna and Yuri weren't in on it?"

He shook his head. "All the better for my plan."

"Do you think Martin is buying it?"

"I honestly can't say. I don't know him as well as I used to."

I thought about that. He was playing a dangerous game. But still, Martin couldn't have changed totally. It was still very clear he had a soft spot for Joo-won. Pushing me away made sense, but Joo-won would have to do more than that. I wasn't a big fan of what kind of acts he'd have to do to get Martin off his guard. I wanted to forgive Joo-won, but I didn't want to give in to his plan. I hated it. "What about this?" I waved my wrist in front of him.

His brows furrowed in concern. He really didn't want to get rid of this thing. He grabbed my wrist and gave a small kiss over where the tattoo lay, sending a shiver through me. "I can remove it. But I'd rather not because of Martin. Does it bother you that much?" He looked back at me, and there was a vulnerability in his eyes I'd never seen.

I wanted to fall into those eyes, wrap my arms around him. I wanted to give in, but I couldn't. It wasn't the tattoo itself. Heck, I couldn't even see it. More so the act behind it. "Being claimed is a big deal. I'd like to go into such an act as a willing participant. That didn't happen here. It makes me feel like I'm a possession."

He tilted his head to the side and studied my hand as he analyzed my words. He grazed an index finger over my wrist, and I fought like hell not to react, but the electricity shocked my core. There was no cocky smile on his face at what he

195

was doing, he just seemed fixated by me, as if he needed to feel me. "I understand. That was not respectful of me. You are my equal. I should not have made you feel any other way."

I dropped my shoulders, satisfied. "K, you get the point. I'll keep it."

He gave a raised brow with a look of shock before quickly turning changing to his old smug smile. "You like being claimed by me," he said more than asked. "Maybe you even love me?"

I rolled my eyes. Did I care for him? Certainly, but that wouldn't change my thinking about love. Just the thought of being any kind of queen to him made me jittery. "It's an extra connection to have, so it can't hurt. Don't get a big head, this is simply practical." I shoved him lightly on the chest. "Now go back to your open house. Free the poor soul you were torturing. For now, I'll keep my distance or be more discrete. Tell Yuri and Senna about it so they won't keep coming here asking me to save you."

He lost his smile, eyes wistful. More show of emotion that sent my heart beating rapidly. "They care that much?"

"You know they do. We all do."

He placed his hand over his heart, eyes squinted at me with appreciation, before bowing and leaving.

I sighed, flopping down on my couch. I cared about him. More than I wanted to admit. I would have helped with the curse even if I didn't owe him a favor, and I wasn't going to let him fail now.

CHAPTER 16

A few weeks passed since my visit with Joo-won, and I couldn't say it was easy. Life was going normally, which was nice, but I missed him. This wasn't a new feeling. I missed him from time to time, but before, I was still sorting out my feelings for Charles, starting up my business and finding a cure for Joo-won's curse. Plus, I could also see him whenever I wanted. With us having to stay apart, I didn't have that luxury. Further, with things settling down with my business and his curse lifted, I had more time to think about him. And I thought about him a lot.

He wasn't a jerk. Nor was he the ever-cool elven king he'd pretended to be this past year. Seeing him all those weeks ago show worry and nervousness, such vulnerability, actually made me even more conflicted. I may not have agreed with his methods to protect me, but I did believe he wanted me safe. It made me like him more. I had fallen for him. I learned nothing.

My phone chimed, and I looked on the kitchen counter where it lay as I filled my glass with water, already overflowing while I was lost in thought. It was the front desk of my apartment building telling me I got mail.

I didn't get much mail anymore. My email was still greatly used, but hard mail wasn't as popular. Magic teleportation helped a lot with the delivery of packages and such. However, not all towns or people used that service. Not only was it pricier, but not every town had magic to even access technology. Therefore, old-school snail mail was still in use. Just not in our town.

So, when the guy at the front desk of my apartment called to say that I received mail service, I was puzzled. I hadn't ordered anything, however, the front desk was very clear that a mail carrier, dressed in a federation postal uniform, had dropped it off at the entrance to town.

There was no from address on it, which got me highly suspicious. I decided to open it up in the lobby and placed a ward around it before doing so. The package was a small square box in shiny black wrapping with gold designs. My name and address were on it, right down to my apartment number. I never gave out my apartment number. When my packages teleported, they showed up in a mailing center at the town entrance and then went through testing to ensure nothing foul was in it. We were justifiably paranoid here. From there, our local letter carriers delivered the packages.

Who knew my exact address? Just because the federation mail service had dropped it off didn't mean the package originated in a federation town. Someone could have simply gone to the postal office and mailed it from there.

I had to know what was inside, but I was still hesitant, even though it had already been magically accessed.

I sat back on the lobby couch, rubbing my chin as I continued to stare at the package on the coffee table. Well, I couldn't keep staring at it all day.

I carefully unwrapped the package and then quickly leaned back as something sprung up. A golden butterfly flew out. It looked so real except for the coloring. How the hell had it survived in the box?

It fluttered towards me, and I let out a yelp, jumping up and running towards the door. Did I mention how much I hate bugs? Yes, golden butterflies were included in that.

The sliding glass doors opened, and the insect flew away out of eyesight. I turned back to the box and hesitantly looked inside, afraid of another bug attack. However, inside was just a golden piece of paper, folded in half. I picked it up, it felt heavy, and the paper was thick. Wait, was this paper? Was it really gold?

I opened the paper and inside. It was an invitation to attend and be a vendor at a festival set for the following Saturday. From Martin.

～

*C*harles studied the invitation, eyes narrowed. "Did this dude really write, 'attendance is mandatory?' What does he think this is? Work? He your boss?"

I crossed my arms, gnawing on the inside of my cheek as I watched him study the invitation in my living room.

Charles passed the invitation to Erik, who looked it over. "This is an obvious trap. What does Joo-won say?"

I shrugged. I didn't need Joo-won to tell me it was a trap. I emailed him as soon as I got the invite, but he hadn't replied. "I'm waiting for him to get back to me. I would never go to this thing without talking to him. He knows Martin better than I do. I did look it up online, and it seems legit."

Erik growled. "After all you've told us about him, there's no way you can go."

Charles scratched his chin, leaning against a wall. "Except, what if her not going starts a battle? The rest of that invitation states that her non-attendance will mean that they are enemies. He could start an attack. According to Senna, Martin has a large tribe."

Would Martin really fight me because I didn't go to his festival? He barely tolerated me. I'd think he wouldn't want me around at all.

Erik put the invitation down on my dining room table. "Let them try."

I shook my head. He could be so confident, but he was a smart guy. He knew better than to just ignore this. "We can't have them bring any trouble to this town. This is my issue."

He glared at me. "It's our issue. You're our friend and a member of The Six. If you get threatened, we all get threatened."

"As comforting as that is, we still have to deal with this, and we aren't in full power right now. Sure, we can call Faith and Felix back from whatever mission they're on, and we have tons of allies, but after fighting the original soulmates, we can't keep pulling people to fight."

Charles raised a finger as if waiting to be called. "I know this isn't a popular suggestion, but maybe we should wake Amina and Phillip. Have them help us with this. We can put them back to sleep after we get rid of this guy."

Erik side-eyed Charles, his face a mask of pure displeasure. "We are not waking them up before we have a cure, only for them to fight then put back to sleep. That is selfish and cruel. They are more than soldiers. She is more."

His voice trailed off, and I could hear the ache he was feeling even in the silence. He could function, he could father their adopted child, he could work but he was still in pain. I could feel the hurt any time anyone even mentioned Amina's name.

I was actually surprised Charles would even suggest such a thing. I looked to him, and Charles hung his head, hands stuffed in his pocket. "You sound just as worried as Joo-won," I stated.

He looked at me with concerned eyes. His suggestion had not come easy. "I am, Lisa. I don't want to bring people into another fight, but what other options do we have? If we ignore this invitation, we have to be prepared for the consequences. If Joo-won is worried about him, then we can't take this guy lightly."

It was the consequences part I was worried about. "I'm not getting anyone else wrapped up in this, including the soulmates. I think I need to go to Queen Arwa. Maybe she'll have some insight since she's been around. She has to be more powerful than Martin. Not that I'd want to ask her for another favor." I really hated being so indebted. I had to take care of this Martin issue myself. "I think I'm going to have to go to this festival."

Charles pushed away from the wall. "Then I go to. All of us."

I shook my head quickly. "I won't call back the others just to stand at my tent and help me sell dresses. I'll talk to Queen Arwa and get back to you. I kind of brought this mess here, let me figure out how to handle it."

I was proud of myself for being all leader-like.

It gave me heartburn.

⁓

*T*he realm of the seelie fae was one made of rainbows and butterflies. Literally, whatever candy-coated dreams you could imagine, that is what the seelie realm looked like. A bright pink sky, trees so tall they looked like they touched the clouds, sparkling birds and insects humming some cartoonish melody in the air. The streets were pristine marble, and the buildings and houses were domed and equally perfect and clean.

When I stepped through the portal to arrive in Arwa's court, I was greeted by portal guards with welcoming smiles and the backdrop of a large, bold rainbow painting the sky. It was even more perfect a day than the last times I'd visited. I kept waiting to see munchkins sing me a song. However, I got the impression that if I asked the smaller fae for a concert, they'd stomp me down.

Instead, I gave a greeting to the guards and began to head to the castle.

"One moment!" said a female fae. She was short with large green eyes, frizzy, orange hair and big ears. I dared not assume that because she was small, she wasn't formidable. Fae held power in their magic, and some allowed for them to transform. You would think you were going to battle a kitten and end up fighting a lion.

I raised my shoulders, startled by her call. "Yes?"

"The elven king, Joo-won, is here. We were told to tell you so that you wouldn't be surprised."

What was he doing here? Was he seeking assistance from Arwa? Would it be risky to be here at the same time?

I gave a smile of thanks and headed through town to the castle. When I finally arrived to the large ivory building behind golden gates, I was easily let in and escorted to Queen Arwa's meeting room where the queen, Joo-won and Bella, my fae mentor, were already seated.

The group was in the maroon-colored room sitting in one of the many plush, velvet seats. A tray of teas and an array of cookies were spread on the golden coffee table in front of them.

I curtsied when I entered the room. Something I always did because I thought you did such in front of a queen. Arwa always said it wasn't necessary, but it was habit now.

Joo-won chuckled.

My heart raced as soon as our eyes made contact.

He smiled, his face seeming to light up, and I returned it with ease, finding myself walking towards him before looking to the others in the room.

I quickly shook my head and reversed course, instead, sitting down on a chaise lounge between the queen and Joo-won's seats.

I looked to Arwa, and she gave me a knowing smile. She was all too familiar of my situation with Joo-won. She sipped her tea, as poised and graceful as always in a turquoise beaded gown with matching hijab. A crystal crown sat perched on top of her head. "What a lovely day for visitors," she exclaimed, placing her teacup on the saucer on her lap.

I nodded. "It's pretty surreal here. I'm sorry to come by on short notice." I glanced over to Joo-won, who was still looking at me with emotion-heavy eyes. I wanted to keep starring at him, but things would get awkward for Arwa and Bella then. "I'm thinking we're here for the same reasons."

"He wants to protect you. He's grown quite sweet."

I couldn't believe he came all this way after I already told him I was capable on my own. Clearly, he wasn't one who listened. And yet, I wasn't surprised.

Arwa placed her teacup on the coffee table, never losing her elegant posture as she moved. "Before you arrived, Joo-won informed us of the dinner that Martin is organizing. You have a right to be concerned. We have been keeping a watchful eye on him since he escaped his prison. And what we have discovered has been quite troubling." She looked over to Joo-won with pressed lips. "I hadn't made you aware before due to your relationship with him. I wasn't sure if you still maintained any sort of loyalty to him."

Joo-won leaned back in his seat, crossing his legs. He

had his perfected poker face back on, and I had no idea what could have been running through his head at Arwa admitting that she had known of Martin being up to no good all this time. I suspect he believed she had every right to be cautious. I understood it. She had a very shaky truce with an unseelie fae and a neutral elf. Neither really trustworthy. "I was the one who locked him up, but I suppose I understand. You were just about to tell me of your findings."

Bella adjusted in her seat, her bright honey eyes filled with excitement. I had a feeling she really enjoyed being in the mix of things. "He moved fast when he was freed. He committed some crimes. Really capitalized on magic returning. But it wasn't until he started growing in his own magical strength that things started to really take off."

I shook my head, curious. "How did he grow in magic? A bond pairing? A spell?"

"We aren't certain. We can't find anyone he bonded to. It was most likely a spell. A potion or amulet."

Joo-won uncrossed his legs, face still neutral but eyes cold. "I've never seen him with any particular jewelry, but he could have it under an invisibility spell. What strength has he grown, exactly?"

It was a simple question with a large answer. Power was a term we used as a catch-all, but it held so many levels. Physical strength, a large or powerful following, mental magic. Mental magic had massive possibilities. And even within types of powers, there were levels.

Joo-won was a powerful elf. He'd come from an ancient line of such elves. However, he was already weakened by the curse and my control. Martin, from what I'd been told, had no exceptional power before now. At least not enough to be stronger than Joo-won. Now he had some type of enhancement just as Joo-won was weaker. They were either even in strength or Joo-won was at a serious disadvantage.

Arwa threw her hands out to the side. "Enough to make him formidable.

I thought about our attack in New York. Since first learning of Martin's power, I'd always suspected he was connected to it, but it didn't make sense that he could change bugs and rodents, only control them. "Since he's grown in strength, could that mean he could have power over weres that are of the rodent variety? Like rats? And could he now make them stronger?"

Bella nodded, hands clasped tightly in front of her. She still seemed way too excited. "We suspect. We've also heard rumors, but have not witnessed, tales of modified pests. Strange creatures. He's using them to attack towns. Steal riches. He's demolished villages that were very dear to us. He and his followers and creatures have left towns without resources like locusts. He is spreading his nightmare and attacks at random. He has no loyalty or just cause."

I scrunched my face up, not liking where this was going. In the very back of my mind, I had hoped Martin had turned a new leaf and was simply a disagreeable person. But no, he was a monster, and he thought we were too stupid to see. I had to know what I was up against. "Define modified and strange."

"Bugs that are larger than usual or suddenly dangerous where they weren't before. Creatures that have never been seen in nature before. Almost like hybrids. But that could simply be from the return of magic and that he's powerful enough to even control supernatural creatures."

"What was the alternative?"

"That he created these things."

It was one thing to control bugs, another thing to make scary bugs. He'd have his own endless supply. What if he decided to attack us with bugs? I would die. I would actually lose my heartbeat and bid farewell to the world. I turned to Joo-won. "Do you know anything about that?"

He really did look like he was going to burst. His eyes were almost red with rage, normally full lips a thin line. Martin was one-upping him, and I was sure he didn't like it. "I do not." He said in a tight voice. "He only ever had control of natural bugs and rodents. He could modify them slightly, but he never could make them bigger or hybrid. He definitely could not conjure them."

"You suspected nothing?" Ok, I knew I was poking the bear at this point, but I could hardly believe Joo-won, in all his wisdom and cunning, had simply let down his guard around this guy.

His face didn't give away any new annoyance. "I, of course, suspected he had a new power source. This was why I wanted to keep you away. I've been holding him close to try to determine more."

"So, you were never entertaining the idea that he could break your curse?"

"I didn't doubt that he could, but I did not want his help there."

That did make me feel a little better that even though my cure for him hadn't been totally risk-free, he still wouldn't have gone for whatever Martin would offer.

Arwa leaned over to pick up her tea, and a tiny sprite, the color of the blue sky, fluttered towards the cup. They, I couldn't discern the gender of the faerie from my distance because it was so small, wrapped their arms around the cup, which was practically the same size as the creature, and seconds later fluttered away. I followed the tiny faerie until I saw them, along with a small collection of other faeries, huddled together, silently by the window. How had I missed those fae before?

Arwa picked up the saucer with the cup. "Thank you for warming the tea."

That was a useful power to have. Who needed a microwave?

Ok, back to the issue at hand. "What is this guy's endgame?" I asked, turning away from the faeries. "Is it one of the three Rs?"

Arwa raised a brow. "I'm not familiar with the three Rs."

"Revenge on someone, Ruling everyone, or Running amok." I'd come up with that idea and was quite proud of it.

No one else seemed to be excited by my terms, but Joo-won tilted his head, considering my statement. "All three. He was one who always wanted to be at the top, and he didn't care about rules or morals. And of course, I would never believe he's fully forgiven me."

I placed a hand to my cheek, my mind racing with thoughts. "Do you think he knows you suspect him of being up to something?"

"I would think him foolish if he didn't."

"Then what is his end game with you and me? Why would he want me at this festival he puts on? I know he's a businessman, but I don't think he'd put our issues aside just to turn a profit."

Joo-won rested his head on the back of the chair. His composure was continuing to break in front of me, and while mostly I didn't mind, his concern over Martin did make me more antsy. "At the smallest level, he simply wants revenge, and he is using you as a pawn. While I believe that is a part of it all, I fear he has something bigger going on."

As much as I'd love to say I was just a nobody, the reality was, as part of The Six, I was a target. "He could see me as a threat to stop whatever he's up to. If one of The Six dies, then we are no longer as powerful. Our bond would be gone. He's taking a preemptive strike."

Arwa nodded. "That would be most probable. If you are no longer all alive, then you all would lose the power of The Six. The biggest threat to those who wish evil would be gone for good."

"What is he up to? Why would he want to take us out? We are helpful to humanity. Did he want those original soulmates ruling the world?"

Joo-won crossed his arms, still looking upward. "No. He would have hated being so controlled. But, as you guessed, he would also see you as being an obstacle to whatever insidious thing he is planning. Not to mention, that there are groups who are seeking to tear you all apart. They've put out rewards for taking one or more of you out. He likes a profit."

I raised my brows, not surprised, but still bothered by that fact. There were actual groups out there plotting our demise. Erik and Charles had mentioned such before. It was why whenever I, or any of The Six, left town, I had to have an entourage.

Charles had kept saying we were like the Justice League or the Avengers or some comic book foolishness. He claimed there were bound to be supervillains and their henchmen who had us on their radar. Then he mentioned something about looking for the Joker to his Batman, and I tuned him out.

I glanced over to Joo-won. "Why didn't you tell me anything about this?"

He didn't look at me. "Because things had become more silent since Amina's slumber. The longer she sleeps, the less of a threat you seem. However, I would never have my guard down and am paying attention. So are town leaders who I have communicated with often about this."

"Still would have been nice if you had clued me in."

He ran a hand through his thick hair and finally glanced

over to me, the blue in his eyes brightening. He was about to be playful again. I was starting to figure him out. "Would you have liked to know, butterfly? This is not your line of business. You aren't a part of your council. We thought we were doing you a service, as they say, by allowing you to live normally as a business owner. I know that is your passion. Not these dark tactics and politics."

I dropped my shoulders. He had a point. I still couldn't get used to the idea of him looking out for me without me knowing all this time, like some benevolent being. "Thank you." I looked down at my clasped hands. He was right about me. I did just want to be normal and stay out of this crazy, horrifying fighting. However, I wasn't chosen to be a passive bystander. "But I have to know about these things. It wasn't what I signed up for, but it's what I'm a part of. I have to do the dangerous stuff in between my daily duties. Superman got to be a reporter, but he also had to save the world." And damn it, I'd been hanging around Charles too much. I must never let him know I said that.

Joo-won gave me a smirk, and as cocky as it looked, it also calmed me a little. His confidence was contagious. And right now, I needed all I could get. I looked over to Bella, who had been observing us with glazed, lovey eyes all this time. She'd never been a big Joo-won fan, but since he'd proven himself, battling Misandre and Lorenzo, she'd come to his side. "Can you tell me, how legit is this festival thing?" I asked her.

She gave a curt nod, composing herself. "Right, it's actually quite successful. He's been doing it for a few years now, several times a year but in different large towns all over the world. It's well attended and profitable. People are always looking for ways to bring back aspects of the Pre-World. He tapped into it really well by making it an eclectic blend of all that Pre-World nostalgia. Live music, food stands, fair games, arts and fashion selling booths. It goes on for the whole weekend. Local hotels even make profits from all the people who come to visit, sell or perform."

I tapped my chin. There were smaller such events in the area that happened several times a year, and it was great for business. I made a killing at the last one. I was surprised I hadn't heard of it before, but then again, I was a new business owner, and the years before this past one, I'd been just trying to survive. Not everyone got back on their feet at the same pace. It seemed our Martin was a quick rebounder.

"You'd probably do really well at this event." She gave a little chuckle. "Of course, he's probably using this festival as a front for something illegal as well. I don't think it's doing well enough for him to go legit."

I didn't think so either. "Yeah, and a great opportunity for some underworld villain to snatch me up. Maybe we should go just to try to stop whatever this event is a front for."

Arwa tapped her fingers on the arm of her chair. "That's a smart idea. And to not go would visit possible violence on your town and I understand you don't want that. I will send some of my people to attend. You will be heavily guarded. I would think having you attacked would be bad for business, so it won't be an obvious assault. It's better to go in with open eyes than wait for him to come to you later."

While that did make sense, I still felt bad that she was going to lend us any of her people to help. This wasn't her fight. "You don't have to help me."

Arwa stood up. "I realize that, my dear. However, Martin is a larger threat. I cannot allow him to gain any more control. I don't have to know what he is up to to know that I don't want him doing it. I know enough to know he means no good for any of us, not just you. Besides," she gave a soft smile and looked over to Joo-won, who was sitting upright again, and then back to me. "Joo-won is my ally, and so are you. I will do everything in my power to make sure we all remain strong."

Joo-won bowed his head to her. "Thank you."

"With that in mind, some time ago, you both sought my assistance in providing a cure for Joo-won's curse." She looked to Bella, who moved to a side table beside her chair and picked up a small box big enough to hold a necklace. "My people did find a potion to return your strength and break the control. However, it comes at a great risk, and I would not advise you use it unless there is a dire need."

Joo-won stood up as Bella passed him the box. He opened it to find what appeared to be a fancy perfume container holding a green liquid. "Why wouldn't you advise I use this?"

Bella sighed, taking a step back from him. "Because it will most likely kill you. The risk is high. We used it on volunteers only. Those who were already facing death that we could not cure. Just one of our test subjects is still living. Others survived for months only to then die out of the blue. Others died within hours. All did get super strong, so that part worked, and they were resistant to control."

Well, that didn't sound like a good bargain. He could go back to his old self only to drop dead a couple of hours later. When would that ever be worth it?

Bella raised her shoulders and reached out her hands. Her eyes were worried, and it looked like she wanted to grab the box back from him. She glanced over to me, as if apologetic for even giving him the potion. "We're still working on perfecting it, but with all that's going on, I guess it would be good to have this in your back pocket."

Joo-won gave Bella a bow, and I shook my head, standing. "No, there is no back pocket for this. If he is in a situation where he has to take this, then we are screwed. With all the powerful people we know, he should never have to risk his life with this."

Arwa gave an understanding nod. "I agree, but we didn't want to make that decision."

Joo-won walked closer to me but did not reach for me, just stood beside me so that I could feel the heat of him. Heat that I wanted wrapped around me. "Do not worry about me, butterfly. I will not leave you."

How could he possibly know that? No one ever knew that. Amina didn't know she was going to have to put herself in a coma. We'd thought we could avoid it. Charles didn't know he would get killed and then reanimated. My ex-boyfriend didn't know he would die. My parents and siblings didn't know they were going to die because of the Sickness and so many other horrors of this world. Nothing was guaranteed.

I opened my mouth, but Bella cut in, giving me a look of understanding. "For all we know, he could be the one to survive it just fine. We just had to tell him of the risk."

Arwa walked over to me and placed a hand on my shoulder. "Let's give you two some privacy. Stay as long as you'd like. I know you dream of quiet times but be thankful for the quiet you have had all these months. Our world now is made of moments of calm. Never take them for granted and enjoy them when they arrive for however long they stay. This too shall pass, and a quiet moment will return, and then it will end. Such is the life we have. But for those moments where there is love, love hard. For what are we without it?" She looked between Joo-won and me before turning and leaving, the other fae following.

CHAPTER 17

As soon as the door closed, Joo-won pulled me to him in an embrace. I had expected a kiss, but instead, he hugged me tightly to him. I could smell the sweet oak and whiskey scent of him as I buried my face into his chest. He ran a hand lightly from the top of my head to the middle of my back. His touch felt so comforting, I wanted to relax into him, but instead, I clung to the back of his shirt, cherishing the moment.

We stayed like this for a while, not speaking until he finally broke the silence. "I've missed you. Have you missed me, butterfly?"

"A little," I mumbled into his chest. Of course, I missed him dearly, but the teasing side of me loved to see him squirm a bit. I couldn't have him get too cocky.

He groaned, letting go of me. "Well, that won't do. Shall I disappear so you'll have more time to miss me properly?"

Ok, playtime was over. I'd been thinking about this man for so long now, I wasn't going to let him just disappear, thinking I didn't care. Not after all he'd done to show he cared. I yanked him closer to me. "I was just joking. Don't–"

He didn't wait for me to finish speaking. Instead, he

grabbed my face and planted a soul-stealing kiss on my lips. My legs weakened, and I bent at the knees. Instead of falling, he wrapped an arm around my back and held me to him. When our breathing showed itself a necessity, I reluctantly pulled away from him.

He gave a short chuckle. "How am I going to let you go again?"

I shrugged, still speechless from the intensity of that kiss. I had no desire to leave him.

He brushed a strand of hair from my face. "Do you doubt how much I love you?"

My heart panged. That word again. That aching feeling that it brought with it. I closed my eyes tightly, no longer wanting to see the passion in those alien eyes of his. Did I doubt him? No. Not anymore. If this was one long game of his to break down my wall, he had the patience of Job. Still, I couldn't ignore the fear that such a declaration kept pressing on me.

"Look at me...please," he said, the quiet baritone of his voice thrumming my spine.

I did as he asked, sucking in a breath as he gave me the slightest of smiles. Even that little grin felt so heart-stabbing. "There, you are. The most beautiful eyes. I know we have to be apart for a while, but don't run from me permanently. I want you, and if you can't tell by now, I'm a patient man. I'm going to make sure that this all works out. I will right my wrong."

I shook my head slowly. "What was your wrong?"

"I helped make him who he was. I encouraged his cruelty long ago, and I should have killed him, not lock him up. I had the power then, and I did nothing."

"You cared about him."

"I was foolish. I didn't want to make the tough decisions."

"It's hard turning on a friend."

"You did."

I winced. I knew he was talking about me banishing Amina without her knowing why. I still regretted how I'd handled that.

He rubbed my arm. "No, that wasn't what I meant. You knew you had to make a hard decision that could have ruined your relationship forever. Perhaps it permanently damaged your relationship with Charles, much to my benefit. But you did what needed to be done."

While true, it didn't match his situation. "Joo-won, me banishing Amina and you killing Martin are two different things. I can't say I would kill her or any of my friends."

"Still, I will do what needs to be done."

I didn't like the tone in his voice. It sounded very ominous. I already knew where this was going. "You aren't taking the potion."

His grin widened. What was so funny? "Ah, so you care if I die?"

I poked him in the chest, bubbling with annoyance. He was going to make me admit my feelings, and I wasn't ready. I didn't do well with feelings. I made rash decisions that hurt people with feelings. "Maybe. Yes."

"She must love me."

"She must not want her friend to die."

He sucked in a breath and clutched at his chest. "Friend? She wounds me with her words."

I covered my eyes with my hands. I really hated admitting my feelings to him, but I needed him to understand that I was serious. "You're more than a friend, and you know it. Maybe I'm starting to get used to you. Maybe I would be devastated if something happened to you."

He hummed, and the sound vibrated in my chest, weakening me again.

He gently grabbed my hands, moving them away from my face. "Devastated. That's a strong wrong."

He put my hands to his broad shoulders and brought his own to my waist. I looked down at my feet, feeling awkward. I liked him, but it hurt. Liking anyone now was scary business.

"Butterfly, it's okay to like me," he said in a gentle voice.

I shook my head. "No. No, it's not. Not if you die. Promise me you won't take the potion. Wait for them to perfect it."

He tilted his head to the side, and his lids lowered slightly. I had a good feeling he was not going to agree to my request. "Tell me you love me."

"Did you hear nothing I said?"

He leaned forward, the heat of him falling over me like a thick blanket in the cold. "I won't make promises I can't keep. I can't wait to hear you say it." He then kissed my cheek and backed away, turning into a portal that appeared behind him.

The man had a way with an exit. He was going to devastate me. I just knew it.

～

*T*he festival was more than I could have imagined, and it was hard to believe that it wasn't legit. Located in Baltimore City, not far from Joo-won's town, which I was sure was purposeful, the area was packed with people. I couldn't recall the last time I'd been to anything so bustling in the area. It covered several streets and grassy areas filled with storefronts and restaurants. It really was an outdoor street festival. There were vendors, games, carnival rides, and performers everywhere. Adults, teens and children. Music and laughter. The smell of all sorts of foods filled the air. If I hadn't known Martin was behind this, I would have been overjoyed. It seemed people were really having fun.

However, I was so nervous I could barely concentrate as customers came over to our space to browse our goods and haggle. Luckily, I had a sales associate with me. Charles and Erik were also there, but they were perched around the booth more like bodyguards. I was also aware that several women and some men slowed down their walking to check them out, and it might have drawn me a bit of business. Again, if I was in a better state, I would have capitalized on that.

We were already on day two of the event with no mishaps. I'd been doing exceedingly well, which gave me a nice confidence boost. If the world hadn't gone to crap, maybe I could have been a celebrity stylist. Still, that didn't mean that things were okay. I'd seen no sign of Martin or his cronies, but I had no doubt they were watching. Since he voluntold me to be here, I knew he was checking. But if he wasn't going to try something, why was I here? There had to be a catch somewhere. I couldn't imagine he was doing this as a sign of goodwill. He was probably planning to rob me of my profits or tarnish my name. Or most likely kill me in some public sacrificial ritual. I was betting on the latter.

A tall paper cup filled with what appeared to be lemonade was shoved in front of my face. I glanced at Charles with raised brows.

He shook the cup. "You gonna take it? It's cold."

I leaned back. "You trust eating or drinking anything here?"

He slurped his own drink, giving me very unconcerned eyes. Of course, he wouldn't be worried. He was an undead vampire with an iron stomach.

He rolled his eyes. "Everyone else seems to be just fine."

I took the drink and peered down at it before sniffing it.

Lavender and Lemon. My mouth practically watered. "That doesn't mean it's safe.

Erik walked over to us with angry eyes. It didn't mean he was angry, that was just his neutral face. He was lucky he was handsome. "I just sold a top."

I made an o shape with my mouth. I hadn't expected him to do more than scowl at people passing by. "A blouse or a T-shirt?"

He scrunched his face and dropped his mouth open as if I'd just asked him to multiply 900 times 160 in his head. "Is there a difference?"

Charles made an over-dramatic gasp and touched his chest. "How could you ask that? Of course, there's a difference."

I knew he was mocking me, but I gave him a nod of thanks. I decided an explanation would be a waste of time to Erik, who had already moved on, returning to surveying the perimeter. "How much did you sell it for?"

Haggling was encouraged here, and I was open to it within reason. I knew my sales associate would know what "within reason" meant, but I wasn't sure Erik did, even though I had explained it carefully to both him and Charles should they need to assist.

Erik gave an exasperated sigh. Was my question that challenging? "The full price."

I raised an eyebrow. "Impressive. She or He didn't ask for a discount?"

"Yes."

I guess I was going to have to pull a discussion out of him today. "And then what happened?"

"I said no. He said it was lucky I was cute, and then he paid."

Really, he didn't even have to try. He could have the worst customer service, and he would still become

218

employee-of-the month based on sales alone. "Can you work for me part-time?"

He gave me deadpan eyes, arms folded over his chest. "Why would I torture myself like that? I thought we were friends."

Was this his attempt at a joke? Every once in a while, when the stars were aligned, Erik would loosen up and be a fun guy. Less so nowadays with Amina asleep, but he still had his moments. This was one. "Was that a funny? Were you being funny? How fun?"

He opened his mouth for what I hoped was a witty retort but paused, straightening up and as he looked to his right down the street of vendor tents.

I moved to the entrance of my tent, Charles to my side, and I looked down the street. A thick fog moved towards us. It was currently about half a block away, but it was not slow-moving. How had we not noticed? We had not prepared for fog today. But it fell under weird, and that meant we had to up our alert and get out.

"Is that a supernatural fog?" my new sales associate, Veronica, asked, standing behind me. "The weather was supposed to be perfect today."

I shrugged. "How predictable is anything nowadays?"

Charles shook his head. "I've never seen a fog that thick. It's like a wall."

The band closest to us stopped playing, and we heard a few shouts of concern.

Erik turned to us, a dark look in his eyes. "We should leave."

"Why? It's just fog. It might pass over us quickly based on how fast it's moving."

"We didn't even want to be here. This gives Lisa a good excuse to leave."

Veronica sighed, flipping her long blond hair over her

shoulder. "But we're making a killing here. It'd be foolish not to finish the day out."

Things began to quiet around us as the fog rolled in as if noise would disrupt it. Patrons went inside the shops and restaurants located around the tents and booths, waiting it out.

I bit my lip. From a business perspective, she had a point. If the fog blew over quickly, and the crowd still stuck around, it'd be silly to leave. However, if it didn't, then we wouldn't be getting any sales anyway. We could wait a few minutes to see how long it stayed. Then again, this could be the catch from Martin I'd been waiting for. Up until now, everything had been just perfect. Now we got this weird fog. I'd been in supernatural fog before. Charles was right. It did usually move fast and not stay long. It wasn't uncommon for this time of year. The time before the seasons changed.

Veronica pushed her head out past me. "No one's screaming, so there's nothing in the fog. It's probably just a weather thing."

The fog was now only a couple of tents away now. I had to make a decision. Erik grabbed my wrist. "Teleport us out," he barked. He glanced at Charles and then tapped the side of his head. "Let me know if things change in ten minutes."

Charles nodded, eyes wide. "Yeah, thanks for leaving me in the terrifying mist."

Guess I wasn't going to be making the decision. Erik was the former military and bodyguard and the current sheriff in our town. He knew best. I began to teleport us away. "Veronica, I'm giving you hazard pay for this."

When we got back to my place, Erik immediately went to the window. I assumed he was checking to see if the fog had gotten out this far. It wasn't unheard of to have a statewide supernatural fog. However, it was clear outside.

He stayed facing the balcony, hands clasped behind his back. "You ever thought of just leaving him for good?"

I already knew who he was talking about, and I wasn't surprised he would feel that way. Joo-won hadn't ever done him any favors. "You really hate him."

He turned his head to the side, still facing away. "He almost killed me, tried to kill Amina. I understand he came to our side, but that doesn't mean you have to date him. He's brought you nothing but trouble. At some point, you have to call it quits."

If I were another person and that person told me about her relationship with Joo-won, I might give her the same advice. Was his world just too dangerous for there to be any peace with us? I thought of how he looked at me the last time I'd seen him. Like I was the most precious thing in the world to him. I recalled all that he'd been doing to protect me, even during the soulmate wars. He'd kept me safe from anyone who tried to harm me. He'd risked his life to rescue me from Lorenzo's torture even though Lorenzo was supposed to be his ally at the time. It was hard to think such devotion was something to quit. "He told me he loved me."

Erik turned to me. "And that's fine, but what do you feel? Do you love him too?"

I looked away from him and sat down on the couch. I couldn't say anything about how I was feeling out loud. That made it real, and it was too terrifying when there was a man out there who could tear us apart.

"If you can't say it then ask yourself if it's worth it. You've repaid any debt you owe him. We've had enough fighting to last us a life time. I've tried to talk Felix out of his fighting."

I rolled my eyes. Erik was being heartless, which made no sense because his love for Amina was impressively strong. "Felix is fighting with and for the woman he loves."

Erik took in a deep breath, stuffing his hands in his pocket. "Yeah, but at least he openly admits his feelings."

I snorted. They expected me to fit a pattern, but they hadn't taken my journey. "Yeah, well, he didn't watch the person he loved die in front of him."

"Charles came back."

I rubbed my scalp, feeling frustrated. Erik knew a lot about me, but there were things I didn't talk about, things I didn't even like to recall on my own. If I focused too much on my life in the Pre-World or even the early years after the Event, I wouldn't move forward. I needed to be happy, and that could only happen if I started over. Since I was paranormal now, I would live longer. I couldn't carry all that pain with me all that time. However, Erik was judging me. He thought I either didn't really care about Joo-won and what happened to him or that Charles' human death had given me a sort of PTSD. While what happened to Charles hadn't helped things, it wasn't my only trauma.

"It's more than Charles. I had another boyfriend who died in front of me. We were together before the Event. When things went to hell, his place was the first one I ran to. I got there just in time to find him in front of his apartment door, getting eaten alive by a werewolf. And I couldn't do anything then either. Just watched as the wolf bit into his head, finally killing him. I threw up and then ran like a coward." In my mind, I pretended he died of the Sickness. I thought it would help erase the terrible image of him getting eaten from my memory. It didn't.

Erik lowered his shoulders and walked towards me, but I took a step back. I didn't want to be comforted because then I would start crying, and I didn't want that. Didn't have the energy for that right now. I cried so much then. I still cried over him, still had nightmares. When Charles was killed, the trauma just came racing back, but I didn't want to face it.

And I definitely didn't want to acknowledge the coincidence of losing yet another boyfriend to this horror-filled world.

"You weren't a coward, Lisa. You didn't know of your powers then."

I didn't want to hear that. It just made me feel useless. "I couldn't help him, and I couldn't help Charles. Or anyone in my family."

Erik tilted his head back, folding his lips in before speaking. I knew he was going to give me some words of wisdom soon like the big brother I imagined him to be. "I get it now. You think helping to take down Martin is some sort of misplaced redemption. Nothing that happened before was your fault or your responsibility. Lorenzo almost killed Joo-won, but you helped save him. Again, you did your part. Your conscious should be clear."

I wrapped my arms around myself, feeling weak and vulnerable. I hated being this way. I didn't like feeling so on display. Erik was usually safe because he wasn't a talker. Now he had me sharing my feelings. I guess Amina had rubbed off on him. Guess I had to open up to my "big brother." "It's more than that. Admitting my feelings just feels like opening myself up to pain, and I don't have the best track record with men. Maybe you're right, maybe I should steer clear of Joo-won. I also hate giving Martin what he wants."

Erik sat down on my couch, resting his forearms on his thighs. He didn't speak, and for a moment, I thought we were done with the conversation until he spoke again. "Being with Amina is hard. Not because of who she is as a person. That's the easiest part. Our moments together..." He trailed off, but the slight smile on his lips and the glint in his eyes made it clear that those moments were magical for him. It was touching to see the grumpy bear's heart melt. "But we haven't had a lot of peace in the almost two years since I've met her. She was banished for months, and she's been in this sleep for almost a year. We've technically been apart longer than we've been together. And even during the times we were both in the same town, there was turmoil around us. The former pack leader, the original soulmates, Phillip. But the good times are worth it. I look forward to her waking up and us just doing nothing together."

I didn't say anything, just looked at him with sympathetic eyes. What he was going through seemed so impossible, but his love gave me hope. It was admirable, and I would only hope someone would love me, like he loved her.

"I'm sharing this because I want you to know that I understand the challenges of love. I understand heartache. You don't have to agree with me about Joo-won. It's none of my business, really. But if you like the guy, then stop letting fear hold you back."

"What if I'm just bad luck with guys I love?"

Coast is clear! Charles' voice rang through our minds. *The fog is dissipating near us, and the crowd is still out. I can see further up the block that things are back to normal.*

I did a little jig, glad to stop the deep heartfelt talk. It was making me sad, and I hated that emotion the most. "Therapy session is over, let's go!"

~

*W*hen we returned to the fair, the fog was barely a mist now, and things appeared back to normal as the crowd began to move and music blared once again.

"Well, that was weird and uneventful," I commented, surveying my tent at the remaining items. We still had half a day left, but I was beginning to want to leave now.

Charles shrugged. "Better than monsters coming out of the fog. I saw that in a movie once. And in reality, about several years ago. The mist just swallowed a person whole, and we never saw them again."

Victoria tapped him on the shoulder with a sweet smile. "Ok, let's save that talk for later so we don't scare off the customers? K? Bye."

Just as I was about to agree, a cold, wet breeze hit the air. I spun around as the mist thickened to a fog once more. "What in the hell?"

Charles swore. "Come on, man. This shit is unnecessary."

I waved my hand in front of my face, knowing it would do no good. I couldn't see anything now. The music still played, and I could still hear the crowd around us. They were all as mystified as us regarding this temperamental fog.

The fog was so thick, I felt like I could part it with my hands, but it was just air. I could see nothing but fog. Not even the outlines of Erik, Charles or Veronica. It felt weird being stuck out in it.

I balled my hands into fists and tried to teleport. Try being the operative word because I couldn't get out. "I can't teleport."

"Shit," I heard Erik swear. "The fog's muting our powers. You didn't feel this before, Charles?"

I heard Charles mumble something unintelligible, an irritated tone to his voice. "Dude, no. There wasn't a reason at the time for me to test my powers, it was calm."

We'd left before the fog got to us last time, so we didn't know then. A regular supernatural fog didn't mute powers. It was just an annoyance, and the danger came in the fact that you couldn't see through it, just like a normal weather-related fog. If the fog was muting powers, it could only mean that it was conjured, and someone very powerful was able to make it suppress powers. Now there were many beings in this world who could find use to do something like this.

Even your regular humans could get this kind of assistance so they could come in and commit crimes on an even playing field with us paranormals. However, I wasn't going to play naïve today. I was already on high alert, and these events had never had any danger in their history, so there could only be one cause here.

Martin.

CHAPTER 18

a hand grabbed my own, and before I could hope that it was Erik or Charles, I felt my body being propelled backwards by a strong wind. The movement only lasted a short while, and I dropped to the ground. The hand holding on to me let go, and I turned to find the source, but I couldn't see. I blew a wind around me, and the fog quickly cleared out, but I was no longer in my vendor tent with the others. I was standing in a dense forest. The trees were so tall and thick that I could not see the sky above me. The area was absolutely quiet. I heard no animals scurrying or chirping, not even the wind.

Then suddenly, the crunching of leaves under feet behind me. I spun around but saw no one through the overgrown plant-life. The barest of breaths tickled the back of my neck, and slapped at it running forward before turning.

Martin stood there, rocking back and forth on his heels, hands clasped behind his back. He gave me a wink with a pleased grin on his face. "I thought perhaps I would not be successful in getting you alone. But determination is what makes us winners, oui?"

Panic tried to squeeze my heart, but I shrugged it away. I

would not let this man scare me. I'd faced much worse. I think. Sort of. "What do you want from me? Joo-won and I aren't together anymore."

He opened his mouth, lips still upturned but those large haunting eyes crinkling at the corners. He paused before speaking, accessing me. "I am never one to blame a woman for a man's behavior. It is such a limited way of thinking. Men are thinking creatures who have ruled the world. Yet, when a man does wrong, we blame the woman as if she could bewitch him. If women were truly that powerful over a man without the benefit of magic, shouldn't they have been running things all along? No, men must take responsibility for their own actions. You are not responsible for Joo-won's changing."

I crossed my arms. Where was he going with this? While I didn't disagree with his logic, I was sure he didn't come here to talk about sexism and the male patriarchy. "That's mighty woke of you but doesn't exactly answer my question."

"Misandre had always said that you bewitched Joo-won. I thought she gave you too much credit."

I stiffened. He knew Misandre? Had they been working together behind Joo-won's back? Joo-won never mentioned Martin until recently, so it was highly unlikely that Joo-won knew Martin was in play so close to home. However, Misandre was very possessive of Joo-won, and they were friends of sorts. Why would she work with Martin? Perhaps she'd gone to him after I came into the picture, and her alliance to Joo-won had shifted. Was Martin after me as revenge for killing Misandre? Did he know where that asshole Lorenzo was? Why was he admitting he knew Misandre? I wanted to ask so many questions, but I thought I'd get more answers by remaining silent.

Martin pointed a finger at me and did a circular motion

with his index finger. "I can see your mind spinning with questions. You are, perhaps, shocked that I knew Misandre? We were both scorned lovers of Joo-won. Enemy of my enemy is my friend, oui? But no, Joo-won is not my enemy. Even after all he has done to me, I cannot break the bond that we have built. I only want to return to it. But he is not the man that I knew. I saw him changing when Yuri and then Senna came along, but now he is almost unrecognizable. You didn't change him. Or bewitch him. But you were the final nail in the coffin."

Just great, he had really grabbed me to get rid of his competition. "So, is this the part where you try to kill me in hopes that he goes back to his old self? Misandre tried, it didn't work."

He chuckled, crossing his arms with a confident air. "How cocky. It's sexy. I get why he finds you intriguing. But as I have said, you must not take responsibility for Joo-won's actions. He is his own person."

He suddenly disappeared, and I turned in a circle, expecting him to pop up behind me and stab me in the back.

A whistle sounded above me.

I looked up just in time to see him jump down from a branch several feet up. I tried to teleport and cursed when it didn't work, remembering that my magic was muted. Martin tackled me to the ground. I expected the impact to be hard, but it was soft instead, the dirt cushioning the fall like a bed of pillows. How odd.

However, I didn't have time to focus on the physics of this strange place's environment. Martin positioned himself above me, balanced on his arms at the sides of my head and his body between my legs. His long brown hair hung around his face like a draped towel, and his lavender eyes practically glowed in the darkened forest. It was both terrifying and beautiful. His eyes, I mean, not the being beneath him on the dirty ground. I like my hot bad boys like the next person, but Joo-won was enough, and this guy was way too dangerous.

"Have you had a threesome?" Martin asked.

"Seriously?" He was really all over the place. One moment, I thought he was going to kill me, and now he was talking about sex? I was thoroughly confused here. What the actual hell was his end game? I hated being confused.

The scent of him, a coffee and bourbon blend, surrounded me, sparking a fire in the pit of my stomach against my will. I truly hated that he had this kind of effect on me.

He pushed down against me, moving his mouth to my ear. "He loves you, even when you aren't together. He loves you. Even when you have control over him, his heart is still yours. He gave you up because he thought I would hurt you. He never said as much, but it is true. I wish to know why he loves you." He moved back and looked down at me, his eyes seemed truly curious, but how could I answer him?

I didn't think any answer would satisfy Martin. Joo-won's affections for me were different from whatever they had together. "I don't know," I whispered. "Martin, I don't know what you want from, me but I don't have anything to give to you. You wanted Joo-won and me apart. We are. You wanted me here. I'm here."

He looked away from my face, balanced on one hand as he used his right to trace a finger over my exposed collar bone. I wiggled under him to fight the pleasurable feeling his touch brought. I didn't have to see his eyes to know that he was toying with me like a cat and a mouse. I didn't want to be the mouse.

"I could break you. As a Six, you are strong, I don't doubt that you are strong. But I could break you, and if I did, it would destroy him. It would be my greatest revenge, and yet, I'd find no peace in it. I don't want revenge. Not anymore. It is a pedestrian goal. I loved him. More than you could possibly understand. He broke me, and yet, I open myself to that pain again because to be with him is rapturous. You will come to understand the joy and pain of loving him."

Now this was surprising. I expected him to want some form of payback. I wasn't sure I believed him. I hesitantly reached up and touched his chin, turning his face back towards me. I parted my lips in surprise to those lavender eyes of his glazed in tears. Whatever he was feeling, it seemed real and intense. A tear dropped from his eye and splashed against my cheek.

He reached down and wiped it away with a gentle hand I had not expected. "But I would have him back. Even if it were to require your love."

I scrunched my face. Was he implying what I thought he was implying? This was a total 180 from what I imagined. "Are you saying you want a relationship with both of us? Like a polyamorous relationship?"

His eyes glowed with an edge of excitement that made me look away. "Could that happen? I think to myself, why fight? I do enough fighting in my life. I could love you, instead. I don't think that would be terrible."

Admittedly, a fire lit in my core at the idea of being surrounded and loved by both of those beautiful men, but logic stamped it out just as strongly. Besides the possible drama it would add to my life, there was the bigger issue of him being an all-around bad guy who I couldn't trust and whose actions I could never approve of.

Then again, could I get him to stop whatever possible evil he was planning if I presented myself as being on his team? Perhaps, Joo-won and I together could get Martin to back down. There would be no bloodshed, no lives threatened. Just thinking of that plan sounded ludicrous in my head. I couldn't trust Martin. He was being manipulative. He was probably testing me. I needed to play this smart but leave room for possibilities.

"Could you ever love me?" I asked. My eyes widened so that I could give him the most innocent look I could muster.

He smiled, and there was nothing creepy about it. Shit, he looked innocent himself. How many people had fallen and gotten hurt or worse because of that face? "I could try. If you would let me."

It felt like I was walking a tight rope and could fall at any moment. Like I was playing in a lion's den. I couldn't ignore the idea that he only wanted me so that he could control Joo-won. Then again, maybe I could turn the tables on him and take control. "I can't be with someone who hurts innocent people."

He hung his head to the side, his hair covering half his face, but I could still see his gentle smile. "I can promise you I will hurt no innocents. I've avoided killing anyone myself, and those in my company who have, I have punished."

Was he saying he wasn't behind the attacks on Niles' people, but that, instead, it was his flunkies who acted on their own? I wasn't sure I believed that and would have to investigate that truthfulness later. "I don't know that I believe you."

"A fair position. I must prove myself. I have sins that time cannot make up for. I know that I may not be appealing to you, but I promise I can be good to you, for you. I can help you with your business. Make you rich."

I folded my arms. I didn't care about his help there. For my plan to work, I couldn't give in to him easily. He had to believe that I could give in to him. He might have thought I was stupid enough to believe he would genuinely go good just to have a part of Joo-won, but I wouldn't think so fool-ishly of him. If I was going to get him to relax around me and find his secrets, he had to believe he could truly win me over.

"I'd rather you stop invading towns and stealing."

He rolled to my side in a quick movement. "Done."

"Because of me?"

He rested on his side, head perched on his hand. "Because I was already going that route. No worries, I will prove it."

"I look forward to that."

He gave me a boyish smile that tugged at me. "I'm happy, Lisa. You are giving me a chance. Even if it is to stop me from doing the evil you think that I am up to. You are open to sharing. I did not think that possible."

I shrugged. "Well, you don't know me."

"Right, but now I want to know even more. You have intrigued me." He jumped up in one fluid motion like some kind of supernatural gymnast. He offered me a hand, and I reached out, practically floating to my feet from the power of his grasp.

I had to admit, he had me curious as well. Either he was a master manipulator or really that much in love with Joo-won. I would find out. "Same."

"Well, we both have our motives. I want Joo-won. You want me to go legit, as they say. Perhaps, in the middle, we will find love."

My nerves were rattled for many reasons, but I stuttered out a 'yes' in affirmation.

He tilted his head back, searching my eyes under lazy lids. "Your friends will be mad when I return you, but hope-fully you will explain my offer to them."

"They wouldn't understand." That part was true. They wouldn't understand or believe me. If I was going to sell this proposition, I had to sprinkle in some truth. "I don't even know if Joo-won would."

Martin flashed me teeth. "He would. We aren't strangers to such arrangements."

I pressed my lips together in annoyance. The man really did get around. Then again, he was old as hell. I suppose variety was the spice of his very long life. Still, it seemed odd that Joo-won hadn't proposed this to me if he was so down with it. "Joo-won never said."

"Because he feared you wouldn't agree to it. You're more traditional. Delicate. That's why he calls you butterfly."

Was that the reason for that pet name? He thought I was dainty and weak? Something beautiful that could be crushed easily. Why was I listening to this guy? I shook my head of the thought. "So, you think by proposing this idea to me, it would go over easier with Joo-won?"

Martin gave a shrug but didn't respond.

In truth, it made sense. The whole thing was stupidly plausible. "You really want peace with me?"

"I would have Joo-won no other way."

I took in a deep breath and gave him my best confident smile. "Let me talk to Joo-won about it. I'd much rather be your friend than your enemy."

"Oh, my dear, that pleases me greatly. This Thursday evening, you, me, Joo-won. Dinner. I'll assume you'll have spoken to him by then."

I had to keep up the ruse that Joo-won and I were on the outs. "He doesn't respond to me when I reach out."

Martin gave me a condescending grin, like he knew better. "He will this time." He then snapped his fingers, and the thick fog returned, swirling around us.

∾

*W*hen I returned back to my tent, the space was in chaos. The event had gone on without any trouble but my disappearance.

When I got home, Erik and Charles refused to leave until I told them what happened. This was after Charles did a magic check to ensure I wasn't compromised in any way before returning to our town. I wouldn't give them any answers until Joo-won arrived, who I reached out to with the necklace he'd given me. I only wanted to talk once about this.

He appeared, crouched in front of me while I sat on the couch. I almost kicked my leg out and hit him in surprise. "I think you do this to scare me."

He didn't smile at my joke, his eyes were as serious as they'd ever been. "Are you alright?"

I nodded, inwardly happy that he seemed so worried. "He didn't hurt me. We only talked."

Joo-won, still crouched in front of me, rubbed my thigh. Not in a romantic way, more as a comfort, his eyes still concerned. It squeezed my heart a little. "What did he want?"

"A truce of sorts. He thinks we should be friends." I glanced over at Erik and Charles when I said the word friends. I then went into modified detail of our talk.

Joo-won stood up and sat down beside me, not speaking. He had to know I wasn't telling the full truth.

Charles blew out an unnecessary breath and glanced around at us. "I think we all can say he's up to something. The fact that he didn't hurt you is interesting, but he's trying to get your guard down because he needs you for something. And it could mean access to The Six or the new soulmates. He is not a friend. I'm not putting him on the V.I.P.

list."

Erik gave a curt nod. "I agree. He wants to be your friend, make him a pen pal."

I shifted in my seat, refocusing the group. "The fact that he was friends with Misandre is the troubling part. I didn't ask him about Lorenzo, but maybe he knows where he is. It might be a good idea to pretend to be his...friend to get some intel on what he's up to and to find Lorenzo. I could even get him to be a better man. And I know that's a stretch, but I'm tired of the bloodshed. Let's see if this works."

"Why don't we just kill him?"

I glared at Erik. That was his answer to everything. "You know, we don't have to be a bull in a china shop about everything."

He shook his head, not impressed with my analogy. "After everything we've gone through, I think we have to be. I was nice to the former alpha here, and during that time, he murdered people. And the fight with the first soulmates killed so many people. I can't put the town at risk like that. Not anymore. We eliminate threats, not rehabilitate them."

"I understand how you feel, Erik, but he's not threatening the town. We don't really know what he's doing. It's not as public as what the soulmates were doing. We can't just kill the guy before we know. Not everything is a nail for you to hammer, and that's the last analogy I'll make for the night, I swear."

He threw his hands up. "I don't have time for this. Don't do stupid shit." He looked over to Joo-won, pointing at him. "Make sure she doesn't do stupid shit."

Joo-won nodded with focused eyes. "Yes. I will make sure she doesn't do the shit that is stupid."

Erik rolled his eyes and headed to my front door. Charles followed him out, pausing before he reached the door. "Don't make yourself vulnerable to preserve the peace. We gotta save Amina, and we need you safe to do that."

He didn't wait for me to respond and left.

He was right. I did have a strong feeling they wouldn't totally be on board with my line of thinking. It was risky. However, I didn't think our role as The Six was to go out and fight and kill everything. We had a strong ability to bring out the good in those we cared about. Amina had helped Phillip, Felix had helped his girlfriend and I had helped Joo-won. There were others we'd won over as well just through talking. We didn't have to kick everyone's ass to get them to stop being evil. I wasn't saying that Martin would be just like that. And I certainly wasn't going to use my body to get him that way. I'd have to figure that part out.

I felt Joo-won's eyes bore into the side of my head, and a dread sunk in me as I realized now was the part where I told him the whole truth.

"What really happened?" he asked in a calm tone.

I sighed and replayed the events exactly as they happened. During the time, Joo-won showed me no expression. Really, if I ever chose to play poker, it would not be against him.

He leaned towards me slowly, searching my eyes. "Would you kiss him?"

So not the question I was expecting him to ask. "Why are you asking me that?"

"Because if you are going to try your foolish plan, you have to make it believable."

I knew that was part of it all, and I thought I could. Anything more was pushing it, and I'd have to get what I needed before that time.

Joo-won didn't wait for me to respond. "This is not what I want for you, butterfly. Why?"

I grabbed his hand. "I want to find Lorenzo. I want to

237

stop Martin with the least amount of bloodshed possible. So you think my plan could work?"

"I think it's worth trying to get information about Lorenzo. However, I think his plan will not be something you can resolve."

"Why?"

He brushed a strand of hair from my face, his skin soft against my cheek. "Because he most likely has no deeply thought-out plan. Martin is a rule breaker. He loves inciting chaos to those in power, comfort and privilege. That is his purpose. Wherever there is order, that will be the place of most risk. This federation would be his target."

"That's over half the country."

"Yes, which is why you cannot resolve this without major bloodshed and battle."

I rubbed my temple. "He's doing all this to get at the establishment? If the Event couldn't do it for good, what makes him think he can? Do you think it's plausible that we can change his mind about things?"

Joo-won leaned back against the couch. "He is very stubborn. Even I could not stop him from his destructive ways. He is not a puppy you can train, Lisa. He is dangerous, and he is damaged, butterfly."

At his mentioning of my pet name, I recalled Martin's words and got instantly defensive. "I'm not weak and delicate."

He trailed a finger up and down my arm. "I call you butterfly not because you are weak but because you are beautiful and precious to me. This plan of yours worries me, but it is something you cannot do alone. We try it but not for long."

I gave him a wide smile, soothed by his words. I was too relieved that he would be helping me. This wouldn't work otherwise, and I wanted to try it my way just once.

"I am most worried for you. I don't want him to make you uncomfortable."

I was sure that couldn't be avoided for my plan to work. "Will he want to have sex with me? He asked me about a threesome."

Joo-won raised his brows. "Yes, he would want to, but he would respect how slow you take things. If he had any ethics, it would be that."

I balled my fist together trying to steal my nerves. Joo-won would never do this plan if I looked scared. At this point, I thought it was our best bet to handle Martin. "I can do it. For a little bit. If it gets weird, I'll end it."

"We test this out slowly. I'll keep my eyes on him. I will let no harm come to you, and I'll swallow my jealousy."

I was going to try to take out a bad guy and find my mortal enemy with love and affection. Who *was* I?

CHAPTER 19

To my absolute relief, Martin chose for us to have dinner somewhere public. Specifically, it was in an Italian restaurant in Joo-won's area. I could assume he chose this location because he didn't want to give away his own home. Joo-won had mentioned that he hadn't seen Martin's home yet.

Whatever the case, my hope was that being in public and in Joo-won's territory meant he wouldn't try anything funky. When I arrived, Joo-won and Martin were already there, seated in a more private area in the back. They both looked stupidly gorgeous, and as I walked towards them, I couldn't help but notice the tons of wanton eyes on them from other patrons and staff. I was sure they were wondering how I ended up so lucky to be having dinner with such hotties. If only they knew.

I sat down at the small round table between the men.

Joo-won reached his hand out to me.

Martin took my other hand. He leaned forward and kissed my knuckles, and I almost gasped. His lips were like silk brushing against my skin. He would be more trouble than I thought.

"You look delectable." His eyes glowed brilliantly as he spoke, and I was really certain I knew how he wooed those he set his sights on.

Joo-won raised a dark eyebrow as if noticing my reaction and whispered a kiss against my cheek that sent shivers tripping down my spine. "She's always beautiful." He searched my eyes.

I was okay. I felt like I was going to be desert, but I was going to be okay. I could do this.

Martin poured me a glass of wine as I looked over the menu, not speaking. I really couldn't see the menu, my eyes were glazed with how I would play out this night. I still half-expected Martin to suddenly shank me. I couldn't imagine ever letting my guard down around him. When the waiter came, I ordered a pasta I'd eaten in the past, hoping it was on the menu because I never focused long enough to check.

When he left, Martin brushed a hand lightly over mine, and it took all my willpower to not jump at his touch. "Relax, beautiful. I don't bite. Although I do nibble." He chuckled at his own joke, and I gave him a tight smile in return.

I fanned a hand in front of my face, feeling the heat rise in my body from their intense gazes. "I'm sorry. This is weird. I'm nervous. I've never been out on a date with two men at the same time. Well, there was that one time I did that speed dating event. Does that count?" I got to chattering when I was nervous. It was authentically me, and it also made things more believable. Martin would get suspicious if I was too casual about this. From what little he knew of me, he would know I wasn't that cavalier about anything. Not as a member of The Six.

He bit his lower lip and shook his head. "Oh, I'm going to have fun with you."

Oh no. What did fun mean to him? *Don't freak out, Lisa.*

He's trying to get a response out of you. I clasped my hands together on the table, getting into my serious mode. "Joo-won and I spoke about it. I'm still not certain about this, but the world is crazy and different. Maybe it's time I get out of my comfort zone emotionally as well. I'm still trying to figure you out."

He snorted. "I am not an easy person to figure out, ma cherie. I take pride in that. But I will bring nothing but excitement and passion into your life. Joo-won can tell you that." He looked over to my elf, squinting slightly, as if he was trying to break into Joo-won's mind and awaken a fire.

Joo-won straightened in his chair, not rising to any bait Martin was giving him. "This is true. For better or worse."

"I have to admit a truth," Martin began. "I'm not certain either of this arrangement, but what's the harm in trying. I certainly can't lose anything more."

The silence that came after his statement seemed to imply that we could. After all, whether it was fake or not, I wasn't sure how comfortable I would be with seeing Joo-won with someone else, man or woman. And I already knew that I was the exception to Joo-won's sharing rule. Would we disrupt a good thing we were growing by doing this? Even if it was fake?

Joo-won opened his hand resting on the table towards Martin, who took it readily. He then grabbed my hand. He quickly kissed both our hands before speaking. "We will be fine. I'm curious how this will work."

He was curious. Martin was excited. I was terrified.

By the time we'd finished our food and were on our second bottle of wine, I was surprised to find I was more comfortable. I knew it had everything to do with Joo-won, but Martin really was on his best behavior. Was this the man that Joo-won had liked? He was actually charming, if I didn't think about him being a dangerous snake.

Martin sat back, throwing an arm on the back of his chair. He looked at Joo-won and me, raising his brows and running his tongue back and forth slowly over his lower lip. The movement was sexy as hell, and I already knew he was thinking something very not PG. "Let's go dancing."

Whew, okay that wasn't so bad.

"I want to see how your body moves."

I nearly choked on the wine I was sipping. I'd forgotten how sexual the fae and elves could be. Looks like the night would get a lot more interesting.

～

*J*oo-won did not dance. He just sat at a table and starred at Martin and me on the dance floor. But Martin could dance. Very well. It felt almost exhibitionist.

The club was fancy, with wall-to-wall tinted windows overlooking the Inner Harbor at the base of an upscale hotel. It was busy for a work night, but who knows what schedule an elven town had. Luckily, tomorrow was my off day because I didn't know when this night would end. And I was having a surprisingly good time with Martin. I hadn't drank that much. Why was I having fun with him?

Martin moved behind me to a slow R&B song the DJ was playing in the darkened space. "Where's your head at, ma cherie?" The coolness of his breath against my ear gave me a tingle in places I didn't expect. Stupid nerves.

"Nowhere, just having fun." I looked over to Joo-won, willing him to come to us but he remained seated, giving us intense eyes. Ok, he was falling out of character. I think. My mind wasn't as sharp anymore. Why couldn't I hold my liquor anymore? I hadn't drank that much.

"I think our lover is not happy," Martin mused. "Perhaps

we can get him to join us." He then turned me to him. "I'm going to kiss you now. Stop me if you don't want to."

My mind raced with a response. He was trying to make Joo-won jealous. I got it. However, Martin still confused me. He seemed so at ease with himself. No, I had to play the game like he did. I couldn't drag this out.

I gave him a curt nod, and soon, his lips were on mine. My mind screamed with fear and excitement. Would he bite my lips? Stab me in the gut while my mind was preoccupied?

He did none of those things. Instead, his lips were surprisingly warm and soft, and his kiss was slow and playful. He licked at my upper lip before sucking on it and moving to do the same with my bottom lip. My lower half betrayed me, and I pressed into his kiss, enjoying his flavor and the feeling he brought me. I pressed my hands on his toned arms as he ground against me to the beat of the song.

I soon felt hands on my waist and a hard chest behind me. Then the familiar and now comforting scent of Joo-won took over. He kissed my collarbone, and I trembled. With him swaying his hips behind me and Martin darn near dry humping me in the front, my cheeks began to flush with maybe a little lust and a whole lot of embarrassment. We were putting on a show here.

Then again, as I stole a glance around me, pretty much everyone was dancing suggestively to the now slow house music. What kind of club was this? Where was the upbeat, fast tempo? I caught people making out on and off the dance floor. Some were a thin strip of clothing away from public intercourse. What was in the liquor here?

"Maybe we should take a break," I said breathlessly. I could already feel Joo-won getting excited behind me as I moved against him to the beat. Why was I grinding like a cat in heat? I stood still, regaining control of my body. "Anyone else hot? It's hot in here. I need to cool down. Get some water. Lots of water."

I tore away from them and practically galloped to the bar. A bartender with eyes the color of burnt orange eventually got to me and seemed a bit dismayed that all I asked for was a water. "Sorry, I can't hold my liquor like I used to. This stuff is going straight to my head."

She chuckled and shook her head. "You're not elven. Our liquor is strong, and the drinks here have a special aphrodisiac. It's meant to make you a little hot and bothered, as the humans say."

Say what now? "So, these drinks are spiked with horny juice?"

She snorted. "That's a way of putting it. Of course, it might affect you more."

I touched my chest, slightly offended that she considered me a weakling. I prided myself on being able to handle my liquor. Of course, that was a whole apocalypse ago. "I'm fae. We're like cousins."

She shrugged. "Still not exactly elven. The water should help, but why kill your buzz? You've got two hot guys with you. I'm jealous." She then winked and moved away to help another patron.

I grabbed my water and began to gulp it down. I needed to be clear-headed not horny. I turned to look back on the dance floor. Joo-won and Martin were no longer there, and I could see them sitting back down at a table, Martin leaning very close to Joo-won and whispering something in his ear or kissing his ear. I couldn't tell from this angle. And Joo-won's eyes were closed. He looked too relaxed. This was his town, he had to know about the drinks here. Why hadn't he told me? How was he going to look out for me if he was busy getting horny high as well?

When I arrived, Martin was still talking, arm draped

over my elf's shoulder. Joo-won had a closed-lipped smile on his face. The pair looked way too cozy. I kicked Joo-won's foot with my own. "Why did no one tell me about the drinks in this place? I've been set up."

Martin looked up at me, looking relaxed and unbothered. "How are you feeling, ma cherie? This place should make you relaxed. We're having fun, no?"

I didn't want to have too much fun with him. To let my guard down could mean death or some form of treachery I didn't want. I flopped down next to Joo-won. "Fun is irrelevant," I replied before turning and poking Joo-won in his toned chest. "Why does a place like this exist?"

He pulled me close to him and licked my upper lip, sending my stomach to tightening. Oh, he was a sly one. Taking us to this place was either a test to see how far I would go with my plan that he already hated, or he was trying to get Martin relaxed enough to spill some tea. Probably both. "Because elves like fun. All forms of it. Didn't you know?" He gave me a questioning look like it was so obvious and then pulled me onto his lap in one supernaturally swift movement.

I gave his chest a weak slap, although I enjoyed the closeness. "Excuse me, some of us aren't well versed in elven lore."

Martin leaned forward and rubbed my knee with a lazy smile on his lips. "Seems we have a lot to teach you. Just relax and enjoy yourself." He moved his other hand to Joo-won's knee and similarly touched him.

Joo-won was unfazed because he started nibbling on my neck. My eyes fluttered closed at the feel of his lips on my skin, my core tingling yet again. He was playing his role a little too good. I could barely focus. When was this water going to kick in?

"Maybe we should resign for the night at your place?"

Martin suggested, looking over to Joo-won with suggestive eyes.

Alarms blared in my head. "There is only one bed in Joo-won's suite." This was an already known fact, but one I decided needed to be said aloud.

Martin moved his hand farther up my thigh, and my legs automatically spread at his touch. Damn you body! "Yes, this is correct. Are you scared to be in bed with me? I know you've shared a bed with Joo-won before."

I gulped. Yes, and it was just to sleep. Okay, there was some teenage making out going on, but I had never had sex with him. Our first time together would not involve Martin. "Yes, I understand, but I'm not ready for anything more."

Martin lowered his head, seeming to understand. "Then we won't do anything more. But I want to grow a connection with you. We are having such a great night, let's end it comfortably together. My word is my bond, I will not do anything you don't want." He glanced over to Joo-won. "He would cut off my hands if I tried." He then stood up. "I will settle the bill. Talk about me while I'm gone."

As soon as he was out of hopeful earshot, I plucked Joo-won on the forehead. He wrinkled his face, shaking his head. "Why?"

I huffed. "I am not prepared, and you aren't watching my back."

He relaxed his face, dropping his shoulders. "I am watching all sides of you, butterfly. I am merely playing my role."

"Well, you're playing it too well."

He cocked a brow. "That would be a good thing, no? Isn't this what you wanted?"

Oh, he really was trying to teach me a lesson. He didn't think I was strong enough to get through my plan. Well, I was. Kind of. "Are we really going to have a slumber party at your place tonight?"

"We can end the night now. I don't want you uncomfortable."

I gnawed at the inside of my cheek, thinking. So far, things were going well. It might set us back to stop now. "We can make a lot of progress if we continue to bond tonight." I glanced at Joo-won sideways. "And you're sure you're okay with him touching me and kissing me?"

He ran a comforting hand up and down my back. "I am doing my best to be comfortable with it. Are you okay with him touching me? He has been more respectful in that sense. I think he is trying to take things slow for your sake."

"Why is he being so mindful?"

Joo-won looked over to the bar to ensure Martin was still there. "Because he is playing the same game we are. The saying, 'the flies come with the honey,' comes to mind."

I frowned. "You mean, you get more flies with honey. Which I never understood, by the way, because who is trying to catch flies."

"To get rid of them. Like a trap."

I tilted my head. "That seems so obvious that I feel stupid for not knowing. And yes, I figured he is playing nice so my defenses will come down and he can get what he wants."

"He is very good with that. Better than me. It worked well in our past. But he knows I know what he is doing, so whatever he is planning, it will not come quick. He will push your boundaries so you have to set them. Don't worry about how I feel."

I scoffed. How could I not? This whole thing felt wrong. "It's not just about how you feel about him touching me. Maybe I'm getting jealous about the way he's touching you. I mean, you're the one with actual history with him. What if you change your mind about him and want to get back together? Maybe I'm too vanilla for you."

He let out a breathy laugh. "You don't know my feelings for you at all, do you? I'd thought I'd done a better job at showing you, but clearly, I haven't." He gently grabbed my chin and studied my eyes. "You are in my system, Lisa. Even if you can't admit how you feel about me, that doesn't change how I feel about you. It's been a year since I've known you, and we haven't even had sex, and I will continue to wait for you. I want you. Nothing and no one can change my mind. Not even a past lover. Do you understand now?"

He said it with such command and confidence that how could I not understand? I suppose I always did. If I didn't, I was just being willfully ignorant. I was just being stubborn. I nodded silently, the tingle in my stomach growing from his words. He was making me a puddle in his lap. It was almost overwhelming the intensity of his words and the way he looked at me.

"Say it out loud that you understand."

My first instinct was to argue and be my cocky self with him, but I really didn't want to. He was crystal clear, and the instant calm I felt at his declaration couldn't be ignored. "I understand," I whispered. I wasn't breathing until he ran one of his large hands down my back again, and then I relaxed into him.

"Do not worry. I have you," he said softly in my ear.

~

*J*oo-won had a California king bed, and it was large enough that we technically didn't have to touch, but Joo-won held me against his chest while Martin had me throw a leg over his as he gently stroked my hair. They were both emanating a comfortable

249

heat, and I couldn't say I wasn't super relaxed. However, with us all contented with the magical alcohol and bonding so well, I thought maybe I could squeeze a bit of information from Martin now. I didn't want to play the long game with him because I did have my limits.

I scooted closer to Martin, sensing more of him on my thigh than I had anticipated. I ran a hand down his toned back, feeling the muscles flex as he moved his arm. His skin was just as soft as I expected. "Who would have thought a month or so ago that we would end up here like this."

He placed his lips on the top of my head. "Certainly not me. But so far, I am happy we have decided to be more mature."

"If Misandre was alive, she'd have a fit."

His chest moved up and down in a soft chuckle. "First you take her Joo-won, then capture my interest. She would be enraged."

I so wanted to know what they were linked up for, but I needed to really play this smart. Strategy wasn't my specialty, but Joo-won and I had talked about how to ease into the information and what to seek first. "Hey, what about Lorenzo? He's still your ally, right? Won't this arrangement affect that? You know he tried to eat me for dinner."

He kissed me again, pulling more of me to him, and I found myself not minding it. He was deceptively intoxicating. "Yes, he mentioned. He is a savage."

"So, you don't like him either?"

"If he is an enemy to you, he is now an enemy to me."

Well, that was unexpected. He was willing to give up his friend just because of me? He hadn't even done so for Joo-won. He was probably lying. I had no way of proving it. "Are you for real? We just now became friends." I looked up at him, searching his face in the dark with my fae eyes.

He gently stroked my cheek with his knuckles. "There is

no honor among thieves. I could never trust him. It is my understanding that he didn't even try to help Misandre before you killed her, and then he ran away."

Okay, maybe he would open up. So now it was time to ask him directly. "Would you tell me where he is?"

His body seemed to harden, and for a moment, I thought he was going to get angry. Joo-won's frame also stayed very still behind me as we waited for his answer.

"Now, ma cherie, I have not seen him in ages. And even if I did, I would not easily betray him. Only if he were to attempt to harm you now would I intervene."

I moved my hand to his chest and slowly, I mean really slowly, dragged my fingernails lightly downwards. I felt him clench under my fingers. "You aren't saying that you don't know, though. You couldn't give me a hint?"

"Aw, are you attempting to seduce me for information? Clever girl. But you'll have to be more enticing than that."

My eyes widened, and I wiggled back from him a bit to feel Joo-won against my back again. This was getting a bit much. What exactly did he think I was willing to do to get this information? My limit was starting to get reached because I didn't think I could keep my hands moving downward. I could kiss him, but I wasn't sure he'd give in for just that.

I felt Joo-won shift behind me and move a hand past me. Soon after, I heard Martin suck in a breath. "Give my butterfly what she wants."

Martin groaned in response, and my mind spun with ideas of what was happening. Jealousy suddenly attacked me, and I wiggled uncomfortably between them.

Martin chuckled. "Calm down, ma cherie, he isn't touching me."

Joo-won moved his hand to my hip, and I soon felt his

lips on my neck. "I'm using magic," he mumbled into my skin.

While that was better, I still didn't like it. I decided then and there that I did not like sharing Joo-won, even if it was pretend. Even if it was with another person who was absolutely gorgeous and a superb kisser, minus the evil past. It was also at that moment that I realized that whatever feelings I was fighting for Joo-won, I had already lost the battle. I was now swimming in a sea of emotion for him. Game over.

I huffed and sat up, scooting awkwardly to the foot of the bed. I had to get away and breathe. What was I thinking doing this? I wasn't as tough as I pretended to be. Not that anyone actually thought I was tough anyway.

"Don't leave," Martin suddenly called. "I will tell you this. Lorenzo is in an enchanted forest. Not my own."

I turned back towards them, the space I had just vacated remained. "What is an enchanted forest? Is it a real place or just one of the forests with supernatural stuff in it?"

Martin patted his chest. "Lay on me, and I'll answer your question."

I squinted my eyes at him. He really was trying to force this bond. I didn't believe it was all just to regain Joo-won's affections. After all these years and all the betrayal, did Martin really love Joo-won that much to put himself through this? No, I knew better. He was setting us up for pain. I would end this before it got that far, but first, I'd get my information.

I reluctantly moved back on the bed and laid my head down on his chest. It was firm like I thought it would be. I said nothing, waiting for my answer. Joo-won's hand was on my back rubbing gently, to relax me. no doubt.

Martin's chest rose up slowly and down, and the movement along with Joo-won's hand was ultimately relaxing.

Elven trickery. "A regular forest with supernatural life in it is not enchanted. Enchanted is more purposeful. Some being has placed magic on it."

"So, the place you sent me to was made by your magic?"

"A friend made it for me."

"Why?"

He didn't answer immediately. This would probably be because it was a secret, and he was doing something more in that forest. "I store things there."

I raised my brows, surprised he would tell me that much. Joo-won paused rubbing my back for a second but didn't speak. Fine, I would be the nosey one. "Like what?"

"Valuables. It's also a good place to go into hiding. You can't find it."

"That's the enchanted part."

"Oui."

"And you didn't put Lorenzo in hiding there?"

"Like I said, it's not my own."

"What other allies could that creeper possibly have?"

He shrugged. "He is quite handsome and has a force of ghouls who follow him. It makes him appealing to those who would have need. So even if you find this enchanted forest, expect it to be full of his people. It would probably be their home for them to come and go as they please."

I bit my lip in thought. It would not be surprising to find that Lorenzo had the help of a witch to make him a hiding place. But the more likely prospect was that this forest was made for or even by Misandre. She was scary and smart, and Lorenzo was one of her closest confidants. He would know how to access it. I didn't need to start with finding out who made him a forest, I needed to find out who made Misandre a forest. For all I knew, she could have made it herself, although I had no idea if fae could even make enchanted forests. I'd have to ask Joo-won later. We also had some of Misandre's people who survived our last battle still in lock-up back in Silver Spring and our ally government town, Hagerstown. We'd been trying for a while now to get them to say where Lorenzo had taken off to, but no one talked, no matter how much pressure was put on them.

Then again, fae were a very tricky group. Those raised fae, unlike me, had a culture of being very specific with words. That's why you could never make deals with them, particularly the neutral or unseelie ones. They thrived on loopholes, and it was your own fault for not catching all possibilities. You needed a lawyer to draw out a contract with them, and even then, that lawyer better make that agreement airtight. That was all to say that if we asked the captured fae where Lorenzo was, they would even tell us. But if we asked them if he was in a very specific place, they might be more inclined to make a bargain. Perhaps for release. We'd return them to the old court they came from.

I wasn't sure of any of this, but it was better than nothing. I wanted to leave right now and go question the fae we had captured. Most of the fae fighting for Misandre took off when she died, but the few who weren't so lucky were clogging up the cells. It would probably be a benefit to release them back once we got our answer because they were a drain on our resources. Some suggested we move to death as punishment, but we hadn't agreed to that yet. So now they were just sitting in cells, coming out to do odd jobs that weren't as desirable. It wasn't to say they weren't a danger, but they weren't to us. They wouldn't attack without a leader, and Misandre's old court did not have us in their sights.

Martin moved my leg so that it was over his again. He really either liked me on him, or he was making me as vulnerable as possible. I was betting on the latter. "No more questions for me?"

"You sure you can't tell me where he is?"

"If he comes out of hiding and I learn of it, it might not be so hidden."

The way he said it gave me pause. Was he indirectly saying he would rat out Lorenzo if he left the enchanted forest? Why? If I questioned him on it, he might not be forthcoming. I waited for Joo-won to speak, but he didn't. I expected my silence on this was a good thing. I decided to shift my questions, and then perhaps I'd get more answers with that. I was doing a lot of thinking from such a long day and with drinks that had pretty much worn off now. "What did you want from Misandre? Did you work with the original soulmates too?"

I felt a base of a grumble in his chest. "You truly don't know a thing about me. I bow down to no one, and those soulmates wanted a hierarchy of power that left them at the top and the rest within their confines. I worked with Misandre because she was powerful and had access to certain things that I needed."

Cryptic answer, but it made sense. She probably helped him commit crimes or gave him the ability to do so. It was interesting that she didn't demand his loyalty then as a subordinate to the first soulmates. Or perhaps he did give his loyalty in exchange for her services. Only he betrayed her later. "So, you wanted us to win?"

"As a neutral observer, I was slightly impartial."

"You could have helped. What if we would have lost?"

"Who says I didn't help?"

Huh. It was true that I didn't know every single ally we had out there who had battled on our side. I wasn't part of the crew that went out to form alliances. It was very plausible that he *had* helped us. However, wouldn't Joo-won have mentioned that? It really seemed like the elven gathering was the first time Joo-won had seen Martin in ages. And if

Joo-won didn't know, why had Martin kept it secret? Perhaps he was lying.

"So you were there?"

"Yes. My people and I. I was concealed because I didn't want to be found out by Misandre or Lorenzo. I had heard Joo-won had backed out, but then I saw him come to the rescue in the final hour."

"You saw him back then?" I turned my head slightly towards Joo-won. "Did you know?"

Joo-won threw an arm over his eyes. It was late, and I figured he was getting tired. "Recently, he mentioned fighting on our side."

I laid my head back on Martin's chest. That made him less of an asshole but still dangerous. "Why didn't you reach out to Joo-won then? I can understand you remaining back when you were friendly with Misandre and after you thought he'd broken the alliance, but it's been almost a year since the fight, and you waited until the gathering to say anything to him. What's up with that?"

"In the Pre-world, were you a reporter? You like to ask the tough questions."

"No, but I'm nosey by nature, so it's ingrained."

He chuckled at that. "I wasn't sure I was ready to see him then."

That made sense without further explanation. They were estranged for lack of a better word. Despite that, he had fought on our side after hearing whatever bullshit Misandre was sputtering.

"Any more questions?"

Hell yeah. Like what was his real plan. But I would let it go for tonight. I had to ask the right questions at the right time, and I think I'd pushed as far as was reasonable for the day. "Tons, but it's getting late."

He gave me a slight squeeze. "Very well. Rest. I promise I won't kill you in your sleep."

No, he wouldn't because I'd warded myself, and Joo-won had added a protection spell. "Thanks for the soothing words for the night."

He gave a light snort. "I was hoping for equal assurances."

"I have no reason to harm you, Martin. I hope it stays that way." I did mean that, even though it felt unlikely.

CHAPTER 20

A week passed, and although none of our captured fae in Silver Spring admitted to knowing about an enchanted forest housing Lorenzo, Hagerstown was able to find success. Once the question was posed to the small collection of faeries imprisoned there, they all but beat each other up to take the offer of return to the unseelie realm. The new governor of the town agreed to let the least objectionable fae free once we confirmed their story.

While on the surface it seemed unfair to let so many go in exchange for one ghoul, this ghoul was high ranking and extremely powerful. Lorenzo was a big threat. Loose ends that had to be cut. Plus, he, along with Misandre, was responsible for killing their former leader as well as many others in their town.

What I couldn't understand was if they were that eager to give up the ghoul, why be so quiet all this time waiting for the exact, right question? Were fae that damn specific? I sure wasn't. Then again, I was raised human.

Two days later, we were on our way to find or kill Lorenzo.

I pressed my head against the passenger side window,

staring out at what appeared to be a vast field of thick, tall grass across the street from our car. Beyond that maze of greenery was supposed to be the entrance to Lorenzo's enchanted forest. It was night, and the whole thing looked like a scary Halloween maze lit only by the moon and stars.

Of course, playing the waiting game also allowed for my mind to travel back to my night with Martin and Joo-won. In fact, that was just the start. I'd spent practically every evening with them, and I was beginning to feel...conflicted. Martin had been nothing but kind and gentle with me. He never pushed for anything more than I was ready for, and he kept his charm. I caught myself forgetting that he was a murderous criminal. It was disturbing.

Charles thrummed his fingers on the steering wheel to a beat in his head. "What if this is a trap?"

I blinked my eyes rapidly, getting my head back in the current situation. "It probably is. Joo-won is bringing his people. And we can fan out and cover more ground that way. Listen to me, sounding all military and stuff. Erik must be rubbing off on me."

Charles snorted. "So, when is your boyfriend and company getting here for this trap Martin and the fae set up for us?"

"We're right here," I heard Senna say behind me.

I screamed and spun around in my seat as Charles jumped and bumped his head on the roof of the car.

Senna, Yuri and Joo-won were seated in the back, looking like the cover of a cool band album or some fashion ad.

"Why?" Charles shouted.

Senna leaned forward and playfully squeezed his shoulder. "Joo-won said you would enjoy it."

Joo-won tapped his chin and gave a quizzical look. "I apologize. I meant to say *I* would enjoy it."

Charles grumbled a curse, squinting his eyes at Joo-won in the rear-view mirror. "What's the plan?"

"We have my elves in the field now, searching for the entrance."

Nice to know they were doing some of the hefty work. "Do you think this is real? Any way to tell if it's a trap?"

He looked out of the window, his chin resting on his fist, elbow perched on the window ledge. "Since we're neutral, we have a good sense of finding dark or light aura. If the magic is there, we'd be able to tell what kind it is. Unless it was masked."

Charles blew a raspberry. "Well, that's helpful."

Yuri opened the car door and got out, holding it open for Senna, who was seated in the middle. The rest of us got out as well.

Once we found the entrance, I didn't really have a plan. I wasn't sure if we should give our hand away and all go in together or if we should quietly enter in stages. I didn't want Lorenzo knowing we were here and running away again. This could be our only chance. We had the cloak of night on our side, but ghouls were supernatural, and it didn't mean they couldn't see anything. I just hoped they didn't have any surveillance out there. Maybe Lorenzo wasn't that smart. He never seemed to be.

Joo-won walked over to me. I felt his pinkie moving over the back of my hand, and despite how miniature the move was, my stomach did a happy wiggle in acceptance of this small affection. It was odd that I was finding just as much comfort in this touch as a kiss. Obviously elven trickery, I foolishly told myself, knowing better.

"Did you want to talk about the other night with Martin?" he said in a low voice.

I felt my cheeks flush, remembering the dancing and the making out and...other things. No, I did not want to talk about it. Especially not around Charles. "No, and you know that. You had plenty of time to bring it up earlier. You just like seeing me blush."

He looked skyward. "Was it too much for you?"

"Now that I don't have the haze of elven liquor in my system, some of the memories were...I don't want to talk about it." I moved my hand from him and crossed my arms. I wasn't uncomfortable with what had happened, but I was a tad, ok a lot, embarrassed.

He gave a deep chuckle. "I'll make sure you aren't in such a situation again with him. You got the information you needed from him, so this friendship with him ends now, yes?"

While that was true, I wasn't sure how it would go down if I suddenly backed away from Martin either. It wasn't that we were at the point of no return, but I'm sure it wouldn't improve relations. I decided we would have to get more into that discussion once we resolved the Lorenzo matter. One beast at a time. "What will we do when we find the entrance to the enchanted forest?"

"We all go in together. Including my people."

That was different than what I was thinking. "So, no waves?"

He shook his head. "Lorenzo is smart enough to know we wouldn't come alone, and if we enter in separate waves, it will only be easier for him to try to take us down. We need to show our full force. We aren't coming for negotiations. Although I wouldn't mind if he provided us some information on Martin."

At the mention of the elf's name, my mind perked up. "Should we tell Lorenzo that Martin gave us the clue to find him? Maybe play them against each other like the cops do on the TV shows?"

Joo-won slightly lifted the corners of his mouth in

amusement. "I'd like that outcome, but we must remember our truce with Martin. We don't want to openly toss him under the truck."

I giggled, remembering that American slang was not his specialty. "I think you mean, throw him under the bus. But I get what you mean. We'll have to find another way to get him to betray Martin. Maybe an offer."

"No. I will not negotiate with that abomination. He tried to eat you. I will never get over that. We will not allow him to live just because of Martin."

There was a steely look in his eyes when he spoke, and I knew not to argue about it. He was absolutely right. I wasn't jumping up and down to let Lorenzo slide. I wasn't violent, but I dreamed of his death.

Over an hour passed before any movement happened.

An elven male jogged over to us. "My King, we believe we have found the entrance. We couldn't remove the ward, but we did weaken it. You can move through it, but it will be uncomfortable."

Joo-won gave a curt nod. "Very good. Round everyone up and tell them to stand at the entrance but to not go inside."

We began to walk through the grassy field, elves making a clear route for Joo-won and the rest of us as we walked behind them.

Charles huffed behind me, soon running up to my side. "This reminds me of that scene in Jurassic Park Two, The Lost World, when dudes were running through that tall grass and then started getting snatched up by the veloci-raptors."

I shot him an incredulous look. While his comparison was ridiculously spot on, I definitely did not want to hear that right now. "Seriously?"

He waved a dismissive hand at me. "I know, I know, I'm a nerd."

"That is something that has never been lost on me or bothered me." I patted his shoulder. "You know that. It's just that when you're in a situation where it could really happen, we don't need to talk about it."

He pointed at me. "Fair point."

Senna, walking in front of us, turned slightly. "That was one of my favorite scenes."

Charles leaned back. "Whoa, whoa, whoa. You know that movie?"

Senna cocked a brow and twisted her lips before responding. "You think because we're elves, we don't know popular culture? Only Joo-won is outdated like that."

I stole a glance at Joo-won, who looked unbothered by her statement. I mean, she wasn't wrong, and I figured he agreed.

Charles moved to her side. "My kind of girl."

"Woman," Senna corrected him.

She was such a class act.

He gave her a salute. "Yes, ma'am. My kind of woman."

I felt like I should have been jealous that they seemed to hit it off so well, but I honestly enjoyed that possible pairing. I guess I had officially moved on. Growth.

After what felt like thirty minutes of walking, we stopped at what looked like a dark, creepy forest I'd find in a horror movie. I half expected some boogeyman to pop out and chase us down. It was darker and denser than Martin's forest by ten-fold.

Charles cleared his throat and glanced over at us. "We sure about this?"

I raised a brow. I was as nervous as he sounded, but I was going to annoy him and play it cool. "You are an undead vampire mage. Are you really scared to go in?"

He gave a snort and glanced quickly over to Senna. Oh, I was embarrassing him in front of his new crush. "No. I'm not scared of anything. Things are scared of me. Let's get this over with, please."

Joo-won raised his hand in the air and then pointed forward. And just like that, every elf around us started marching forward through the ward and into the forest. Passing through the ward was not an easy process, as we were warned. It felt like I was entering an oven, except we weren't getting burned. Then there was the force pushing against us like a sea of water. I couldn't move easily. For a short moment, I was suffocating, but Joo-won wrapped his hand around mine and pulled me through quickly.

When we made it through, I bent forward, resting my hands on my knees and taking deep breaths. I felt like I'd run a marathon in just a matter of seconds.

Joo-won leaned over me, patting my back. "It'll pass very soon." He seemed totally unaffected.

How was he so strong? Wasn't he supposed to have diminished powers? "You aren't affected?"

"I have many years of practice pushing through wards. I've developed a tolerance to many of them."

Well, that made sense. He was a former professional thief. Breaking through wards was his specialty.

Once everyone made it through, we began to move forward in the darkness. If it wasn't for my faerie eyes, I'd be moving blindly. We could have added light, but we didn't want to be too obvious with our presence. Although I was sure, whoever had made that ward could feel us entering. Then again, ghouls didn't have that power, so it was possible that whoever made it for Lorenzo wasn't there to warn him.

The forest was quiet. I mean, not even the sound of insects and animals or even the wind. The only sound came from us. Where was Lorenzo? Did he have a camp or something more formal out here? Perhaps a village? Ghouls weren't silent stalkers. They were very similar to vampires, except they ate the flesh of the dead instead of blood and had coal black eyes. They wouldn't just be sitting around doing nothing. Unless they were all in hiding, ready to jump us. Or, perhaps we weren't even close to where they resided in this creepy forest.

"I wonder how large this forest is?" I whispered. We could be wandering for days here. Maybe Lorenzo and his ghouls wouldn't jump out and attack. Maybe they'd just sit back and watch us get lost.

"I am not sure. We are definitely at risk. As I explained before, we planned this journey. However, you did not want me to send any elves in to do surveillance."

"I didn't want to give up the element of surprise. We've lost enough time as it is. We don't even know if he's still in here."

"This is very true. We can set up camp in here if need be. There are provisions for such."

Charles moved over to us. "No one said anything about spending the night in this hell hole." He tripped over a branch and cursed.

"We must prepare for all possibilities. There will be no return here."

A loud chirping-like sound filled the air suddenly. No, not chirping, more like crickets but not crickets. It reminded me of the sounds of summers pasts. The sound of cicadas. Except this was even louder than I could recall them ever being. People were actually shouting to be heard, and then I saw a group of elves who were forging ahead of us run our way.

I froze in fear. "Why are they running towards us?"

Charles turned to me. "Nope, nope, nope. Run now, ask questions later." He spun me around. "Teleport us the hell out of here. When you see a mass of people running in fear, we don't investigate."

I nodded. He was absolutely right. That was horror movie 101 logic. I pushed my hands out to teleport us, but nothing happened. I tried again, pushing my power out. Still nothing.

Charles looked down at me in concern. "What's the hold-up?"

Yuri appeared beside us, looking over to Joo-won, who was trying, and also failing, to open a portal out of here. "King, we must take cover." He looked wide-eyed and sounded out of breath.

Senna spun in circles and then stopped covering her mouth as she looked behind us. "Oh no!"

Yuri nodded. "It's a brood of cicadas. They are coming our way."

Charles scrunched his face. "We're running from harmless blind bugs?"

Yuri began to jog forward in the direction of the entrance, and we all followed, not asking questions. "They are supernatural and as large as a chair each."

I ran even faster. Regular cicadas that came out every so often would have sent me racing through the forest, but giant ones were even more nightmarish. Then I heard the screams. I made the unfortunate decision to look behind me and saw several of the most horrifying creatures in my life lift several elves into the air and fly away. They were indeed cicadas. Kind of. They had the same bulging red eyes and translucent wings. Their body was the same shape as a typical cicada, except they were humongous.

What fresh hell was this? Why were giant cicadas a thing? This had to be Martin's doing. I wasn't surprised, but I was disappointed for some odd reason. I think I really had started to like him.

I sucked in a breath and looked around at the chaos for my plan of attack. Why were they snatching us and carrying us away? Cicadas were supposed to be harmless? I knew it was a lie. Nothing that scary looking could be any good. I didn't even want to know what they were doing with the poor souls they were snatching away. I just didn't want to be one of them. Why the hell wasn't our teleport powers working?

I heard high pitch scream near me and turned to see Charles duck as several got closer to us. Was that him? "They aren't blind!" He started blasting away with his modified gun, dropping bugs. "How many of them are there? It's never-ending. Why would Martin make something like this?"

Regular cicadas just bumped into people, they didn't move with purpose to come for us. These seemed very purposeful.

"Get down!" Joo-won shouted before pushing me to the ground and laying over me.

There was nowhere to hide. Why couldn't we be in the tall grass again? All there was were trees in here. That wouldn't do any good for long because these suckers flew. We army crawled to a nearby wide oak-looking tree, still moving low to the ground. By now, the other elves in the area were fighting back with their various magics and weaponry. And they were getting a good chunk of those monsters. At least our other magic still worked.

Yuri jumped up when one came our way and swung his sword, slicing it in half. Senna moved to her feet and pressed her back to his as they began to slice and dice the giant offenders, getting splashed in big bug gore. It was vomitous.

"I hate fucking bugs!" Senna screamed like a wild banshee as she swung out her sword to annihilate another creature.

I moved under Joo-won. I couldn't lay here helplessly.

He moved from over me, not saying a word as he withdrew his glowing blue sword, remaining by my side. He should know by now that I wasn't a princess to sit helplessly by, even if it was bugs. Giant. Ugly. People stealing bugs. I was not going to vomit. But it was an infestation. A biblical plague. My mind screamed.

I took in a deep breath and lifted my hands. Electricity shot into the sky, lightning crackled. My lightning. It moved through the sky in zigzag patterns before branching out and zapping the flying creatures, roasting them until they burned and dropped to the ground dead.

Yuri jumped back as a bug beast dropped in front of him. "Most efficient little faerie." He gave me an impressed thumbs up. "You are the badass."

I gave him an appreciative wink, then looked around, readying myself for the next wave of flying nightmares. I spotted a bug zooming down out of the sky towards Senna, and I focused my lightning, this time from my fingers, at the bug. "Get away from her, you bitch!" I screamed with all my might.

The bug shook in the air at my magic and blackened, dropping several feet away from Senna. I smiled, satisfied. "I always wanted to say that."

Charles gave me a fist bump. "Look at you, all Ripley in *Aliens*. Yeah, in case you didn't know, you're a nerd, too. Welcome to the club."

I curtsied. "Thanks for the invite."

Charles' eyes widened. "Duck!"

I moved to drop to my knees, but I was too late as I felt stabbing pricks on my back, and suddenly, I was lifted high into the air with an almost light speed. I wiggled and screamed, the call of the monster cicada loud in my ear.

I raised my hands up and zapped the creature, and it actually screamed a terrifying, alien shriek before letting me go. I fell towards the ground, my stomach lurching. I couldn't figure out a way to properly brace for this kind of fall. It would hurt. Maybe I could still die. I was so high. My life flashed before my eyes, and I was pissed because I was supposed to live a long one, but now I would die young for even a regular human.

Then arms caught me in mid-air. Joo-won. It was not romantic. He flung me over his shoulder fireman style as we descended and stabbed his glowing sword upward, slicing into the belly of the giant cicada I'd just zapped as it bore down towards us. A wash of nauseating bug gore fell over us, and I fought the urge to hurl as he landed us down on the ground with ease.

Joo-won lowered to his knee, and I got off his shoulder, looking around the area in wide-eyed horror. He was a foul-smelling mess, just like I was, yet even in bug slime, he looked good. He gave me a smile as he stood up, seemingly unaffected by being covered in goo.

"Thank you." I closed my eyes and shivered beneath the cold slime. I refused to stay like this. I waved a hand over my body, and once again, I was shiny and clean. I sighed, satisfied, and opened my eyes to see Joo-won still messy. "No cleaning magic for you?"

He shook his head. "It's a waste of energy. I need my full strength."

I sucked my teeth. "Could have told me that earlier. Anyway, how'd you catch me in the sky? Elves don't fly."

He turned, surveying our surroundings. I didn't hear any more monster cicadas, but that didn't mean more weren't coming. "I didn't fly. I jumped. I have the ability to jump extremely high." He tilted his head. "I thought you knew? And did you think I would let my butterfly get hurt?"

I smiled and gave him a quick kiss on the cheek.

Senna cursed, wiping bug juice, or whatever it was, out

of hair. "I am not okay. I would have preferred the veloci-raptors."

Charles pouted and shook his head. "Nah, I can guarantee you these cicadas were better."

Yuri patted her back and then quickly lifted his hand as he looked at the slime now attached to it. He wiped his hand on his pant leg in disgust. "I think we are in the clear now. I don't hear anymore."

Senna muttered something unintelligible before washing herself in cleaning magic.

Joo-won nodded. "We must find the elves they took away. They may plan to harvest them so they could still be alive."

Those around us nodded in agreement, and we once again pushed forward.

We didn't get too far when we were greeted by the very being we came to see.

Lorenzo.

CHAPTER 21

*L*orenzo stepped through the blanket of darkness, and I wondered if he'd been there the whole time. He had his hands in the pocket of his dark jeans, looking all too comfortable. He paired a deep V-cut dark T-shirt with his jeans, and his jet-black hair was smoothed back from his olive-toned face. He looked healthy and relaxed, like he'd just come back from vacation. That pissed me off.

I raised my hands, connecting with my lightning still in the air, and then dropped it down. The conjured magic bounced off of him. No damage. Damn it, he was warded.

He tsk-tsked. "And here I thought we could have a mature conversation."

Joo-won took a step forward. "You just sent a horde of flying beasts at us. If you wanted cordial, you should have greeted us earlier."

Lorenzo removed his hands from his pockets and tapped his narrow nose in mock confusion. "But you were trespassing."

This man was insane, and I had very little patience. I wanted to call him a coward, but I knew that wouldn't help things. Since I couldn't outright kill him until I got that damn ward down, I'd have to find another use for him. He was going to give me information about Martin. "There wasn't exactly a door to knock on."

He gave me a bored look, midnight eyes sleepy. "Cute," he stated as he surveyed our small army. "I assume you came to kill me?"

He sure didn't look threatened. How many ghouls did he have with him, hiding in the darkness?

Yuri made a grumbling noise. "No, we came to have a party."

Lorenzo chuckled baring a mouth full of razor-sharp teeth. They were tiny now, but they would grow when he attacked. There was never any love lost between Lorenzo and Yuri. Especially when Lorenzo openly flirted with Senna which I was told he had a knack for doing back when Misandre and Joo-won were on good terms. "Nice to see you again, elven brown-noser." He glanced over to Senna, who was standing next to Yuri, and blew her a kiss. "What a waste."

She raised her sword, and Joo-won put an arm in front of her to stop her from attacking. "I hope you've been enjoying your time in hiding. We've come to ruin your fun."

"Is that so?" The ghoul scratched his neck as he considered us. "You didn't bring all of your warriors. Sure you have enough?"

Joo-won smirked. "More than enough. You lost many people fighting for Misandre. Hiding out here, I'm sure you weren't gathering more."

Yuri humphed. "And even if you did, ghouls are easy to defeat. The bugs were more challenging."

Lorenzo growled at that attack, and I wondered if that meant there was some truth to what the elves were saying. Ghouls had speed and strength, and while that was formidable, they didn't have magic. Of course, we were making a lot of assumptions. We really didn't know what his full power base was. He was warded, and he had giant cicadas on his side. He didn't have magic, so how was he able to do all that? "Did Martin make these bugs for you? Where did they take our people?"

The ghoul shrugged. "It doesn't matter who made the bugs. They are mine. And your friends could be in the trees, underground. Who knows? Better find them quick, though."

While my rational mind tried to remember that cicadas didn't eat people, I had to remember that we weren't dealing with the creatures I used to run from in circles when I was a kid. We were dealing with monsters who very well could be carnivorous or worse, bury their eggs in the captured elves for them to come burrowing out of in the future. I nearly gagged at the image in my head. "Who is helping you with this magic?"

"Well, Food, why would I tell you anything."

I blinked my eyes, a little taken back. Did he just call me food? Another reminder to when he chained me up and sliced my skin off, eating it in front of my face like I was a turkey. Ok, that put me in a rage again. "Look, you rotten, corpse eater, if you have any hope of not dying a slow, painful death, then I'd advise you to answer our damn questions. Or you'll find yourself dead like your old pal Misandre."

He gave a nervous glance to the side and crossed his arms, trying this best to look unscared. He could call me names all he wanted, but he had to know that I wasn't a weakling. "I'm not scared of you, fo–"

I raised a hand. "If you finish that sentence, I will tear your tongue out with a hurricane wind. And yes, I realize you have a ward on you, but we'll break it." I tilted my head towards Joo-won. "Did you forget he's the king of breaking wards? Hell, it wasn't even him that weakened the ward for us to get in here."

Lorenzo lowered his head, his black eyes staring at me like scary pools of darkness. "What is it that you want?"

I felt Joo-won's hand on my back, and soon, his head was tilted close to mine. "Ask about Martin. We will work on the ward over him."

That was a plan. Even if Lorenzo didn't tell us what we needed to know, we were going to get that ward down and off him. "Was Misandre the one who boosted Martin's powers?" It made the most sense to me. If he didn't care about serving the soulmates, Martin had to get some other benefit from joining with Misandre. "And be aware that I can sense if you're lying, so don't bother." I really couldn't sense it, but he didn't need to know that.

Lorenzo gave a smirk and shoved his hands back in his pockets. "Fine, I'll play along. Then you'll leave. Let bygones be bygones."

He was insane if he thought we'd leave him here to thrive and without the missing elves at that. I just glared at him but gave no answer to his proposal.

He snarled but began to speak anyway. "Misandre sought Martin out as a back-up for Joo-won. She wanted a powerful elf, and she wasn't sure Joo-won was really the type of elf that she wanted. I always knew he was a goodie-two-shoes." Lorenzo turned his terrifying stare to Joo-won.

As expected, Joo-won did not take the bait and instead waved his hand as if urging Lorenzo to continue.

"She also wanted an elf who could possibly take you out when things started to go south. That grew after you began to show interest in this one." He tilted his head towards me. He really hated to say my name. I suppose it made it easier to consider me food that way. Since his kind ate humans, typically deceased humans, he couldn't very well go around befriending his food source. I guess it made sense in a sick way.

I crossed my arms, thinking about what the ghoul was telling us. Misandre was smart. I never doubted that. Sure, I thought she mostly wanted me dead because I had distracted Joo-won from her, but she wasn't moved by her heart, she was too evil for that. She wanted me dead because it would put her in good favor with the ancient soulmates who wanted my friends and me gone. Power was her ultimate goal, and those soulmates could give it. Therefore, it made sense that she wouldn't blindly go into a relationship of any kind with Joo-won without a back-up plan if she couldn't get what she wanted, which was to marry Joo-won and connect their kingdoms, thus growing power.

When Joo-won stepped away from her, she reached out to Martin to continue her mission. What I couldn't confirm was what Martin got out of the deal. What was this access that she had? "So why did Martin agree to work with her?"

Lorenzo yawned. There was no way he was sleepy, so this was most likely a show of boredom to insult us. "She gave him the power he has that's made him stronger."

Now that was surprising. I knew Misandre was strong, but she was a water fae, giving powers didn't seem to be her specialty. Or was I wrong?

Joo-won tilted his head to the side, clasping his arms behind his back. I guess he wasn't concerned about not being ready to fight anymore. Well, more likely, he wanted Lorenzo to believe he'd let his guard down. "What did Martin give up to allow her to enchant him with such power? Misandre's magic would not let her give such an aid without assistance."

This was the smart question. We already knew Martin was no innocent. He hadn't turned a new leaf, seeking a life of repentance. He was still the same.

Lorenzo nodded as if he, too, understood the importance of that question. "He pledged his loyalty to her. For as long as she was alive, he promised to support her in whatever she did."

Well, that couldn't be right. If that was the case, then wouldn't Misandre have wanted Martin to fight in the soulmate war? Only he said he stayed out of it. No, there was something more that he had to do.

Joo-won shifted in his stance beside me, a restless energy starting to simmer. I think he was just as agitated as me. "What kind of support did that look like?"

"Fighting in any battles and raids she required. Including his people."

Huh, well then maybe Martin didn't lie. He just let us assume what he never said. He said he didn't go to battle against us all those months ago. He didn't say that he didn't allow his people to fight. The turd.

"She wanted you dead, Joo-won, and had planned to have Martin make that happen. It's only fortunate for you that she died before that could happen. Fortunate for me as well. She made a similar deal with me." He lifted his hands to his sides. "And look, even after her death, the power she gave us remains."

Misandre really had been a busy bitch.

"Her loss is very sad." The way Lorenzo said it was anything but sad. He seemed on the verge of laughing.

Yuri grumbled. "You don't sound so sad. Is this how evil mourns?"

Somehow Lorenzo's eyes grew even darker. They were like staring into the void. "Do you honestly think I liked that woman? She broke her promises time and time again. She wanted us just as her foot soldiers. She promised I could rule Hagerstown and then took it over herself."

None of what Lorenzo said was surprising. Honestly,

him even telling us her plans wasn't surprising. He'd joined forces with Misandre because he, too, wanted access. That and she killed lots of people, which gave him an easy food source. However, she never gave him the power he sought. I recalled that when they briefly took over Hagerstown during the time of the ancient soulmates returning, Lorenzo was caught off guard that Misandre proclaimed she was the new leader. Clearly, there was no love lost, although I was sure he wouldn't be this loose-lipped if Misandre was still alive.

Joo-won tilted his head back, observing Lorenzo with those ancient, emotionless eyes. He was thinking up something, and I'd be quiet and give him time. "You are lying about something."

Was he? I had no clue, but I was glad Joo-won could discern the truth. Except what was the lie?

Lorenzo raised a brow, a smirk on his thin lips. "Oh?"

"Yes, it makes no sense that your extra strength would remain after Misandre's death. The spell, good or bad, should always break upon the enchanter's demise." He squinted his eyes. "Unless these enhancements did not come from a spell. No, they came from an object. A bespelled object can remain full of magic even after the enchanter has passed."

Lorenzo's right eye twitched, but he said nothing. A tell? Was Joo-won on to something? "I don't know what you're talking about. It was just her magic. For all I thought of her, Misandre was indeed powerful."

Joo-won shook his head slowly. "Be that as it may, I have lived too many years to be fooled. You have an enchanted object in your possession that maintains your enhanced strength."

Joo-won said it with certainty, and I believed him. If this were true, that meant that Martin had an enchanted object too. And if we found said object, we could probably easily defeat him. Same for Lorenzo.

Lorenzo ran a long tongue over his razored front teeth looking all too nervous. Yup, Joo-won was right. "Think what you want. It ultimately doesn't matter how my powers grew. Just know that I am almost invincible. Even beheading me couldn't keep me down."

Sadly, this was true. I'd pretty much dismembered the guy, and Misandre just put him back together like Humpty Dumpty. You know how annoying it is to kill someone only for them to reappear? And this was the second time that had happened to me. The first time the guy came back and killed Charles. Fortunately, Misandre hadn't reappeared... yet. However, I was keeping my eye out for her even though I had burned her body and we'd spread her ashes in separate parts of the world. One could never be too cautious in the post-apocalypse.

Lorenzo seemed really satisfied with his point because now the nervousness was starting to wear off his face and be replaced with confidence. He put his hands on his waist and looked at us expectedly. "Sooo, now that you have your answers, leave us be."

Senna gave a snort. "There is no way we are leaving you alive here. You are a menace. Even hiding out here. I'm sure you and your people are coming in and out and causing death and destruction."

Lorenzo gave a slight raise of his shoulders, affirming her guess. "So am I to believe that you all are now do-gooders. That's a far cry from when I first met you."

While I was sure that was true, Joo-won and company had proven many times that they were truly idle observers to trouble. There was always a reason that served them for helping, but it sometimes felt like they had to do mental gymnastics to show that they weren't altruistic. Either way, I was glad for it.

I opened my mouth to respond, but Joo-won spoke up first. "Think what you want of us, but I do know that you and your ghouls will not stay in this forest forever. You are barely surviving, living in hiding in the middle of nowhere. I also know you well enough to realize that you will continue to see Lisa and her friends as threats. That you would wish to take them out or gain profit from their demise."

Lorenzo nodded, rubbing his chin. "There is a bounty on their heads in the underground. Killing her or any of them would be advantageous to me."

Wait, what? I had a bounty on my head? And I didn't know it? There was no way Erik didn't know this. He probably kept it from me like he did everything else so I could live close to normal. I glanced up at Joo-won. Did he know? He avoided my eyes, but I knew this wasn't a surprise based on his prior actions. It still felt weird to think anyone could see me as a threat. However, I was walking around talking about killing Lorenzo like I was some enforcer, so I guess it wasn't too surprising.

Lorenzo continued to talk. "However, the fact that I haven't attacked her should let you know that I am not going that route."

Yuri pfft, waving a hand at him as if shooing Lorenzo away. "You haven't attacked because you are weak. You are no more than a dog. Poodle."

Lorenzo growled and took a step towards us. From the darkness behind him, I saw humanoid shadows moving from behind trees. His ghouls. This was about to get ugly.

Joo-won raised a hand to pause the argument. Everyone stopped, including Lorenzo. The stillness in the air seemed to grow as we all watched Joo-won. He looked down at me, studying my eyes. What was he looking for? Did he want me to say whether we should fight or not? I hated fighting with a burning passion. I just wanted to take out Lorenzo and leave the whole battle as a final option.

He looked away from me and rolled his shoulders back. Did he read something in my eyes that would help him decide what we were doing? Hell, I didn't know for sure what we should do. "We leave," he said simply.

He then turned and headed towards where we had arrived. No one asked any questions, including Yuri and Senna. Joo-won was not a coward. He was not afraid of Lorenzo. If he didn't want to fight, there was a reason for that. However, now was not the time to ask.

The ghouls followed us as we headed out of the forest. They didn't attack, just hovered in the shadows, making sure we did what we said we were going to do. It was creepy as hell seeing them peek behind trees or jump above us from tree to tree. We couldn't even see the whites of their eyes because they had none, so they really looked like shadows unless they smiled. If we did see their teeth, they were glowing white points. I couldn't tell how many there were. We really had decimated a great number of Lorenzo's people in the soulmate wars, but still, it seemed like he had a good many followers with him.

Once we exited the forest back into the tall grass, Joo-won stopped walking. He turned back to the forest and dropped to his knees. What was he doing? He dug his fingers into the ground and closed his eyes. Was he trying to break the ward? Or perhaps seal them in? I didn't want to ask and give away his actions to the ghouls inside, not that I could see them anymore. Once we stepped outside of the forest, it just looked like more grass again, but I knew they were there, staring at us. I could feel their slithering aura.

"Until we get our people back, no one will get out of that forest," he announced.

Around me, other elves ran to the ward, forming a long chain around the now invisible forest. They were all on their knees, hands in the dirt as well. They had to be sealing them. Tall blue flames erupted from the ground they were touching, surrounding the enchanted forest. The flames were several stories high, yet the elves did not move. I soon heard several bumping sounds, like bodies slamming against walls. The forest flickered into view. It was very faint, almost transparent. Scenes of ghouls slamming against an invisible wall inside a dark forest shown back at us. Then those scenes would flicker out back into the grass and flames.

They're trapping the ghouls in the forest. The ghouls would die inside if they couldn't get out and cause no more harm. I was only slightly let down that I couldn't get rid of Lorenzo directly but just a tad.

The back of my neck tingled, and I spun around, narrowly missing claws to my face. Lorenzo.

I stumbled back on my butt and then quickly pushed my magic out, sending Lorenzo spinning in a magic wind. Joo-won raced past me and jumped into the air, his blue sword out. He swung his sword into the wind, but it blew him back. I dropped my magic, and Lorenzo fell to the ground, Joo-won following.

Quickly jumping to his feet, Lorenzo pulled out two long blades from what I presumed was his back holster and ran towards Joo-won, moving his sword in a windmill fashion. To my right, I noticed several ghouls running towards Joo-won. It seemed some of the ghouls had gotten out before the ward was completed. They weren't even looking at the other elves. Their aim was Joo-won. Smart.

I shot up and zapped them with my magic, and they fell back, only they didn't stay down. Ghouls weren't easy to kill. That was the annoying part. If you didn't decapitate them or stab them in the brain, they were a tough kill, much like vampires.

I brought down a bolt of lighting and directed it into the head of one of the ghouls. Instantly the bastard fell face forward. I turned to the next ghoul, but Senna had already decapitated it. But we weren't done. Several more were coming towards Joo-won again. They really had a singular mission.

Charles moved to my side, firing his guns until I heard no more sound. "Out of bullets."

I frowned. "Can't you conjure up some more?"

"I have a limit, woman. I already had to use a lot on those damn cicadas. It takes energy. But that's okay." He bared his fangs. "I got back up." He then moved away in a blur of vampiric movement.

Lorenzo sliced into Joo-won's sword arm. Blood spurted out, and I was sure he nicked an artery. Could elves bleed out? Joo-won seemed unaffected as he tossed the sword to his other hand and stabbed at Lorenzo again. Yuri jumped behind him and slashed his sword out at a ghoul who had taken a leap in the air to pounce on Joo-won.

I ran forward and pushed a barrage of magically conjured hail and heavy rain at several more ghouls aiming for Joo-won. The hail took out chunks of the ghouls, and the rain helped to slow their movement and obstruct their vision, even causing many to fall. However, it did not kill them. I hated that my magic wasn't exact. It did great for massive harm, but where you had to make it precise, it was a real pain.

However, I did do some help because it made it easier for the elves to quickly finish the injured ghouls off. I refocused my attention on Joo-won again. A ghoul had gotten through and latched his teeth onto Joo-won's new sword arm. Lorenzo quickly took that moment to bring down his blade, but I swiped my hand out to send him flying on his back.

Lorenzo immediately jumped up and sped towards me, faster than I could keep up with. I pushed my hail towards him, but something slammed into my side, knocking me to the ground. A male ghoul pinned me to the ground, smashing my face into the dirt. Earth crept into my mouth, and I struggled under his grasp, spitting out the dirt as I tried to move. This ghoul was like a bag of boulders, and I was too tiny to think my regular strength would do any good.

I radiated a heat over my body, conjuring my own sun-like rays. The ghoul screeched and jumped off of me.

"Lisa, move!" Joo-won shouted.

I turned to move from the unknown attack, but Joo-won appeared in front of me, pushing his hand back and sending a blast of light from his hand, demolishing several ghouls who were about to pounce on me. I guess they had separated their attack from just aiming for Joo-won to include me now.

However, Joo-won's impressive light show was new to me. "Have I seen you do this before?"

"No. I can only do it once in a while, and it takes much energy," he replied before pushing me to the ground from what could only be another attack.

Before I could complain, I looked up to see Yuri standing in front of Joo-won, his sword in Lorenzo's side. However, it wasn't his sword's placement that had my attention, it was Lorenzo's blade now sticking out of Yuri's chest.

Yuri ignored the blade and swung his sword for another attack. Lorenzo, who looked seriously injured, his body a canvas of blood and cuts, ducked to the side. Yuri stumbled forward, still moving as if he didn't notice the blade.

Joo-won held him steady, moving him to the side. With

his free hand, he pulsed out his power, hitting Lorenzo in the gut, only it didn't dematerialize the ghoul. Instead, there was a large hole in the center of his torso. Lorenzo hunched forward, hand over his stomach in shock.

It appeared Joo-won's special magic was running out of juice. I pelted Lorenzo with more hail, making my rocks larger than normal. He tried his best to dodge them, but he was moving slowly now due to his injuries. I was hoping I could enlarge the wound that Joo-won had already caused, but Lorenzo's movements weren't making it easy, even if they were slow. Fortunately, Senna had already taken a flying leap in the air and was currently dropping down towards Lorenzo, her sword high above her head. The ghoul looked up and moved but not fast enough to miss getting sliced in the shoulder by the blade, nearly tearing his arm off.

Lorenzo grabbed his dangling arm and took off in a blur of movement deep into the grassy maze, too fast to follow.

Senna took a step to follow but paused when we noticed Yuri dropped to his knees, his sword falling from his hands. His eyes were dazed, mouth slacked. He looked exhausted and even paler than usual, if that was possible. "We should go after him."

Joo-won hunched to Yuri's level, grabbing his friend by the shoulders before Yuri could fall forward with the blade still in his chest. Senna appeared in front of them, getting on her knees and laying Yuri's head on her lap. "Don't touch the blade," she shouted, eyes wide and shoulders raised. "It's in his heart."

Joo-won let go of Yuri's shoulders. He floated his hands over the blade, a visible strain in his face. I could see the veins in his neck popping as he gritted his teeth. He was trying to heal Yuri, but how could he do so with the blade still there. A sudden flashback to Charles hit me. What if it was poison?

"You can't heal him that way," I stated, walking over to them.

Joo-won closed his eyes. "I'm moving the sword very slightly and healing as I go. But my energy is low." He said the last part in barely a whisper, and I could feel the frustration emanating through him.

I hovered my hands beside him, and several other elves came over to do the same. The fighting around us had subsided, and we'd successfully defeated any ghouls free from the ward. Lorenzo was still M.I.A.

Senna let out a breath, running a comforting hand through Yuri's damp hair. He didn't look good, and his breathing was horse and short. "His dagger was poisoned. Even if you get it out, we have to cancel the poison."

"Shit," I heard Charles whisper behind me. "And idea what kind of poison?"

I had no doubt he was remembering his own attack from a poisoned blade. If this poison was from hell, the cure would not be simple. I knew from experience it wasn't something I could heal, so what I was doing was the equivalent of a band-aid over a gun-shot wound.

Senna rubbed at her cheeks with the back of her hand, lips pressed tight. "It's not one I know of."

Joo-won balled his hands into fists and growled. "It's from the underworld. The demon Alister gave us all poison as a gift when we were aligned under the original soulmates."

That would make sense. When Joo-won had been a follower of the evil first soulmates, he was considered one of their top commanders along with Misandre, Lorenzo and Alister. Only he and Lorenzo remained, but I wasn't surprised that Alister, a deceased king of the underworld, would have hell poison as a weapon. Alister had given it to another of our enemies who used it to try to kill Amina, killing Charles instead. How generous of that asshole to give such gifts to his cohorts, and now, long after his death, we were still dealing with those consequences.

Yuri opened his eyes, glancing over to Senna. He smiled, blood trickling from his lips. He didn't even look like he was in pain. It was as if the sight of her had numbed him. "I've always been in love with you."

Senna grabbed his hand, still stroking his hair. "Stop talking. You're going to be okay."

His lids drooped, but he kept the lazy smile. "When I first saw you, I thought you were a princess. So beautiful. So smart."

Even so wounded, he fought to remain alert and pour his heart out to her. It was gut-wrenching and beautiful.

Senna's eyes flooded with tears, and I could hear the slight sniffles under her breath. "Yuri."

"I know you don't love me in that way. But I just needed you to know. And to whoever you make a happy man, they better treat you well forever. Or I'll haunt them. I don't know how, but I will learn in the afterlife."

Senna chuckled, and now the tears were flowing down her cheeks in streams. I wasn't much different. I was practically hiccuping from emotion.

"Where is our king?"

Joo-won tapped his shoulder. "I'm here, friend."

Yuri turned his head away from Senna to look at Joo-won. "You are a good king. Thank you for helping me live a good life. I regret nothing. I've lived a long time. This is fine. I never thought I'd have a family. You made it so I did."

Joo-won looked up at the night sky, blinking his eyes rapidly as if to push back tears. "You are not just an excellent soldier and advisor; you are my best friend." He looked down again. "And that's why you aren't going to die today." He waved his hand over Yuri's body.

The elf closed his eyes, his body relaxing.

I narrowed my eyes, looking over the body, confused. He looked dead, but I could see a slight rise and fall of his chest. "What did you do?"

"I put him in a magic sleep. Sleep is healing. But this sleep will pause his injuries. We need to find someone who can fix him. This is not magic that is long-lasting."

Senna looked over to him with raised brows, hands still gripping Yuri tightly. "How much time do we have?"

"One week."

That was hardly enough time. "And if we don't find a cure by then?"

Joo-won didn't look at me, just down at his friend in his enchanted sleep. "Then he will die."

Charles moved behind me, closer to us. He ran a hand over his very tired-looking face. "Amina and Phillip are in a spelled sleep. There isn't a time limit. The original soulmates were under that spell for centuries."

Was he suggesting we put Yuri under that spell instead? It would certainly give us more time. "Can we do that? Put Yuri under the soulmate spell?"

Senna wiped at her face, shaking her head. "No. That spell was made for soulmates. It's not a one size fits all magic. While it's very strong, it's very specific. At least that's what I was told. We could try it, but I wouldn't rely on the extra time."

I looked to Charles. "What about making him a vampire?"

"It cancels out on certain paranormals like elves. It won't work."

Joo-won finally looked up, and I could see that his eyes were bloodshot. I knew he cared about his people, and Yuri was his closest friend, but to see the emotion still devastated me. He was not a hard man. He had heart. "Wake Amina and Phillip up."

I froze. I knew why he would suggest this idea, but we'd already established that it was cruel to wake up the pair any time we had a problem. Plus, we really didn't know what kind of problems that could start. Amina wanted to be put to sleep for a reason. She knew that she was at a high risk of becoming dangerous, just like the original soulmates.

Charles dropped his shoulders, giving Joo-won sympathetic eyes. "I'm sorry, man, but we can't wake my sister up. We promised we wouldn't. We have to find another way."

Joo-won looked unrelenting, his eyes darkening. "This is an emergency."

Charles put his hands out in front of him in surrender. "I'm not trying to be cruel, but there are a lot of emergencies out there. Once we open up that door, it doesn't close. And I'm not going to make my sister some type of workhorse we wake up to do something and then put back to sleep."

"Then leave her awake."

Did Joo-won really not understand the risk? He was there when Amina and Phillip had used their magic to heal a whole town of sick and injured people in one go. Therefore, it was understandable why he believed that they could heal Yuri. However, they had not been there when Amina had bespelled her own brother against his will. She knew her mind was darkening, and Phillip already had his internal battle with good and evil. It had scared them both. The original soulmates started off as helpful and kind, and then it mutated. The same would happen to Amina and Phillip, and they wanted to sleep until we found a way to change their powers and make them less susceptible to wanting to control the world. Therefore, we could absolutely not leave her awake. And we would not use her either.

Joo-won tilted his head, studying us both. "Wake one of them up."

I sighed, touching his shoulder in an attempt to comfort him, although I knew it wouldn't help. I knew nothing would outside of doing what he wanted. "We barely know for sure if the two of them could stop this poison. One of them is highly doubtful. Together, they couldn't stop Charles' hell poison."

"They are stronger than they were then."

I bit my lip, looking down at Yuri which was a mistake because that peaceful face only squeezed my heart tighter. Yuri, who looked cold and emotionless, was actually the heart of the group. We couldn't let him die. However, I knew for certain that Erik wouldn't allow us to wake Amina up. Even Phillip would be problematic. There had to be other options. We knew powerful people. Maybe I could help with the aid of the rest of The Six. We weren't whole, but we still had strength together.

Then a thought popped into my mind. Felix, another Six member, was half angel, half demon, and his girlfriend, Fran, was also half demon, who had access to the under-world. I looked to Charles, a rush of urgency pulsing through me. "We ask Fran and Felix for help. If this is a hell poison, then they can certainly get access to a cure. Let's try that first. We can save him without touching the soulmates."

Joo-won gave a curt nod. "Fine. If it doesn't work, then we wake the soulmates."

He said it so matter-of-factly as if he had the power here. But he didn't. None of us did, and I was afraid to see what would happen if my idea failed.

CHAPTER 22

I won't drag this out because it was a real letdown. Despite Fran and Felix's best efforts, they were unable to cure Yuri. It turns out the hell poison was not fully from hell. Fran determined that it was probably conjured from another realm. My knowledge of the realms was not vast. I knew of the fae realm. Then there was the realm of the angels, the realm of the demons and underworld, the realm of certain gods. Our human realm. But who knew how deep the rabbit hole went? Where the hell had Lorenzo gotten this stuff? We had to find him.

Once my plan failed, Joo-won went M.I.A except for continued visits at the hospital to convince Erik to wake up the soulmates. He had his elves on standby there 24 hours a day. I reached out to Senna to get some updates, and she visited me in my apartment.

She sat at my dining room table, and I passed her a cup of tea, sitting down across from her. "How's he doing?"

Senna shook her head slowly, lips pressed together. "He's broken. He barely sees anyone."

I'd tried to visit with him several times, but he kept

saying he was busy. He was pushing me away, and it hurt like hell. "Why is he pushing us away?"

"Tomorrow, our friend will die. We are running out of hope. He hates to appear weak. And he really is trying to find a cure for Yuri. He's obsessed. That I can understand." She twisted her hands together, looking unsure, which was not a common look for Senna. "I feel like I never truly appreciated Yuri like I should. I feel bad I never returned his feelings for me."

While I could sympathize with her, she didn't owe Yuri her love. Her feelings, or lack thereof, were valid. "Don't let guilt be the guide for your heart. Just because you weren't romantically in love with him doesn't mean you treated him horribly. You cared about him as a friend, and he knew that. He knew the love you had for him."

Senna gave me an absentminded nod, and I was pretty sure she wasn't ready to receive what I was telling her. "We need to find Lorenzo and get the cure."

"What about Martin? Was he any help?"

"None at all. He claims he doesn't know where Lorenzo is now, and nothing he tried for Yuri helped, although he claimed to be tapping all his resources."

"Do you believe him?"

Senna cut her eyes at me. "Absolutely not. I think you guys have been playing a dangerous game with him."

I knew that. My gut was screaming that I could not let my guard down around Martin. But still, he had led us to Lorenzo. "So, what is there left to do? Do we have any leads?"

"No. Although Martin claims he will work his connections. We have other associates looking, especially in other ghoul communities."

"What about the surviving ghouls that were still trapped in that enchanted forest?"

"We have guards on the area day and night, but none of them will turn on their boss, not even in exchange for their freedom. We tried to coerce them to talk when we went in to find our people. We retrieved them, although not all survived. The ghouls are either very scared of Lorenzo or we haven't offered the right incentive."

Freedom seemed like the best incentive to me. What else would be better? "Aren't they on borrowed time? They should be running out of food and air from the smoke of the fire?"

Senna nodded, her eyes looking weary. "Yeah, ghouls can go long periods of time without food and air. We think they are just stalling until the last minute. Once things get dire, they will turn on Lorenzo. However, it will be too late for Yuri to rely on that."

She grasped my hand, a desperate look in her eyes that was very unlike her. I understood it. "Can you try convincing Erik again to wake her up?"

I had been trying. We all had. "I haven't stopped. I got Charles, Faith and Felix on my side to help, but we need Erik. He won't do it. With persistence, it's possible we can wear him down, but it's been six days, and he still won't budge."

"This is our last viable option. Joo-won might take drastic measures to make it happen."

That sounded ominous. "What do you mean by drastic."

"They are already at the hospital. It will get violent. He's been putting it off because we are all friends, but with tomorrow as the last day, he'd start a war to make Erik wake Amina up."

I moved my hand away from her, an icy cold stabbing my spine. "The elves aren't at the hospital in case Erik changes his mind. They are there in position to fight, aren't they?"

Senna furrowed her brows and looked towards my window. "He is desperate."

"It will not end well for him. He has to know that. I should talk to him."

She gave a quick shake of her head. "He won't talk to you. He's kept his distance from you on purpose. You won't change his mind. Focus on changing Erik's."

I had one day left to reason with a stubborn werejackal, or we'd be opening the town up to another battle. Negotiation was never my strong point. This was bad.

~

*E*rik was annoyingly stubborn. Like, I was beginning to hate him. He was confusing his love of Amina with illogical actions. And I was so scared of what Joo-won would do, I didn't even leave the hospital. I just stayed in the waiting area with the elves, keeping an eye on them, Charles at my side.

Joo-won refused to even acknowledge my presence, and every time I or any of us neared him, a gang of elves stood in our way. How was I going to convince this stubborn elf that this was not the way to go? Today was our last day to save Yuri, so I understood his desperation. However, if Erik's pack members showed up, it was going to turn into a full-on shit show. And it wasn't as if I didn't understand Joo-won's position. He'd helped us in the soulmate battle. As allies, we owed giving our all to help him, didn't we? Then again, there had to be a limit. Erik was very protective of Amina. He'd be pissed Joo-won was here causing a commotion related to Amina, and he had already clearly said he was not going to wake her up. Intimidation would not work on Erik.

That day, the elves were very much alert. They had not shown weapons, but we knew they were on them, probably cloaked in an invisibility spell. Joo-won was M.I.A., but I had a good feeling that when he showed today, the fighting would begin. His back was against the wall.

I walked to a vending machine to grab something to drink. My voice was hoarse from my pointless reasoning.

Erik walked to my side, arms crossed and face set on scowl. I was already flinching before he spoke. It would not be good. "Get your goddam boyfriend and his entourage out of here, or I will throw them all in jail."

I scrunched my face and barred my teeth to steel myself for a response. "I don't think you have jurisdiction over them to do that."

He glared down at me, as I expected. His eyes were angry enough to bore a hole through my cranium. "Do I care?"

"Clearly not. And who wants fighting in a hospital?" I rubbed my forehead. "Honestly, I don't know what to do."

"You teleport him and his people out of here, and after that, I'm making sure he's warded from our town. And if he thinks I don't know he's planning to start a fight, he's wrong. My pack is right here. We'll drag them out of this building and make it so they can't fight again."

I sucked in a breath. I knew he wasn't lying. Erik was usually the kick ass now, talk later kind of guy. I also knew he had reached his patience limit with Joo-won. He was actually being a bit accommodating by letting them stay in the hospital this long. That made me think that there was some hope of him changing his mind. "Look, Erik–"

He growled and looked away. "No."

I huffed. "You didn't even hear what I had to say."

"I already know. I've told you no before. Nothing's changed."

I scratched my scalp in frustration. He really was so stubborn. "That is not what Amina would want."

"You know her better than me, now?"

Before I could respond, I felt a hand on my shoulder. I looked up and saw Charles standing there, looking over at the elves with pity. "No, but I do."

Erik raised a brow, face still set in angry mode. "What are you saying, Charles?"

"I'm saying my sister is and has always been a helper. For better or worse. If we let Yuri die without trying everything we can and she wakes up and finds we didn't try to get her help, she'd be pissed."

Erik closed his eyes and rubbed his forehead. "Charles, where is the limit? She can't help everyone. Including all our allies."

Charles leaned against the wall, turning towards Erik. "Yuri's a friend. Not just an ally. We break the rules sometimes. And it's not always fair. It'll piss people off, and we'll just deal with that. Plus, I'd like to see my sister. Wouldn't you want to spend a day with her?"

Erik hung his head, taking in a deep breath. He was pondering Charles' words. This was way further than I'd gotten with all my convincing. Would Erik really give in? Could we even do this without him? "You won't let this go, will you?"

We shook our heads. I put my hands in front of me in a pleading motion. "This is his last day. And I don't want war because we were too selfish to help a close friend. That's not who we are. The Six help."

He glared at the both of us, lips pressed tightly together. "Fine," he said and then walked away.

That was it? That's all he was giving us? "I didn't expect him to cave in that quickly."

Charles patted my back. "No one wants war. And I think he does want to see her again. He was just too selfless to admit it. I don't blame him."

No, I couldn't either.

~

*W*e'd come together, even Felix and Faith. Blake, Phillip's vampire consort, also showed up. There was an electric excitement in the air. We all wanted to see the new soulmates again. Even if for one day. There was plenty good in them both when we'd put them to sleep. One day for them to be awake really wasn't a huge risk. In fact, maybe we could do this every month until we found a cure. Perhaps that was pushing it, but I wanted to see my friend again.

We recited the awakening spell. Several times.

It didn't work.

It wasn't us. Our magic was strong. I thought that maybe the spell itself was no good. Either it was inherently bad or just weak. We'd put a powerful spell on Phillip and Amina to have them sleep, so it was possible the awakening spell we possessed wasn't strong enough. Although we were told it would do the trick. There was only one other option. The spell was good, but Phillip and Amina were refusing to wake up.

When I'd told Senna of our lack of success, she'd proposed that as a possible rationale. We had herded the elves in a vacant hospital room while we attempted to wake up the soulmates, and after our failure, I'd dragged myself to the room to give them the bad news.

However, when I arrived, it was only Senna there, sitting in a chair by the window. When she turned to me, I could see that her electric green eyes were now dull, dark circles shadowing them. Her face was tear-streaked, and I could only imagine how long she'd been crying. "I had a fear that might happen. They asked to be put asleep, after all. Of course they wouldn't want to be woken up," her voice was hoarse, unsurprisingly.

I dabbed at tears in my eyes. I'd started crying after the third recital of the spell. We all did. There was some peace in knowing we could always wake them if we needed to. Now, we didn't even have that power. It was like they were really gone. I could barely breathe thinking of that horrible fact. I pounded at my chest with my fist slowly to push away my pain. "You think they're ignoring us?"

She let out a cough to clear her throat before responding. "It might not be purposeful. They are in a dream state. It might be their subconscious that is ignoring you. Or they could need a navigator. A trusted friend to enter their dream and tell them it's okay to wake up."

I dropped my shoulders, feeling totally helpless. Everyone we knew who could dream walk was either asleep or dead. Erik had communicated with Amina in a dream once, but that was when she wasn't in a magical sleep, and it never happened again. If Erik could enter her mind now, he would have told us. "What do we do? If we do find a cure to break them of the evil that being a soulmate causes, how can we wake them up to let them know? How would we ever convince them? What do we do?"

Senna stood up, her movement slow and almost pained. I hurt just looking at her. "It doesn't matter anymore, Lisa."

I frowned in confusion. We couldn't give up. We had to fight until the very last moment. This was unlike Senna. Where was Joo-won? He wouldn't give up. "How can you say that, Senna?"

She wiped both hands over her face, a movement of pure exhaustion. "Because he's dead. He just died. Our clock ran out and the poison took hold immediately. But thank you for trying." She pushed her hand out, and a portal appeared. She stepped through it wordlessly.

I stumbled to the side, a wave of nausea passing over me. This couldn't be happening. He couldn't be dead. I thought of Yuri's face. He was stoic but sometimes awkward. Intimidating but a romantic at heart. I thought about our time together in New Orleans. I enjoyed shopping with him and hearing stories of his life. And that memory did it. The flood of tears poured down my cheeks, and they wouldn't stop. I pounded my chest with my fist to beat away the growing pain in my heart. However, it didn't work. I felt sick, and my breath came short.

How could I lose yet another person in my life? Just as I was beginning to bond with him. It was cruel.

~

When I was able to make my mind and body work again, I immediately thought of Joo-won and teleported to his hotel. I could only imagine what he must be feeling. However, Joo-won wasn't in his suite when I arrived at the hotel, but I did find him in his office, another repurposed hotel room. I expected him to be at his desk, but instead, he was sitting on the floor, his back to the left side of the clear table. He had one long leg stretched out and the other bent, an arm balanced on the knee. His head hung to his chest, and his normally perfect hair was tousled.

"I asked not to be disturbed," he said in a low growl.

I didn't say anything as I walked over to him. I got on my knees and wrapped my arms around him in a hug, resting his head against my chest.

I felt him sigh in my arms. "Why are you here?" His voice sounded quiet and fragile, and part of my heart cracked.

"I just heard about Yuri. I'm so sorry."

He shifted so that he could wrap his arms around my waist, his head still laying on my chest. I stroked my hand through his hair, and we stayed like that with no words for a minute.

Finally, he began to speak. "I'm not alright."

I lifted my head and looked down at him. He was such a solid, strong man, and for him to admit this just made me admire him more. We all knew he wasn't alright, but he'd been trying to push us away so we wouldn't see. He needed us, and there was nothing wrong with that. "You don't need to be, Joo-won. You don't need to be."

"I let him down," he began, almost robotically as if he was trying to erase any emotion from his voice. "I was not the king that he believed in. I am not strong enough to protect them anymore. They should not follow me."

Well, that I refused to believe. His power lessoning did not make him an unworthy king. I grabbed his face and tilted it up towards me. "Who told you that your ability to be a great king had anything to do with your powers? Great leaders aren't the strongest. That's what they have soldiers for. They don't even have to be the wisest. That's what they have a counsel surrounding them for. But they must be the most thoughtful, and you are. You've made decisions that ended up saving your people from those ruthless original soulmates. And when we were fighting Lorenzo and his ghouls, none of your people died. Yes, many were injured, but they lived because you trained your people to be strong. What makes your kingdom so impressive is because of how you lead. Never doubt that."

Joo-won looked up at me with bloodshot eyes, but even with those tired eyes, I could see what looked like admiration. I had never had anyone look at me like that. In that moment, he looked both vulnerable, strong and beautiful, and I wanted all of it.

Before I could do anything, he moved me to his lap and kissed me deeply. The heat of his mouth pressed against me, sucking on my tongue, gently biting my lips until I felt them swell with passion. I thought I would suffocate, and I didn't care. My stomach clenched from his need, my need, our need. His hands were in my hair, fingers brushed against my scalp to bring me closer to him.

He moved his lips from mine momentarily to kiss my nose, my chin, my jaw, my neck and collar bone. "You are my heart. Do you know that?" he whispered.

I melted at each press of his lips, at the heat from his hands on my back. I was so very tired of fighting my feelings for him. I wanted this man. I wanted the love he was offering. And who was I kidding? I'd fallen for this man so long ago it was comical to keep fighting it. If I'd learn nothing from Yuri, it was to live your truth with no regrets.

"I love you. I love you. I love you." I kept repeating it because my heart felt so full. I wanted him. I wanted nothing else. I had to feel him. I yanked at the end of his black t-shirt and pulled it up, exposing his defined stomach. I ran my hands over his hard abs, his skin flushed with heat.

He suddenly paused and tilted my chin to look at him. He searched my eyes with his own now sparkling ones, saying nothing. However, I knew what he wanted to know without him saying it. He wanted to know if I was sure, and I was. He was a patient man when it came to me, and I knew he'd be fine with waiting longer. But I was sure of him. I was ready. My heart was ready.

I nodded, and he tapped his forehead against mine, and I felt him raise his hand to push out another portal. I knew he wanted to take us to his suite, but I didn't want to move. I wanted him right now, right there. I lowered his hand, and he moved his head back. He cocked a brow with a quizzical look, but there must have been something in my eyes because his own darkened and became all too serious to match the fire of lust in my own.

He closed his portal before lowering me down gently on the carpeted floor. He took his shirt off and then put it behind my head like a pillow. He then moved between my legs, balancing over me on his hands. He leaned down and kissed me again, sucking on my lower lip, which pulled a moan from me. It was like his lips had a direct line to my lower regions. It was insane. As he continued to kiss me, his hands moved up my ribcage until they reached the underside of my breasts. He slowed his movement, as if waiting for permission, but I had no time for that. I arched my back into his hands, and he moved until he was covering my breasts, circling his palm flat against my nipples.

My eyes fluttered against the touch of his mouth and hands, and I lifted up to grind against his slacks, feeling him already alert. He groaned, and that only turned me on more. I circled my hips, frustrated by the amount of clothes we both had on but not wanting him to pull away from all that he was doing.

He grabbed me by my hips, removing his hand from my breast and gave me a glazed stare. Again, I didn't need words to understand that look. If I kept doing what I was doing, the party would not last as long as I hoped. "I can go again all night, but let's not have the first time go that way, butterfly," he said in a thick voice.

I laughed before lifting my hand towards the ceiling in a fist. In an instant, our clothes disappeared through my magic, and I heard him curse as the wetness of my center rubbed over him. I couldn't recall if this was the first time I'd heard him curse. It pleased me. "I'm sorry. Let's save sweet and slow for the next time."

He chuckled before lowering his mouth on one of my exposed nipples, ripping the breath out of me. He twirled his tongue expertly, giving attention to both breasts. My cries filled the silence of the room, my core flooding more. I felt his hands move between us until he was touching me, sending pleasure to my already sensitive nature.

I lifted my head off the floor and looked at him, my eyes blurry with need. "No more waiting."

He gave me a pained look like those were the words he had been waiting to hear for far too long. He then pulled back and entered me. I screamed and dropped my head back to the ground as he continued to move over me with strokes of differing speeds and pressure. It was inhuman. And yes, I knew he wasn't human, but still, I was so amazed. He seemed to hit every sensitive area in me all at once. I moved to suck on the tip of his pointed earlobe, and that set him off as he moved deeper into me. I shut my eyes and wrapped my legs around his waist, trying to match his pushes. He would move impossibly fast and then slow it down at just the right moment.

I soon exploded, reaching my peak. My breath exited me, but he continued, hands caressing me, mouth licking and sucking. I felt like my body was floating. My back itched, but I ignored it, too overcome by my current state of pleasure. Moments later, he cried out, quickening his pace, hips pounding against mine until the movement brought me over again.

He slowed to a gentle lazy pace but did not retreat. He kissed me on the lips again then pulled back with a smile. He looked way too happy in that moment, and I was satisfied that I could bring him this break of peace. "Why are you smiling so hard?"

He looked up over my head. "If you wanted to make love standing up, you could have asked, butterfly."

I squinted my eyes. What was he talking about? And then I looked behind him. Something was off. The room was not right. Things weren't where they should be and were suspended at odd angles. No, wait a minute. I looked slightly behind me. My back was no longer on the carpet, it was against the wall. We were suspended in the air against a wall in the room. And, were those wings? They were large and iridescent. I reached behind me and felt the wings. They were surprisingly tough with ridges, making what felt like circular patterns in the wings. I'd have to get Joo-won to take a picture of them. "I did this?"

Joo-won nodded and kissed my cheek. "We were flying at one point. Elves don't have that ability. Plus, the wings."

I hadn't even felt them come out. Or was that the itch I was ignoring? "Why didn't you say anything?"

He brushed my hair from my face, truly unbothered that we were hanging off the wall like some work of art. "Why would I ruin the moment?"

He had a point there. No need in me freaking out, which I would have. It was actually cool. I was finally a flying faerie like in all the fairytale books. My mind began to ponder all the branding I could do with my wings. Wait, would these things go away? Would I have to design clothes with wing cutouts? Maybe I should anyway. There were a lot of beings who could use them.

Joo-won waved a hand in front of my face. "Did I lose you?"

Yes, yes, he did, but I could refocus. I gave him a mischievous grin. "Well, now that I know I can do this. We should try it again."

He chuckled softly, and I was overjoyed to see him smile. "What position do you want, my love?"

I winked at him. "All of them."

This brought out more laughter from him. "Your wish is my command."

~

y legs were now made of rubber, I was sure of it. And these rubber legs had to take me to the bathroom. It was the middle of the night. I had no clue what time. Joo-won and I had made love countless times, taken a break for food, talked mostly about Yuri, and then went back to making love. I loved it, and now I was spoiled for life. Yet, still, a girl had biological needs, and I had to unhook my body from his.

We were now on his bed, and I rolled to the edge, shivering. He pulled me back to him with a grumble. I didn't want to leave him. I knew he was still suffering, he'd been restless in his sleep, but I would only be gone a few minutes. I leaned back and kissed him on the lips, and the frown on his mouth relaxed. "Be right back."

I plucked his t-shirt from the floor and threw it on before scurrying to the bathroom on said rubber legs. Luckily my wings did retreat. I then practiced pushing them in and out between lovemaking breaks. I was so going to fly everywhere now just for show.

Once nature's call was answered, I washed my hands, already mentally back in the bed entwined with him again. It seemed suspicious to feel this darn giddy.

So of course, when I opened the door to find that I was no longer facing Joo-won's bedroom but rather a sparse, deep red painted room with floating fireballs of light around the walls, I would have loved to say I was surprised. However, I wasn't.

Shit.

I tried to slam the door shut, but a hand stopped it and forcefully pushed it back, sending me stumbling on my bare butt. I backed away in horror as a man stepped into the bathroom.

Lorenzo.

CHAPTER 23

I pushed out my magic, but he slid to the side, missing my electrocution. He tsk-tsked. "Too slow." He raced towards me, and I began to teleport, however, his cold hand wrapped around my ankle and dragged me forward, breaking my teleportation magic.

He was fast, so very fast. My bare skin scraped against the cold tile floor, and my body buzzed in what felt like a static shock as I went across the threshold into the room that was not Joo-won's suite. I zapped my hands out again before I made it all the way over, and Lorenzo shook but held tightly to me. He should have been burning. What was the deal?

He kept dragging me back to me as I cleared the space into the room. "I'm on to you now and got myself warded for an even longer period of time. It was worth the extra expense. You can't hurt me."

Oh, I would hurt him. My magic wasn't weak. I would just have to break down his ward, but it would take more than a minute, and I was now on the other side. He let go of me, and I kicked him in the back of the leg before crawling back to the bathroom, but it was already gone when I turned. Now, instead of a bathroom, I was facing a closed door. I got to my feet and yanked it open. No bathroom. Only a darkened hallway. I decided I'd take my chances, and I moved to exit, slapping against an invisible wall.

Of course, I was trapped.

A cold wind slapped against my bare legs, and I was reminded that I was naked under this flimsy piece of clothing. I ran my hands over my body, covering myself with jeans, a shirt and sneakers.

I heard Lorenzo walk closer to me. "Aww, I thought I'd get a show."

I spun around, striking out against him. "You piece of rotting shit."

He shook against my magic, but still, he didn't get crispy. I pelted him with hail. He lifted his arms over his face and stumbled back but appeared unharmed. Still, that didn't mean that I wasn't harming him.

I conjured a monsoon wrapping him in wind and water. He began to move towards me again, but it was slow, as if he were walking through thick mud. I could see his hair getting wet. Someone's ward was weakening. I turned my back on him and focused on the ward at the door.

Whose place was this? Ghouls didn't have magic other than their strength and speed. Who was helping him? I placed my hands against the translucent wall of magic and focused my remaining energy on the ward, ensuring that my weather magic was still pelting away at Lorenzo.

"You fucking bitch!" he screeched.

I added pelts of ice to the monsoon. His ward would have to crack soon.

I went back to focusing on the other ward and kept pushing my remaining strength into this one. I could only hope it wasn't super strong. I figured if a ward was going to be put up, the best one would surround the building or even a place of imprisonment. This was just what appeared to be a den with only a TV, couch, coffee table and bookshelves.

"I will rip your heart out and eat it while you are alive!" Lorenzo screamed behind me. He sounded closer. That meant he was still moving through my magical storm. I had to get out of here fast before he made good on that threat. "You think that just getting out of this room is enough? You have no idea where you are or what you're up against."

I knew what I was up against now, and I had no interest in dealing with him. I had to get the hell out of wherever this was.

I felt the brush of fingers against my back, and I turned slightly, seeing Lorenzo way too close for comfort. Crap. I looked back at the ward and strained again until my hands suddenly pushed through the wall like it was made of play doh.

I moved through the ward and the unpleasant feeling of the imaginary play doh. It was suffocating. I felt like my face and body were being smushed and squashed. However, it didn't last long, and I was soon on the other side. I raised up another ward to trap Lorenzo in. I then tried to teleport and...nothing. Dang it, of course, my tele-portation magic wouldn't work here. That would be too easy. I guess I'd have to get out of there the old-fashioned way.

I and took off down the dark hall having no idea where I was going. I was just moving by my gut at this point. I tossed a small ball of sunshine in front of me to light my path. I knew it gave my location away, but I could barely see my hand in front of me. I was underground in some sort of windowless hallway and just dark gray cement walls. A basement, most likely, but despite the den I just existed, I couldn't say I was in a house. It could have been an office building, and I was in the warehouse part.

A loud moan broke my thoughts. It sounded like a hurt gorilla. The noise grew louder, so clearly, I was heading towards it. I looked behind me. Maybe the other direction was better. It was just as pitch black, but it was also back towards Lorenzo, and I really didn't want to run into him. I took a hesitant step forward and was greeted by another moan. This time multiple ones. They all sounded like animals, and they all sounded very unhappy.

Was there some kind of zoo in here? I thought I heard birds, crickets, squeaks. Was that a lion?

I turned the corner to my right and paused as I faced another corridor. This time I could see cages on either side. Still no windows, but there were floating orbs of light and a very unpleasant barnyard smell. I covered my nose and mouth and walked forward. I looked to my right in one of the first cages and stifled a scream. What sat in the cage was like nothing I'd ever seen before. It was a gorilla but also a lizard? It was the size of a normal gorilla, but it was covered in hard, bumpy scales. The eyes were very-lizard like and... very sad. The creature looked at me, and a very lizard tongue shot out. Then it recoiled and turned around in its pile of hay, resting.

I looked to the cage across from me and saw what could only be described as a flying tarantula. This time I did scream. The thing was huge. The size of a dining room table and it had translucent wings. It fluttered back and forth in its cell, and I ran past it. Another cell, this time filled with a large tank of water and some sort of giant eel and snake combination. Still another cell with a horse and hawk hybrid. And another with an ant head and body of a rat. Also, very large.

The whole room was filled with giant hybrid animals. This

was nightmarish and sad. I was never a big animal person, but I didn't want them hurt either. I used to always hate going to the zoo because I found the whole thing depressing. The poor animals were drugged up and locked in these confined spaces, some all alone. It looked boring and lonely. It always gave me an unsettling feeling. I felt the same now. None of the animals looked aggressive. They weren't clawing out at me. In fact, many of them sounded like they were whining.

"Who did this to you?" I asked, not expecting any kind of answer. I needed to get the hell out of here, but I also would feel like a jerk if I left these creatures locked up like this. Not that I was excited about unleashing a flying spider, and I did not want to touch that giant eel thing to take it to the ocean or wherever it came from. I would need help. I couldn't do this alone.

Then again, I couldn't leave either. The thought hit me like lead. Lorenzo had to be stopped. He'd killed Yuri and so many others. I needed to finish the ghoul off once and for all. I was always running from something. Maybe it was time to run towards something. I was strong. Lorenzo didn't seem to fear me. He easily called me food. I didn't appear to be a threat to him, yet I knew I wasn't someone to easily be defeated. I'd been kidnapped so many times. Had beings literally try to eat me alive several times. I was not prey. I needed to stop acting like it. I didn't want to keep waiting until my back was against the wall to fight or love anymore.

I took in a deep breath. It was time to take control. I spun around and headed back out of the corridor. It was time to off Lorenzo. Then I'd get the hell out of here and get some backup to set these creatures free. Well, most of them. I was seriously concerned about that flying tarantula. It might need to stay where it was.

A shadow appeared at the end of the corridor, and I

steeled myself, ready for a fight. It looked like the outline of a man, but I couldn't tell if it was Lorenzo. I'd expected to see those glowing sharp teeth. There wasn't a way out behind me, so I was cornered. Just what I didn't want. Just when a girl was ready to bring the fight, the fight came to me.

Only it wasn't Lorenzo who appeared.

It was Martin.

I narrowed my eyes. What was he doing here? This was no coincidence. He had clearly lied to us about still maintaining contact with Lorenzo all this time.

He gave me what appeared to be a sympathetic smile, shrugging. "I'm sorry you're here, Lisa. Lorenzo is not a smart fellow."

I was not buying his friendly act. "What are you doing here? Let me guess, is this your lair?"

He chuckled. "Lair. You make me sound like some comic book villain."

I didn't think I was too far off. I didn't answer him and instead just gave him a hard stare.

He bowed his head. "Yes, this is my building. This area is my...community. I regret ever letting Lorenzo know where I stayed." He tossed a hand out. "But we were supposed to be allies, so what can you do?"

I looked around the room. "What kind of foolishness are you up to here?"

"Just entertaining some hobbies."

Hobbies? Harming animals was a hobby to him? I sighed, still perturbed by my disappointment. He'd stayed true to his character, I wasn't fooled, but I was still conflicted. I wanted so much for him to be someone we could rehabilitate. Especially with Yuri gone. However, I knew for certain that wouldn't happen now. "This is a sick hobby. Now I understand why you never invited us over. Why do this?"

Martin walked further in, ignoring the creatures. "I can see the disappointment in your eyes. You don't approve."

"You're hurting these animals."

He looked around at them, eyes unperturbed. "I am improving them."

I snorted, placing my hands on my hips. He really was full of shit. There was no way I believed him. "Except for that spider, they were all fine to begin with. Just the way nature intended. You are destroying them. How'd you even do this, to begin with? I thought you only had magic over rodents and insects."

He reached a hand out to me, his face now a mask of remorse. "Please, let's talk somewhere else."

"No."

He lowered his hand. "I do hate that I've disappointed you. That brings me no joy. Very well, my magic has increased. I might have been a bit less than forthcoming on just how much I've been enhanced by Misandre's magic. I can control all animals."

I squinted my eyes, knowing he wouldn't tell me everything, so I would put together the rest of the pieces. "You do more than control them. You also manipulate their bodies. Maybe even conjure them. When we were in that enchanted forest, we were attacked by giant cicadas. Was that you?"

He raised his hands in surrender. "I'm sorry, beautiful. I had gifted Lorenzo those well before I met you."

"Right. And you didn't think to warn us?"

He lowered his head, and his long hair fell over part of his face, leaving one eye uncovered. "You didn't tell me you'd found him, which I was also hurt by. But you knew it wouldn't be easy getting to him. And you won. No one got hurt – well, almost no one. Poor Yuri. He was a good man.

How about you teleport back to Joo-won, who I am sure is going crazy with you gone, ma cherie."

There was an urgency to his voice that made me wonder if he really wanted to just get rid of me. Which, of course, made me suspicious. I touched the emerald pendant around my neck. If Martin was saying I could teleport out, then the ward blocking me from earlier had to be down. That also meant that I could get Joo-won here. Backup would be nice. I touched my invisible tattooed wrist for good measure. Having a connection to him wasn't so bad, and if that failed, I could tap into my telepathy with members of The Six. In the meantime, I was going to get to the bottom of what this elf was really up to.

"There's something I don't understand, Martin."

He cocked a brow, expectantly. "Yes, what is it?"

"These creatures aren't here just for your amusement. That would be a waste. No, you want to send them out to the world to help cause trouble. Giving those gross bugs to Lorenzo was the start of something. You're making these things and then giving them to people to cause destruction to anything orderly. You brought those rodents to Manhattan."

He walked towards me slowly. "You surprise me. You're much more than a pretty face. I'm really beginning to understand why Joo-won has fallen in love with you. How entertaining." He rubbed his chin, squinting at me in study. "Yes, I assisted that rat pack. At a high price. I don't gift my hard work away. Profits must be made. In that case, they wanted some enhanced rodents to help them in their dispute with that vampire's town. It was just an unfortunate coincidence that you were there."

"And you just had to help the bad guys. You're like an illegal arms dealer or something."

I didn't move from him as he came to face me. I would not run in fear. I was powerful too.

He reached a hand up to me, eyes still deceptively sorrowful. He touched my cheek with his palm, lips slightly upturned. "I'm just trying to survive."

I frowned, hating that instead of fear, I found the touch of him welcoming. Why was my mind so resistant to hating him? Was it magic, or was I that taken with him?

I grabbed his hand but did not move it away. "There are other ways."

He bit his lip. "I like my way. Ah, the look on your face breaks my heart. How can I make it up to you?"

Did he really care about my opinion? At this stage, what was the need to keep up the phony friend act? I wondered how far I could push him. "Where is Lorenzo's power object? Since you're such best friends, he would have told you, right?"

"You think you would be able to defeat him?"

Ok, they really did think I was a weakling. I held in my temper, not rising to his insult. "I literally broke him once. I can do it again. Permanently this time."

He lowered his hand from my face, and my conflicted feelings felt the absence of his touch. "Normally, I would help you in any way I could, but you see, if I gave away the whereabouts of his object, I'd be putting myself at risk as well. Not that I don't trust you, but we're still learning each other."

Now, why would that be? Were the objects held in the same place? That would be stupid. While I wasn't convinced that Lorenzo had much of a brain, I did think Martin had some smarts. However, maybe he had underestimated my brain. I didn't skip college because I didn't have an intellect. I just liked fashion and beauty more. He'd given away a clue unintentionally. And it was all I needed.

Their enchanted objects were most likely not in the same exact location. No, they were in similar locations.

Their bodies.

If Martin told me that, then I'd know how to make him weaker. Still, he'd told me enough.

Time to kill a ghoul.

CHAPTER 24

I walked forward, intending to inch by him to return to Lorenzo. I would magically rip him apart bit by bit. Although Martin was still a problem, it wasn't as immediate as Lorenzo, and I had no plans to do anything against Martin, if I could help it, without going over a plan with Joo-won. I didn't want to be the one to kill his friend, even if he was corrupt. Not after Yuri.

Martin grabbed my wrist before I could fully get past him. His large lavender eyes were almost vacant now, but he had that smile still plastered there. "Where are you going?"

I gulped, feeling nervous despite my internal pep-talk. I could be strong and still have fear, couldn't I? "I'm going to kill Lorenzo. Is that a problem? Or are you still trying to protect your alleged not best friend?"

Something flashed beneath his eyes. Excitement. Did he like my bitchiness? "Ah, *ma cherie*, while I love your zeal, you should really get back to Joo-won. I am sure he is worried."

I shook my arm free of him. Why was he trying to get me out of there? Was he going to pick up and move operations as soon as I left so there would be no evidence of what he'd been up to? Had he actually let Lorenzo escape, and he just didn't want me to know? "What? New clients coming, and you don't want me here for that?"

He gave me a disappointed pout. "I thought we were getting along. Why change that for us?"

"Because I don't get along with criminals? You told me you would change. Of course, you lied."

He looked up at the ceiling, laughing. "Where are the laws, *ma cherie*? The world is different now. Free. We can do what we want."

"There is still right and wrong. Good and evil. And there are many communities, including a whole federation in this country, that have a set of laws that we abide by. None of them would allow making weapons out of creatures."

He gave me a skeptical look, top lip turned up. "You can't be so naïve. You think your government would not pay the highest bidder for such things? Not that I would ever help them." He gave a grimace. He really did hate law and order. "This world wants to become a beautiful mix of chaos. Why fight it? Live as you please. Gain the riches, the love, the pain, the power that you want."

He was actually crazy. I'd always thought it, but I was pretty sure now. Perhaps being locked away alone all that time had done more harm than good. "Look at what you've done. When will it be enough? What's your end game?"

He scoffed. "End? Why does a finale need to happen? You search for a reason where none needs to exist."

"What you're doing sounds tiring. And it's wrong. Nigel's town is a good thing. People need structure and safety. Chaos is harmful. A lot of people were injured from that attack. Same with those bugs. And what dangerous people are you selling these creatures to? What you are making has harmed innocent people. And you've profited from it. Your kingdom has grown because of the places you've destroyed with creatures like these. You may not care about good and evil, but I care about life and death. You just bring death, and I won't allow it anymore."

He gave me a slow clap, poking his lips out as if he was amazed and impressed by my speech. I knew he wasn't. He was a condescending asshole.

"So hopeful. So idealistic. Now I fully understand why you are part of The Six. It's amazing to see someone so powerful be so uncorrupted."

Well, at least he was acknowledging my strength.

"Let's just agree to disagree."

I rolled my eyes. And now he was back to thinking I was stupid. "That's not how it works."

"Who says? I can make sure nothing I make harms you and your allies, and you can let me be."

I took several steps away from him, growing tired of this pointless conversation. We were never going to be on the same page. "The world is my ally."

He snorted. "That makes me sick to my stomach. You are being unreasonable."

"No deal," I replied before teleporting away.

I reappeared in front of where I had locked up Lorenzo. Only he was not there. Big surprise. He didn't have the magic to break wards, so it was fair to say that Martin had let him out. Clearly, they were still partners in crime. Only I couldn't figure out why Martin had then led us to Lorenzo's hideaway.

The hairs on the back of my neck went up, and I ran forward into the room, not looking behind me. I'd learned my lesson by now that my magical body knew when to get the hell out of the way. I spun around and thrust my magic out, lightning pouring through my fingers.

Lorenzo spun to the side, then raised his hand towards

me, and before I could move, I felt sharp pricks pierce my thighs, stomach and arms. The hell? I looked down to see what looked like large black thorns over my body.

I looked back up at the ghoul, and he had his hands up, his black nails growing in sharp daggers. They looked just like what was stuck in me. "Eww, eww, eww, eww, eww. These are your nails?" I banished the nails out of my skin and stumbled backward, feeling woozy. And of course, they would be poisoned. Damn it. I hoped this wasn't the same hell poison. "Your power is lame, you vulture," I shouted before sending a barrage of fiery hail his way.

He shouted in rage as he tried in vain to dodge being pelted. The lava hail wasn't killing him, but at least I could see that his protective ward was gone. Seems I had successfully weakened it, and whatever time extension he had on it wasn't that long.

Sharp cramps tightened my stomach, bending me forward. It felt like several needles were stabbing away at me from the inside. I so did not need this. What kind of poison was in me? I was not going to pass out from this thing. I'd wake up dead if I did, and I know how nonsensical that sounded. The point was I didn't want to wake up to this guy munching on my thigh. I had to get rid of him now before this poison did whatever it was trying to do. If I was going out, I was a least going to take him with me.

I pushed out a hurricane wind towards him as soon as I saw him pushing through my hail. I was lucky I could use multiple weather magic going at once. I needed to conjure the storm of a century to get rid of this guy. I could conjure anything dealing with the seasons. Weather could be destructive. Lorenzo was not a great fighter. He was just league with the right people. If Misandre had not put him back together, he would have still been in pieces in that cell.

The muscles in my calves tingled, weakening. He might

not be strong, but this poison wasn't a joke. Time was ticking away. *Think, Lisa, think.* Lorenzo was starting to move towards me again, this time at a normal pace which was still slow for him, considering he could move as fast as light, but not slow enough for me.

I pushed my arms out to the side and closed my eyes, focusing above me. I thought of earlier with Joo-won. I could float or fly then. I could do it now. I was a faerie. Flight was foundational, and now that I knew I could, I could do it again. The familiar itch returned, and soon, my wings sprouted out, carrying me to the ceiling.

I looked down and found Lorenzo looking up at me with raised brows. "Surprise, bitch!" I called before wrapping his body with ropes of lightning, digging into his skin. He strained to break free, but I wouldn't let him go. I pushed more power out, wiping a tornado around him that would suck out his air. Ghouls, as far as I knew, still needed air to breathe. Then again, I'd never studied them to know for sure. He had been torn apart and put back together, who knew what Lorenzo could survive.

Lorenzo choked out a cough but then glared up at me with angry eyes. Well, his eyes always looked angry to me. "You have to come better than this." He hissed. Maybe he didn't need air.

He broke his arms free of my lightning, my magic dissipating to the sides. I could see that his clothes were badly burned and bloody. My lightning had been digging into him, and the cuts looked deep. Still, they weren't enough.

Lorenzo shot his hands out, and his thorny claws came my way. I flew to another part of the room, only grazed in the arm by a claw. He raced towards the couch and jumped up before leaping forward and grabbing my ankle. I could fly, but my speed still couldn't match his.

He yanked me towards him as I tried to push forward, but he was stronger. He dropped to the ground as I struggled. I kicked my other leg out at his head, but he gnashed my calf with his teeth, tearing into my flesh.

This would not be my life. I was not going to continue to get bit like some piece of chicken. I pushed a force of wind around myself, and it propelled me forward, tearing me away from him.

Lorenzo smacked his bloody lips. "Tasty as always."

I wanted to tear his teeth out. I could tear his teeth out. It was time to bring hurricane Lisa to reality. Hurricane winds were destructive. They tore up houses and tossed cars. Mine would do the same. I clapped my hands together, and my destructive wind tossed him against a far wall like a rag doll. But I wasn't done. I clasped my hands tightly together.

I thought of all the horrors this asshole had caused. The people he killed. People I knew and cared about. I hated killing, but I would like it today.

Lorenzo thrashed against the wall, but he would not get away. My wind would not let him. "You're not going to win this. Martin won't save you. He sent us right to you. He's playing you."

He sneered at me, unmoved by my words. His voice cut against the wind, and he spoke in breathing gulps. "You think he isn't playing *you*? Everything that bastard has done has been to get rid of you. He wanted to claim innocent, so he made sure he wasn't the one doing the work. The attack in New York. Sending you to me. Sending me to you at Joo-won's place. All him. He was hoping I'd off you."

I couldn't say I was surprised, but it still pissed me off to have it confirmed. Of course, it also made sense why he didn't try to kill me when I spent the night. If he did get his hands dirty, then Joo-won would never forgive him. Best to be the one who comforted Joo-won over my demise and get him back that way. "Oh, I know he is a fucker but so are you. And I'm not the one who is about to die. You killed my friend."

His face scrunched up, and he cried out, still trying to move against my high-pressure wind. Bones began to break in his arms and legs. He spat and screamed. "I'm ready for death. Your fear of dying is what makes you weak. Go ahead and kill me. I've done what I came to do. I'm glad that icy bastard finally died."

He didn't say me as well. Did that mean that my poison was different? A dull headache banged at the back of my head, and my nausea returned. I knew my time was limited.

He couldn't beat me, and he knew it. He didn't even try to bargain for his life. He was giving up. His body began to cave inwards, bones continuing to crack in his face and torso. His eyes, already dripping blood, tore from the sockets. His neck snapped and hung to the side on his shoulder, but he was still alert. He wasn't dying. In fact, it looked like his bones were already repairing!

And then I saw it, a glowing green light shining from inside his chest through a deep cut that I had given him earlier with my lightning. What was this?

I balled my fist and punched forward, conjuring a ball of hail the size of a tennis ball. It shot forward towards the green light, tearing through his chest. Lorenzo screamed a guttural cry, his body shaking even harder against my wind pressure. And then the light was gone.

Something clanged to the floor, and I narrowed my eyes to see what appeared to be a small black rock. I lowered to the ground and put my hand out, the object floating towards me, soon sitting in the palm of my hand. It felt smooth and unassuming, but I knew it had to be the enchanted object.

I released Lorenzo, who fell to the ground, not moving. I

didn't need to kick him to know he was dead. He was going to be dead today. I shot a ball of sun fire at him, and instantly, his body ignited in flames. I didn't care if anything burned around him. It was Martin's house and the whole place could burn.

CHAPTER 25

I left the fire burning behind me after confirming that Lorenzo was now nothing but ash. A loud thump from above, off to my left, caught my attention, and I turned down the hall in hopes to find a staircase. I wasn't going to leave. I wanted to tear it all down. Martin wanted chaos; I would give it to him.

Just as I hoped, I found a door opening up to a stairwell. I quickly climbed them, emerging to the first floor of what appeared to be the lobby of a glass building. And near the front entrance was a madhouse of elves and creatures fighting. Joo-won's people and Martin's. I looked through the chaos to find them but had no success. Then I heard shouting from behind me as two men spilled onto the floor of a corridor holding several sets of elevators.

Joo-won and Martin.

They were both bloodied. And they were fighting each other. What had I missed?

I ran over to Joo-won and helped him up. He did not look good. He was holding his side, so perhaps he had broken ribs, and his face was a mess of bruises, cuts and blood. He actually looked worse than Martin.

I hovered my hands over his injuries. "Why are you two fighting? Did he tell you about what he's doing?" His wounds weren't healing nearly fast enough, and I figured that might be because I was poisoned and trying to heal my own issues. This was problematic.

Joo-won sucked in a breath as I healed him. "I thought he had harmed you. I didn't believe him when he denied it."

He looked over my shoulder at Martin, I presumed. "You step any closer, and I will rip your throat out."

I heard Martin snicker, but he didn't move. I was guessing it was because he was trying to heal up himself and needed the break.

Joo-won clasped my hands in his, bringing my attention to his eyes. He shook his head. "Don't use up all your energy on me. You don't look too good."

I smirked even though he was absolutely right. I felt like roadkill. "Sorry, I forgot to put on my makeup before I left your place."

Joo-won surveyed me, frowning at my bloody leg. "Did you kill him?"

I didn't have to guess if he meant Lorenzo, there was nobody else we wanted dead more. "Yes, sir. And he won't be coming back."

He tapped his forehead on mine. "Thank you. Now, go home and heal."

I shook my head. He was crazy if he thought I was leaving him now. "I brought you here with the necklace. How selfish would I be for leaving you and your people to fight while I go?" I turned towards Martin. "Call your people off? Let's just keep it between us, shall we?"

Martin spit blood out on the floor beside him. How classy. "Now, why would I do that?" He wiped his mouth.

"Because you claim to care about us. Correction, you

325

care about Joo-won. Your BFF Lorenzo gave away your dirty secrets before he died."

Martin rolled his eyes. "Of course, that vulture would. I was really hoping you would have killed him in that forest. He was a loser, and he was cutting into my profits." He waved his hand in front of his face, visibly annoyed despite his injuries. "Well, at least you got him now. Better late than never."

This guy was a real piece of shit. Did he ever get his hands dirty? "Now that I took out Lorenzo, I'm going to shut your little operation down. You've caused enough destruction, and you won't be reasoned with."

He gaped at me, but it was clearly mocking because his brows raised, and he hardly looked concerned. "How are you going to do that, ma cherie? Do yourself a favor and turn away. Go back to your little shop."

He really was not threatened by me. I'd have to show him. I lifted my hands, sparks of lightning surrounded them, reaching up past my elbows.

Joo-won placed a hand on my shoulder. I looked up at him, and he still looked pale and sweaty. He had to have internal injuries, and his own magic wasn't healing things fast enough. He gave me a slight shake of the head, and I knew instantly that he wanted me to back down so he could handle it. I really itched to zap Martin one time, but I understood Joo-won's desire to resolve the Martin problem once and for all, on his own.

He looked up over to Martin, eyes neutral but cold. "I not allow you to continue your destruction."

Martin sneered at him. "I hate what you've become. You would have never turned down an opportunity like this. I was giving you forgiveness by asking you to join my business. We would have made a great team again. We could have been so much more. I loved you. Do you care so little for me after all this time?" His voice broke, and the anger left his face. His brows scrunched together over saddened eyes, mouth pressed tight.

Joo-won swayed slightly, pain softening his cold eyes. "It doesn't matter how I feel. You know that. As it was then and so it is now, I cannot allow your chaos to continue. I am enjoying this new world. My people are flourishing. I find that I want to be a part of it now. I want to protect it."

As he spoke, there seemed to be an almost shock in his voice, as if he were surprising himself by his words. Despite the grave situation, it brought a tiny smile to my mouth to see that he was indeed becoming a good guy.

Martin sniffed and wiped at his eyes, but I caught the tears before he cleared them. "I thought of your death for decades. I couldn't understand you. Couldn't understand how someone I thought I knew as well as I knew myself could turn his back on me and treat me so cruelly. Then I hoped for death. I thought you might regret your actions and be tormented by what you had done if I was no more. And then I tried to understand. If I did, I could better accept my fate. For a while, I foolishly allowed myself to believe that I was wrong. When I was freed, I didn't even seek revenge. I wanted to rebuild and be worthy of your love. " He raised his face towards the ceiling, his long hair falling back off his shoulders.

"And then, I saw that you had moved on. You had not suffered. You had stopped caring about me. Perhaps you had never loved me at all. Misandre showed me your truth, whether she meant to or not." He looked over to me. "She poisoned you."

Ah, so this was about jealousy and me. Didn't he know that I couldn't hold that kind of power over Joo-won? He made his own decisions. If I was so strong, he would never have almost killed Erik and Amina, among other evil deeds.

I could feel the tension radiating off of Joo-won. He was preparing himself to attack. So was I. I'd powered my lightning down, but my palms were itching to zap something.

Joo-won gave a deep sigh, moving slightly in front of me. "Martin, Lisa is no poison. You were. I was so enamored by you that I turned a blind eye to your cruelty. I let it go on too long. The fact that I didn't kill you before showed how much you were a weakness to me. I will not make that mistake again."

Martin gave a soft chuckle. His head was now lowered, and I could not see his eyes. "I suppose then, we are at an impasse. It pains me that I will have to kill you now. Stop me." He said the last sentence as more of a plea instead of a dare or demand. He may not have wanted to kill Joo-won, but he would. He loved his own selfish interest more.

Joo-won adjusted in his stance. He hadn't killed Martin in the past. Couldn't do it. Would he be able to now, despite his words? "Try your best."

"You can barely stand. It would be so easy."

Martin raced towards us. He pushed me aside, sending me into the nearest wall so hard the plaster broke. I was sure I'd be feeling that for a while. I gathered myself just in time to see him try to stab Joo-won in the stomach with a jagged-looking dagger.

However, Joo-won had grasped the blade of the dagger, preventing it from sinking in. He struggled to push it away, hands bloodied from the deep cuts he was gaining. He kicked a foot out, connecting with Martin's privates, and the other elf stumbled back.

I zapped him with my magic. If he was warded like Lorenzo, it was long since gone because he shook with my electrocution. Smoke rose from him, his mouth foaming with saliva. The scent of burnt flesh permeated the air. I had to kill him fast before his minions noticed their ruler getting toasted.

And then my magic went out. Just died, like the power was shut off. A cramp seized my body, going beyond my stomach, sending me doubling forward. I could feel it in my arms, calves, and back, reminding me that I was poisoned and it was depleting, correction, had depleted my powers. Even from his non-existent grave, Lorenzo was tormenting me. I wanted to kill him all over again.

Martin dropped to his knees, still singed but alive. Before I could figure out my next move, Joo-won zoomed past me with his glowing blue sword in the air, impaling Martin in the chest.

Instead of dying, Martin sucked in a deep breath and flipped backwards with the sword still in his chest. Seriously? How was this dude so mobile? He could have at least staggered to the side and coughed up blood like normal people.

He clapped his hands together and grinned at us with bloody teeth. Okay, at least he was bleeding internally. He tore the sword out of his chest and tossed it aside before waving his hand over what should have been life-threatening injuries. Before our eyes, he began to heal. Crap. How were we going to beat this guy? I was tapped out of power while this poison was in me, and Joo-won was already power depleted even before he started to fight.

Time to call the crew. I mentally sent an S.O.S call out to the other members of The Six. Instantly I could hear their voices in my head.

I need to borrow some strength. I've been poisoned. My power is gone. It's a whole thing. I said in my head.

Where are you? Charles' voice rang out.

At Martin's, and I have no idea where that is, but I'm with Joo-won and his tribe, so we have the numbers.

Can you ask Joo-won? We can get there and help. Charles added.

Actually, Faith and I are in the middle of a battle ourselves, Felix cut in.

Is it more important than helping Lisa? Erik questioned

I sighed. Time was ticking here. Just some power is all I need.

Ok, people, by the time you all gather together and figure out how to teleport somewhere that you've never been, I will be dead. Just fuel me up with some energy.

Uh, we have been. Faith stated in my mind. *Just because we're talking doesn't mean we didn't hear you the first time.*

I certainly didn't feel energized. I still felt like I needed to go to sleep for a couple of days. And I needed to sit down. That wasn't good.

I don't feel anything. Maybe it's the poison.

Maybe it's because The Six aren't all awake. Charles guessed.

Amina being asleep was more of a problem than we imagined, and we couldn't wake her up, so we were stuck.

Ok, so maybe you guys do need to come here.

I looked over to Joo-won, who now had his sword again and was busy fending off Martin's attacks. I really didn't want to bother him. I raced past them in search of Senna or another elf on our side. I quickly spotted Senna in the middle of the action. I didn't want to bother her either, but we needed to do something. I picked up a sword lying beside a deceased elf and raced into the madness.

"Senna, on your left!" I shouted, and she turned, fighting off another elf with her sword. I got her right side and clanged my sword against an enemy elf having very little idea what I was doing. I'd been doing some sword training but not enough to feel confident in myself.

"Do you know where we are? I need to tell Charles so

they can help." I dodged the elf's sword attack, starting to break a sweat. "We're having a hard time with Martin."

Senna stabbed her attacking elf in the heart then spun towards me. "Duck."

I did as she demanded, and she quickly beheaded my elf. Damn, she was good.

She tilted her head back towards Joo-won. "Help him. I'll get the others. I'll be back in five."

She was such a boss. I gave her a quick nod and ran back to the elevators, sword still in my hand. Before I could make it all the way back, the ground began to rumble. I moved to the nearest wall to maintain my balance. "What in the world?"

And just like that, a door opened up, and out poured all of the horrific creatures locked up below. Even the giant eel snake slithered out.

I could have died then and there. I did scream. A lot. And then that giant flying spider started to come my way. "Oh, no. God, please bring down a giant can of bug spraaaay!" I dropped to the floor and swung my sword above my head in a circle, screaming the whole time.

The spider dived down towards me, and I swung upward with more purpose. Why was this spider coming for me? Weren't bugs supposed to be more afraid of us than we were of them? The lies!

"This is a freaking nightmare!" I shouted as the spider hovered over me, its many eyes staring down at me. And then it opened its giant mouth, exposing monstrous teeth.

I would not go out like this. Having my head bit off by a giant spider fly. I summoned all the courage I had just as it continued its descent ,and I stabbed my sword upward, sliding it across the spider's abdomen. Yellowish liquid gore poured out of it and all over me. I ran backwards to avoid the spider dropping on me. And drop it did, splattering to the ground in a tangled mess.

I could have vomited from the sight and the smell. The smell on me. And I had no magic to glamour myself clean. Why?

I wiped my face with the back of my hand and looked on at Joo-won just in time to see Martin stab him in the side with a dagger. Joo-won wasn't able to stop him this time, and his right arm was hanging loosely at his side. Possibly broken.

I raced towards them with the last of my strength and stabbed Martin in the back with my sword. I yanked my sword out, ready to strike again, but Martin spun around, eyes enraged. "You just won't go away, will you?"

I needed to give Joo-won a moment to heal. If he kept going as it was, he wouldn't make it. I really needed the others to show up because taking Martin on without my magic was not a smart idea. "I'm not a coward."

"No, you're stupid."

How rude. I pointed my sword at him. Was I really going to fight this guy? Maybe he was right, I was stupid. But I was also very much in love with Joo-won, and I didn't have it in me to watch him die. Look at me. Growing before my death.

I stuck my sword at him, and he quickly ducked before landing a rib-breaking punch to my side. The pain vibrated through my body, but I held on to my sword in spite of my agony. I leaned against the wall, clutching my left side. "Didn't anyone ever tell you it was rude to hit a woman?" I wheezed out. Crap, it hurt to even take a breath.

Martin smiled. "Yes, and I never listened."

I slashed my sword out again, ignoring my growing pain. He tried to move, but my sword did catch him across the left side of his face. That was not enough damage, but it seemed to really piss him off. The wound wasn't healing as fast as before. Was he getting drained of energy, or was this sword laced with something?

I didn't have time to ponder that because he slammed against me, grabbing the sword holding my wrist and squeezing. He sneered at me. "You are a little bitch."

"You dusty fuck."

He kept squeezing my wrist, any tighter, and my bones would break.. I let out a scream, dropping my sword in pain, and he let me go. But this was not over. I did not get this far being a damsel. I kneed him in the crotch with all my might, and he let go of me, hunching forward. I then did a high kick to the side of his head, crying out in agony as the movement aggravated my broken ribs.

He stumbled sideways but did not fall. I lunged for my sword, preparing to behead him like I saw Senna doing, only my right hand was no good and my left hand was pretty weak. I tried anyway, but Martin had already recovered and swatted my blade away with ease. "I'm going to kill you now."

Movement behind him caught my attention. I saw Joo-won race towards us, a look of scary determination on his face. His injuries were healing before my very eyes. What the?

He grabbed Martin around the waist and slammed him down on the concrete floor. I could have sworn I heard bone crack. Martin pushed his hand out against Joo-won's neck, squeezing, but the elven king didn't even bother to move his hand. He brought down another dagger, longer than the one used on him, and plunged it into Martin's heart, over and over again. I could hear the metal of the dagger actually scrapping the tile floor.

Martin's body spasmed under him, blood shooting out of his mouth. So, the other elf was not indestructible? And now I could clearly see why a fully powered Joo-won led the group. There was no time for Martin to recover, and Joo-won's movements were almost as fast as a vampire's or ghoul's. He cut, slashed, stabbed until there was nothing but a gaping wound where Martin's destroyed heart now sat. Martin dropped his hand to the floor, but there was life still in him. His eyes roamed around unfocused. I wanted them to die out.

Joo-won then dug his hand into Martin's chest and pulled out a black stone. Much like the one in Lorenzo's body. His enchantment. He tossed it towards me, and I caught it, stuffing it in my pocket.

Martin's body lay still, his mouth open wide, eyes large in a frozen mask of what looked like fear. Fear of death. Joo-won reached over, grabbing his sword on the ground nearby, and swiftly beheaded Martin. He rose and stepped on the bodiless head, smashing it several times.

Gross.

Joo-won then walked over to me, assessing me before hovering his hands over my body. I felt his cool healing magic move through my system, healing me of the poison and my broken bones. How had he done this? Where had this power come from?

Oh no.

"Joo-won, tell me you didn't take Arwa's cure."

He didn't answer me for a long moment, just continued to heal me. "You would have died."

I punched him in the shoulder, feeling a wave of sorrow grip me. "It can kill you."

He gave me a gentle smile. "I'm not dead yet."

How could he smile? "You could literally drop dead any moment. How could you do this?" I clutched my chest, feeling my breath coming short even though my ribs were now healed.

Joo-won lost his smile, placing a hand on my cheek. His

eyes searched mine as if wanting to see my pain. "I could not lose you, Lisa. Do you not understand how much I love you?"

I wiped at the tears, blood and gore from my face, hands shaking in despair. I felt like I was dying. I needed him to live. I needed him. "Don't you understand how much I love *you*? I can't lose anyone else. This can't continue to be my journey."

I shook my head, letting my tears wet my cheeks. I was tired. I was so very tired. I understood why Joo-won did what he did. I wasn't foolish. However, it didn't mean I liked it or wanted it. I hated Martin even more now. Hated that he, like Lorenzo, had found a way to affect us even after his death. Why couldn't we be happy? Why did someone always have to be taken away from me? Joo-won had been so patient with me, and now we could only have minutes before he suddenly dropped dead without any notice.

Then I would be alone. Without him. Without my heart. The thought made me nauseous.

Joo-won leaned forward, giving me a slow, soft kiss on my forehead. "What choice do we have? I would give my life to protect you always. That will always be a certainty."

Blood dripped from his nose, and I gasped. He frowned and wiped at it, looking down at the blood with a questioning gaze.

"Are you okay?" I asked. I'd never seen Joo-won with a nosebleed. It was a very un-elven thing. My mind started panicking. It had to be the effects of the cure. Was this the first sign that it would kill him?

Joo-won looked back at me, a smile planted on his face again. He was covering up his worry, but I wasn't buying it. He had been pretty bloodied up until that moment from all the fighting, but it didn't mean this was from the battle.

335

"Even covered in whatever that is, you look beautiful." He wiped my cheek and looked at the gross grime on his hand.

"I killed a giant spider."

He nodded, looking at the elevators. I looked as well, readying myself for another attack, but there was nothing. "Remember when we first met, I would send you all those gifts. Jewelry, flowers, clothes, food... You returned everything except the food. You know I actually baked them?"

I sighed. I knew this. He had cooked many times for me since then. Why was he bringing this up now? I grabbed his hand with both of my own, trying to comfort both him and myself.

He squinted his eyes, smile still in place. Why did he look so damn happy? "I can't wait to cook for you again."

"Ok, and you can do that. We just need to get you looked at by Bella and make sure everything is okay."

"Marry me."

My heart stopped. Was he being serious right now? Could I say yes? I was so overwhelmed with everything. My mind could barely process all that just happened. And Joo-won did not look good. Sure, his injuries were healing, but he looked ashen ,and there was a dullness in his eyes that I'd never seen before. Usually, those marble eyes were lit from within. Even when he gave me deadpan eyes, I still saw the internal control. Now he looked out of sorts. It was breaking my heart. What the hell did this so-called cure do to him?

Joo-won swiped his hand over me, and I was clean once more. "There, even more beautiful. Do you want a diamond or something more unique?"

"Whatever you want to give me," I replied in a small voice, trying not to make it tremble.

"I'll have to get a bigger place for us. I liked the hotel life, but there are some luxury apartments we can move into."

He turned his head and coughed into his hand. When he looked down at it, we saw blood. He swiped his hand, and his palm was magically cleared of the blood. I felt like I was going to pass out from the growing panic swelling inside me.

Joo-won looked behind me, not seeming to notice what was happening to him. "Fighting is over, but there are several large beasts roaming around."

I didn't turn to look. They weren't my concern right now.

"Ah, now I see the spider you killed. Impressive, buttercup."

My heart sank. Buttercup? Something was happening to his mind, and I wasn't sure if the blood, coupled with the disorientation and lack of coherence, were part of it. I wasn't going to wait anymore.

I summoned a portal to the fae realm and took us through. He didn't fight me, which was also odd. I would have thought he'd want to be with his people and assess the injured, but he seemed totally unfazed.

Once the portal guards approved our presence, I teleported us to Bella's treehouse community. Luckily, she was home, and she quickly let us in.

I sat Joo-won down on her couch and stood next to Bella, who was currently studying him. "He took the cure to get his full strength back. Now he's bleeding from his nose and mouth and talking weird. What does this mean?" I asked.

She sighed and stood up straight. "The magic is breaking him from the inside out. This is what we were afraid of." She turned to me with sympathetic eyes. "I'm sorry, Lisa."

Anger bubbled in me. I was so mad that this happened. I didn't want to hear sorry. I wanted to hear that she could fix him. "Can you cure him?"

She dropped her shoulders, looking back at Joo-won,

who laid back on the couch, looking very relaxed as he looked out the wall of floor to ceiling windows in Bella's home. "We haven't been successful with that yet. There isn't anything I can do. But he has time. If it were more immediate, he'd be dying now. He might have months."

I let out a shuddering cry. I was overwhelmed. Just as I got him. Just as we were finally in a place that was long overdue, I would lose him. The fates were too cruel to me. What kind of undeserved karma was this? I wouldn't let him go. "We don't know how many months he has, but can he be put to sleep while we find a cure? The elven sleep only lasts seven days, but we can keep putting him under since the illness is slow-moving." We had to try something. Anything.

Bella pressed her lips together and gave a curt nod. "We can try that. His situation is better than Yuri's since it's not dire. We might even be able to keep him in the sleep for longer because of that. And we will work nonstop to find a cure."

I wiped away a tear that escaped my eyes. "I have faith in you."

Joo-won looked up at us. He suddenly looked very coherent, eyes bright and shining. "And if I don't survive, you will be strong. You were always strong, Lisa."

A flood of tears blurred my vision. Just what I didn't want. How could I be strong and cry like this? How could I be strong when my heart was breaking? "I don't think I have it in me anymore. It's too much."

He got up and wrapped his arms around me. "You were willing to die to save me. It is not too much for you. And if I go, you will be okay. Trust me on this."

He seemed so sure of this. Of me. I wanted to be just as strong. I wanted to have his faith. My luck had to change. I deserved my happily ever after. "Ok, and I like diamonds."

He gave me questioning eyes for a moment, and then

recognition took hold. He smiled once more. "Then I will get my butterfly the best diamonds I can find."

He then kissed me, and for a moment, I truly believed everything would be okay. Then the light in his eyes dulled, and he returned to the couch, peacefully looking out of the windows, ignoring the blood dripping from his nose.

EPILOGUE

TEN MONTHS LATER

*M*y alarm blared loudly next to my head, and I slammed my hand down on it to silence it. It was just barely light out, and I swung my legs to the side of the bed, swinging my feet to quickly get my body moving.

Once I was able to get out of bed, I went to the bathroom and took a shower, readying myself for the day. When I stepped out of the hot shower, feeling more rejuvenated, I jumped slightly, finding Joo-won standing there, leaning against the sink with his usual cocky smile.

I sighed and rolled my eyes. "Like what you see?"

He didn't respond, just continued to stare at me. His usual, as if he couldn't get enough of seeing me. I didn't mind.

"You know, I really wish you would stop scaring me like this. I didn't even hear the bathroom door open."

My eyes watered, and I blinked rapidly to push the tears back. "You know it's Senna's birthday today. We're taking her out to dinner against her will. She'll be like what, 200 years old? Finding a birthday present for her was very stressful." My voice shook, and I coughed before moving to sit on my covered toilet seat to begin my lotion ritual.

Joo-won's eyes followed me to my seat next to the sink, but he still didn't speak. He never did. I had no expectations that would happen.

I grabbed the lotion from my counter and sighed. "It was good seeing you today."

I reached out to touch him, and he dissipated before my eyes before I could make contact.

"Bye," I whispered to the empty room.

I grinned, refusing to be sad today. The dreams or visions of Joo-won used to hurt. Some days they still did. Most days, I loved seeing his face. It brought me a sort of peace. I wasn't ready to give up on him being healed. My heart didn't grow numb as time passed, but I did have to fight the hopelessness.

I had not seen Joo-won since he went to sleep. We knew Bella was awakening him and putting him back to sleep. She was able to grow the length of time for his slumber to a month, but about two months ago, she informed us that the sleep spell was no longer holding as long. She stated that soon it would not work at all. Time was running out, and that frightened me.

Each time he awoke, we asked to see him, but Bella informed us that he refused. The hope hurt. Not seeing him hurt. He knew this and was keeping his distance to protect our hearts, but it wasn't working.

It would be easier, less painful, to move on. However, that was the old me. The new me – the me that wasn't afraid to love anymore was going to fight to hold onto him. The new me was going to have faith.

So for now, I would smile at my Joo-won visions. And sometimes I would talk to them. For now, this was all that I had.

*S*enna blew out the candle on her slice of chocolate cake then pushed the plate away before crossing her arms. She looked absolutely miserable, and that was only added to her all-black wardrobe, which had become her stable for this almost full year. Today she was wearing a black pants suit and a black fascinator with a net covering her face.

I huffed, annoyed with her lack of enjoyment. "I thought you liked chocolate cake. And couldn't you have worn something other than black today? It is your birthday, after all."

She rolled her eyes, looking around at the elves passing by in her town as we sat outside of a restaurant front patio that evening. "I did not want to come to this. You all forced me."

Charles, who was sitting beside her, rubbed her back. "You needed a break. I know running the tribe is a lot of work."

"You have no idea. And my advisors aren't as good as Yuri and I were to Joo-won." She placed her head in her hands, elbows on the table. "You have no idea how exhausting this is. People want to test my strength because they falsely believe I am not strong enough. Then we merged with Martin's people, and I'm still regretting that. I'm trying to keep us all together."

I reached over and patted her arm. I knew she had a lot on her plate, but I also didn't want to see her burn herself out. She was a powerful elf, but she wasn't invincible. "We can help anyway you need us to, but we also are going to look out for you. We're your friends. Friends who want you to wear something other than black sometime."

She lifted her head to give me a glare. "I am in mourning."

There, that pang again in my heart. It was still so fresh. Yuri's death was still too painful.

"I understand about Yuri. I do. I can only imagine with how long you've known him how that feels. But Joo-won is not dead."

"Aren't you stressed? Did Bella tell you that they can't do the sleep spell anymore on him after this one? That it won't take? Don't you care?"

I removed my hand from hers and sat back in my chair. She had no idea how I was struggling. Not a day passed that I didn't think of my elf. I fought misery constantly. Fought what felt like an unjustified fate on a daily basis. "Of course, I care about Joo-won. I love him. I hate that so much time has passed with no cure. I'm terrified." I looked down at my hands on the table, feeling the nausea from my heartbreak rise. "I have vivid dreams about him all the time. We're so happy in them, and when I wake up and find out that he isn't with me, I feel absolutely sick."

Senna frowned and pressed a hand to her chest as she listened. Her eyes watered, and she wiped the tears away with her other hand, not speaking.

I continued, welcoming the release of what I'd been holding inside. Before, just the thought of talking about it made me cry. Erik, who had a closer understanding of what I was going through, tried to offer an ear, but it felt like it would only hurt us both more to talk about how the people we loved couldn't be with us. Now I was ready to share to heal. "Sometimes, I think I see him when I'm out. I have embarrassed myself many a time, calling out his name to the wrong person. Even at home or when I visit his place, I see him. It's like he haunts me. Only he isn't dead. I've just had to accept that my mind wants to see him and will do what it wants to make that happen. And sometimes...sometimes seeing the visions of him makes me happy."

343

A tear splashed on my hand, and I looked at it like it was a foreign substance. I didn't want to cry. I wanted to be happy. I was supposed to be strong. And I was.

Charles rapped the table with his knuckles, his eyes wide and determined. "We're going to find a way to save him before the time is up. I'm searching. And I work best under pressure." He gave us his little boy grin, and I was reminded of why I always liked him. He had a way of bringing a light heart to a dark situation.

Senna's phone rang, and she let out a curse as she looked down at it. "I'm beginning to think people are making up things to cause me headaches. I should just kick them out." She pushed back her chair and looked at us. "Please, someone eat this cake."

I shook my head. "I'll get it wrapped up and drop it off at your place. You're going to want it later."

Charles chuckled and stood up. "She sure will. I'll come with you, Sen. I know I'm not an elf, but I'm your support."

She cut her eyes at him, lips twisted. "Not your duty."

He rolled his shoulders back, crossing his arms over his chest. "As the prospective man in your life, it kind of is."

Senna snorted. "Not true. We've talked about this."

He quickly held up his hand. "Ok, today, on your birthday, let your wall down. Let me be there for you. I don't think Yuri would want you pushing everyone away. He gave me his blessing."

She dropped her mouth open. "I don't recall him doing that."

Charles coughed into his fist. "He said it in a light whisper. Let's go." He moved her towards the sidewalk as she gave him a look full of skepticism.

They were cute together, but I already knew Senna was walking the same route as me, pushing people away because she was afraid to love and lose again. I really hoped she came to her senses soon because Charles was a good man.

I waved the bill in the air. "No worries, my treat!" Business had been good lately, and it was the only thing holding me together. I might as well do something nice with it. Although I did donate to a lot of charities.

I wrote my credit information in the bill. I'd opened up a credit in this town not long ago to make it easier. Despite Joo-won being gone, I still visited. Also, these elves were very fashionable, and they liked my goods.

I sat back, sipping the rest of my wine as I looked on at elves passing by. Everyone seemed so content. Life had been peaceful lately. I suppose I didn't blame them. The town had grown, and Senna was maintaining law and order, although they had no idea how hard she worked. They were finally stationary, and the world was getting more and more settled. We were all becoming somewhat pedestrian as the months and years passed. We'd never go back to the old ways, but we were finding more avenues for normalizing, even as nonhumans.

A woman walked by wearing a dress from my shop, and I pointed at her. "Love your dress."

She flashed me a grin and bowed her head in thanks as she continued to walk. It was nice seeing my work on the street. It made me feel like a celebrity in my head.

A man walked down the sidewalk towards me. Jet black hair styled expertly, a crisp white shirt, and well-tailored royal blue pants covered his body and those shocking turquoise eyes.

Joo-won.

I smiled as I looked at my latest imagination of him. I had long ago decided that this would be my response. It made the continued image of him easier for my heart. It was a trick of the mind, but I would no longer call it cruel.

My imaginary Joo-won sat down across from me. He looked so handsome and confident as always. "You look beautiful as ever, butterfly."

I stuck my tongue out at it. It really didn't matter how I reacted. It wasn't real. Then again, my imaginary Joo-won never talked before. Not while I was awake. Had talking about him changed things?

My imaginary Joo-won cocked a brow. "Not the reaction I was expecting, but I'll accept it."

I leaned forward on the table. "You aren't real. You are a figment of my imagination. And now I look like I'm talking to myself."

My imaginary Joo-won tilted his head back slightly in understanding. "Ah, I can promise you I'm very much real."

I rolled my eyes. I couldn't have this today. I just needed to go home and sleep. I reached over and plucked my imagination on the forehead to make it disperse and go away. Only my hand didn't hit air. It hit skin – a very hard forehead. I reared back, sucking in a breath. What was this?

My imaginary Joo-won scrunched his face up and rubbed his forehead. "Oww," he said in a deadpan voice.

I scooted back in my chair. "You're real. No, but I would have known. Bella would have called me." Something wasn't right. This was too out of the blue; we should have been prepared. This was something else. "You're a shapeshifter." That was the only explanation. Shapeshifters could take the form of anything.

The shapeshifter gave me an incredulous look. His brows raised. "I am not a shapeshifter, and I think you know that."

He waved his hand, brushing his hand against my invisible tattoo. My skin tingled, sending heated vibrations throughout my body. I shivered, adjusting in my chair. I licked my lips and looked around, hoping I didn't look too inappropriate.

He smirked at me. That familiar face that I loved to get annoyed by. "A shapeshifter would not be able to do that."

He was right, they wouldn't be able to do that. It was really him. I could feel my heart speed up, the thumping loud in my ears. "Bella cured me. She hadn't been telling you she was having any more progress because she didn't want to get your hopes up, especially with me refusing to see you. When they awakened me and found that the cure worked, I asked them to let me tell you myself. I know–"

I let out a sob, my throat dry. I'd been crying this whole time. I wasn't even sure when it started, but I couldn't stop the tears from coming now.

He paused, his eyes softening before he reached over with both hands, wiping my face. I frowned, confused for a moment, until I realized he was wiping away my tears.

"I missed you," I croaked out. A wash of relief fell over me, and it almost felt surreal. I didn't even want to blink, afraid he'd disappear, and this was really all in my head. But I knew I wasn't having a psychotic break. Joo-won was real, and he was here right with me.

Joo-won got up from the table and moved in front of me before getting on one knee. Perhaps I could have fainted then, but that would require me again to lose sight of him, so I sat rigid and wide-eyed. I couldn't breathe.

He pulled out a small gold box.

I pressed my lips tightly as he opened it. I actually gasped. The shine from the diamond nearly blinded me. It looked magical, and therefore, I was sure magic had touched it.

He cleared his throat, actually looking nervous. It was cute. "Lisa Xu, my butterfly–"

"Yes," I shouted.

His lips twitched in a small sideways grin. "Would you–"

"Yes."

He chuckled and shook his head. "Marry me?"

I raised my arms above my head. "Yes, yes, yes, yes, yes!"

His shoulders dropped, a look of satisfaction on his face, eyes crinkling with his grin. Then he placed that beautiful ring on my finger, and I could have screamed. Okay, I was pretty sure I was already screaming.

Elves around us clapped in congratulations and then surprise at Joo-won's return.

My life was not perfect. It never would be. I had no doubt that as a member of the special Six, sent to protect the world, and now a queen to an elven king, I'd face many more obstacles. But somehow, I'd found my happiness in this crazy new world. I'd carved out some normalcy. My fate had finally changed.

Perhaps happily ever afters did exist in a post-apocalyptic world.

If you enjoyed Lisa and Joo-won's story, please consider leaving a review on Amazon and Goodreads.

ABOUT THE AUTHOR

C.C. is originally from Baltimore, Maryland, and has actively written fiction since the age of eleven. She's an avid "chick lit" reader and urban fantasy fan. During her days, she works in Civil Rights for the federal government. In her free time, she sings karaoke, travels the globe, and watches too much TV...when she's not writing, of course.

To keep updated on future books and C.C.'s website, go to:
www.ccsolomon.com
CC Solomon: Nerdy Travelista Newsletter
Cat's Corner: New Adult Urban Fantasy and Paranormal
Romance Reader Group

You can also reach C.C. at the following
social media sites:

OTHER BOOKS BY CC SOLOMON

Paranormal World Series:

Mystic Bonds

Mystic Journeys

Mystic Awakenings

Mystic Souls

Mystic Realms: A Novella

Paranormal Times Series:

Mystic Memories/Dark Memories: A Novella

Dark Hauntings

Dark Reckonings: Coming 2022

Dark Powers: Coming 2022

Paranormal Rising Series:

Deathly Touch

Paranormal Lands Standalone Series:

Lightning and Curses

Standalone Novels

Girls of Might and Magic: An Anthology By Diverse Books With
Magic

The Mission